CRITICAL ACCLAIM FOR CHRISTINE MICHELS'S FUTURISTIC ROMANCES

IN FUGITIVE ARMS

"Ms. Michels is growing as a writer by leaps and bounds, combining a fascinating premise with a love story of searing intensity to make your heart soar with delight."
—*Romantic Times*

"Those readers who enjoy an action-packed space-opera romance will find *In Fugitive Arms* a wonderful change of pace."

—*Affaire de Coeur*

"I love the story and applaud Ms. Michels's wonderful imagination. Excellent futuristic-romance adventure."
—*Rendezvous*

"Ms. Michels has created a superb science-fiction romance of galactic proportions."
—*The Talisman*

ASCENT TO THE STARS

"Futuristic romance gets a big boost with the exciting debut of the highly talented Christine Michels, who whisks us off on a fast-paced romp through the stars."
—*Romantic Times*

"Christine Michels skillfully blends a totally realistic alien society with a beautifully believable romance that mixes into a superb novel."

—*Affaire de Coeur*

Futuristic Romance

Love in another time, another place.

IN FUGITIVE ARMS

"Saints alive, sweetheart," he murmured as his breathing slowly returned to normal. "You are one hell of a woman. I think I could get used to this."

Shenda opened her eyes and, in the next instant, bolted upright. Scooting back onto her own side of the tent, she sat staring at him. "This is not going to happen again, Swan. Ever. Do you understand?"

He stared at her, pinning her with those amber-hard eyes. "I was under the impression that you enjoyed it as much as I did."

Heat flooded her face. "That's beside the point. I have no particular use for men, and I refuse to begin a relationship with one. Especially a fugitive."

"Maybe you'd do well to remind yourself of that before you snuggle up next to one again."

In Fugitive Arms

Christine Michels

LOVE SPELL **NEW YORK CITY**

LOVE SPELL®

June 1995

Published by

Dorchester Publishing Co., Inc.
276 Fifth Avenue
New York, NY 10001

Cover Art by John Ennis

Printed in the United States of America.

This one is for Nathan, an avid science fiction/fantasy reader and a wonderful source of otherworldly ideas. Thanks for your input, brother.

Prologue

Torchlight shone from glistening onyx walls like moonlight on night-blackened water as shadowy figures moved in the steps of a rite more than ten thousand years old, its significance long ago lost in the obscurity of time. The incantation of unintelligible syllables echoed and swelled. Tendrils of smoke from burning incense writhed about the domed enclosure like grasping fingers. He looked out over his assembled flock with pride. Of the three directors of the Tridon, he alone had done more to increase their numbers and revive the brotherhood than his two colleagues combined. And the culmination of all their dreams loomed on the horizon like a new day. *A new day*. He liked the analogy, for soon would dawn a new day in the progression of mankind.

Extending his hands, he held them poised above a silver bowl containing a dark, oily liquid. The torchlight licked hungrily at the blood-red ruby stone of the ring on his right hand and, for an instant, his attention focused on it. Then his thoughts moved on. To the knowledge that they had found and were just beginning to comprehend. To the tantalizing power promised by that expanding enlightenment. To the future.

It was past time to right the wrong that had been done them. Their enemies were gone, themselves lost in the mists of time. And now the brotherhood of the Tridon would seek again the strength it had lost in eons past. A strength bound only by the limits of imagination. A strength capable of granting its user virtually unlimited power. Soon it would be theirs to wield, and he would lead his brothers into a new age. *The dawn of eternity*. Words from the ancient writings. Words that haunted him with their elusive promise.

As the murmurs of the congregated brothers surged and swelled around him like ocean waves, nurturing him, he spread his fingers over the bowl and completed the incantation. Slowly, the representation of a city began to form on the surface. It was a place dredged from the depths of his memory. Yet it was like no metropolis he had ever seen with his own eyes. It was a city of gleaming crystalline spires and golden statues. A city whose powerful forces shimmered in the air like heatwaves. A city which had been home to one of his ancestors. The inherited memory enticed him. He was a direct descendant of the original Tridon of Atlantis, and it should have been his city to rule. But his ancestors' enemies had denied him his birthright. His features hardened with determination. He would rebuild the city.

The vision faded and an alteration in the atmosphere signaled the approach of an initiate.

Another whose blood, when subjected to DNA testing, revealed the distinctive strand that proclaimed him a descendant of Atlantis. Lifting his eyes, he studied the man who walked toward him. A man with whom he had been acquainted for years, though he'd never realized the other carried the gene of a true descendant. Tonight, provided he passed the test, this man would join their ranks. And one more component of the plan would fall into place.

One

Like a spherical hell, Sentra hung in its orbit, red and hot against the inky backdrop of space. Persistently bombarded by scorching heat and toxic radiation from the blue-white dwarf sun that held it captive within its gravitational field, the prison world was a dead planet despite its life-sustaining atmosphere. Nothing endured there. Nothing except the prisoners housed beneath its blazing surface, the guards unlucky enough to be stationed there and the heat.

Corporal Shenda Ridell wiped the back of her hand across her sweating brow as she strode Corridor G on rounds. Not even the climatically adaptable Stellar Legion uniforms could adjust to the constant temperature extreme of Sub-Level One. The soles of her boots rang hollowly on the concrete floor, drawing the eyes of sweating inmates too lethargic to care that their only escape from Sub-level One, known as Death Row, lay through the thick metal door at the end of the corridor. Or perhaps they actually looked forward to their escape from Purgatory through death. Purgatory. That's what the inmates called Sentra. Shenda concurred.

Grimacing as a trickle of perspiration wormed its way down between her breasts, she fervently wished she'd drawn duty on Sub-Level Two, where the temperature would be at least ten degrees cooler. She hadn't, though, and in all likelihood never would. Her superiors had always seemed determined to forestall any cries of preferential treatment, and she accepted that reality as the price she must pay for her chosen career.

But she had never before been assigned to Sentra. Quarks! What a hellhole! She had never realized how debilitating heat could be. For the first time, if the opportunity had arisen, she would gladly have accepted a little special treatment. Unfortunately, none would be forthcoming. And her tour of *active* duty had just begun. The opportunity to return to her normal position within the Legion—as a navigator and astronomer in the Stellar Exploration Corps posted to Space Station Apollo—lay months away. To maintain their combat readiness, all Legionnaires were required to take a six-month tour of active combat duty once in every two-year cycle. The two years had rolled around and Shenda had had to give up her computers, charts and telescopes to don a stunner, a laser and combat fatigues.

As a fashion statement, the uniform left a lot to be desired. The primary color was the exact terracotta shade of Sentra's red sands. Blotches of light tan created the traditional camouflage effect. She imagined the reaction of the fashion consultant her father had hired back on Earth, and almost grinned. Poor Father. She could feel almost sorry for him. All his attempts to create the consummate statesman's daughter had come to naught, for Shenda had refused to become a pretty ornament for him to display at society functions. By the age of 14 she had already attended enough of them to know that she would sooner die as the result of some risk she might face as a Legionnaire in space than die of boredom on some dignitary's arm.

"Attention!" The voice emerged simultaneously from the prison intercom system, and her wrist terminal. Shenda glanced up at the nearest monitor. The control room supervisor—a black man Shenda knew only as *Lieutenant*—was on screen. He didn't seem to be suffering from the heat in the least, Shenda noted with some acerbity. But then, unlike most of the complex, the control room was air-conditioned.

"Attention! Corporal Ridell, Corridor G." No mistake about it, that was her.

Shenda halted and depressed the button on her wrist terminal to initiate private communication. The main monitor returned to displaying the prison corridor, and the lieutenant's face appeared in miniature on the tiny screen on Shenda's wrist. "Yes, sir."

"We lost exterior video feed three minutes ago, and now we've lost the vid from Corridor E as well. Check it out, will you?"

"Corridor E is not in my sector, sir."

The lieutenant sighed. "I'm aware of that, Corporal. We can't reach Samson. His terminal may be malfunctioning. You are closer to Corridor E than anyone else, Ridell. You have your orders."

Shenda grimaced inwardly. "Yes, sir." Dammit to hell! The extra three corridors she would have to walk would lengthen her shift considerably, and she was already dying of thirst.

Shenda entered Corridor E, noting at a glance that there was no sign of Samson. The video feed was indeed dead; the monitors attached to the elaborate security system displayed nothing but visual static. Frowning, Shenda searched the overhead tracks for the nearest roving camera. It hung silent, its normally active lens-piece frozen in place. Why? Curiously, she approached the closest monitor and examined the secondary video-eye. Lacking the range of the overhead cameras and designed primarily for inter-terminal communication, it normally operated as backup for the overheads. It, too, was dead. Sighing as she realized there would be no simple solution to the problem, Shenda licked her dry lips and removed her tool-belt.

"Attention, Private!" A voice suddenly blared very near her ear, startling her. "Sub-Level One, Corridor D. Computer scan cannot read your identity tags." The lieutenant's commanding voice emerged from terminal speakers all along the corridor. "Please adjust them outside your uniform *now.*"

Although she was neither a private nor in Corridor D, which was a wide, gently sloping hall that angled toward the surface, Shenda found herself glancing down to ensure that her own dogtags rested outside her uniform as required for identification purposes. *Must be another prisoner arriving,* she mused. Corridor D was the closest access to the thruster pads and, for that reason, was used exclusively for bringing in additional prisoners or rotating prison personnel off-planet. Since the next rotation of guards would not occur for another month, the only reason for a private to be

17

in Corridor D would be as part of an escort for an incoming prisoner.

Shenda studied the vid unit. A wire dangled from it. Overheated? She depressed the button for terminal-to-terminal restricted audio link. "Lieutenant, this is Corporal Ridell. Do you read?"

"Affirmative, Corporal. What did you find?"

"A disconnected wire, sir." She studied the end. Surprise made her glance sharply around. "It looks like it may have been cut." Who could have cut it? The prisoners remained safely in their cells and, according to the cell-door lights overhead, the doors remained securely locked.

There was a pause. "I don't like the sound of that, Corporal. We have been unable to locate Private Samson." There was another pause and his words became more distant as the lieutenant talked to someone other than Shenda. "Have we identified that private in Corridor D?" A pause. "Well, why the hell not? Somebody must know the guy." Shenda heard the unintelligible murmur of an answering voice. "Ridell!"

"Here, sir."

"We've now lost the vid feed from Corridor D as well. Is it possible that D's audio is malfunctioning?"

Shenda considered, working while she talked. "Even if it is, it's right around the corner. Anyone in there should be able to hear the audio from the terminal at the junction."

The lieutenant didn't respond immediately. Finally, he said, "Can you repair the vid?"

"The overheads will have to wait for a tech, sir. But I'm splicing this unit now. Just two more units and I'll have all the backup vid working anyway."

"Good. I want you to walk the corridor, exercising extreme caution until reinforcements arrive. Do you understand?"

Shenda looked up at the monitor as the lieutenant's handsome visage flickered on. "Understood, sir. Do you have video?"

"Affirmative, Corporal. Keep me posted."

Shenda nodded and stepped away from the terminal. So where was Private Samson? Frowning, she picked up her tool belt and began walking toward the next vid unit. She didn't like the feel of this.

An inmate coughed.

Suddenly, Shenda sensed an alteration in the atmosphere: the electrical charge preceding a storm. She looked to the cells on her right, peering beyond the bars constructed of sheenless metal alloy—no costly laser grids here; they weren't considered necessary when the surface temperature could kill an escapee in as little as 24 hours. Nerves tingling with the awareness of a danger she couldn't identify, Shenda studied the inmates as she slowed her stride. Although they still reclined in apparent lethargy, there was something different about them. Did they seem less listless?

One of the prisoners met her eyes as she passed, and suddenly she knew what it was that permeated the rank prison air. Excitement! The inmates were excited. Why?

A prison break? A riot? Impossible! More than 50 years ago, Earth had experienced a number of costly and deadly prison revolts. It was they, in fact, that had sparked the construction of this facility. And in all the years that the Sentran prison had been in operation, not a single prisoner had escaped. The small percentage that had successfully overpowered guards and escaped the facility proper, had died on the surface. So what was fueling the convicts with excitement? Shenda removed the stunner from her belt, palming it, and cautiously moved on.

Her eyes fell on a prisoner in a cell a little ahead, just opposite the junction. She slowed her pace. Unlike the others, this man no longer lounged lethargically on his cot. Gripping the bars of his cell, he peered intently at her from beneath lowered brows. Dark brown hair hung in sweaty tendrils to his shoulders, and at least two days of growth stubbled his strong jawline.

Although Shenda was accustomed to seeing the male prisoners on Sentra clad in nothing more than loincloths, for some reason this man seemed more naked than had the others. Masculinity positively oozed from every pore. He was a large-framed man, over six feet, with a powerful, athletic musculature. His darkly tanned skin bespoke either regular injections of melanin or considerable time spent in a shipboard sunbed. In the next instant his weight shifted and she caught a glimpse of a white hip and a very definite demarcation line on his upper thigh. She promptly altered her assessment. This man had spent considerable time beneath the filtered rays of a *real* sun.

As she drew nearer his cell, Shenda met his gaze. His eyes, dark and unfathomable, as cold as the depths of space, glistened, not with excitement, but with something else. Fierce determination? Challenge? A shiver worked its way up Shenda's spine. Something was definitely wrong here, but she was at a loss to determine what it could be. She eyed the inmate warily. Checked the security light over his cell door: red. It was fine. Returned her eyes to the felon.

Feeling inexplicably threatened as though some

aspect of him completely negated the security represented by the bars of his cell, Shenda swallowed. But it was more than just his unkempt appearance and powerful physique which influenced her. Rather, it was something that emanated from him: a force, present in every prideful line of his body, unconsciously projected, demanding respect.

She struggled to classify him. He had a fighting man's physique, and a commander's stance. She'd wager a month's credit that this man was no ordinary murderer. A *mercenary* captain? The mere thought curled her lip in disgust. Mercenaries. Murderers for hire to the highest bidder, usually in the employ of one of the highly competitive exploration and mining companies.

The lieutenant's voice boomed through the complex again, startling her. "Private! You must identify yourself immediately!"

Shenda realized that it had been little more than a minute since she'd last spoken to the lieutenant, yet the charged atmosphere had slowed time. And suddenly she knew from which direction the threat would come: Corridor D. The *surface*? But with the exterior vid out, they were blind to the nature of that threat. She checked the single working monitor. No lights flashed to signal the triggering of a silent alarm, so even though support personnel were en route, security still didn't perceive a major threat. Quarks! Couldn't they feel it?

As she approached the junction to Corridor D, her wariness increased tenfold and the malfunctioning vid units were forgotten. Shenda circled wide, away from the junction and nearer the wall of cells, although she carefully remained beyond the reach of this particular cell's menacing inhabitant.

She could see no one in the corridor. Yet, rather than assuage her fears, that observation only exacerbated them. Suddenly a deep vibration rumbled through the complex. Within mere fractions of a second, the sound grew from a rumble to a terrifying roar. Before her mind could begin to identify the sound as that of an explosion, the floor bucked beneath her feet. Off balance, she was thrown aside like a child's toy to strike the bars of the nearest enclosure with jarring intensity. Her tool-belt fell from nerveless fingers. Her head snapped back. Her teeth clamped down on soft tissue, filling her mouth with the salty taste of blood from her lacerated tongue. And a large forearm wedged itself beneath her chin, restricting her breathing, holding her immobile against the unyielding alloy of the cell bars. Fear raced through her, swift and instinctive. And with it, the cold clarity of thought that a Stellar Legionnaire must always have in times of stress.

Not for the first time, Shenda decried the regulations stating that prison inmates need not be fitted with crime-deterrent capsules. However, since the capsules had been designed as a means of alleviating overcrowded prisons on Earth by providing a system wherein many criminals could be allowed to remain within society, inmates fell outside the guidelines.

Bureaucratic idiots! Had the convicts been fitted with the capsules, the prison's central computer could have detonated them at the first sign of trouble. The prisoner would be either executed or—if his crime was a lesser one and he'd been fitted with one of the newly designed stun-capsules—rendered insensible. Such a capability would have terminated any uprising in its infancy. But there would be no help coming from the central computer. Shenda was on her own until the additional guards arrived from the bowels of the prison complex. If they *could* arrive. The explosion had sounded as though it had issued from deep beneath them.

Ignoring the chaotic din that surrounded her—men's voices raised in anger, in supplication, in elation, issuing orders—Shenda concentrated on her own perilous situation. As the odor of male perspiration enveloped her, she lifted her left hand to claw at the muscled forearm pressed against her throat. With her right hand, she carefully angled the stunner in her palm back to strike at her captor.

"I wouldn't." The growled words grated along her nerve endings like sandpaper. Something cold touched her temple. She looked out of the corner of her eye to see her own laser, suddenly alien and deadly, pressed to the side of her head. A hard chunk of ice settled in the pit of her stomach. "Hand it over," the inmate demanded in a bass rumble. She hesitated, desperately seeking another avenue. "Now!" His arm pressed more firmly against her throat, cutting off her breathing.

Reluctantly, battling a darkness that hovered on the edges of her consciousness like a vulture, Shenda passed him the stunner. Immediately his grip slackened enough for her to draw a shallow breath. What did he think he was going to gain by taking her hostage? she wondered. She couldn't even open the cell door; it took a special key to override the computer, and guards never carried them.

Another explosion roared through the complex, rattling her teeth in her jaws. They lost overhead lighting. As the emergency lighting kicked in, bathing everything in a surreal red glow, bits of concrete crumbled away from the ceiling, creating a cloud of dust that threatened to choke off the little breathing capability she still possessed. Her nails raked desperately at the muscle-corded arm across her throat, and she was rewarded by a slight relaxation of the constriction.

How long would it take for reinforcements to arrive? And what would happen to her, a hostage to a condemned man, when they did?

Shenda had little time to wonder further about her fate. In the next instant the red light over her captor's cell door transformed to green, and Shenda knew with a sickening sense of dread that the enclosure was no longer secure. She glanced to the side with her peripheral vision, and saw that a similar occurrence marked the release of cell doors all along Corridor E. Stars! It wasn't possible!

Had she been playing a game of Galactic Exchange at that point, she would not have wagered so much as a single day's credit on the anticipation of a long life.

"I must release you in order to open the cell door. You will do exactly as you are told or you will die. Is that understood?" Despite the deep, animalistic tone of her captor's voice, he spoke with the precision of an educated man.

Shenda nodded as much as was possible with his arm wedged beneath her chin. He must have felt her compliance because he released her almost instantly. Shenda gulped two quick dust-laden breaths and, coughing, watched her captor slide open his cell door. Wait. Watch. But, the muzzle of the laser did not waver.

Scrutinizing her captor thoroughly, she noted

the name recorded on the waistband of his loincloth: *SWAN*. Perspiration ran in small rivulets down Swan's body, beading in glistening drops on the hair of his chest. Large pectoral muscles and a flat stomach ridged with sinew vaunted a strength Shenda suspected was not overstated.

Without allowing the laser to falter by so much as a millimeter, he cast a glance at the working monitor. Shenda followed his gaze. Hope blossomed. The silent alarm had been triggered. Now, the number of reinforcements enroute would quadruple . . . provided they could find a means to get here that had not been cut off by the explosions.

Swan reached for her, grasped her arm and jerked her roughly in front of him, obviously intending to use her as a shield. Since he towered a whole head over her own five feet six inches, and Legionnaires carried laser weaponry equipped with precision sighting, she wouldn't be a very effective buffer if they managed to get a clear view of his head for more than a couple of seconds. But she didn't feel inclined to point that out.

Once again Swan's left arm encircled her, this time at shoulder level, merely holding her before him. The sheer size and overpowering masculinity of her captor began to sabotage Shenda's innate assertiveness. She could feel his powerful pectoral muscles flexing against her shoulder blades; his rock-solid biceps against her breast. Rather than controlling her by means of near strangulation, he relied more heavily on the threat of the laser at her throat. "We're leaving." He directed her toward Corridor D.

Shenda stared in disbelief at the access to the corridor. The gates hadn't worked. They were supposed to lower into place, isolating individual prison sectors at the first sign of trouble. Stars! What else could go wrong?

And then the realization of where Corridor D led penetrated. The surface! "Are you insane?" she demanded hoarsely of her captor. "You can't last thirty-six hours aboveground." She refused to say *we,* as though doing so would in some way acknowledge the possibility of such a horrid end to her life. "The sun will bake you to death."

"I don't plan on being there that long. Now shut up and move!" To emphasize his order, he pressed the muzzle of the weapon against her throat a little more forcefully and swung her off her feet to point her in the direction he wanted to go. Stepping over heaved and ruptured concrete flooring, Shenda began walking.

A tide of half-naked shouting men, all racing toward the surface and the dubious promise of freedom, surged around them. Even had Shenda been able to break away, she would have been carried along by the force. Although partially shielded by her captor's big body, Shenda found herself battered by sharp elbows and the clawing nails of hands fighting to grab anything or anyone in order to pull themselves through the crush to freedom. The temperature, augmented by the proximity of milling bodies, rose to the point of being suffocating. Corridor D had never seemed so long.

Suddenly, off to one side, Shenda caught sight of a Legionnaire uniform. Elation rose within her. "Over here," she shouted, forgetting, for an instant, the danger presented by the weapon at her throat. She struggled frantically in Swan's grasp, determined to free an arm and attract her colleague's attention. And then, the incongruity of the Legionnaire's presence *here* struck her. The prisoners seemed not in the least bothered by his proximity.

As she stared, she met the young Legionnaire's eyes. The excitement mirrored there was identical to that in the eyes of the escaping inmates surging around her. Shenda's heart sank. A collaborator, she realized; or an impostor.

The Legionnaire's eyes moved beyond her to Swan. A brilliant smile split his face and he snapped a salute. Then, turning his attention back toward their rear, he watched for the pursuit that would, sooner or later, materialize. Soon enough? Shenda wondered.

Off to the right, she noticed another fraudulent Legionnaire hugging the wall and watching the sea of humanity pass. Within moments another . . . and another. By the time they reached the enormous double doors at the end of Corridor D, beyond which lay the surface of Sentra, Shenda had counted eight such Legionnaires, one of whom had been a female.

The doors opened ahead of them. A blast of heat at least ten degrees warmer than the 35-degree centigrade temperature of Sub-Level One struck Shenda in the face.

Suddenly the female Legionnaire materialized beside them. "What about them?" she shouted at Swan, gesturing at the prisoners surging around them.

"They're on their own." Swan's loud response vibrated Shenda's eardrums. "They have a pilot. If they can get to one of the guards transports, they might make it."

The woman nodded. She looked at Shenda with solemn, unreadable eyes. Then, returning her gaze to Swan, she nodded slightly and turned her attention forward. A shiver, ominous and cold despite the heat, worked its way up Shenda's spine.

Now that they were outside, the compression of humanity eased. A large quantum-style ship awaited them on the nearest thrust pad. Sleek and as black as the night sky, it would be nearly invisible against the jet background of space. Like a pirate's ship. Shenda swallowed. Ah, quarks! Given a choice between a pirate and a mercenary, she'd take a mercenary any day. At least he would have a code of honor, convoluted though it might be.

Two

Suddenly, laser fire erupted behind them. Yes! Ignoring the weapon Swan held to her throat, preferring the certainty of death here, as a Legionnaire, to the uncertainty of her fate as the victim of pirates, Shenda began to struggle in earnest. Determined to slow her captor, she had just begun to twist in his grasp, seeking some sign of her colleagues, when a high-pitched shriek grated along her nerve endings, making her teeth ache.

"Swan," it said. Before Shenda had a chance to do more than turn her head forward again, something swooped in her face. She felt the scrape of leathery wings against her cheeks. Heard the hawk-like scream of the name "Swan" in her eardrums. Felt the touch of something warm and scaly against her forehead. And froze. What was it?

Slowly, carefully, she turned her head to the left. Some type of winged reptile sat on Swan's naked shoulder. It was about the size of a domestic cat. But beyond that the resemblance to any creature Shenda had ever seen ended; unless you took into account the renderings she'd seen of mythical dragons. In reality, it resembled those more closely than anything.

Two enormous taloned feet dug into the bare flesh of Swan's shoulder. Iridescent fishlike scales in metallic shades of gold, silver and copper covered its body and whip-like tail. As though prepared for flight, its leathery wings extended away from its body, allowing the brilliant Sentran sun to pierce the transparent yellow-gold flesh. It revealed a delicate bone structure and a tracery of black veining. In the next instant, the creature cocked its bird-like head, opened its mouth and flicked her cheek with a long, forked tongue. Tasting her? Shenda gritted her teeth and managed to suppress a shudder, but it wasn't easy.

"What . . . what is it?" she asked, barely conscious of having spoken aloud as, with a combination of horror and fascination, she eyed its tiny mouth full of needle-sharp teeth. Her attention completely focused on the creature, she didn't realize that she had gone compliant in her captor's grasp, or that they drew ever nearer his ship.

Swan sensed the question more than heard it. "A Morar," he shouted distractedly as he turned to look back the way they had come. His people, although returning the prison guards' laser fire, were in full retreat. One of them screamed as a blast struck his thigh. He fell back, and another immediately moved forward to take his place. Another blast made it through, striking the ship near Swan's right shoulder in a shower of sparks. They didn't have much time. He looked down at the woman he held captive.

"Swan!" a female bellow came from the open hatch of his ship. He recognized Brie Tanner, ex-Legionnaire sergeant extraordinaire. "Get in here. We have to go. Now!" When she was stressed, Brie was the bossiest woman this side of Pluto, but she was also one of the smartest. Which was why, of all of his people, only Brie could get away with speaking to him that way.

Swan cast another glance at his retreating rescuers. Brie was right.

Having heard Brie's yell, his captive began to struggle again in earnest. A booted foot slammed painfully into his naked shin. Swan glanced down at the tight knot of midnight black hair perched atop the corporal's head. She'd pulled it so tight that it actually seemed to draw the outer corners of her eyes up. In the next instant he realized that he was staring directly into his captive's desperate, green eyes. Saints! She would have to look at him now. Gritting his teeth against some foreign emotion that threatened his purpose, Swan raised his fist and clipped her on the jaw. As she sagged in his grasp, he shoved the laser into the waistband of the prison loincloth. Then, lifting her in his arms, he ran up the gangway into the ship.

Placing the woman hastily on the cot in his cabin, Swan strapped her into place. Then, removing the clinging Morar from his shoulder, he set it on a stand designed for the purpose. "Watch her, Tlic. Let me know when she wakes up."

Tlic responded with an indecipherable squawk as Swan secured the door. Drawing the laser weapon from his waistband, he raced back to provide what aid he could to his small band of ex-Legionnaires. His people, the able supporting the wounded, were almost upon him. Firing around the edge of the hatch, he laid down a cover of laser fire. A prison guard fell. Another stepped over him to take his place. And again Swan fired. He had to give his rescuers time to make their way up the gangway. Thank the stars, it was a short one.

"We're in. Close the hatch," Billy shouted as she reached to pull Leverton and Drusiak into the ship.

Swan pulled the lever. "Hatch closing," he yelled in response. Something struck the side of the ship, louder and with more force than any laser. A shower of sparks from traumatized overhead wiring rained down on his naked torso. Brushing at the cinders, Swan considered the damage to his *Raven*, and gritted his teeth against the spate of curses hovering on his tongue.

"That was blaster fire," Steve Houston said, identifying the nature of the difference for them. "Grenades are only a minute away, guys." Steve knew Legionnaire fighting techniques better than most of the others. His major discipline with the Stellar Legion prior to the squad's desertion had been combat procedure.

"Get us out of here, Brie, or we won't be going anywhere," Mike Obherst bellowed toward the corridor mike.

In the next second, thrusters fired and the ship lifted. Another hit from a blaster rocked the craft. "Come on, Brie," Swan muttered under his breath.

Shuddering, the ship began to move forward. Unlike a skimmer or a scout ship, the *Raven* was a mid-size, quantum-style craft with the capacity to carry as many as 30 passengers. It was the largest ship capable of landing directly on-world. Anything larger required a space dock from which passengers or cargo would be shuttled to a planet's surface. Although it was as swift in space as either of its smaller counterparts, the size of the quantum-style ships made them more ponderous in takeoff.

Breathing heavily in the thick, hot air, Swan observed Andrew Tucker lending support to the wounded Striker as they moved down the narrow corridor in search of a vacant compartment. Kneeling next to Choban, their resident medic, Swan asked, "How many wounded?"

"Out of the eight who went in, five are wounded," Choban said. "But most aren't bad." He held up Obherst's hand to display a bloody, mangled finger.

Swan looked into Mike Obherst's eyes and saw the pain there. He didn't believe him when he smiled and said, "It hasn't started to hurt yet."

Reaching out, he laid a hand on Obherst's shoulder. The gesture spoke more eloquently than words.

Obherst grinned through his pain. "Anytime, boss."

Swan returned his gaze to Choban. "Samson?" he asked.

"Clipped him a good one and stuffed him in a storage closet," Choban responded. "They'll never know he was one of us."

With a grim smile, Swan nodded. "Good."

Slowly, the noise of the exploding fire of blasters faded as the *Raven* moved beyond the range of the smaller weapons. Now if only they could beat the grenades. "Booster rockets in fifteen seconds, guys," Brie warned. "Automatic cabin pressure equalization and life support systems engaged. Brace yourselves."

Somebody passed Swan a pair of magnetic gravity boots for his bare feet. Although the *Raven* was capable of producing enough artificial gravity to keep its crew's feet on the floor, its strength was minimal and the gravity boots provided a more natural environment. Swan secured his feet in them and, with no time to do anything else, joined the remaining crew members as they braced themselves in the narrow passageway. Gripping the metal handles which lined the ship's halls at waist height, they pressed their feet against the opposite wall for stability.

The boosters fired. An explosion of sound permeated the craft, making even shouted conversation impossible. Swan felt his skin tighten against the bone structure of his face. Felt the vibration of the craft radiate through him. Felt the exact pattern of the rivets and ridges of the bulkhead mapping themselves into the flesh of his naked back. It became an effort to force his lungs to move against the weight on his chest. The torturous ascent lasted forever.

Forever was only a few long minutes. Slowly the pressure eased. "We have orbit, guys," Brie's voice said through the speakers, labored and a bit breathless. "But don't start celebrating yet. Looks like somebody was up here waiting for us. Logan, you'd better get up here."

"Yeah." Swan's mouth was as dry as sunwarmed stone and the word emerged as a rasp. Swallowing, he tried again. "On my way."

A minute later, Swan stepped onto the bridge. The wide panorama of star-studded space stretched out before them. Freedom—if he could manage to hold on to it.

"Here." Brie's strident voice focused his attention on the screen near her right hand. A large blip tracked across the screen on a path which would intercept theirs in mere minutes. A definite threat. Another smaller blip following their flight path almost exactly rose from the surface of Sentra. It might be escaping prisoners, but then again it might not.

Quickly seating himself in the pilot's seat, Swan began studying readouts. Placing his palm on the identification plate imbedded into the console, he waited impatiently while the computer completed palm-print verification. The few seconds seemed like an hour as he watched the blips tracking ever nearer. A green light flashed.

"Verbal response mode," he snapped. The tension in his muscles increased rapidly in proportion to the nearness of the blip on the screen.

Almost immediately, a precise female voice, only faintly recognizable as mechanized, replied. "Verbal response mode activated. It is good to see you, Commander Swan."

Logan ignored the pleasantries. "Lais, identify the ship currently on intercept course with *Raven*." L.A.I.S. (pronounced lace) was an acronym for Lindell's Artificial Intelligence Systems.

A schematic diagram flashed up on a screen to his left. "It is the star-cruiser *Trojan I*, standard Legion design. They will be within firing range within three minutes."

What the hell was a star-cruiser doing here? Shouldn't they be off chasing pirates or saving the galaxy from the privateers funded by one of Earth's more rebellious jurisdictions? He tried to remember who it was who had been the thorn in the side of Earth's coalition presidency the last time he'd paid any attention to Earth's news. The Brazilians, he thought. So why wasn't the *Trojan* hunting Brazilian privateers? "Brie, transmit the identity of our passenger."

"What good will that do?"

"Just do it, Brie," he snapped.

"Yes, sir."

Swan smiled grimly as he watched Brie's fingers fly over the console. *Raven* still wasn't in the clear, but he'd bet his life on the fact that the warship wouldn't fire on them. Not now when they knew the identity of Swan's hostage. It gave him a few precious minutes.

He focused on the computer monitor. "Lais, how long do we have until *Trojan I* is within interception range?"

"Eleven point three six minutes."

"Locate a lane for the leap," Logan said, referring to one of the plentiful and naturally occurring wrinkles in the fabric of space. "And plot a course for Fortuna." The discovery of the lanes, scarcely more than a hundred years ago, and the fractionally more recent development of a means to detect them easily, had revolutionized space travel. But the fact that the lanes occurred naturally meant that their locations were completely unpredictable. He sent a prayer winging its way to the saints that there would be a lane near . . . very near.

"Computing."

A number flashed up on the screen. "I have located a lane ten point seven-five minutes away. However, there is a twenty-five percent instability quotient."

They couldn't wait for stable lane. "Initiate," Swan barked as he scanned the data filling the screen. Talk about cutting it close. He depressed the intercom button on the console. "Ten minutes to hyperspace, guys," he announced. His voice was strong and controlled. "Strap yourselves in." A chorus of affirmative responses sounded from various parts of the ship. The monstrous starcruiser loomed ever larger on the screen. "And pray," he murmured in afterthought to no one in particular as he terminated communication.

"Mass restriction activated. We will achieve space-time escape velocity in . . . eight minutes." Lights flashed in sequences too rapid for the human eye to follow as Lais computed. A second later, she spoke again. "Assuming that the lanes do not shift during our flight, the course to Fortuna will require two leaps. We will be in hyperspace for four point seven-five hours ship-time on the first leap before emerging into standard space."

"Acknowledged," Logan said. Abruptly, the ship rocked violently. Bracing himself, he scanned the console for an explanation.

Lais interpreted the readout simultaneously. "I am registering disrupter fire across our bow, Commander. The source is *Trojan I. Raven* has not sustained damage."

"Understood," Logan responded. They had no option. "Proceed with the leap."

The noise within the ship gradually increased to a point that precluded unnecessary conversation. Both Logan and Brie donned helmets which allowed them to maintain direct contact with the computer and each other. Although designed to protect the wearer, the helmets were, in effect, computer terminals. Even the visors had been designed to function as miniature computer monitors when necessary.

Logan watched the stars and distant planets move past the steelglass viewscreen at an ever increasing speed until they became nothing more than tiny streaks of light. The star-cruiser, looming ever nearer, continued to torment its smaller prey with tooth-rattling blasts as it attempted to bully the *Raven* into abandoning its escape. Observing the inexorable progress of *Trojan I*, Logan squeezed the arms of his seat and suppressed the urge to bellow in frustration. "Come on," he murmured, gritting his teeth. "Come on."

"Please be prepared for the leap," Lais said in his ear.

There was an instant of wrenching dislocation. A moment when the physical aspects of his body had no place, occupied no time, did not exist. Pain was non-existent. Time became meaningless. Fear was everything. Not the fear of death, but the fear of having never been. Fear of nothingness. Fear that he would be lost forever in that dark, mystical fabric of the universe where time and space were no more. It was always the same. Although they ignored it as best they could, few could control the instinctive terror that gripped them in that instant. And then, mercifully, it began to fade.

"Space-time curvature is nearing completion," Lais informed them.

From the enormous bridge of the *Trojan I,* Captain Carvell stood before the large steelglass viewscreen and stared, with a sense of fatalistic doom, at the spot where the *Raven* had disappeared. Behind him ten feet and down three steps, he could hear the murmurs of his crew as they went about their duties. Good people, all. Nearer, within four feet, he could feel the presence of two others at his back: a tall blond man, immaculate in a white uniform, and his aide, impeccably dressed in blue. Both had embarked with the *Trojan* in an unofficial capacity, as *observers.* Yet Carvell knew well that the man behind him held the power to make or break careers. The charismatic Commissioner of Justice, Darren Marnier, was the type of man whom millions would follow blindly to their deaths were he to ask it of them. Even now, Carvell could scarcely reconcile his own changed feelings for the man with the aura Marnier exuded. The contrast was so great that, at one point, Carvell had actually wondered if there might be something wrong with his own perceptions. How could he despise a man that everyone admired? But there was no mistake. Believing Marnier to be the benevolent man he depicted himself to be, Carvell had allowed his own career to be helped along through the auspices of the Commissioner of Justice. He had been reminded of that just recently. The reminder had carried a subtle menace that Carvell could not ignore. He swallowed, forcing himself to acknowledge the fact that a moment of weakness in his life had resulted in a debt which would never be cleared.

Girding himself for the repercussions which might follow his loss of the *Raven*, he tuned his ears to the soft-voiced conversation behind him. "It would seem that the intelligence report we received concerning Swan's imminent rescue came a little late." The voice belonged to the man in blue. Carvell had forgotten his name, but he remembered his penetrating dark-eyed gaze.

"Mmmmm," came the thoughtful response. "Deliberately, do you think, Phillip?"

There was a pause. "I can't be certain."

Slowly, Captain Carvell turned to face the tall man in white and his unnerving companion. The *Raven* was gone. There was nothing that could be done about that now. "I'm sorry, sir. Without disabling the ship, there was little else to be done."

Pale blue eyes studied him expressionlessly for endless moments. "You will yet have your opportunity to capture Swan, Captain. Set course for Fortuna by the fastest route you can find."

Carvell chafed at being used. He had never been

any man's tool. But escaping this situation would take some thought. In the meantime, he had little choice but to continue as he was. Gritting his teeth, he nodded and responded as expected. "Yes, sir." He wondered what Fortuna held in store for them.

Logan sighed with heartfelt gratitude as all noise within the ship abruptly ceased. "We have achieved hyperspace," Lais stated unnecessarily. "Total elapsed ship time to Fortuna is estimated at sixteen point two hours. Did you wish to program a destination time?"

Logan glanced at the console. Time compression was not recommended; it invariably caused headaches ranging from mild to crippling in nature, and sometimes generated unexplained psychoses in crew members. To avoid this, ships usually attempted to approximate arrival time in relation to the actual elapsed ship time while in hyperspace. However, in this instance Logan couldn't help but feel the risk of compression was warranted. "How long did you say we'd be in normal space between leaps?"

"Current estimate is fifty-three point five minutes."

Logan considered. "Program destination time for sixty minutes from now. However, if for any reason we are in normal space for longer than fifty-four minutes, readjust destination time accordingly."

Experience had proven countless times that it was fatal to attempt to arrive at a destination *before* you had actually left another part of space. Those who had tried, without fail, had disappeared forever. Scientists called it Paradox, a phenomenon put forth by nature to ensure the integrity of the space-time continuum; Swan called it scary. Although he wanted to lose as little time as possible in returning home—he didn't want to emerge from hyperspace to find a star-cruiser full of Legionnaires already waiting for them—neither did he want to cut it too close. The 60 minutes should be enough to allow for a margin of error and still enable them to escape the star-cruiser following them.

"Affirmative," Lais responded. "Current projected arrival time in Fortuna space will be 11.48.27."

Swan checked the console display. "Confirmed," he said, removing the helmet. Relaxing slightly, he turned his attention to his copilot, who had likewise removed her headgear.

"And after Fortuna?" she asked. "Where are you taking us, Logan?" The use of his first name gave her away. Brie was worried.

He looked at her. She was broad-shouldered for a woman, with a solid body and slightly stocky build. Not unattractive by any means, but certainly no beauty. Then again, she was not the type of woman who cared. It was Brie who had approached him when she and her small band of Legionnaires had been forgotten and abandoned, without credit for their services, on Fortuna. Who knows what had happened? Possibly a computer glitch somewhere. But the Stellar Legion's loss was his gain. Logan had never had cause to regret hiring the small band when they'd decided to transfer their loyalties to someone who would not forget them when it came time to compensate them for their services. "Nowhere, Brie. You're staying home."

"On Fortuna?" she asked incredulously. "But . . ."

Swan stared her argument down before it emerged. He knew from experience that he had to be firm with Brie at the onset. "Was there something you wanted to say, Sergeant?"

Brie hesitated, but forged on. "Yes, sir. I'd like to point out that Fortuna is the first place they'll look for us."

Logan sighed. She was, after all, concerned for *his* safety. "Fortuna is the first place they'll look for *me*, Brie, not us. There is no reason why all of you should become fugitives. They have no proof to link any of you to me or to the prison break. By the time we reach Fortuna, accelerated healing will have erased most outward signs of injury, so provided you aren't harboring me, you won't be in any danger. Besides, I need you people there to protect my interests." His thoughts turned to the man who had become his nemesis. Logan still found it difficult to accept the knowledge that the people's best hope for a humanitarian politician was in fact a criminal. How could a man so charismatic, so polished, so seemingly righteous and honorable, enthrall people so thoroughly that none even suspected his rotten core? One thing was certain, despite the difference in their status, Logan Swan would not go down without a fight.

Logan looked at Brie. "I'm only going home long enough to retrieve the tracker and make some plans. Although we know who is stealing the artifacts, unfortunately we don't know where he's taking them." He thought that, perhaps, Lilah could have told him. But after sentencing him to death by betraying him to authorities in exchange for who-knows-what from Marnier, the woman who had been Logan's lover had disappeared. Forcing the bitterness and hurt from his mind, he looked at Brie. "As soon as I've arrived at a workable plan I go on alone."

Brie nodded, although she didn't look happy. "I understand." She cleared her throat and studied some instruments. "How much of the data we sent through Tlic actually got to you?"

Logan frowned as he requested additional navigational options from Lais, hoping to find a faster route. "Most of it, I should think."

He had a rather unique relationship to the Fortunan Morar. A few years earlier, he'd been stung by it and managed to survive. An uncommon occurrence. In addition to rendering him resistant to Morar venom, the happenstance had forged a link between himself and Tlic that had enabled him to see through the Morar's eyes and hear through its ears. Distance seemed to have no effect whatsoever on this capability. However, by human standards, the Morar's piercing vision was distorted, which made some things unrecognizable to Logan. Likewise, the Morar's hearing, although acute, was slightly off when relayed to a human mind. He had no idea why he'd been stung. When one took into account the number of people with whom they came into contact, Morars actually stung very few. Some medical scientists theorized that the stinging was actually some type of selective process initiated by the Morars in an attempt to forge a link with the human species. However, the Morars did sting in self-defense as well—horses, who for some reason intensely disliked Morars, were often stung.

Logan focused on Brie's question. "Why do you ask?" he said.

Brie cleared her throat. "I told you when the monitors went down in Corridor E they'd send the nearest guard to check it out. You got that. Right?"

Swan nodded. Brie continued. "Well, when computer scheduling revealed the identity of the guard most likely to draw that duty, I suggested you use her as a hostage to get you *to* the ship." Swan caught the unspoken meaning—*to* the ship, not *on* the ship—and began to understand where Brie was taking the conversation.

Swan sighed. "As the daughter of the Commissioner of Interstellar Affairs, His Excellency Harris Ridell, our Shenda Ridell made an excellent hostage to get me *to* the ship, I agree with you. Although, as it turned out, the blasts were so effective I hardly needed her. But there is something about her that you didn't tell me. Something that I learned myself while on trial."

"What is that?"

"According to the latest entertainment gossip, Shenda Ridell is also expected to be formally affianced to the Commissioner of Justice, one Darren Marnier, in the very near future."

Brie stared at him. Slowly, she closed her eyes. "Stars!" she breathed on a sigh.

Logan smiled grimly. "Exactly. Ms. Ridell is the closest thing to a life insurance policy that I'm likely to get."

"You intend to ransom her to him?"

Swan shrugged as he stared through the viewscreen with a hard, vengeful gaze. "Whatever it takes, Brie." He scanned the computer data and typed in some codes. "Whatever it takes," he murmured again. He was painfully aware that the mere act of bringing her aboard was likely to increase the manpower employed to hunt him down at least tenfold. And yet, as he so often did, Logan relied on his instincts. They told him the woman would prove useful. He looked at Brie. "Having someone with us whose life is not expendable has already bought us some time. At least they didn't shoot us out of the sky."

He looked at the universe displayed in all its splendor beyond the viewscreen, and realized how much he had taken for granted. "Unfortunately, time is one commodity I don't have much of."

There was a pause. "It's getting worse?" Brie asked quietly.

Dread gripped his throat in icy fingers, making speech impossible. He nodded and stared silently, sightlessly through the viewscreen at the timeless mists of hyperspace until the grip on his larynx loosened. "If we don't find that damned statue, I wouldn't bet on a long life."

"Do you have any idea how long you have?" she asked.

Swan shrugged. "Before I was incarcerated for trial, Lais projected twelve to fourteen weeks. That leaves me four weeks, six if I'm lucky."

Brie nodded solemnly. "You're sure there's nothing else we can do to help?"

Swan shook his head and concentrated on relegating the paralyzing fear to a distant part of his mind. He had to concentrate on surviving the next few hours before he could worry about the rest of his life. Methodically, he immersed himself in work as he continued making computer calculations. Although they were not yet safe from pursuers, he already felt at home. The *Raven* was his, and he knew her better than anyone else. Submerging himself in work, Logan managed to keep his mind blessedly off of his problems for almost two hours. Then, his intellect sought a new focus and found one. "So, Brie, what can you tell me about our passenger?"

Brie, her warm brown eyes focused straight ahead, didn't respond. Logan followed her gaze.

The heavens beyond the viewscreen now consisted of beautiful pastel mists swirling in ever-changing patterns against a blackness deeper than anything ever seen. Timelessness. Hyperspace. Suspension of all sense of motion. The known universe cloaked in mystery, hidden beyond the range of the human eye. Navigation was accomplished by coordinates only.

A second later, Brie surfaced from her trance, raked a hand over her close-cropped brown hair, and looked at him. "Sorry. What did you say?"

Logan frowned. What was it he'd said? Oh, yes. "What can you tell me about Shenda Ridell? You were once in the same squad, weren't you?" As a Legionnaire, Corporal Shenda Ridell was his enemy. As Marnier's fiancée, she was doubly so. Logan needed to know everything he could about her.

"Yeah." Brie nodded, and drew her brows together slightly in concentration. "What do you want to know? The general gossip? Or what I *personally* know?"

"Both."

She sighed again. "Okay. I might as well start with what I know. It's probably shorter."

Brie stroked her right eyebrow, a habit she had when thoughtful. "Before we ever saw her, we all knew who she was and that she would be joining our squad. Rumor had preceded her. We were prepared to hate her for the preferential treatment we were certain she'd get. But despite that, I eventually grew to . . . respect Shenda."

Logan noted the pause, and read it. "But you didn't like her?"

"I didn't get to know her well enough to decide if I liked her. Nobody did. Even when she joined group activities, she was never really one of us. A couple of the others tried to befriend her. From what I could tell, it never worked."

"So how did she earn your respect?"

Brie looked out the viewscreen and shrugged. "She never complained. Not once in the entire tour of active duty. And believe me, some of the garbage assignments they gave her would have made *me* complain."

Logan frowned. "What do you mean? I thought you said you expected her to receive special treatment."

Brie swiveled her seat toward him. "I did. We all did. You know, promotions she didn't deserve, that kind of thing." She shrugged. "But it never happened. The sergeant, and even the lieutenant, seemed determined to prove that they couldn't be bought." She shrugged and looked at Logan. "Personally, I know that wasn't true, so they must have had another reason for the way they treated her. I suspect now that they might have been paid to try to drive her out of the Legion. But what it came down to was that she always received the worst assignments. Without fail. And she never complained."

"You make her sound like a saint or something."

Brie snorted. "She's too damn cold to be a saint. Like I said, she never lets anyone close. She does her job—and does it damned well—but she never does more than her job. She takes *duty* very seriously, so she's reliable in a crisis, but she never offers help beyond the scope of duty requirements and never asks for it. At the time that I knew her, she had no friends. None. She didn't even date. Whether she finally developed a friend or two, I don't know. I suppose she must have if she's engaged."

Logan drummed his fingers on the arm of his

seat. So Shenda Ridell was a loner. Not particularly good material for a Legionnaire unit. To create a squad that operated with the precision of a well-oiled machine, individuality often had to be sacrificed. "All right. So what did the gossip have to say about her?"

Brie removed the container of water attached to the underside of the console and sucked a mouthful through the straw before answering. Finished, she capped the container and allowed it to drop slowly to the floor rather than replacing it. "Her mother died when she was quite young. Four or five, I think. She was raised by a series of nannies before being sent to boarding school, where she spent her early years. In adolescence, her father removed her from school and hired a succession of tutors to educate her at home. Rumor offered two explanations. Number one was that he missed her so much, he decided he wanted her living at home. Number two said that he was trying to turn her into the perfect accessory for his career. Harris Ridell is a charismatic man well liked by a lot of people, so most seemed to buy into explanation number one." Brie eyed the water container on the floor as though it were a Sentran rat. "From where I sit, I see a man fueled by ambition and little else, so . . . I tend to buy into reason number two."

Logan frowned. Brie was an excellent judge of character. She never made snap judgments, and he'd rarely known her to be wrong. "So how the hell did she end up as a Legionnaire? Her father couldn't have approved!"

Brie smiled. "Remember that ancient saying: *Like father, like daughter*?" Logan nodded, and she continued. "Well, I think His Excellency raised a child who's just as cold and tough as he is. She certainly has the same unswerving dedication to a cause. Although, to give her the benefit of the doubt, I would hazard to say that in her case her motivations may be a little less self-serving." She looked at Swan. "I think Shenda decided what she wanted, and she went for it. Daddy couldn't stop her."

If Brie had accurately assessed Shenda's character, then Ms. Ridell must have felt there was some personal gain in becoming a Legionnaire. Swan wondered what she'd gained that had been worth all the garbage assignments. "How could a young woman have circumvented the power held by a man like Harris Ridell?" he mused aloud.

"Honestly? I don't know. One short-lived rumor had it that she sent a vid-disk to an ex-journalist— a man her father had ruined over some political fiasco—with instructions that if she ever disappeared in questionable circumstances the video record was to be released to the press within thirty days. Not even the gossips dared to speculate as to what might be on that disk, though." Abruptly, she looked sharply at Swan. "Quarks! If that rumor carries even a shred of truth, Daddy is going to be absolutely frantic to get her back."

Logan closed his eyes briefly and then looked at Brie again. "So what you're telling me is that there is no love lost between His Excellency and his daughter."

Brie shrugged. "Only Shenda could answer that," she said. "They *are* the only family each other has. And from what I've heard, Shenda goes home every year for her vacation, so there must be something there. Personally, though, even if love is there, I don't think they *like* each other much."

"Let's say the rumor about the vid-disk is wrong, and assume that Harris Ridell and Shenda hate each other. Do you think there's a possibility that he won't be looking for her as energetically as we had supposed?"

Brie stroked her eyebrow. Finally, she sighed. "I don't think it will make any difference. He's enormously ambitious and constantly in the public eye. Politically, he can't afford to be seen as doing less than his utmost to regain his daughter."

"Of course." Logan rubbed at an itch on his chest, and realized that he was still half naked. He desperately needed a shower and some clean clothing, but he wanted to know everything he could about his pretty hostage before he spoke with her. "What about Marnier?" His lip curled as he said the name. "Anything new on him?"

Brie shook her head. "Sorry. Nothing of any use to us on the legal networks. I'm planning on accessing the Sub-Net computer archives to find out everything I can."

Logan nodded. "Do that. Let me know if you come up with anything . . . new." He finished the final word in a murmur as a feather-light touch in his mind informed him that Tlic was attempting to make contact. Closing his eyes, he found himself suddenly seeing his cabin with a Morar's vision. Colors were either muted, or non-existent. The human form lying on his bunk was elongated and angular.

His captive stirred, moaned slightly and brought her hand to her forehead. Opening her eyes, she appeared slightly confused as she stared at the ceiling. Then, slowly, her expression cleared. She tried to jerk to a sitting position, but was halted by the safety straps across her body. A minute later, she released the fastenings and, using them to steady herself, swung her legs over the side of the bed. Catching sight of the Morar, she froze.

"She awake?" Brie's voice drew Logan back.

He opened his eyes and nodded. "I think I'll go take a shower and then have a talk with her." He rose.

"Swan . . . ?"

He looked back at Brie. "Yeah."

"She's still a full-fledged Legionnaire with a sworn duty: to recapture and return you to authorities. I know real well the type of indoctrination she's had and the creed she's adopted. The sanctity of life—her own or anybody else's—ranks well down on her list of priorities. Duty is at the top. It'll take a lot to change that. Don't underestimate her."

Logan nodded. "I hear you."

Three

Holding onto the berth to steady herself in the low gravity, Shenda cautiously took her eyes off of the creature long enough to take in her surroundings. The chamber was not as small as some cabins she'd seen, but space was definitely limited. Attached to the floor near the head of the bunk, very near the creature's perch, sat a pair of magnetized gravity boots. Directly across from the narrow berth, a floor-to-ceiling cabinet full of drawers and doors created a wall, concealing the bulkhead. To the right of the cabinet, a small table and two small stools occupied the space nearest the door. Across from the table, at the foot of the bunk on which she sat, was another door. Probably a lavatory. On the wall behind her, an upper berth, currently retracted, occupied a depression. The chamber was positively spartan . . . very similar to her own quarters.

She swung her gaze back to the creature—what

had her captor called it? A More? No, a Morar. That was it. The Morar's strange beak-like mouth hung open, displaying a number of needle-sharp teeth. The tip of its forked tongue lolled from its mouth. Shenda wondered what it would do if she rose to go to the washroom. She needed a drink. Her throat was so dry she couldn't swallow. Even recycled and purified ship water, tasteless though it was, would be better than nothing.

Slowly, carefully, she moved along the berth until she could grasp the gravity boots. After removing her own Legion-issued footwear, she slid her feet into the heavier, slightly too large gravity boots and fastened them securely. The Morar observed without a change in expression. Cautiously, Shenda rose. The Morar cocked its head, watching her with depthless golden eyes, and drew its tongue back into its mouth.

"Easy," she whispered, sliding her feet slowly along the floor, gradually increasing the distance between them. "Easy." Any second she expected to hear that nerve-grating shriek and see those powerful talons directed at her face. It didn't happen. Within a minute that seemed like an hour, she reached the lavatory door. The door slid aside with a soft whisper as the sensor registered her presence. It *was* a lav. Thank the stars!

Turning on the tap, Shenda sucked a few mouthfuls of water from her cupped palms. Her thirst alleviated if not quenched, the next thought that entered her mind was escape. Somehow, she had to escape this band of fraudulent Legionnaires and return the convict, Swan, to Sentra. Or failing Sentra, at least deliver him into the hands of justice. The problem was, she couldn't arrive at a workable plan until she knew more about her captors. Who were they? Despite the appearance of the ship, Shenda realized on reflection that pirates were rarely so well organized. Why had she been taken? What did they hope to gain? And the most important question of all: Where were they headed?

When she emerged from the lav a moment later, it was to see her captor standing in the center of the small cabin. Shenda drew up instantly. His attire, consisting of the prison loincloth and a pair of mid-calf-height black gravity boots, would have looked hilarious on a man less certain of himself. But Shenda did not find anything about this man the least bit amusing. He dwarfed the small cabin. Wide shoulders, powerful arms and solid pectoral muscles all bespoke a man who was no stranger to physical labor. And his strength did not reside exclusively in his upper body by any means. Narrow hips rode strong thighs ridged with corded muscle. No, when the opportunity arose for her to conquer this man, it would definitely have to be by stealth and technique for, in a contest of strength, she didn't stand a chance. Firmly believing, however, that the most effective defense was a good offense, Shenda faced him with all the outward calm of a Legionnaire and the hauteur of a woman raised in upper society. "Who are you?" she demanded. "Where are you taking me?"

To her surprise, Swan turned his back to her as though she represented no more threat than a child, and pulled open a drawer in the cabinet. The gesture irritated her, as perhaps it was meant to do. She would not make the mistake of believing she was dealing with an uneducated felon here. Before her stood the first man who had ever successfully escaped the confines of Sentra. At the moment, he would not be wary of her Legionnaire fighting capabilities because he knew that, in space, she had nowhere to go, no means of escape. And it was possible that he too possessed more than rudimentary fighting skills. His companions, after all, had successfully played the part of Legionnaires long enough to cripple Sentra's costly defense system.

A faint rustle from the Morar drew her eyes. *And* there was the creature. She wondered if it provided protection for its master. Warily, thoughtfully, she took a couple of steps into the room.

When Swan turned to face her he held a small stack of black cloth, which Shenda assumed to be clothing, in his hands. "My name is Logan Swan," he responded in a deep rumble. His eyes, two hard chips of topaz stone, glared at her from beneath thick black brows. "But I think you know that. If by asking who I am you are, in fact, wondering what I *do*, I am an archeologist. I live and work on the planet Fortuna. *That* is where I'm taking you."

Archeologist! Fortuna! He could not have thrown her more off stride had he presented her with irrefutable documents proving he was a long-lost relative. Her mind grappled to bring to the fore everything she knew about the planet.

Fortuna. Earth's first, and thus far, only colony world. Colonization had not gone smoothly. The colony, barely 125 years old, had been muttering about secession for the last 80 years. But with an entire world population of less than three million people, and with the still-primitive conditions which were the norm on the planet, Fortuna simply didn't have the strength to demand its independence too loudly. If all that Shenda had heard from Legionnaires who'd been stationed there on duty rotation was true, it was the last place in the galaxy she wanted to go.

"Why—" But Shenda got no further.

Raising a restraining hand, he stopped her. "Further conversation can wait until I've showered and changed." He began to walk toward the lavatory . . . toward her. Every square inch of his large frame radiated menace and leashed violence. The urge to step hastily out of his way, to avoid contact, tore through her. She fought it. Be damned if she'd retreat from a convict. He halted in front of her; a scant six inches separated them. "Make yourself at home." His bass voice seemed suddenly different. More . . . intimate than threatening. She could feel the heat of his near-naked body. Smell the tangy scent of male perspiration. Hear the faint rustle of the clothing in his hands and the squeak of his boots as his weight shifted. Shenda felt strangely breathless, and she wondered absently about the quality of the life-support systems.

"In that cabinet"—he gestured with his chin toward a large square door in the wall of cabinets—"you'll find a beverage and snack dispenser." He studied her for a moment, and Shenda found herself captured by his eyes. Eyes the color of the potent whiskey her father had always favored. Swan extended his right hand toward her face. She felt the heat of it hovering near her cheek. *If he so much as touched her* . . . The half-formed threat wavered in her mind incomplete, halted by a strange fluttering sensation in her stomach. Shenda swallowed, unable to break the magnetic hold of his gaze.

And then, dropping his hand slightly, Swan extended it palm up and said, "I'll take the wrist terminal. I wouldn't want you getting yourself into trouble should we happen to get within range of a Legion ship."

"What . . . oh." Welcoming the distraction, Shenda looked down at the terminal in reflection. She considered the minute chance that the device would prove beneficial to her in any way, and realized it really wasn't worth attempting to make a stand over. "Here." She unstrapped the unit and deposited it in his outstretched hand.

He nodded in acknowledgment. "Don't try to leave the cabin," he cautioned. "The computer will prevent it." Turning, he entered the lav.

Shenda found herself sighing in relief as she watched the lavatory door whisper closed. What the hell was the matter with her? She should have been more forceful, demanded an explanation without delay. For some reason, her iron will had deserted her when she needed it most. She refused to consider fear as the explanation. Her captor might be dark and dangerous, but she doubted that he could match some of the people of her acquaintance for sheer ruthlessness.

As Logan locked the door, he shook his head. A moment ago, he had had the strongest urge to undo that ridiculously tight knot of hair atop Shenda Ridell's head and see if the outer corners of her bright, emerald eyes retained their exotic upward cast. How long was that midnight black hair? he wondered. And what would it feel like to wrap his fingers in it? The urge made him realize something that had been overshadowed by other concerns up to this point. He was attracted to Shenda Ridell. *Very* attracted to her. And the woman was engaged to his enemy! In love with his enemy!

Saints alive! He really *was* beginning to develop a self-destructive tendency when it came to women. While he was still coming to terms with the perfidy of one treacherous female, his hormones were already angling for another just like her. Quarks! They were even connected to the same man. Marnier. Logan frowned. He had yet to discover the *exact* nature of Lilah's association with the man.

Still frowning, he set his clean clothes on a stand, removed the gravity boots and filthy prison loincloth, and stepped into the shower, sealing the enclosure. As the chemical-laden recycled water began to swirl around him, forced into motion by compressed air, Swan soaped the dried sweat from his flesh and considered. When it came to women, Swan had never been blatantly licentious—*business before pleasure* had been pounded into his head at a young age by both his father and his grandfather—but neither was he used to denying himself when the inclination did strike.

He'd always enjoyed the pursuit of a woman as much as the possession. And for the most part, they had found him attractive, so he hadn't often had to deal with rejection. The fact that his lovely captive was an enemy, as likely to cut his heart out as to fall for his charm, somehow only added to her appeal. Add to that the knowledge that seducing her would accord him a small measure of vengeance against the man who'd had him imprisoned, and the idea became positively enticing.

After all, he had no intention of becoming celibate. There was absolutely nothing wrong with two mature individuals seeking mutual satisfaction from each other. Good, pure, honest sex. He grinned, and then immediately sobered. He'd almost allowed himself to forget that other danger he faced. He could almost feel the nameless, faceless shadow of Death hovering behind him. Time was the most precious commodity he possessed, and he couldn't risk losing sight of that. He had to find the figurine, save his life, and clear his name. Yet if his imminent death was inevitable, neither did he want to meet it without knowing, once again, the ecstasy of a woman's responsive embrace. He would seduce Shenda Ridell before he turned her over to her fiancé, but not yet. Not while the duties of commanding a ship might interrupt him at any moment. Part of the satisfaction in seducing her would be making certain she never forgot him. He wanted her to remember his hands on her body whenever Marnier touched her; to picture his face when she closed her eyes; to dream of him. His eyes glistened with the force of his hatred, and he smiled a cold hard smile. Such revenge would be sweet indeed. Then he dismissed all thought from his mind. Letting the warm water beat down on him, for a long time he immersed himself in the simple, mindless enjoyment of washing all traces of the Sentran prison from his flesh.

As he donned his clothing, Swan considered the immediate future. The arrangements for having her fiancé ransom Shenda Ridell would take careful planning. Dealings with men like Marnier were uncertain at best. It was risky even to attempt to arrange such an exchange, but necessary. He simply could not stake his life on the tracker alone. It was a simple mechanical device much too easy to circumvent.

An hour later Shenda watched with something akin to amazement, as a grim-faced Swan emerged from the lavatory and walked across the small stateroom to lock her wrist terminal away in one of his cabinets. He looked . . . commanding. Black trousers hugged his narrow hips and muscular thighs like a second skin. His dark brown hair, still overlong, was combed back from his forehead to brush the collar of his black shirt. A silver Com-cel had been attached to the auricle and lobe of his left ear, the two pieces interconnected by a delicate silver chain. Commonly worn by ship's personnel, the device, programmed with the identities of other Com-cel wearers, enabled private audio communication with the mere mention of the wearer's name.

Raising her eyes to his now clean-shaven face, Shenda suppressed a shiver as she met unfathomable, dark eyes beneath thick, black, lowered brows. How was it that he held so easily what others aspired to and never achieved? she wondered. And what type of power was it? Presence? Charisma? Whatever it was, it was that indefinable something that cowed enemies and demanded respect. The aura of one to whom others looked for leadership and protection. And it was an influence to which Shenda vowed not to succumb. To regain her aplomb, she averted her gaze, sipped at the container of fruit juice she'd requested from the dispenser and turned her mind back to going over what she knew of Fortuna and its people.

In barely four generations, the Fortunan people had become virtually alien, the product of a primitive and dangerous world. Because the large equipment needed to build decent roads and carve civilization from a hostile landscape had been too costly and difficult to transport, much of what had been required by the early Fortunans had been transported in pieces, or not at all. As a result, those colonists who stayed had opted for a much simpler and much harder lifestyle. They possessed no motorized land vehicles, traveling from place to place by the archaic means of horseback, something Shenda could scarcely imagine, having only seen the uncomfortable-looking creatures on holos or entertainment vids. If she recalled correctly, Fortunans *did* accomplish longer trips by skimmer, but there apparently were not enough of these to matter.

In the short time they'd been on the planet, the Fortunan people had become as barbaric and unmanageable as the world they called home. They refused to avail themselves of genetic screening to ensure that their offspring enjoyed all the benefits of the progress made in human engineering. The entire general populace seemed to carry weapons of one type or another for protection from who knows what. And they had developed a strange belief system or sect known as the Kanisi which governed their lives, including legislating and administering their government. Beyond that, Shenda knew almost nothing about Fortuna. All of which added up to one thing: She had no idea who or what she was dealing with.

Swan took the stool across from her, startling her from her thoughts. Shenda looked up quickly, only to have her gaze intercepted. Tarnished gold locked on gleaming emerald with an almost audible click. She immediately sensed a threat to her personal space. Despite the separation of the small table, it felt as though he stood a mere fraction of an inch away from her.

"Earlier, you were about to ask *why* I took you with me. Correct?" His bass voice washed over her, pulled at her with the deceptively gentle tug of an undercurrent. Shenda found herself studying his mouth, watching the way it moved as it formed the words. She noticed the deep depression immediately beneath the center of his lower lip that lent his mouth the illusion of being fuller

61

than it was, almost pouty. She saw the shadow of his shaven whiskers lurking beneath the skin. Noted a faint cleft in his chin.

"Ms. Ridell . . . ?"

Shenda started, and struggled to conceal it. She recalled his question, and thanked the stars that she hadn't been so distracted that she'd missed it entirely. "Please, call me either Corporal or Ridell. Drop the *Ms.*" She cleared her throat. "And the answer is yes." She leaned back slightly on her stool, distancing herself. "I want to know what you think you can possibly gain by taking me hostage."

Swan studied her for a moment. Finally, he nodded. "It's quite simple really. I'm going to ransom you for an important item that was stolen from me."

"You must be joking."

Swan rose and stalked to the end of the small room before pivoting to face her. "I assure you, I'm deadly serious."

"Ransom me to whom?" she demanded. "The Legion is not in the habit of paying to retrieve its people. And if you're considering my father . . . well, there is very little chance of a payoff from that quarter either. He detests being blackmailed."

"Actually, I was thinking of approaching your fiancé."

Shenda frowned. "What are you talking about? I don't have a fiancé."

"It was on the entertainment news vid not too long ago. I am not mistaken."

Suddenly, Shenda had a premonition of disaster. "What is the name of this man I am to marry?" she asked quietly.

"Darren Marnier, Commissioner of Justice."

Shenda blanched, and struggled to conceal it,

as her mind raced to cope with this new development. Marnier, the golden boy of politics, had approached her with his proposal the last time she'd been home. Refusing to take him seriously, she had laughed and walked away. A mistake. Marnier was nothing if not a master of manipulation. Unfortunately, only a handful of people knew that. Shenda had neglected to consider the possibility that he might try to force her to marry him.

But how? She'd been on guard against coercion almost all her life. What could he possibly have found out about her that would give him the means to threaten her into marriage? She had no friends that could be used against her. No nefarious deeds in her past or terrible secrets. . . . Oh, stars! She was wrong. There was *one* secret. One so precious that she had all but blocked it from her conscious mind. Fear flared in her mind.

Damn! She should have dealt with Marnier in no uncertain terms when he'd initially couched his ridiculous proposal. She had allowed herself to forget that Marnier's gall was matched only by his ambition. To him, she was just an asset with a father who'd gained considerable power and all the right connections in the last few years. She was not his first choice for wife, but the others had escaped him. She had underestimated just how desperate he was to acquire the veneer of the honorable family man. And now, he'd outmaneuvered her by leaking news of an impending marriage to the media. If Shenda refused to marry him, she would embarrass both Marnier and her father publicly. A situation that she had been in with her father before and survived barely. But Marnier was another matter. She dared not embarrass him publicly, without some type of insurance to keep him leashed. Especially not until she knew for certain what he thought could force her to marry him. It could simply be a threat to her own life, in which case, if she opposed him openly, she had little doubt that some docking bay clerk would find her lifeless body, devoid of all valuables, discarded among the refuse for disintegration. But it was the other possibility that terrified her. Had Marnier found her child? The son whose existence she had kept secret from everyone?

She had to think her way out of this mess. The last thing she wanted was to be ransomed by Marnier. Yet she dared not let her captor know that. If she gave away the truth, she would negate her value to him—become expendable. So she would have to play the part of a fiancée while somehow ensuring that Marnier did not ransom her. She'd rather take her chances in the clutches of a convicted felon, an unknown quantity, than be handed into the ruthless hands of the Commissioner of Justice, Darren Marnier.

Her mind raced at breakneck speed seeking alternatives, finding them, and then discarding them as unworkable almost immediately. She could not pretend to be deeply in love with Marnier; her captor was an intelligent man and would soon see through her performance. So she would impersonate a woman about to marry for convenience, a marriage for political and social gain. *That* she could do. Maybe.

The irony of the situation did not escape her. In taking her hostage, her captor had alerted her to Marnier's scheming and saved her—at least temporarily—from a fate she viewed as almost worse than death. Provided, of course, that her menacing captor did not kill her himself.

As she struggled to absorb and deal with the situation in which she found herself, Shenda looked away from Swan. "So," she said, "Darren leaked that to the media already. I thought we'd agreed to wait a while." She took a deep breath. She had to find out what article Marnier had in his possession that Swan needed so desperately, and hope that a course of action presented itself. Taking her courage in hand, she met Swan's gaze. "What exactly is it you're exchanging me for?"

Swan's hard, penetrating gaze raked her from head to toe. Finally he shrugged. "Nothing terribly valuable to anyone but me, I assure you. A small winged figurine."

"If it's not valuable, then why would someone have gone to the trouble of stealing it?"

Swan's expression cooled a degree. "Why don't you ask your fiancé that, Ms. Ridell." Reaching out, he stroked the leathery wing of his Morar. "And you needn't look so worried. I'm certain your fiancé will eventually return it to me in exchange for returning you to his arms. Love can be a powerful motivation."

Shenda choked back a mirthless laugh. Love? Marnier would be the last person in the universe to learn the meaning of the word. Dammit! Somehow, she had to get Swan to tell her his story. She couldn't hope to circumvent Marnier without understanding the ramifications of the situation she was in. Desperation clawed at her. "Please . . ." She forced the word past the constriction of pride in her throat. The plea emerged on a croak. "You have taken me hostage. I need to understand this."

Swan looked over his shoulder at her, considering her for endless moments with an enigmatic gaze, and she wasn't certain whether her entreaty had fallen on deaf ears or not. Then, his posture rigid, the muscles of his broad back tense, he turned back to consider the Morar. Finally, he spoke. "I don't believe the theft of the figurine itself meant anything in particular. Its confiscation was merely part of a larger campaign." He fell silent.

"I don't understand."

Swan raked her with his potent, observant gaze. "I guess it can't hurt," he murmured a moment later as he turned to face her. "As I told you, I am an archeologist on Fortuna, as was my father before me, and his father before him. In fact, my grandfather was one of the original colonists who emigrated from Earth. Fortuna is an archeological treasure that even Earth's politicians can understand. Scarcely five hundred years separate the disappearance of intelligent life on Fortuna from our arrival. The cities of our predecessors are incredible treasure troves of information which we have barely begun to decipher, let alone comprehend."

Swan sighed and began pacing. "However, as Fortunans we lack funding, and often find it necessary to finance our archeological enterprises by selling off certain artifacts to museums and the occasional private collector. Most of these buyers are, naturally, on Earth. For years now, partial shipments, and in a couple of instances entire shipments, have disappeared. These thefts gradually increased in number, and I hired private investigators." He glanced at Shenda. "They brought me nothing but bills for expenses incurred.

"Then, a short time ago, the insurance companies refused to insure us further. Since I could not afford to ship uninsured artifacts, I began selling items through catalog. I required fifty percent payment in advance, and insisted that the buyer insure the shipment of the particular item from his end."

Swan opened a drawer near the Morar's perch, removed a container and extended it toward the creature. Shenda watched as it extended its long tongue down the length of what appeared to be a slightly enlarged straw.

"This system worked well for a while," Swan continued. "Although some thefts still occurred, I received at least a substantial partial payment, and the insured buyer suffered no loss other than that of the item he'd desired." When the creature withdrew its tongue, Swan replaced the container and turned to face her. Frowning, he strode back across the room and sat again on the stool across from her, folding his hands into fists on the table before him.

Shenda began to get impatient. She rose to lean against the door, distancing herself from the disturbing proximity of her captor. "Look, I don't see how this relates to me, or to Darren Marnier, for that matter."

Swan looked at her with those hooded eyes and suddenly she felt guilty. As though she'd committed a breach of etiquette that he'd not believed possible of her. Shenda gritted her teeth. She didn't like being made to feel like a recalcitrant child. "You asked—no, begged—to be granted understanding, Ms. Ridell," he said. "I can't possibly make you understand without relaying the entire story. Do you want to hear it or not?"

Shenda drew a breath, compressing her lips against the retort she wanted to make, and nodded.

Swan's lips lifted slightly in what might have been an attempt at a smile, and he resumed. "The last shipment was the one that created most of my present difficulties. It was a large shipment destined for the International Museum. The museum insured it and, as agreed, credited me with a substantial partial payment in advance." Swan looked at Shenda, pinning her with his penetrating gaze.

"The complete shipment was stolen, Corporal. I was accused of stealing it back and killing the museum's two guards in the process. Piracy and murder. A number of the less valuable articles in the shipment were conveniently found in a little-used wine cellar in my home on Fortuna. It was enough to convict me."

So, like every criminal, he professed his innocence. And he, no doubt, expected her to take him at his word when a court of law had convicted him. With an almost superhuman effort, Shenda managed to still her tongue. She could not afford to anger him.

Swan looked toward the ceiling. "But most important of all, one particular figurine ended up in that shipment that was not to have been sold at all. We know this because during my trial the information was revealed by one of the dockhands. He had apparently noticed that the lid of one of the crates had come loose, and seeking to resecure it, had accidentally popped it off. He accurately described this figurine. Yet the figure had not been in my catalog, and had been seen by only a handful of my people." Abruptly, he lowered his head and pinned Shenda with his gaze. "That is the figurine you are being ransomed for, Shenda. I need it back. Urgently."

Shenda bristled at the familiarity implied by his use of her first name, yet she had no choice but to overlook it. "If that is so, you must believe that somehow Darren Marnier is behind the thefts."

Shenda raised an incredulous brow. "Is that right?"

"Look." Obviously agitated, he rose and stalked toward her. "We *know* who is arranging the thefts. We had a tracking device hidden in one of the items in that last shipment. When the shipment was reported stolen, I followed the signal to Nigeur." Nigeur, a small moon in a star system near the Space Station Apollo, was used primarily as a holding station for goods awaiting transport. "It was there that I discovered the name of my nemesis. Unfortunately, it was also there that I was captured and charged. Now, I need to discover what happened to my shipment when it left Nigeur. I *must* find the figurine."

"And Marnier, I suppose, is also responsible for your imprisonment."

"Precisely."

Shenda continued to stare at Swan as she attempted to absorb and decipher all the implications of his revelation. It didn't particularly surprise her that Marnier might have involved himself in theft. He was characteristically predisposed to avarice. What eluded her was his purpose. The man had no *need* to steal anything. He could buy it. But what she had to concentrate on at the moment was her own precarious position.

Swan urgently needed a particular figurine back. No doubt to satisfy some powerful and irate buyer. And for that, he was going to ruin her life by selling her to Marnier, thereby placing her in Marnier's debt and giving the Commissioner of Justice the opportunity to use whatever means of coercion he'd planned on using to force her into marriage. But Swan's motives could not concern her. Somehow, she had to convince him that she was worth more to him in person . . . and alive, than she was as goods for ransom.

"You're telling me that my fiancé, the Commissioner of Justice, our most popular politician, is a criminal?"

"That's right."

Taking her life in her hands, Shenda plunged into the role she knew she must play. "I don't believe you, Swan." She shook her head. "For some reason that escapes me, you're lying."

Swan shrugged and turned away. "Suit yourself. You asked."

"But you've planted a seed of doubt in my mind." Shenda swallowed, and her heart began to pound erratically in her chest. This was the riskiest part of her plan. The part where she would either convince Swan of her sincerity or . . . or insure that she was ransomed. "How can I marry a man who might be . . . a criminal?"

Swan turned slowly back to face her, an equal measure of surprise and cynical suspicion on his face. "Pardon me?"

Taking a deep breath, Shenda plunged on. "I am a Stellar Legionnaire, Swan. Sworn to *uphold the law in the pursuit of peace and justice for all humankind.* That vow is extremely important to me." She saw the disbelief register in Swan's eyes and forged on, taking a slightly different tack, before her courage could desert her. "I agreed to marry Darren because of the . . . the social status of being, not only the daughter of the Commissioner of Interstellar Affairs, but the wife of the Commissioner of Justice. Can you imagine what the discovery of Darren being involved in illicit activities could mean to that position?" She saw some of the skepticism begin to fade from Swan's eyes and knew she had taken the right approach. He obviously had a very low opinion of her character.

Now to convince him of the rest. "Give me the opportunity, as a Stellar Legionnaire, to do my duty. In the process of pursuing justice, I can learn just what kind of man my fiancé is . . . *before* I marry him."

Swan considered her with hooded, expressionless eyes. "Just what did you have in mind, Ms. Ridell?"

Shenda rose to pace the small stateroom. If any of what Swan had said was true, he had just given Shenda enough information to destroy Marnier's entire political career, as well as a means of preserving her life and her secret. Provided, of course, that she managed to get the information and the proof, quickly, into the right hands. She needed Swan to allow her to accompany him in retrieving his artifact, thereby giving her the opportunity to gather the information she needed on Marnier. Then, when it was all over, she could turn Swan over to the authorities and allow him to sue for a re-trial based on any new evidence they discovered. It was a perfect plan . . . if she could just convince Swan to go along with it. Her stomach was tied in knots. "I can help you find your figurine. I know more about Darren than most people."

Logan stared at her. He was crazy to consider her proposal for so much as a second. If the woman was avaricious enough to turn on her own fiancé, she'd turn him in without a qualm. He couldn't trust her. Yet the thought of Marnier's own fiancée being instrumental in his downfall was . . . appealing. Not to mention the fact that going along with her plan would give Logan more time with her. That alone would frustrate Commissioner Marnier.

"Well, Ms. Ridell." Swan pinned her with his

gaze. "Let's see just how cooperative you can be. Tell me, why would your fiancé be stealing artifacts? And more importantly, where would he take them?"

Shenda hesitated, her mind suddenly filled with the realization that she was about to align herself with an escaped convict, a fugitive from justice. She rubbed her jaw and winced as she encountered a bruise. The bruise *he* had given her. The thought occurred to her for the first time that maybe she was being manipulated. She had only Swan's word that Marnier had announced an impending engagement. The apparent coldness between herself and Marnier had been open to public speculation at times. Had someone dug beneath the surface to discover more? Unlikely . . . but possible nonetheless. Although she had no alternative for the moment but to proceed on the assumption that Swan was being truthful, she would keep the possibility of subterfuge in mind. "Darren has three residences," she said. "One on Earth, one on Space Station Apollo, and another on Olympus. He could have other residences I know nothing about, but I don't think so. I imagine he would take anything of value to him to one of his homes. As for why he would be stealing artifacts, I haven't the vaguest idea. He certainly has enough credits to buy anything he wants."

Swan shook his head. His hard, disturbing gaze fixed on her with the watchfulness of a predator. He was testing her. "Not necessarily, Shenda. To avid collectors, some articles are considered priceless and not for sale at any price."

Swan studied her grimly a moment more before turning to pace the chamber.

Shenda stared at him. He was so . . . big. So hard and cold. She was suddenly almost as afraid of his acquiescence as she was of his refusal. But she could not allow herself to be ransomed by Marnier. Her nerves stretched to the breaking point as Swan continued to pace. "Well?" she said finally into the protracted silence.

He pivoted to face her. His brows lowered until his eyes looked like twin dark stones. He stalked toward her, halting a scant six inches away. She could feel the heat of his body. Sense the tension in him. "I don't trust you, Ms. Ridell." His lips twisted with derision on the word *trust*. "And I'm warning you, I can make your stay very unpleasant if treachery is your game. I'm a desperate man, Shenda. My life and everything I hold dear are at stake." Grasping her arm in his left hand, he reached out with his right hand to grip her throat. His hold was firm, but not painful. "Do you have any idea what a desperate man is capable of?" His low, intimate tone soothed, belying the nature of his words as his thumb moved on the flesh beneath her ear in a gesture that would, in another situation, have been a caress.

And once again Shenda found that her breathing was affected. She felt almost lightheaded. How ridiculous! It was as though Swan's proximity made her nervous, and yet, the sensation was different. Suddenly, memory struck with all the pain and viciousness of an attack dog.

Nine years ago, she had felt this same breathless excitement. It had happened when a man ten years her senior had entered her life. He had taken her love and all she'd had to offer. And Shenda, more the fool she, had dared to believe that her feelings were returned. A scant three months after their tempestuous and secret affair had begun, he had left, crushing her tender heart beneath the heel of his boot as he closed the door in her face.

He had political ambitions, he'd said; he hadn't the time for a relationship; he was not ready for a wife and could not afford *the scandal of a mistress*.

Yet, the memory that seared her mind like a caustic chemical was not his treatment of her, but her own reaction. Throwing pride to the winds, she had screamed and cried and cajoled and even begged him to return her love, to keep her in his life in *any* capacity. And he had scorned her for her childishness, her lack of refinement. How could she have sacrificed her pride, her dignity so thoroughly? The pain of that rejection was as fresh as it had been that day. And Shenda had never forgiven herself for giving him another weapon with which to wound her. She could only be thankful for whatever instinct it was that had prevented her from attempting to use her pregnancy to hold him. Although young and afraid, she had borne the secret, the shame, and her child alone. And she had been spared the pain her mother had been unable to endure, the pain of having her child used against her.

Perhaps the greatest irony of all lay in the fact that the man who'd walked out of her life then was the same man who now attempted to manipulate her into marrying him. When Darren Marnier had rejected her, Shenda had vowed that she would never again be fool enough to believe herself in love with another man. Never again would she give a man the means to hurt her so devastatingly. Never again would she allow her pride to be trampled for the sake of an emotional attachment. Instead, like a man, she would be governed by ambition, not emotion. She would concentrate on obtaining what she wanted. She would learn to play the game . . . and *win*.

She had never had any trouble keeping that

vow. Even when the most charming of men had set out to seduce her, she had not been affected. Men, quite simply, had never again sparked even the slightest interest in her. Until now . . . How could her body betray her like this?

She looked into potent whiskey eyes and felt a fluttering deep in her abdomen that had nothing to do with fear. Her pulse raced as his warm breath caressed her face. Her breasts tingled as his strong warm hand stroked the flesh of her neck, a neck that suddenly felt very fragile and delicate. Her lungs constricted until she felt certain she'd faint from lack of oxygen. It was a sensual betrayal she had not expected. Did not know how to deal with. But, she knew she couldn't allow it. *Wouldn't* allow it. She would rather die than risk losing her soul in another one-sided affair. It would be less painful.

Falling back on instincts that had been honed over the six years she'd spent in the Legion, Shenda retaliated. In one swift smooth move, Shenda drew a small weapon from its place of concealment in the belt of her uniform and placed it firmly against Swan's chest. She had only to depress the button on the crescent-shaped metal object in her palm, and a razor-sharp four-inch blade would pierce his heart.

She met his eyes. Fought the magnetic pull and read the realization of his position mirrored there. In the instant it would take him to snap her neck, she could end his life. A draw.

Shenda smiled a mirthless smile. "Do you have any idea what a cornered Legionnaire is capable of?" she asked in return, hating the strange huskiness of her voice. "I don't trust you either, Swan. But we don't have to trust each other to work together toward a common goal: collecting evidence to either prove or disprove Marnier's involvement in the theft of your artifacts."

They stood unmoving, trapped by a stalemate of their own making. "Why are you so anxious to help me?" he asked. His intent stare raked her features, watching for the slightest hint of dishonesty.

"I've told you. I cannot allow myself to be disgraced by marriage to a criminal."

"That's a very shallow reason, Corporal." His deep bass voice washed over her seductively.

She shrugged it off, holding his gaze, knowing that everything rode on the outcome of this confrontation. "I can't help that."

"Very well, Ms. Ridell." Slowly, warily, Swan loosened his grip on her throat and backed away a step. "I'll take that," he said, extending his hand for the blade.

Shenda's pride balked at being disarmed, but once again she had little choice. She was on *his* ship, surrounded by *his* mercenaries, or whatever they called themselves, and at *his* mercy. She placed the blade in his hand.

"I will accept your proposal," he said. "For the moment. If I discover at any time that you are lying . . . I promise you, you will regret it."

"Understood." She met his gaze unflinchingly. She could not allow him to think of her as an underling. Nor could she allow him the opportunity to devastate her senses again. "One thing, Swan. We are partners in this. You are never to lay a hand on me again. Is that clear?"

With a hard look and a sharp nod, he acknowledged her statement. "Do you have any others?" he asked, indicating the blade in his hand.

She shook her head.

"I can have you searched, you know."

Gritting her teeth, she bent and removed another small blade from a concealed pocket in her trouser leg. "There!" she said, slapping it into his palm with ill temper. "That's it."

"It had better be." He moved to the center of the room and unlocked a cabinet, into which he deposited her weapons. After locking it again, he turned toward her.

A tonal ring sounded, signaling an impending announcement. "We will be re-entering normal space in one minute," said a computerized female voice.

Swan touched his ear, activating the Com-cel. "Swan to Brie?"

"Yes, Commander." Brie was often more formal when using communications devices than in person.

"Let me know if there are any Legion cruisers within range. And keep an eye out for the *Trojan*. We have to assume they're on our tails. It's unlikely that they would have chosen the same lane as we did, but we can't afford to take chances."

"Acknowledged, sir. Out."

"Out," Logan echoed, giving the verbal command for the Com-cel to discontinue reception. Looking at Shenda, he gestured toward a stool and said, "Sit down. We're about to reenter normal space." Although the reentry was never as bad as the exit, Logan found that standing through the process tended to give him a headache.

Shenda followed his advice and resumed her position on the stool. Swan had taken no more than a couple of steps toward her when she sensed something wrong. He opened his mouth as though to say something, but the words never emerged. An expression of dread crossed his face. He cried out, but the sound was faint and hollow, as though echoing through a bottle. And then, incredibly, he began to fade away. She could see *through* him to the Morar sitting on its perch.

Holy Stars! Shenda swallowed, staring in astonishment as her captor slowly faded into oblivion. "It's not possible," she whispered, continuing to stare at the spot. *People don't just disappear.* She denied the evidence of her eyes. There had to be an explanation. She rose to study the area where he had last stood.

There had been talk for centuries of creating matter-transference equipment which could reduce a living being to its molecular structure and then reassemble the person or animal at another location. Had they finally created such a thing? But if they had, why had Swan looked so frightened?

Shenda sucked in her bottom lip thoughtfully. A secret government device possibly? Had a pursuing cruiser plucked Swan from his ship to return him to prison? She shook her head. No, she would have heard about any such device if they had one. It just didn't make sense.

Quarks! This was downright spooky, and she didn't spook easily. She squatted to examine the floor, looking for any hint of a mechanical device. Nothing. She was just about to rise when she noticed a strange tingling in the air in front of her. Almost immediately, she began to see the faint outline of a pair of black gravity boots topped by black trousers.

The tingling grew almost painful. "What the hell?" Shenda leapt back, rising to her feet in the same motion. A second later, her captor rematerialized. He looked pale, shaken and weak.

As soon as he'd fully emerged from whatever place he'd gone, he grabbed her arm for support.

Shenda led him to the stool.

He looked up at her, his aggressive masculine features stark and pale. "Like I said, Shenda, I'm a desperate man. Attempt to double-cross me and the next time that happens, I'll take you with me."

Four

Curiosity overriding everything else, Shenda chose to ignore his antagonistic comment and knelt before him. "What happened?"

"That's the hell of it," he said. "I don't know . . . not really." Demons haunted the depths of his eyes as he met her gaze, and Shenda felt a curious tightening in her chest. Some dormant instinct within her stirred and she felt the insane desire to hold him, to cradle his head against her breasts and comfort him . . . to care for him. Impossible! She fought the reaction. The man was a convict . . . and a colonial at that. She didn't even know him. And she certainly had no desire to know him.

Shenda concentrated on his words, read the hesitation in his voice. "But you have a theory?" She rose to resume the seat across the table from him, distancing herself from him and her own inexplicable reaction to him.

He nodded. "It first happened when a friend and I were working in the ruins on Fortuna. We were exploring the carvings on a pedestal, trying to interpret them. Chance removed a figurine of a pair of golden wings from a pedestal to examine it and . . ." Swan massaged his temple and cleared his throat. "He dropped the figurine and . . . disappeared. Nobody has seen him since.

"I was about six or seven feet away when it happened. Without thinking, I rushed toward him and entered the area of effect. As I tried to grab him, I felt a painful tingling sensation, like hundreds of hot microscopic needles penetrating the skin, and then . . . the world, everything tangible, faded away. I had no idea how long I was gone, it could have been minutes or days. According to my assistants, none of whom were within range of the effect, it was mere seconds." Abruptly, he looked at Shenda. "The same thing has been happening ever since. And, each time it happens it takes longer to . . . re-materialize. One day, I won't make it back."

Shenda frowned. "So what do you think happens? What is it?"

"I think it's some kind of alien transporter. After all, Earth's scientists have been working on that theory for centuries. So far they've been unable to complete the transfers with any consistency, but that doesn't mean that it's not possible."

Shenda nodded thoughtfully; the scientific curiosity that had prompted her to pursue astronomy shifted into high gear. "That's the first thing that came to my mind when I saw you disappear. But if this happened initially on Fortuna, how can it possibly affect you here?"

"I don't know." Swan shrugged. "The only explanation I can come up with is that maybe, that first time it dematerialized me, it did something that would allow it to home in on me until it could complete the transfer."

"Possibly," Shenda agreed as her gaze turned inward, seeking possibilities. "The figurine that your friend—what was his name?"

"Chance . . . Chance Barrington."

Shenda nodded. "The figurine that Chance picked up to trigger this . . . energy is the same one you're trying to get back from Darren, isn't it?"

Swan nodded. "That's right."

"What do you plan to do with it when you get it back?"

"I'm going to put it back on that damn pedestal and hope that it reverses the effect, whatever it is. I'm not willing to bet my life on the theory that the thing *is* a transfer beam. Or even if it is, that it still works properly after sitting dormant for more than five hundred years. And if the thing does complete its transfer, where exactly will I end up?" He shook his head. "No, thanks."

Shenda studied him thoughtfully. His color was beginning to come back and he looked less shaken. She could now understand why he was so desperate to retrieve the figurine. To find yourself fading away repeatedly and not know when or *if* you'll ever come back had to be a thoroughly terrifying experience. Still, an incorrigibly adventurous part of her couldn't help wondering what was at the other end of that alien energy field . . . whatever it was.

"What if we retrieve the artifact and you disappear before you can replace it?"

"Then you, Corporal, will never fulfill your duty in returning me to justice. Or"—he shrugged—"accomplish whatever ulterior plan it is you have."

Shenda grinned wryly. "You don't trust me much, do you?"

Logan considered her and shook his head. "Hardly at all," he agreed.

He studied her face, her brilliant green eyes, and wondered if that was guile he saw in their depths. Whatever her reasons, if their partnership worked, her help could save considerable time over the alternative of arranging an exchange. And time was exceedingly precious to him at the moment.

"Brie to Commander Swan," Brie's voice said through the Com-cel.

He raised his hand to his ear to touch the device and trigger its reception of his voice. "Go ahead, Brie."

"There *is* a Legionnaire star-cruiser in this sector. Lais identifies it as the *Viking*. It does not appear to have noticed us. There is no sign of *Trojan I*."

"Good. Stay as unobtrusive as you can. Is there a terminal in this sector?" Terminals had been designed primarily to monitor imports from and exports to the many mining operations within the galaxy and, of course, Fortuna. They also served as off-loading and on-loading points for freighters transferring goods. The terminals themselves stocked a few supplies—for sale at exorbitant prices—provided rescue services, and liked to flex their bureaucratic muscle on occasion by demanding licenses and, in the case of freighters, shipping authorizations.

"Yes, sir. Terminal Electra."

"Avoid it; we don't want their sensors picking us up and some bored controller hailing you."

"Yes, sir. Brie out."

"Out." Logan looked at Shenda. "I really should

be on the bridge right now. Would you care to join me?"

His offer surprised her. It was a gesture of trust that she had not expected yet. Or was it? "Why?" she asked, eyeing him suspiciously.

"Because I want you where I can keep an eye on you."

Shenda nodded. "That's what I thought."

"Come then." Grasping her right elbow, he escorted her through the door and into the corridor. In that instant, as she felt the heat of his hand burning through the fabric of her uniform, she barely suppressed the urge to jerk her arm from his grasp. But now that circumstances had conspired to make them reluctant allies, outright animosity no longer could be a component of their relationship. To pull away from him would reveal a weakness. And ally or not, he was still an adversary.

Oblivious to her inner turmoil, Logan released her arm and began making cordial conversation as they started down the corridor. "You're on the *Raven*." His tone was smooth and deep. "I commissioned her direct from the manufacturer five years ago. She cost me a small fortune, but she's worth every penny."

Shenda forced herself to disregard her inexplicable awareness of the man at her side and concentrate on the conversation. The corridor they walked was bright, in good repair, and spotlessly clean. "Your appreciation shows," she responded. Years of listening with half an ear to boring politicians and self-important ladies stood her in good stead. No matter how distracted she was, she rarely lost the thread of a conversation.

He smiled slightly. "Are you a pilot, Ms. Ridell?"

"No. I can fly when I have to—and I'm fairly

proficient in a scout—but I prefer to leave it to others when I have a choice."

"Ah, I have a tachyon-style scout at home." His eyes gleamed with enthusiasm as he looked down at her. "I call her the *Eagle*."

"You own *two* ships?" Shenda asked incredulously. Privately owned and operated ships were becoming more common—a circumstance which was proving to be a nightmare for the traffic controllers at Space Stations Apollo and Olympus, whose facilities had not kept pace with the demand. However, the majority of the space vessels crowding the lanes still tended to be owned by corporations who maintained fleets for use by personnel. The discovery that a colonist privately owned *two* ships stunned her.

"Yes, I do," he confirmed, smiling slightly at her expression.

"Why?"

"Why not?" he asked in return. "I love ships. I love flying. I love space. It only makes sense. If I hadn't been raised with a career as an archeologist ready and waiting for me, I might very well have been a pilot." They reached an intersection in the corridor and Swan, once again, grasped her elbow to guide her to the right.

The heat of his hand sent tingles traveling up her arm. "Archeology must be more lucrative than I'd thought," she said.

"Not really," Swan rejoined. "Although the scientific journals do pay well for articles revealing my discoveries. My family and I own considerable land and we put it to good use. Diversification is the key to survival on Fortuna. We raise some of the strongest, most reliable horses available on the planet. We have one of the largest corundum mines in the sector. And . . . we export large quantities of potatoes." He paused at another junction, indicating with a gesture that she should precede him to their left. "Besides, the *Eagle* wasn't that costly. I had the parts imported and I put her together myself."

Shenda stopped dead and looked back over her shoulder. "*You* built a ship?"

Swan placed his hand against the small of her back to urge her forward again. His touch was electric, and as Shenda hastily stepped forward, he shot her a quizzical glance before answering her incredulous question. "I did. Don't look so surprised, Shenda."

Dammit! She didn't like the way he said her name; it sounded too . . . personal.

He continued. "I have a multitude of interests, and I've been fortunate enough to be able to indulge many of them. It's a freedom that I cherish."

They stepped through a doorway. "And here we are," Logan said, "the bridge of the *Raven*. I believe you know Sergeant Brie Tanner. Or should I say ex-sergeant, since she has chosen to leave the Legion. Brie . . . Corporal Shenda Ridell." He observed the two women closely.

Shenda reacted first. Although she betrayed a half moment's surprise at encountering an acquaintance, she recovered quickly. "Tanner." She nodded slightly in a gesture as cool and regal as any Logan had ever seen. Her guard was definitely up. "I hadn't connected Swan's use of the name Brie with you. I should have. It explains why your people were able to pass themselves as Legionnaires so successfully."

"Ridell." Brie returned Shenda's cool acknowledgment in full measure. "It's been a long time."

"Yes," Shenda agreed. "It has. It's nice to see you again."

Logan decided now was the time to interrupt, before the pleasantries, such as they were, deteriorated. "Ms. Ridell, you may have a seat over there." He indicated a vacant chair situated at a currently unmanned station before taking his own seat and checking the readings coming through on his console. They had traveled for almost an hour when he heard a warning from Lais and an exclamation from Brie in quick succession. "What is it?" he demanded.

"We've just been tagged by a random scan from the *Viking*," Brie responded, her fingers flying over the console pad. "Lais, activate Echo."

"Activating."

"Change course point three-five degrees."

Lais apprised them of their new heading. "Confirmed," Logan said. He studied the instruments. The *Viking* appeared to be concentrating several electromagnetic scans toward the same region where they'd initially tagged the *Raven*. "Looks like they didn't have time to get an exact fix on us before you activated the Echo. Good work."

Brie nodded. "Let's hope it keeps on working."

"Beginning acceleration for the leap," Lais said. "Mass restriction activated."

Logan studied the ghost ships on the monitor, all emitting signals that made them seem as concrete and tangible as the *Raven* herself. Only a detailed computer analysis, or physical contact, would reveal them as counterfeits. Lais had provided them with 12 ghostly echoes of the *Raven* . . . and time. The time it would take for the *Viking* and the personnel at Electra to sort them out. Hopefully it would enable them to complete the distance to the next leap-point unchallenged. He looked at the clock, then triggered the intercom. "Twelve minutes to hyperspace, people. Settle in." He looked at Brie. "So far, so good."

"Yeah," she said, holding up two pairs of crossed fingers. Then, as the acceleration of the *Raven* began to be noticeable in its noise level, she again donned her helmet.

Suddenly remembering his passenger, Logan looked back over his shoulder. "You all right, Shenda?" Her lips tightened slightly as he spoke her given name, and he surmised that she didn't appreciate his lack of formality. Too bad.

"Of course," she answered shortly.

"Strap yourself in then," he directed as he, too, pulled his headgear on.

In the next five minutes, Logan watched seven of the twelve echo ships disappear from the display as Lais monitored the progress her counterpart on the *Viking* made in isolating their position. Damn! They were penetrating the deception too quickly. He glanced at Brie. Tension thinned her lips into a rigid line as she, too, observed. In the next instant, two more ships blinked out. The clock read five minutes, 32 seconds to hyperspace.

Logan scanned the data filling the various screens on his console and began to relax slightly. Even if the *Viking* identified them within the next second, they were beyond the interception range of her tractor beam. Although they had not reached the outermost range of her disrupters, he was banking on the supposition that the warrant for his arrest included the information that he had in his possession a valuable hostage—a hostage without whom he now realized he would not have survived. The *Trojan I* had been on top of them too quickly, almost as though it had expected something to happen. Thank the stars for strong instincts, he mused. Once again, they had served him well.

Four minutes, 13 seconds. Two more ships disappeared from the monitor. Three minutes, 25 seconds. The last ship winked out.

"Attention! Unidentified vessel, heading Gamma, Alpha, five-three-nine-one. Transmit your certification number immediately." The demand came from a forgotten entity: Terminal Electra.

"Quarks!" Brie swore. "What next? Intensify rear shields!" she barked at Lais.

The clock read two minutes, six seconds.

"Attention! Unidentified vessel. You have thirty seconds to transmit your certification number or you will be fired upon."

Brie swore again.

"Go ahead and transmit the dammed number," Logan said. "They'll know we're wanted, but the terminal police don't have time to intercept us anyway."

"Please be prepared for the leap," Lais said as Brie complied with Terminal Electra's demand.

A moment later, Logan's fingers dug into the padding on the arms of his chair as the *Raven* leapt through a rent in the fabric of space and all that was tangible, both mentally and physically, faded into nothingness.

"Space-time curvature is complete," Lais said as the sudden cessation of sound deafened them. "We will arrive in Fortunan space in approximately twelve point one seven hours ship time."

Logan and Brie removed their helmets almost simultaneously. Swiveling in his chair, he achieved a vantage point that would allow him to look at both Brie and Shenda. "Well, people, we have twelve stress-free hours. I suggest we use them wisely." He paused and directed his next words to Brie alone. "I want you to leave

Lais in control, get yourself something to eat and a few hours rest."

Brie nodded. "I could use a break."

"I could use a decent meal myself," Logan remarked. "Prison fare is not known for its palatability." He looked at Shenda. "Would you care to join us, Shenda?" he asked, purposely using her first name, not because he wanted to annoy her, but because he refused to allow her to distance herself from him through formality. It was easier to betray someone whom you did not *see* as a person.

She was too tense to be hungry, but she felt irritatingly unclean. She decided to test Swan's determination to keep her in his sight. "Actually," she replied, "I'd like a shower and a change of clothing first, if you have anything available. I'm feeling a bit sticky, and who knows when I'll have another opportunity."

He studied her, his hard, golden eyes stripping away flesh and bone to bare her soul. Finally, he nodded slightly. "I think that can be arranged. What do you think, Brie?"

Brie looked Shenda over with an assessing gaze. "She's probably about the same size as Billy."

Swan nodded and tapped the Com-cel. "Swan to Billy."

"Go ahead, Commander," Billy's high, girlish voice said a second later.

"Would you happen to have something you could lend our guest to wear? She would like to freshen up."

There was a pause. "Sure, Commander. But it's not a uniform." Most of the Legionnaires Swan had hired now wore civilian clothing.

"I'm certain it will be fine, Billy. Could you send it to my quarters, please?"

"You got it. Billy out."

"Out," Swan echoed.

"So, then . . . everything's arranged. Brie and I will go on to the galley."

"I appreciate it. Thank you."

Swan nodded acknowledgment of her courtesy. "When you've finished, you may join us if you like." He didn't trust her, but there was little risk involved in affording her a little freedom. She would not have access to any sensitive or critical areas of the ship. "You need only turn left instead of right when you leave the stateroom, descend the first companionway on your left, and then enter the first door on your right to find the galley.

"Or if you prefer," Swan continued, "you can settle for a snack from the dispenser in my quarters. I leave it up to you." He rose and indicated with a gesture that Brie and Shenda should precede him from the bridge.

Stopping briefly at the door to his stateroom, Swan had Shenda place her hand on the sensor and instructed the computer to give her access to the room. He then directed her to place her palm over the sensor a second time to check it. The door opened. "Good." Swan smiled. "You should find the clothing Billy sent for you in the apparel dispenser." He nodded at the wall of cabinets. "We'll see you later."

Shenda nodded, concealing her discomfort. She much preferred an openly adversarial relationship to this courteous, cautious mistrust. But fate had decreed otherwise.

Preoccupied by thoughts concerning the hazards of aligning herself with a man like Swan, and the peril of being sought by Marnier, she made her way to the lav. Closing the door, she leaned against it and sighed. Her head ached. Reaching up, she released her hair from its knot, combed her fingers through it and massaged her scalp. Ah, much better. She eyed the tiny shower enclosure with anticipation and began to disrobe.

She decided she could do without the bulky gravity boots for the shower. It wasn't as if she'd float off without them, and it would be impossible to thoroughly enjoy her shower with them on. After discarding them, she stripped off her soiled uniform. Leaving it in a heap on the floor, she stepped into the shower enclosure, programmed the temperature and water pressure according to her personal preference and activated the shower. Instantly, the artificially fresh smell of biochemically purified ship's water surrounded her, and the scent of Sentra and perspiration, real or imagined, began to fade. Heaven! If she never saw that godforsaken planet again, it would be too soon.

Indulging herself, Shenda lathered suds over her body and through her hair twice before deciding she'd had enough. Then, shutting off the water, she triggered the dryer. The warm air caressed her body and sent her long hair floating around the enclosure as though it had a life of its own. Mmmm. Comfort. She could almost sleep.

With a start Shenda realized that she had indeed allowed herself to drift into a half-waking state. How much time had she squandered? Her stomach rumbled, reminding her that she still hadn't eaten a midday meal. Deactivating the dryer, she stepped from the shower and . . . discovered she had no clean clothing to put on.

"Dammit!" she scowled. She'd been so preoccupied that she'd forgotten to remove the clothing from the dispenser. Now what? She eyed her malodorous uniform distastefully. She did *not* want to put it back on, even for a minute.

After donning the gravity boots so that the slightest force wouldn't send her careening into walls, she opened the door of the lavatory and peered cautiously out into the main stateroom. Its only occupant was the Morar. Shenda looked at the wall chronometer and saw 25 minutes had passed. She eyed the dispenser across the room. Should she risk it? Surely Swan wouldn't return to his cabin yet.

Again she scowled. How could she have been so stupid? Oh, well, there was nothing to be done about it now. She poked her head around the frame of the door again to look at the Morar. "Close your eyes," she demanded. To her absolute surprise, it complied. "And don't open them again until I say it's all right," she added for good measure.

Then, with a deep breath for courage, Shenda streaked across the stateroom to the dispenser as quickly as the heavy gravity boots would allow, opened the cabinet, and grabbed the small pile of neatly folded clothing lying there. It was midnight blue. Shaking it out quickly, she held it up in front of her. A jumpsuit. And it *did* look like it would fit, thank heavens.

She was just about to examine the garment for fastenings when a soft whoosh to her right established her worst fears as fact: The stateroom door had opened. As Swan filled the doorway, she frantically clutched the jumpsuit to her body. Afflicted with mutual paralysis, they stared at each other in shock.

Shenda recovered first. "Get out!" she shrieked even as she began backing desperately toward the still-open door of the lav. "Get out!" But the idiot remained frozen in place, his tawny eyes clinging to her with a predatory intensity that made her heart stutter. Just before the lav door whisked shut, shielding her from his eyes, Shenda felt certain she'd seen the beginnings of a smile on his lips. Damn him to hell!

Smiling, Logan stared at the closed lavatory door, still not quite able to come to grips with the vision he'd just had. Could it possibly have been Corporal Shenda Ridell who'd stood before him, delicate white shoulders framed by a gossamer cloud of ink-black hair? In the few spare seconds she'd stood before him, he'd memorized several characteristics which he knew would torment him in the nights to come.

The small globe of an ivory-skinned breast just barely visible beneath her arm as she held the jumpsuit over her breasts. The sensuous curve of a pale-skinned hip and thigh as she backed away from him. A fleeting glimpse of high, firm white buttocks as she reached the lav and turned slightly to slap at the sensor, closing the door. Logan swallowed, suddenly painfully aware of just how long it had been since he'd been with a woman. Two months was a long time. He needed a drink.

As he moved toward the dispenser, he considered the idea of leaving before Shenda emerged from the lav. An instant later, he decided against it. She was going to have to face him eventually, and waiting would probably only make the task more difficult. His lips twitched as he remembered the horrified expression in her bright emerald eyes. And now he knew the answers to the two questions that had plagued him. Her eyes did retain their exotic upward cast even when her hair was down. And her abundant wavy hair reached almost to her waist. Beautiful. As Logan sipped at a glass of potent Fortunan brandy, the reason for his sudden return to his quarters reared its head.

Marnier. Even as he wished for her presence, the door to the lav opened and Shenda stepped into the room. Her hair once again neatly secured in the tight little knot atop her head, she looked regal and unapproachable . . . only two bright spots of color high on her cheeks betrayed her.

"You look very nice," he said, hoping to put her at ease, although the comment was hardly a fabrication. Billy's snug blue jumpsuit looked wonderful on Shenda. As his gaze drifted over her tiny waist and the flare of her hips, he couldn't help but remember the fleeting glimpse he'd caught of those same sensuous curves without the barrier of clothing.

Her face flamed a little more brightly, but she nodded once, with cool dignity, and said, "Thank you," in a cultured, melodious tone.

The heightened color in her cheeks, the slight quiver of her full lips, the fleeting glimpse of a vulnerability that she kept carefully hidden, all captivated him. As the color in her face continued to rise and she cleared her throat, nervously smoothing a non-existent hair back from her face, Logan realized with a start that he was staring. Raising his glass to his lips, he took a large swallow of brandy and welcomed the burn as it made its way to his stomach. "Would you care for a drink?"

"No, thank you."

"I'd like to speak with you a moment." With a gesture, he invited her to sit.

"What about?" She sat on one of the two stools available.

Taking the seat across from her, Logan took another sip of his drink and studied the bottom of his glass for a moment before responding. Finally he said simply, "Marnier."

"What about him?"

"Have you ever heard of the Obsidian Order?" Logan watched her carefully.

Shenda returned his gaze thoughtfully. "No, I don't think so. Should I have?"

Logan shrugged. "I don't know. According to the computer archives Brie accessed, the name has appeared twice on underground news broadcasts. Once in connection with Marnier alone, and once concerning Marnier and . . . your father." Shenda's expression of thoughtful interest did not change. "Yet according to every source that Brie could think to access, no such organization exists today."

"That *is* strange," Shenda murmured. She drew circles on the table's surface with her finger. "But no . . . I'm certain that, if I'd heard of it, I would have remembered."

"I'd like to know exactly what the Obsidian Order is, if it exists and *where* they meet. Short of trying to find the author of the unauthorized press release, do you have any suggestions?"

"Well," Shenda responded, "if my father is involved with the organization, I can probably find some reference to it on our home computer. My father is a meticulous record keeper."

"If it's possible, we'll have Lais establish access for you, although we may have to wait for a return to standard space." Jump satellite access from hyperspace, although possible, was extremely unreliable. Logan rose. "Have you eaten something?"

Shenda shook her head. "No, but I'd like to." She rose from her chair just as Logan took a step toward the door, and suddenly . . . they found themselves standing a scant handsbreadth apart. Too close. Much too close for sanity. "Shenda . . ." Her name emerged as a husky murmur, startling

Logan himself, and he forgot what he'd meant to say. Her beauty reached out to captivate him . . . seduce him with the promise of rapture.

Shenda found herself staring into potent whiskey eyes, held captive by the mesmerizing fire in their depths. A strange tightness gripped her chest, constricted her breathing. *Danger!* her brain screamed. Adrenaline flooded her system. She felt suddenly lightheaded. *Run!* But it was too late. Even as she sought the strength to force her legs to move, Swan's darkly handsome visage swooped down on hers.

Shenda's senses exploded in a maelstrom of sensation at the gentle touch of his lips on hers. Her heart pounded. Her breath quickened. Her pulse leapt erratically. She could no more have backed away than she could have stopped breathing. She felt his arms encircle her, his hands caress her back, his thighs press against hers. The heat of his body soothed her and she wanted only to burrow into his arms. Thought fled. Instinct alone remained. Of their own accord, her arms rose to wrap themselves around his neck.

His tongue probed gently, coaxingly at her lips. Powerless to deny the subtle supplication, she opened to him. As his tongue invaded, his embrace tightened. His powerful arms crushed her to him, making her feel small and fragile, calling to the ultra-feminine core of her that even six years in the military had not eradicated. In the next instant, he shifted her body slightly in his hold, and Shenda jumped at the electric touch of his heavy muscled thigh coming into contact with that most secret part of her. She felt a strong, almost painful, stirring deep in her belly. Molten heat raced through her, and the little that remained of her faculties evaporated.

His lips left hers, trailing gently over her cheek and into her hairline. Lost in sensation, Shenda rested her head in the hollow beneath his chin. He muttered something in a bass rumble that she felt rather than heard. And then, reason intruded and she tensed. What was she doing? This man was an escaped convict. He had taken her prisoner and had planned to ransom her. Her only value to him lay in her ability to help him retrieve his precious figurine. Any kind of relationship between them would have been out of the question, even had she wanted one. Which she most certainly did not. The chaotic sensations raging through her body proclaimed her a liar, but she ignored them. Pride reared its stately head and lashed her with its spiky tail. She *would not* make a fool of herself over another man. Ever.

"Let me go." She was amazed at the composed tone of her voice.

Logan looked down at her. Need blazed through him like a prairie fire. He was swollen and hard with wanting her. Yet she was right. The desire had to be denied. The place and the time were wrong. He was captaining a ship in an unstable lane that could collapse at any time—hopefully with enough warning to allow them to return to normal space. He was responsible for the lives of ten people who had risked their own lives in order to rescue him. And he was determined that, when he did make love to Shenda Ridell, she would want him badly . . . very badly. The need to take something that was precious to Marnier and make it his own burned virulently in Logan's gut. He had never believed he was the type of person to seek revenge . . . until he had been wronged.

Angry with himself for relinquishing the iron

grip he normally maintained on his self-control, he curled his lips in mirthless self-derision. Looking down at her, he hooked a single strand of loose hair behind her ear. "Another time perhaps."

Taking a deep breath, Shenda gathered her fragmented dignity and pushed herself away from the man who had almost caused her to make a fool of herself for the second time. She hated him for that. "I don't think so. I thought we had agreed that you were not to touch me."

Five

Logan stared into eyes as cold as twin chips of green ice and smiled disarmingly. "So we did. It slipped my mind. I apologize." But he exulted in the knowledge that her initial response to his kiss indicated a reciprocated, if unwanted, attraction. Eventually, he would have Ms. Shenda Ridell.

"Please remember it in the future." Her eyes shot daggers at him, and her tone was enough to shave two degrees off the temperature of the room. He suspected that, had she been on firmer footing, he would have been subjected to a formidable display of temper.

"I'll do my best," he lied. "Excuse me, I'm needed on the bridge." He was lying about that, too, at the moment, but he had to get somewhere where the possibility of making love couldn't torment him. "In the meantime, if you want a meal, I suggest you eat and avail yourself of the time to rest while you have it. Later, you may join us on the bridge or return here as you prefer." Moving past her—he noticed that she hastily stepped back to avoid contact—he triggered the sensor plate on the door and stepped into the corridor. "If you would like to try your hand at finding out more about the Obsidian Order, you may ask Billy to assist you in attempting to access a jump satellite. I'll see you later." At her curt, wordless nod, he smiled slightly and left her to her own devices.

Shenda chafed at her seclusion. She despised having nothing to do. She had eaten, she had rested as well as possible beneath the watchful gaze of the Morar, and she had taken Swan's advice to seek out Billy. Unfortunately, all their attempts to access a jump satellite had proved unsuccessful. She paced to the other end of the tiny cabin for the hundredth time. There was no help for it. She was going to have to join Swan on the bridge. Even his company was preferable to going slowly, mind-numbingly insane.

Eleven hours from the time he had left Shenda, a footstep roused Logan from the light doze he'd fallen into in his chair. He turned. "Brie." He greeted his second-in-command with a nod as she stepped onto the bridge. "Did you have a good rest?"

She nodded. "Sure did."

"That's good." Logan watched her take her seat and strap herself in.

"Five minutes to the Argus Star System," Lais announced. "We will be in Fortunan space in seven minutes. One minute to emergence," Lais informed them. A minute later, the universe appeared with a suddenness that almost stole his breath away. And there before him was the binary star system known as Argus. The giant Red Sun and its yellow Dwarf associate held 13 planets and 25 moons within their grasp. The enormous blue-green world that occupied the fifth planetary position in orbit around the red sun was home. Fortuna. He had rarely seen a more welcome sight. But there was no time to enjoy it.

Massaging the nagging ache between his brows, a result of the time compression, he focused on his console. "Start the Echo, Brie." Without waiting to observe the fulfillment of the order, he spoke to the computer. "Lais, I want a secure communications channel. Use that new scrambling system we installed."

"Secure channel available, Commander. What is the call destination?"

Brie interrupted before Swan could respond. "Swan, the *Trojan I* has just emerged behind us." She pointed to a sector on their port side.

"Is the Echo in operation?"

She nodded.

"Then we should have a few minutes. Let's hope that Marnier's feelings for his bride-to-be haven't undergone any radical changes in the last few hours. But keep an eye on the Echoes," he cautioned before turning his attention back to the computer. "Lais, place that call *home*, please. Immediately."

"Destination computer does not answer," she said a moment later.

Logan frowned. "Try again."

A moment later. "Destination computer responding."

His mother's attractive features appeared on the monitor. "Logan! Thank the saints!" she exclaimed before he could get a word out. "We were so worried. Your father has been sending letters of protest and demands for a re-trial to every receptive computer within the government from Earth to Olympus. Then, just a minute ago, we received the news that you had escaped. We've been ordered to refuse you sanctuary or face severe punitive action. They implied that they could confiscate our property, Logan. Can you believe that?" His mother's agitation remained engraved on her face.

"Nobody is going to take anything, Mother," he assured her. "As soon as we land in Santon, my people and I are heading home. I need supplies for a few days, and a couple of horses. I'll have the Legionnaires stay with you to protect our interests."

"Your father has already activated the guardians. But how will you get through security in Santon? Won't customs have received orders to arrest you?"

"I'm sure they have, Mother. But since when do Fortunan officials take orders from Earth officials without unraveling enough red tape to smother a colony of Morars?"

"You think they'll ignore the order long enough for you to escape?"

"I'm banking on it. I'm a Fortunan citizen. You saw the petition that they sent to court, Mother. How many Fortunans believed that I should have been tried by an Earth court? How many believed I was guilty?"

His mother's face cleared slightly. "You're right. They won't just hand you over." Then she frowned again. "But I want you to come here for supplies rather than going home. We'll have everything ready for you. It'll save time."

"I don't want to jeopardize your safety."

"You won't. The Legionnaires know better than

to harm innocent Fortunan citizens. The political repercussions would be too great. We'll be waiting for you here." His father moved into view, and Logan was able to see two of the four faces most dear to him in all the universe. Only his sister, Larissa, and his grandfather, Zach, were missing.

"I heard the last little bit, Logan. Take care, son," he said. "Remember, we're always here for you if you need us. No matter what."

His throat suddenly too tight for speech, Logan nodded and depressed a button to disconnect. His parents' faces faded from the screen. Turning to Brie, he noticed peripherally that Shenda had joined them on the bridge. He nodded acknowledgment, wondering how much she had heard and if it mattered. Then, he gave a mental shrug. There was nothing he could do about it now anyway. "How are the Echoes doing, Brie?"

"Not great. Only seven left."

"Incoming communication," Lais announced. "An open message to the *Raven*." An open message was one that was neither directional nor a scrambled call; it could be received by any ship in the sector.

Logan turned back to the monitor to see Marnier's face appear on screen. He stared in disbelief. Marnier had come after him himself! Unheard of! What was going on here?

"Commander Logan Swan, this is Commissioner of Justice Darren Marnier." As if there was anybody in the galaxy who didn't *know* the face on the screen. Logan's lip curled with the force of his dislike. "You have kidnapped a government employee. If you do not return your hostage unharmed and surrender immediately, damages for the cost incurred in your pursuit may be exacted from your personal estate." Marnier paused for effect. "You cannot escape. However, there is no need to risk the lives of your friends. If you give yourself up to me immediately, I will guarantee amnesty to all those involved in your . . . shall we say, unauthorized release. You have one minute to signal your acceptance of these terms."

The screen went blank. Logan stared at it for a second and turned to Brie. "It's your call, Brie. If we're lucky, we can still get you people away from the ship before the Legionnaires descend on it. There'll be nothing to link you to my *unauthorized release*. But . . . the possibility remains that you could be caught. Do you want to accept Marnier at his word and agree to his amnesty?"

Brie looked at him incredulously. "Don't be absurd, Swan. We just went through hell to get you out of that prison. Besides, a man like Marnier does not keep his word." She directed a stony glance over her shoulder at Shenda.

Swan nodded and smiled. "I had to ask, Brie. In case there were any second thoughts." He stared once more at the darkened monitor screen. "Hell! I wish I could tell that bastard exactly what he can do with his offer." Unfortunately, responding to the message would give the *Trojan I* a fix on their position, totally negating any time advantage granted them by the Echoes. "No offense, Ms. Ridell," he said over his shoulder.

"None taken," she responded with automatic cold formality.

Logan studied the information screens. They would be entering the Fortunan atmosphere in two minutes.

"We're down to two Echoes," Brie informed him.

* * *

His hands clasped behind his back, Marnier stood rigidly on the platform before the gigantic steelglass viewscreen. Not a single platinum hair was out of place. Not a wrinkle or a spot marred the immaculate white of his uniform. Not a trace of compassion or emotion showed on his coldly handsome face. It was an image he cultivated. Sending his gaze beyond his reflection to the blackness of space and the huge blue-green Fortunan globe, Darren wondered where the colonist was. He had known Swan wouldn't respond. But the gesture was one that had to be made. He was, after all, the Commissioner of Justice, the people's humanitarian champion.

He turned to face Captain Carvell, and indicated with a gesture that he wished to converse privately. "Have we isolated the location of the *Raven* yet?" he asked in an undertone.

"Shortly, sir," Carvell responded. "We are down to one Echo."

Marnier considered his options. He didn't trust the Fortunan authorities to follow his directives. They'd exhibited far too prevalent a tendency toward insubordination in the past. So, he needed some insurance that Swan would not escape him.

"Captain, before the *Raven* reaches the surface, I want the ship severely disabled. Not *destroyed*. I want no lives lost. But I want to ensure that the ship will not be leaving the planet again within the near future. Do I make myself clear?"

As Captain Carvell met his gaze, disbelief shone in his eyes. "What you ask is . . ." Something gave him pause.

Marnier raised an eyebrow. "Yes?"

The captain cleared his throat. "What you ask will be extremely difficult, sir."

Marnier nodded. "I'm aware of that, Captain.

Have I overestimated your capabilities?"

Captain Carvell appeared to consider his answer. "Of course not, sir. It will be done as you order. The *Raven* will not leave the planet again without extensive repairs."

"Good." Marnier allowed himself a small smile of triumph before turning back to view the Fortunan planet, dismissing Carvell with the move. His eyes narrowed. Shenda was out there, and that infuriated him. She was not irreplaceable in the vast scheme of things. No one was. There were others like her, he was certain. But he had neither the time nor the patience to seek them out. Shenda Ridell would make the perfect wife. Suddenly the irony of that discovery struck him. Fate was a practical joker without equal. He laughed silently.

And just as quickly his mirth faded. How had Swan happened to take hostage the one person whom Marnier would not sacrifice easily? It was no accident, he was certain. Perhaps he had made an error in judgment by announcing his engagement to Ms. Ridell so precipitously.

No. He negated the thought as soon as it occurred. He had needed to force Shenda into taking his proposal seriously without resorting to bribery. A tactic which he was certain would not work with Shenda in any case. He had counted on discovering her deepest, darkest secret to use as . . . persuasion. Everybody had a secret. The problem was, she was one of the few people he'd had investigated whose secret he'd been unable to discover. Which meant that, as yet, he hadn't been able to obtain any real leverage. And with the exception of a short period of seven months in her mid-teens, her life appeared to be an open book. He still had his people trying to uncover exactly where Shenda Ridell had been during those missing months. As far as her father knew, she'd returned to boarding school for a short stint to study a subject for which there'd been no tutor available. As far as the boarding school was concerned, she'd been home. So . . . Shenda had apparently disappeared for those seven months. Why? The timing did not escape him. It had been shortly after the termination of their relationship and her emotional . . . breakdown. Depression? he wondered with a frown. Was Shenda hiding mental instability? He'd have it checked.

In the meantime, he would deal with the colonial bastard, and all his plans would remain on track. He did not doubt for one moment that somehow he would get what he wanted. After all, Swan could not possibly suspect Shenda's real worth. Could he? No, impossible! Yet, the audacity of this colonial barbarian astounded Marnier. And that alone gave him pause. There was little that had the capacity to shock him anymore. People were usually quite predictable, and because of that, controllable. This Swan character was an unknown quantity—for the moment.

Darren's thoughts turned to his growing collection of artifacts. Some he'd purchased legitimately, though anonymously, through one of his many business interests. Those that he had been unable to purchase, he'd arranged to . . . appropriate. Why had Swan followed a few stolen artifacts to Nigeur? Did he have some idea as to the true value of the articles stolen? And if he did, why had he chosen to sell them in the first place?

Only one of the artifacts in Marnier's possession had never appeared in one of Swan's catalogues. A statuette of a pair of golden wings which appeared to have strong significance according to the writings trapped within the large crystal Darren had seized. Was it the winged figurine that Swan had pursued so doggedly? If so, then he would have to know or at least suspect the power it held. In order to do that, he would have to have divined its use from the crystal. Yet if he had known the true value of the crystal, he would not have sold it. Would he? It was a puzzle, and Darren didn't like puzzles. He had attempted to wrest the answers from his source on Fortuna, but had been unable to obtain any satisfactory explanations. The source had, perhaps, outlived usefulness.

Regardless, there was no way that he could allow Swan to retrieve any of the articles now in his possession . . . not even in exchange for Shenda, if ransom was Swan's plan. Their potential was too great, their value inestimable. And if Swan *had* seen the crystal, perhaps learned its secrets before putting it up for sale, he could not be allowed to live. Anyone not an acknowledged member of the Order who had had access to the crystal must die. The risk that Swan might have learned something of its precious knowledge was too great. Marnier would never share it. It would be his and his alone. Soon, he would rule the galaxy . . . the universe. And none would stop him.

"Fire disrupters on my mark." The loud command drew him from his reverie, and he realized that he could actually see the *Raven* plunging toward the planet's surface in a desperate bid for freedom. Swan would not escape.

"The last Echo is gone, Commander. Dammit!" Without a pause Brie directed her next comment to the computer. "Lais, intensify power to rear shields." She looked back at Swan. "We're under attack."

"We are under attack," Lais automatically echoed Brie's words over the ship intercom. "Please brace yourself."

The blast struck so near the ship that Swan felt the repercussions of the shock waves in his bones. "That was close!" Logan's mind raced. "What's he up to?" he asked no one in particular.

"Although he does his best to hide it, Marnier hates colonists," Shenda interjected from her seat at the inactive navigator's station. "If I were to hazard a guess, I'd say that he knows of that Fortunan tendency you spoke of earlier. You know, the red tape. And he's taking out a little insurance that you won't escape. As long as you're on the surface of the planet, he'll be pretty confident that his people will catch up with you eventually."

"So you think he's shooting to maim."

Shenda nodded. "That's my guess."

"He must have some amazing gunners in his command." Logan narrowed his eyes thoughtfully. "All right. Lais, I want you to transmit all of your data, with the exception of the guidance, defense and communication systems, into the helmets for later retrieval. Erase all data storage areas as you transfer. We don't want to leave them anything to find."

"Acknowledged. Transfer begun. Be advised that I am initiating the deceleration system now."

"We're abandoning the *Raven*?" Brie asked, donning one of the said helmets.

Logan's expression was homicidal. "I don't think they're going to give us a choice." He tossed the other helmet to Shenda. "Here, you might need this. If we crash, try not to bang your head too hard. The data in that helmet will be irretrievable if you do."

"Right," Shenda returned drily.

"I am tracking incoming disrupter fire," Lais announced.

"Evasive?" Swan barked.

"Evasive maneuvers are limited while in deceleration mode," Lais responded. The blast struck an instant later. Their shields flickered beneath the force, allowing the deadly beam to penetrate. Metal screamed. The ship shuddered. Alarms sounded.

"Guidance systems are inoperable," Lais informed them in her calm computerized voice. "We are out of control."

"So much for not killing us," Logan muttered, watching as the *Raven* ate up the miles remaining between them and the surface of the planet at an astonishing rate. Although deceleration was in progress, without guidance they could not position the Raven properly for thruster use. A situation not exactly conducive to survival.

"If you take manual control, I can be your guidance system," Shenda shouted above the chaos. "Turn on the externals."

Logan considered the possibility of treachery for a split second, and dismissed it. Flicking a switch, he activated the archaic cameras needed for manual guidance and glanced over to make certain that the screens at Shenda's terminal now held images.

"We still have stabilizers," Shenda said. "We're all right."

Logan depressed a switch and a pair of large dials emerged from the surface of the console before him. "Lais, patch manual control through to me and give Brie override capabilities on the deceleration system."

"Acknowledged."

"What are the coordinates for the thruster pads?" Shenda asked. Brie shouted them to her. Shenda shook her head. "We're not going to make it. I need a large clear area. We'll have to land her the old-fashioned way." The old-fashioned way meant that they would have to use the ship's downward thrusters alone to slow the ship enough to land without crashing. Since the docking bays were unreachable, they would be unable to avail themselves of the upward thrust available from the pads there.

The largest clear area Logan knew of was the pastureland on his family's ranch a few miles out of the city. It was slightly closer and, since they needed to go there anyway, it was the logical choice. *If* they could reach it. Continuing to adjust the dials in his hands according to Shenda's shouted directions, he yelled the new set of coordinates to her and watched as she calculated. "Can we make it?" he asked a moment later.

She frowned. "It might be pushing it a bit, but I think so."

"Let's do it."

"We have a five percent increase in hull temperature," Lais announced.

Brie checked her console. "Nothing to worry about," Brie yelled over the ever-increasing noise of descent. "We might get a bit warm, but we'll be on the surface long before we sustain heat damage."

Although the speed of their fall declined as the decelerators did their job, for some reason it seemed that the ground continued to rise up to meet them at an astonishing rate. Perhaps it was because Swan knew there were no ground thrusters. Trying to ignore the view through the steelglass, Swan continued to make adjustments to the settings of the dials in his hands at Shenda's instruction. "Adjust right—left point three seven degrees." He turned the right dial a fraction of a turn to the left. Shifting his attention just for an instant, he triggered the intercom. "Brace for impact, people," he yelled over the sound of the shrieking ship.

"Fire forward thrusters on my mark," Shenda shouted to Brie. "Five—four—three—two—one—mark." The thrusters fired and their descent to the Fortunan surface slowed, allowing the ship to level off. "Fire rear thrusters!"

Three minutes later, the ship came to rest with a hard, bone-jarring thump and the terrible sound of rending metal. The *Raven* was hopelessly crippled. But they were alive. Or were they? Logan's thoughts turned to the people he couldn't see. "Swan to Choban," he called via the Com-cel. "How is everybody?"

"A few bumps and bruises, sir. Some migraines. Maybe a couple of loose teeth. But we're ready to move."

"Let's do it then. Swan out." He looked at Shenda and Brie. "We have a bit of a walk ahead of us. The ranch is in the valley over that next rise." He pointed through the viewscreen, pitted and scarred by their rough landing but still intact. "We'd better change our footwear"—he indicated the gravity boots, which would be inordinately cumbersome in a gravity environment—"and be on our way."

Minutes later, holding her helmet in her hands, Shenda studied the area as Swan's people exited the ship and began making their way across the grassy plain in the direction of the rise. Large rocky boulders had been strewn haphazardly across the flatlands as if by a giant hand, and the occasional gigantic tree spread its branches in a circle wide enough to encompass an entire scout ship. It was a bright day, the pale white-blue sky overhead virtually cloudless, although a bank of muddy clouds hovered on the horizon. To someone who had spent most of her life on space stations or within Earth's atmospheric domes, the world around her seemed vast and . . . empty.

Her gaze switched to Swan's people. They wore civilian clothing now and carried few belongings, so they must have left their Legionnaire uniforms aboard the ship for Marnier and his guard to find. Her own uniform had been left behind, probably still in a heap in Swan's quarters. It didn't concern her. What did concern her was the fact that Swan seemed to be taking his time in collecting her combat boots and his Morar from his cabin. And since he was by definition her captor, she felt obliged to wait for him. The trouble was that Shenda was just as anxious as the rest of them to put some distance between herself and a possible encounter with the Legionnaires under Marnier's command.

Where was Swan?

A moment later he emerged, the miniature dragon clinging to his shoulder. His eyes scanned the group of people trailing off toward the rise before coming to rest on her. His expression was cool and enigmatic. "Is something wrong?" she asked as he continued to stare at her. She noticed that he'd removed the Com-cel from his ear.

"I half expected to find that you had gone into hiding to await the arrival of your fiancé. Instead,

I find you calmly standing here waiting for me. Why?"

Shenda returned his stare. "We made an agreement. Remember? I stand by my duty. Besides, I need my boots," she responded, gesturing to the footwear he dangled in his right hand. She had not even considered escape. Fleeing wouldn't do her much good if she didn't have the means to control Marnier's sudden inexplicable obsession with her. And she had begun to wonder if there was something more than a determined desire for a politically important wife behind it.

Swan gave her a skeptical look, but nodded. Trading her the boots for the helmet—Brie had taken the other helmet with her—he waited with obvious impatience while she donned them. Then, grasping her arm he urged her in the direction taken by the others. "We'd better hurry." He cast a wary glance at the sky. "Your boyfriend could be arriving with a shuttle full of armed Legionnaires any second."

Shenda shrugged and ran a couple of steps to keep pace with Swan's long stride. "Possible, but I doubt it," she said. "Darren doesn't like rough landings. They mess up his image. He'll disembark at the station. He could send the squad, though." And she, too, cast a wary glance at the sky.

Swan gave her a sidelong glance, and she realized how her comment must have sounded. It hadn't exactly been something that should have come from the mouth of a man's fiancée. She would have to watch her tongue. Although she had no immediate fear for her life in Swan's hands—dead, she would be of no use to him—he could still attempt to get ransom for her if he mistrusted her motives. And that was the last thing she wanted.

She was still racking her brains, trying to figure out what she could do to reinforce her affianced image, when the Morar on Swan's shoulder startled her by issuing a shrill cry and leaping into the air. She watched the miniature dragon soar into the sky with all the grace of an eagle in flight. "Where's he going?" she asked.

"Home," Swan responded. "To his hive."

"But I thought he was your pet."

Swan shook his head. "Tlic is my friend," he said. "The Morars are hive creatures. They have a very complicated societal structure that we still don't fully understand. He needs to be with his own kind or, eventually, he will just die. He'll come back to me when he wants to visit or . . ." He trailed off and showed no sign of continuing.

"Or what?" Shenda prompted.

The expression on Swan's stony face didn't change, yet Shenda thought he appeared slightly discomfited. "Or . . . when he senses that . . . something important is happening in my life."

"Oh." Shenda cast a glance after the soaring Morar, now only a small dark speck in the sky. She wondered what *something important* might mean and how the Morar would know when that something happened. But a distant flash in the sky distracted her. Marnier? she wondered, and ran a couple of steps to keep pace with Swan.

The *Trojan I* settled into orbit around Fortuna, and Marnier immediately put in another call to the surface city nearest Swan's home, a place called Santon. "This is Commissioner of Justice Darren Marnier. Put me through to Senior Consular Reicher." He'd learned the name of the officer in charge at the station on his previous communication.

A full four minutes later, the face of a dark-haired man in his early forties appeared on the screen. "Commissioner Marnier, a pleasure to make your acquaintance. How may I help you?"

Marnier wasted no time on preamble. "The escaped felon has just landed his craft a short distance from your city. My people and I will be on the surface shortly. We will need a number of skimmers at our disposal."

Reicher's face took on an expression of commiseration. "I'd like to help you, Commissioner. However, due to a chronic problem with supply"—he raised his left eyebrow pointedly—"available skimmers are limited in quantity. I may be able to place one or two at your disposal, but I'm afraid more than that is an impossibility."

Marnier chafed at the lack of deference in the Fortunan official's demeanor, but concealed his annoyance beneath his customary urbanity. "That is unsatisfactory, Consular Reicher. Two skimmers will not accommodate one half of the search party."

"Well, sir, I can probably supply enough horses to outfit your people. That's how we Fortunans do most of our traveling."

"Horses?" Marnier asked incredulously, raising a perfectly shaped brow. "Just what are my people supposed to do with horses? Swan would be on the other side of the planet before they learned how to stay on the beasts."

"I'm sorry, Commissioner," said Reicher, looking anything but sorry. "Perhaps if you could do something to expedite the shipment of skimmers we've had on order for the last two years, I will be able to provide more adequate assistance in the future. But . . . in the meantime"—he shrugged—"I'm afraid there's nothing more I can do."

Marnier gritted his teeth. He refused to allow an upstart colonial to provoke him. "Very well, Consular Reicher." He bared his teeth in a vicious smile. "Have two skimmers awaiting us. We will be disembarking soon."

"You won't want any horses, sir?"

Once again Marnier flashed his cold smile. "Thank you, no. That won't be necessary."

"Then I'll do what I can to have the skimmers ready for you. You *do* have clearance for a military operation on Fortunan soil?"

"Of course, Consular Reicher."

"Ah, good." It was Reicher's turn to flash his teeth in a meaningless smile. "Naturally I will need to see the documentation before I can release the skimmers. And we will require seven hundred thousand trade credits on deposit against any damage the skimmers might incur during your . . . operation."

"Isn't that rather exorbitant?" Marnier asked coolly.

"The price of a skimmer on Fortuna *is* exorbitant, Commissioner. That old saying about supply and demand, you know. We cannot afford to risk our expensive skimmers without substantial compensation should something happen to them. You understand."

"Naturally," Marnier said in soft agreement before flicking the switch to terminate the conversation.

The expression on his face as he turned away from the console was enough to turn Captain Carvell's blood cold. Yet when Marnier did nothing other than rise and stalk rigidly from the bridge,

Carvell couldn't help but allow a small smile of enjoyment to touch his lips.

A few moments later, Shenda and Swan topped the rise. Before them in an enormous valley, golden-green with grass, lay an immense estate. At least it was immense to the eyes of a person who was accustomed to living where space was at a premium. Not even Earth's president could lay claim to a piece of property this vast, she was certain. And the space stations where she was often stationed had been constructed with the idea that most personnel would be rotated off-station at regular intervals. For that reason, quarters—with the exception of those occupied by a few permanent or highly placed personnel—were functional and nothing more.

Shenda couldn't help but stare. To the left sprawled a long, low white building that, from here, looked to be 50 meters long. Beyond it another white building, perhaps half as long and two stories in height, formed an inverted L. To the right, an imposing edifice, obviously a three-story house, sat like an ivory jewel against the blue-green waters of a large pond or lake. White fences crossed and crisscrossed the property, corralling more horses than Shenda could count. Most of them appeared to be black or brown.

"It's beautiful," she said, her voice emerging on a breath of awe.

Swan looked at the panorama before him. He had never lived anywhere else; to him it was just home. And right now he was too impatient to be able to appreciate it fully from another person's perspective, but he nodded agreement. "This is my parents' portion of the property. My own property adjoins it about seven kilometers down the valley." He gestured vaguely to the land lying beyond the small lake before starting firmly on down the hill.

Shenda gaped after him as she rushed to rejoin him. "Your property is seven kilometers away and you said it *joins* your parents'?" she asked breathlessly as she skipped a couple of steps to keep up with him.

He glanced at her. "That's right. This is Fortuna, Shenda. A planet one and a half times the size of Earth with an entire worldwide population that is not even the equivalent of one of Earth's large cities. Land is not in short supply here. Almost everything else is," he admitted with a wry twist of his lips, "but not land."

A couple of moments later, they caught up to Brie and a man Shenda had caught a glimpse of earlier. "Shenda, I'd like to introduce you to Andrew Tucker, one of the best scout pilots in the galaxy." Swan nodded at the man without slackening his pace in the slightest. "Drew, meet Corporal Shenda Ridell."

"Corporal." Tucker nodded coolly in her direction and subjected her to an intense searching gaze.

"Mr. Tucker," Shenda said, echoing his tone. It was quite obvious the man was wary of her. She couldn't blame him, she supposed. Given the same situation, she wouldn't trust her either.

Minutes later, the small group finished descending the lengthy, gently sloped hill and approached the front of the long low building. Tucker disappeared inside. Swan turned to Shenda. "Wait here with Brie while Tucker and I saddle a couple of horses." He glanced at Brie. "I'd like to speak with you again before I leave." He passed the helmet he'd carried from the *Raven* to her.

Taking it, she dangled a helmet from each hand. "Sure," she said, nodding.

"Horses?" Shenda said incredulously. "You're going to ride?"

Swan paused in midstep. "Of course. Horses are the primary means of travel on Fortuna."

"Oh." Although intellectually she had known that, somehow she still hadn't been prepared for the actuality. "But I thought that, since you owned ships, you would have provided yourself with skimmers as well."

Swan nodded. "We do own a couple of skimmers, but they are much too valuable to the daily running of operations to take for any extended period of time."

"I see." Not knowing what else to say, she watched her captor disappear into the shadowy interior of the building, which, if she recalled her lessons, was called a stable. The pungent aroma of horse manure combined with that of fresh-cut hay hovered in the air. Shenda sniffed. The scent wasn't so much unpleasant as unusual. Abruptly another thing Swan had said replayed in her mind. *A couple of horses.* Suddenly apprehensive, she turned to Brie. "If Tucker and Swan are taking horses, what are the rest of us going to do?"

Brie looked at her expressionlessly. "*Tucker* and Swan aren't taking horses. *You* and Swan are. The rest of us are staying at the ranch as backup for the Kanisian guardians."

Shenda blanched. It was worse than she thought. "That's impossible."

"Why?" Brie looked honestly confused.

How could Shenda tell her that she was almost as afraid of spending time alone with Swan as she was of facing Marnier? "I . . . I can't ride," Shenda blurted, hoping she'd managed to keep the desperation she felt from her tone.

Brie smiled. "You'll learn. Believe me. It might be painful, but you'll learn."

"I don't understand."

Brie waved a hand. "Forget it. Listen, I want to make something clear to you." She looked back the way they had come, her gaze clinging to the horizon. "Swan is a very special man. When our squad was abandoned here, hated by most Fortunans as representatives of a foreign government, he hired us." She looked back at Shenda. "I just want you to understand that, if Swan should end up back in the hands of the authorities, you're gonna have a bunch of real upset ex-Legionnaires to answer to. You understand me?"

Shenda met her gaze openly. "I understand." She had no intention of turning Swan over to authorities until she had the proof against Marnier. Such proof, if it truly existed, would ensure Swan's eventual release in any case.

Brie studied her for a moment and then, apparently satisfied, nodded once. "Good."

A moment later Tucker and Swan emerged leading two handsome horses. One was tall, sleek and almost pure black. The other, slightly smaller, was a dark coffee brown with a black mane and tail and a small white star in the center of her forehead. Shenda swallowed. Not only did she not want to learn how to ride a horse at this particular point in her life, but she did not want to go off alone with Swan to . . . wherever the hell he planned on going.

"Swan," she called. "May I speak with you a moment?" She moved off to one side, out of range of Brie's hearing.

Swan cast an anxious glance at the sky and then, with the lines of a frown fixed firmly between his brows, joined her. "What is it, Shenda?"

She forced herself to meet his hard gaze. "Look! I hate to disabuse you of what you no doubt consider an ingenious strategy, but if you think I'm going to roam the outback of some primitive world alone with you—on horseback, no less— you are absolutely insane."

"No, *you* look, Ms. Ridell," he said. His features looked as though they'd been carved from granite. "Marnier and his people will probably be here at the ranch in less than an hour. If you're serious about abiding by the agreement we made, we have to leave. Now! Horseback is the only way. You either come willingly, or I will confine you until an exchange can be arranged with Marnier. Either way, I'm afraid you have little choice but to ride a horse into the *outback* with me. Do you understand?"

Shenda tried to stare him down, but his implacable gaze didn't waver.

"I need your answer *now*, Ms. Ridell. We're wasting time."

"I understand," she hissed through gritted teeth, hating him.

"Good." His lips curved in a smile that didn't quite reach his tawny eyes. He moved back to finish readying the horses. Taking the two helmets from Brie, he secured them together by means of a rope and draped them over the horse's rump behind the saddle.

Six

A minute later, Swan turned to her. "Ready?" he asked with false pleasantness.

No! A part of her wanted to run as fast as her legs could carry her, but since that was impossible, she merely nodded and stepped forward. The horseback riding she could look on as an adventure despite the allusion Brie had made to pain. But her association with Logan Swan was quite another matter. She was fast beginning to despise the colonial and his overbearing manner.

However . . . as Swan placed his large hands on her waist to aid her in mounting the horse, Shenda once again became painfully aware of him as a man. Why, dammit? She didn't need or want men in her life. Yet despite the assertion of her conscious mind, Shenda could not help turning to watch Swan mount the enormous black beast he had chosen to ride. She noticed that he now had a laser and another unidentifiable object, which she supposed must also be a weapon of some type, holstered on a belt at his waist. But that observance barely registered; it was the simple automatic result of her training.

What *did* register was the way the fabric of his black shirt stretched taut over his broad back as he pulled himself onto the horse. The picture of him swinging one leg over the beast with a grace that suggested he was quite at home on horseback engraved itself in her mind. She watched as he settled his narrow hips into the contrivance on the horse's back and gathered the reins in large, work-roughened hands. The horse tossed its head and whinnied in objection, sidestepping in a manner that suggested it would very much like to argue its servitude. Swan gripped the beast's sides between his muscular thighs and calmed it by leaning forward to stroke its neck with one tanned, long-fingered hand. And then, as he looked up, his gaze met and trapped Shenda's.

Unbidden, unwelcome, came the memory of how it had felt to have him kiss her. He was a beast. An arrogant, domineering convict. But if one discounted his too-aggressive facial features, she couldn't deny that he was one of the most physically attractive men she had ever had the misfortune to come across.

"Is something wrong?" he asked.

Shenda started, and deliberately redirected her thinking. She would never again allow a man to mean something to her. Never. "I . . . I was just wondering why you're taking the helmets." She gestured to the headgear hanging on either side of his horse's hindquarters. Although she couldn't have cared less at the moment, she desperately hoped that he would accept her question at face value.

"So I can load the data into my scout."

"Of course." Shenda nodded her understanding, and Swan turned his attention to Brie.

"Rotate your people in shifts as you see fit. Send a couple of them to my place, if you can spare them. There isn't as much to protect there, but I wouldn't mind having someone there. As soon as things are reasonably secure here, you'd better return half the squad to the site. I don't like the idea of it being unprotected."

Brie nodded. "You've got it. Don't worry about anything. Just get that statue back."

Logan looked down at Tucker. "The tracker?"

"Hidden under the console on the *Eagle*. You can't miss it if you know it's there. And I put the ship to bed like a baby when I got back. Knew you'd want me to take care of her for you."

Swan smiled. "Thanks again, Drew. I'm glad you were with me." Tucker had been his pilot when, following the emissions of the tracker, he had landed on the Nigeur moon seeking the figurine. When he had been caught and arrested, Tucker, obeying orders, had escaped and secreted the small scout ship.

"Anytime, Boss." He held out his hand and Swan reached across his body, leaning down slightly, to grasp it. "Take care."

Nodding, Logan moved forward to grasp the reins of Shenda's horse and wrap them around the horn of his saddle. "Your horse's name is Midnight Star," he said to her. "We call her Star. For the first while, I want you to hang on to the pommel while I lead her. Later, if there's time, I'll show you the rudiments of horsemanship."

Shenda frowned inwardly. She suspected that he was deliberately keeping her dependent on him because he didn't trust her. But understanding the necessity for speed, she merely nodded her agreement. As the horse started forward, Shenda made a grab for the saddle. Whew! As new experiences went, this one had to rank among the most unusual.

A few minutes later they turned down a lane bordered by enormous trees and approached the white house she had seen from atop the hill. Looking even larger than it had from above, it basked in the shade of a grove of immense trees by the lake. Enormous white pillars soared a full two-and-one-half stories skyward to support an ornate portico. A wide staircase led up from ground level to two handsomely carved wooden doors set directly in the center of the facade. Numerous pots of colorful plants and flowers set in stone planters charmed and welcomed.

"It's beautiful," Shenda breathed. "But what's it made of?"

"Wood. Importing building supplies from Earth is next to impossible, and since we're right on the edge of a rain forest here, wood was the natural alternative." He looked at her. "Ever seen a rain forest?"

Shenda shook her head. "They have a few preserves left on Earth, but I never found the time to visit them."

"We'll be riding through one for the next couple of days, so you'll have your chance."

"Couple of days?" Shenda said incredulously. The intriguing idea that it could take two days to travel through a rain forest warred for supremacy with the realization that she would be spending two days alone with Swan in the wilds.

He nodded. "And that's crossing it at its narrowest point. If you were to follow it inland, it would take weeks to come out of it." Suddenly perceiving

Shenda's worried expression, he asked, "Is something wrong?"

Yes. But she couldn't admit to the real fear that plagued her: that she was terrified of spending the night alone in a rain forest with a man who did devastating things to her senses. So she said, "What about Marnier?"

Swan stretched his lips into the semblance of a smile. The coldness of the gesture combined with the icy hardness of his eyes was almost enough to make Shenda shudder. And once again, she wondered about the wisdom of aligning herself with a convict. "Nobody will be following us in there, except on horseback. And if they do, they'll be slower than we are." Grasping the horn of his saddle, he dismounted. "Wait here a moment. I just have to pick up some supplies."

As he started walking toward the house, two people emerged. Even from this distance, Shenda recognized them as the two she had seen on the monitor of the *Raven*: Swan's parents. It was an emotional family greeting, and she averted her eyes to give them privacy as they embraced. When she looked back, Swan was strolling toward her, a pack in each hand.

His parents followed more slowly. "Shenda," said Swan as he secured one of the packs behind her saddle, "I'd like you to meet my parents, David and Callista Swan. Mother . . . Father . . . Ms. Shenda Ridell." Although there was curiosity in their eyes when they looked at her, they merely nodded their acknowledgment. Swan's mother forced a small, strained smile of welcome to her lips, while Swan's father focused his attention on his son.

"You needn't worry about us or things here, son. The guardians are here now and will stay as long as we need them. Just do what you have to to clear your name and come home."

Swan nodded and embraced his father again. Then, thumping him once on the back, he broke away and mounted his horse. "I'll be back as soon as I can."

Turning, Swan headed back the way they had come, but angled to the right, away from the stables and outbuildings. "Swan," Shenda called in a low voice.

He looked back over his shoulder at her as she rode Star to his right and slightly behind him. "Yes?"

"What exactly are the guardians?"

He studied her thoughtfully with his hard golden-eyed gaze, as though considering his reply. Finally he said, "The guardians are the Fortunan equivalent of the Legionnaires or the marines . . . with the exception that they have developed their own combat techniques." That said, he looked anxiously toward the horizon and goaded his horse to a slightly increased pace.

Shenda followed his gaze, but saw nothing amiss. "How does someone become a guardian?" she asked loudly, her voice quavering in response to the jarring movement of the horse beneath her.

Swan ignored her.

"Swan?"

Abruptly he pinned her with his penetrating stare. "Why the interest, Shenda?"

"I'm curious, that's all. I know almost nothing about Fortuna."

"We prefer it that way." He raked her face searchingly with his eyes before looking forward again. Shenda had just resigned herself to remaining uninformed when he began to speak. "Many of the basic principles incorporated into the guardian tenets are taught to our children throughout their schooling. Then, upon the completion of their education, all young people here, male and female, are required to become guardians. The first year of guardianship is devoted entirely to completing their training. The second and third years are donated in service to our world as payment for their education. It works very well."

"So all guardians are young people?" It didn't make sense. Where were the seasoned veterans to lend the benefit of their experience to novices?

"No. Some who find that they are especially suited to the life become career guardians. They are paid for their services, sometimes very well. Some guardians have even begun to be hired off-world to conduct investigations."

"Really?" Shenda looked at him in surprise. "I hadn't heard that."

He shook his head. "You wouldn't have. For the most part, they like to move anonymously. But properly trained and accredited, they are among the best there are."

"So why didn't you hire a guardian to investigate the thefts of your artifacts?"

"I did eventually. After the Earth investigators got nowhere with their inquiries into the crime from that end, I hired Chance Barrington." Chance had been among the best of the guardians. Although he wasn't a native Fortunan, he'd taken the training when he'd emigrated here and discovered that he really took to it. Back on Earth, he'd been a police officer, so he'd already known some of the basics. But it was Chance's fascination with ancient civilizations that had sparked their friendship. Hiding the tracking device in a shipment had been Chance's idea.

"But he picked up that figurine and disappeared

before he could get anywhere with the investigation?"

Swan nodded solemnly and they fell silent. A short time later he gestured toward a dark line on the horizon. "The rain forest," he said. "We'll be entering it in another few minutes. The land we're traveling now has been cleared of the smaller, immature brush that was a precursor to the forest proper." He looked back the way they had come. "It looks like another storm is blowing in from the ocean, too. We could get wet."

Shenda frowned. She remembered seeing the ocean as the *Raven* had been plummeting toward the surface, but she'd thought they'd landed a good distance inland. "How far away is the ocean?" she asked.

"About twenty-five kilometers back," he said. "This ranch land"—he nodded at the grasslands upon which they rode—"occupies a huge plateau. We get lots of rain here, too, but not as much as the rain forest. The clouds blowing in off of the ocean usually hold on to their cargo until they get farther inland."

Shenda nodded and allowed her thoughts to return to the Kanisi and the guardians. Suddenly a question occurred to her. "Swan, are you a guardian?"

He shook his head. "No." In truth, he had thought about becoming a career guardian because he had always enjoyed the physical disciplines. But he'd had too many other interests to devote himself to the rigid training involved. "I simply took the basic training and served my two years like everyone else."

Abruptly he held up a warning hand and tilted his head in a listening gesture. And then she heard it, too. The hum of a skimmer traveling very quickly.

"Lie forward on the horse, wrap your arms around her neck and hang on," he ordered even as he began urging the animals to increased speed. "I want to make the cover of the forest before they see us."

The next few moments were some of the most harrowing of her life. The instant Shenda wrapped her arms around the horse's neck, Star leapt forward. The pommel of the saddle jabbed Shenda in the midriff at every stride, so . . . she tried to shift her position. *That* was when her right foot came out of the stirrup. As she fought to regain control of the apparatus, she found herself slipping from one side of the saddle to the other, expecting a bone-breaking fall at any moment. The jarring ride caused her to bite her tongue; and her hair came out of its controlled knot to fall over her face in an unruly mass. Yet she dared not release her grip on the mare long enough to try to brush it aside. The ride seemed interminable.

Finally, the horrible, bumpy, jolting trip ended. Lifting a shaky hand, she brushed the hair out of her face and studied her surroundings. The first thing her gaze encountered was hundreds of arrow-straight tree trunks. Astonished, she let her eyes follow one of the nearest, seeking its summit. It was lost in the gloom high overhead as hundreds of similar trees spread their branches to trap the sunlight before it reached the ground.

"Stars!" she breathed.

Logan followed her gaze skyward. "Some of these trees are almost five hundred feet tall, although most range around two hundred and fifty."

Pushing herself upright in the saddle, Shenda

winced at a pain in her rib cage. "Will Marnier find us?" she asked.

Swan stared at her, misreading the hopeful note in her voice. "I'm sorry to disappoint you, Shenda, but I'm afraid you'll be spending considerably more time in my company. Whoever was in that skimmer seemed to be heading in the direction of the *Raven* without wasting any time. I'm almost certain they didn't see us."

Shenda nodded, concealing her relief, and brushed ineffectually at the escaping mass of her unruly hair. Dammit! She'd never get it under control without a good brush and a mirror.

"You have beautiful hair," Swan said suddenly. "Why do you hide it?"

Shenda stared at him, pleased by the compliment despite herself. "Because it's impossible to work with it down."

"Too bad." Nudging his horse forward at a sedate walk, he got them moving again.

As they rode into the depths of the temperate jungle, the impenetrable canopy of foliage overhead plunged the forest into a perpetual twilight that not even Fortuna's two suns could penetrate. The air became so moist that beads of water formed on exposed skin and leather. Plants of all kinds—some definitely of the fern genus, but most unidentifiable—grew in pale, phosphorescent clumps on the timberland floor or hung from vines attached to host trees.

A sudden rustling to her right drew Shenda's attention. The fronds of a nearby plant swayed violently. And some of the things she'd heard about the primitive living conditions on Fortuna came to mind. "Swan . . ."

"Yes?"

"What kinds of creatures live in here?" she

asked, not knowing for certain if she wanted to hear the answer.

Unaware of her sudden reticence, he embarked on a dissertation designed to educate and satisfy curiosity. "Mammals, birds, reptiles. Just about anything you can imagine, except snakes. On Fortuna, the only snakes you'll find are water serpents—some of which can grow to tremendous size. None of the species here are identical to those of Earth, naturally, except those we introduced. And the native Fortunan species are slower to reproduce than we expected, so their numbers are fewer than we would have anticipated by Earth standards. Some creatures, like the Morars, appear to be able to change physically to adapt to an environment—even becoming amphibious at times. For the most part, though, life here seems to have followed a similar pattern of development to that of the species found on Earth."

"I see." Shenda peered apprehensively into the depths of the nearest thicket, a clump of orange-tinged luminescent foliage. "Are any of them dangerous?"

"Of course. Many of them are. A Morar sting, for instance, is often deadly. The venom goes directly to the brain and . . . everything shuts down. But they build their hives in the open and don't like forests much. For the most part the deadliest creatures do their utmost to avoid humans."

Shenda stared at Swan in confusion. "If Morars are so deadly, why do you have one for a . . ." She remembered that Swan had insisted the creature was not a *pet*. "A friend," she concluded.

Swan studied her for a moment as though debating something in his mind. Finally he shrugged. "I was stung by Tlic and survived. For some reason that nobody understands, when that happens we become . . . linked to the Morar and, more distantly, to the hive itself."

Fascination made Shenda forget her trepidation for the moment. "What do you mean *linked*?"

Swan sighed and guided his mount around a large clump of mildly poisonous fiddlehead bush. "Morars are telepathic creatures governed by a queen. The queens are never seen. In fact, the only one that has ever been seen was a dying one apparently exiled from her hive. She was quite large, almost as big as Dancer here." He leaned forward to pat the stallion's neck. "Anyway, when I regained consciousness after being stung, I found—like some survivors before me—that I occasionally received images or heard things that I wasn't seeing or hearing with my own senses. In some way, the venom forges a telepathic nexus to the Morar and a more distant one with the hive occupants. I am now immune to the venom of the members of that particular hive, and resistant to the venom of all Morars."

Shenda studied Swan consideringly. "That's how Tlic will know when something important happens in your life," she said, finally understanding Swan's earlier comment. "He can sense things in your mind just as you can receive what's in his."

"That's right."

"That's incredible!" Shenda exclaimed. "How many Fortunans are . . . linked like that?"

Swan shrugged. "Quite a few by now, I imagine. There seem to be at least five to ten people stung every year. Of those that are stung, thirty to forty percent survive. And about fifty percent of the survivors develop the link."

Another rustling drew Shenda's attention, and she looked up to see a cloud of . . . something, its luminous strands reaching, coiling, folding back on themselves. "What is *that*?"

Swan looked up. "Lunar Moss, so named for its particular noctilucent quality. The threads are prized by clothiers for ornamenting fabrics."

Shenda studied the small cloud of bioluminescent thread-moss suspended between the trees. It *was* beautiful. Yet it left her feeling cold. Her instincts told her there was something strange about it, something deadly. The strands that coiled and reached seemed almost to be searching for something. The moss didn't appear to have any roots that she could see. And it had attached only enough of itself to the surrounding trees to be able to hover overhead. "How does it live?" she asked Swan.

Swan looked at her. "You sure you want to know?"

"Yes."

He glanced at the ground beneath the hovering cloud. "This particular specimen hasn't been here very long, or you'd be able to see how it feeds. There'd be a small pile of skeletal remains littering the ground."

Even as he spoke the words, there was a high-pitched shriek as one of the beautiful strands shot down to the ground and came up entwined around a small, desperately struggling, furry creature. Shenda watched, horrified by the animal's helplessness. "What will the moss do to it?"

"As near as we can determine, it will drain the life force from it. Examinations of its victims have never revealed any other explanation for their deaths. As soon as the Terong is dead, the moss will simply drop it."

"Has it ever killed a person?"

Swan shrugged. "Once or twice, I think. But the

victims walked right underneath a very large cloud of the stuff." He nodded over at the moss clump. "A cluster that size isn't capable of holding a person."

"Thank the Stars for that."

They'd drawn ahead of the moss now and Shenda, sparing one last glance over her shoulder at the sinister cloud, was reminded that Swan had said they sometimes used it on clothing. "You'd think that it would lose its luminosity when it died."

"It may. Nobody knows."

Shenda frowned. "What do you mean? I thought you said that clothiers used it."

Swan glanced over at her. "I did. But the strands aren't dead. You can cut them into a thousand pieces, and each piece will develop a life of its own."

"Quarks! Do you mean to tell me that the clothiers are embroidering living strands of that deadly moss into fabrics? And people are actually wearing them?"

Swan nodded, and looked at her as though he didn't quite understand her reaction. "That's right. Once cut off from its cluster, the moss strands grow so extremely slowly that people usually discard the clothing long before it grows enough to even subtly change the shape of the design. And, when the clothing is disposed of, it's burned to kill the moss and prevent the inception of a new moss cluster in a location that could prove dangerous to children or pets." His first genuine smile flickered fleetingly across his face, transforming his features. Unaccountably, it was enough to prompt her heart to constrict strangely. "It's quite safe really," he added.

Studiously ignoring the strange feeling in her

chest, Shenda focused earnestly on the conversation. "How do they manage to harvest it?"

He shrugged. "I haven't the faintest idea. I'm afraid I never bothered to ask. Fashion has never been one of my interests."

"Oh." Shenda fell silent as they progressed through the impenetrable gloom of the old forest. Inexplicably, she found her gaze drawn again and again to the man before her. She admired the curve of his strong jawline as he glanced over his shoulder at her. She appreciated the play of the muscles beneath his shirt as he moved. She watched the movement of the tendons beneath the smooth, tanned skin of his long-fingered hands as he guided Dancer. She wondered what it would feel like to have those hands caress her.

No! With an almost painful effort, Shenda wrenched her thoughts away from Swan. She wouldn't think that way. Nothing good could come of it. Nothing. Resolutely, she focused her eyes on the black tuft of hair that rose up between Star's ears, and refused to so much as glance at Swan.

Time stretched on. The gloom lurking in the shadows of the ancient giants of the forest seemed to reach out to her, attempting to crush her inherent optimism beneath a weight of despondency. Did she really think she could outmaneuver Marnier? The man was a master of manipulation. He could have her killed and her murder investigated in a way that would never reveal the killer as anything more than a phantom on a docking bay.

For the first time in a long time, Shenda keenly felt her lack of friends. To know that you could disappear from the universe without a single person missing you was a sobering thought. And yet, she could not have done anything differently.

Friends would have made her vulnerable, controllable. And she had too much pride to be anyone's puppet. Although her independence had come with a steep price: perennial loneliness. She thought she had grown used to it. Until now.

Overhead, the branches of the trees sighed with melancholy as wind soughed through them. The darkness deepened. The humidity intensified as night drew nearer, causing small droplets of water to drip from above like silent, chilly tears. The accoutrements of solitude.

"We'll have to camp for the night soon, or we won't be able to see," Swan said, turning to look at her.

Shenda nodded. "Sure."

Swan studied her thoughtfully. "Are you all right?"

Shenda made a concentrated effort to shrug off her uncharacteristic depression. Straightening her spine, she met Swan's gaze boldly. "Of course. Why wouldn't I be?"

Swan studied her one more moment as though not quite certain whether to believe her protestation, and then shook his head. "Keep your eyes open for a small clearing."

About ten minutes later, they came across an opening in the jungle of foliage that he deemed suitable. Bringing Dancer to a halt, he dismounted. Then, remembering the fleeting glimpse of pain he'd seen on Shenda's face, he abruptly arrived at a possible explanation for it. "Are you sore?" he asked, approaching Star from the left side.

She looked at him blankly. "Sore?" she echoed.

He nodded. "Horseback riding can become extremely painful if you're not used to it. Let me help you." At her nod, he directed her to free her right foot from the stirrup and swing her leg back over the horse's hind quarters. "That's it," he said, grasping her waist to steady her as she settled her right foot on the ground. "Now, take your left foot out of the stirrup and let go." She did as directed and turned to face him. She looked slightly flushed, but in the deepening darkness, he could have been mistaken. "How do you feel?"

"I think you're right," she said. "I seem to have a few tense muscles."

He nodded. "Unfortunately, I have to warn you that it will get worse before it gets better. By tomorrow morning, you could be quite stiff."

"Great," she responded with a distinct lack of enthusiasm as she looked away, letting her eyes trail slowly over their surroundings.

"Is something the matter?"

"Just checking for Lunar Moss," she said with a shrug.

A grin flickered across his lips and her heart skipped a beat. "I already checked." Walking over to Dancer, he said, "Come on. Let's get these packs unloaded and a camp set up before it gets any darker."

Observing as he loosened the fastenings behind Dancer's saddle and removed the bulky roll of supplies, Shenda turned to Star to mimic his actions. The pack, when it came free, was heavier than she'd expected, and she almost dropped it. Carrying it to the center of the clearing, she joined Swan. He was in the process of spreading out what appeared to be a small plasti-fab tent. Shenda hadn't seen one since her days as a raw recruit at Camp Kilmar on Earth, and said so.

"If you stay on Fortuna any length of time, you'll see quite a few of them," he responded to her observation. "Farmers and ranchers use them when they're out working and can't get back to the house before dark."

Shenda nodded her understanding. "Do you have a flame coil?"

"Over there." He nodded to a package on his left.

Opening the package, Shenda removed three curved brackets and a metallic pancake-like object about 14 inches in diameter. "Any preferences for where you want it?" she asked.

"Just there, in the center, I think."

While she assembled the flame coil on its tripod stand in the center of the small clearing, Shenda found her gaze once again gravitating toward Swan. Impatient with herself, she attempted to rationalize her compulsion. It was only because he was such an incredibly handsome man that she couldn't keep her eyes off him. She was simply reacting like any person compelled to look again and again at a beautiful piece of art. Only Shenda knew that, aesthetically speaking, Logan's features were not quintessentially archetypal of male beauty. He was too rugged, too much a product of primitive Fortuna. So either her tastes were at odds with those of the artists of the day, or there was another reason why she seemed constantly compelled to observe this man with whom she'd reluctantly affiliated herself.

"Just about finished?" His question startled her from her preoccupation, and her gaze suddenly locked with his.

Immediately she felt the effect. Her heart tripped a beat. Her lungs constricted. And heat stained her cheeks. Bless the darkness. "Yes," she said, triggering the switch on the flame coil. Instantly, the flat circular object began to emit a soft red glow and uncoil itself until it resembled a spiraled inverted pyramid.

Finished, she looked over at Swan and the tent he had completed erecting. It looked barely large enough to accommodate one person in a sitting position. If that person chose to recline, Shenda was certain he would be leaving his feet exposed to the vagaries of climate or hostile life forms. Still it was certainly better than nothing. "Is there another tent?" she asked.

Swan shrugged as he moved to the horses and began removing their saddles. "I'm not certain. You'll have to check the other pack. There is a limited amount of space available for supplies, and my parents may have opted to leave a second tent out in favor of other items. Then again, they might not have."

They had. Shenda inventoried the items she'd discovered in the pack that had been on Star. A single large thermal slumber envelope. A compact solar-powered light cell. A large hunting knife. Twine. About 20 small packets of concentrated food rations. An old-fashioned block of bio-soap complete with washcloth. A canteen of fresh water. And a comb.

Sighing, Shenda considered the small collection. Since she had no intention of joining Swan in the tiny tent, she was left with no alternative but to appropriate the slumber bag for her own use. It would keep her warm. But not dry. She looked skyward and saw nothing but impenetrable blackness. As long as the rain Swan had predicted continued to hold off, she'd be fine. She'd survived nights in the open before. She could do it again.

"Hungry?" Swan called.

"Yes. I have some rations here." She gathered up the packages.

Near the penetrating warmth of the flame coil,

they sat down at right angles to each other to examine their hoard. "As meals go, these energy bars can't compare to Virtuoso Cuisine," Logan said, referring to the most famous—and most expensive—dining establishment in the galaxy. "But they beat standard Legion fare, I'm told."

Shenda chose a Vegetable Medley bar. "I'll let you know," she said.

Logan chose the high-protein Nut Medley along with a chunk of jerked Gnoth meat. Biting into the jerky, he watched Shenda. Her hair, still loose after her harrowing ride for safety, billowed around her like a soft dark cloud. He could see that it was completely unmanageable, as she had said. But it was also very, very provocative. He studied her delicate features and wondered again why someone of her standing had joined the Legion.

As though sensing his gaze, she turned toward him. "You're right," she said. "The bar is really quite good."

Swan nodded. "The Isherwood family makes them. I think they'll begin exporting soon." Conversation ebbed and the only sounds were those occurring naturally in the depths of a rain forest: the howls of night hunters, the screams of their victims, and the scurrying sounds produced by each. Logan breached the silence. "May I ask you a question?"

She met his gaze warily. "You can ask, but I'm not guaranteeing I'll answer."

"Fair enough." He studied her delicate features and tried to frame the question nonintrusively. Finally he forged ahead. "I'm curious. What could possibly make an attractive young woman join the Legion when she could have had Earth's society at her feet?"

"I prefer setting it on its ear," Shenda muttered.

"Pardon me?"

She shook her head, negating the importance of her previous statement and stared at the flame coil. Finally, just as Logan was about to give up on a response, she sighed. "You can't aspire to something you already have, Swan. I had wealth, and the fame attached to being a prominent politician's daughter, but it wasn't mine. I was born into it. And as I grew older, I didn't like the strings that came with it.

"So I aspired to have my independence. The Legion gives me that." She looked at him. "I'm an astronomer, you know. I spend my time studying and learning from a constantly changing universe. A universe so vast that we will never know all there is to learn from it, never even find an end to it. That kind of a job tends to add perspective to your life." She looked back at the flame coil. "I joined the Legion to gain my freedom. To earn my *own* living."

"Freedom?" Logan said. "You are the first person I've ever encountered who described the structured environment of a Legionnaire unit as *free*."

Shenda shrugged. "You asked." Clearly that was all she intended to say on the subject. Finishing their meal, they leaned back to enjoy the scent of the night air. Then there was a sudden movement on Shenda's part as she rose and peered off into the gloom, drawing Logan's attention. "Is something the matter?"

"I don't know," she responded hesitantly. "What is that sound?"

Logan cocked his head. At first he heard nothing. Then a distant rumbling reached his ears. "Sounds like thunder to me. Looks like we're going to get that rainstorm after all."

Seven

The ominous rumbling sound reverberated again, and Shenda stared up at the impenetrable curtain of night overhead. She couldn't believe the extent of her ill luck. She felt as though she was being swept along by an inexorable tide, robbed of her free will. And suddenly, she was furious. Pivoting, she faced Swan. "Now what the hell are we going to do?"

His features, red-tinged in the light of the flame coil, showed confusion. "It's just a storm. We'll be fine."

"Oh, yes. We'll be fine," she mimicked. "We only have one slumber bag and one small tent, Mr. Swan. And if you think I'm crawling into that—" —she gestured furiously to the offending piece of shelter—"with *you*, then you're crazier than a short-circuited servo."

"Relax, Ms. Ridell." He returned a credible imitation of her furious formality as he rose to face her. "I've never raped a woman in my life and never will. So if something were to happen in there"—he, too, gestured at the small tent—"it would be because you wanted it to happen."

Shenda stared at him. "You bastard."

"I've been called worse," he said with a shrug. "As much as you might abhor the idea, one way or another we are sharing the tent." He saw her glance at the slumber envelope, and didn't like the speculative expression in her eyes. "*And* the slumber bag," he added. "I refuse to freeze just to pander to some quaint notion you have of preserving your modesty. I intend to get some rest, and I can't do that if I have to wonder what you're up to."

Shenda remained frozen in place, staring at him. The darkness made it difficult to perceive her expression. "Are we clear?" he said. He looked up into the dense blackness overhead. The air had gotten a lot heavier in the last couple of minutes. "We're going to get wet very soon if we don't get settled."

Shenda stalked over to the pile of supplies she'd unpacked, threw the slumber envelope over her shoulder, tucked the light cell beneath her arm and began shoving everything else back into the waterproof pack. That done, she turned to face Swan. He was in the process of checking on the horses and securing their gear. "Just remember our agreement, Swan."

"About what?" he asked, exasperated and a little disgruntled.

"Keep your hands to yourself."

He rose from his squatting position next to the saddles to face her. She looked small and fragile. He was certain he could have shattered the flimsy wall of bravado she'd erected with very little effort. But her pride would have suffered a terrible blow. And for some unfathomable reason, Swan admired her intense pride. "I'll remember," he said. Which did not mean that he intended to abide by it. He had seen the way she'd followed him with her eyes all day. Much as she wanted to deny it, she was almost as attracted to him as he was to her.

"Good." Shenda knelt and crawled into the tent.

Inside the small cramped space, Shenda turned on the light cell and removed her boots, setting them in one corner before hastily arranging the slumber envelope. Then, with one last furious glance at the doorway through which her captor would soon come, she crawled into it, zipped her side closed and firmly shut her eyes. A few minutes later, when she continued to hear Swan moving about the camp instead of crawling into his space in the small shelter, she discovered that her eyes had opened. Slowly her ire faded.

For the first time she acknowledged that some part of her really *was* attracted to Logan Swan. The idea terrified her, and she searched her mind for some explanation for the anomaly. She hadn't had a relationship with a man since she was 16. She was now 25. Perhaps the attraction was simply a product of her biological clock telling her it was time to . . . reproduce.

She remembered that distant time in the past when, after hours of grueling pain, she had held a small bundle of humanity in her arms and kissed her son's warm, fuzzy head for the first and last time. He was eight years old now. And he believed that the woman who'd raised him was his mother. Shenda's arms ached with remembered emptiness. And she prayed with all her heart that Marnier did not know about her son's existence . . . *their* son's existence. But she feared that her prayer would go unanswered. What else could Marnier possibly know that would make him think he could force her to marry him? No, there was a more important question to answer: How would he use her son against her? Shenda tried to anticipate what might come, but found the task impossible.

She turned her thoughts back to the more immediate problem of her strange reaction to Swan. It was probable that, at this time of her life, she would have been attracted to any reasonably handsome man—any man who might have made suitable father material. Shenda had never really considered having another child. Children, like friends, became a weakness that could be exploited. Her own mother's situation had taught her that. But now, for the first time, she wondered if it might be possible to be a parent. Would she be a good one?

The first fat drops of rain began to pound slowly, randomly, on the taut surface of the small tent. It was a cold, lonely sound. An instant later, the tent shook as a large form wielding a light cell crawled into the enclosure. Shenda hastily shut her eyes. She heard the rustle of fabric and prayed that he wasn't undressing; yet she refused to betray her wakeful state by checking. Then, unbidden, a disturbing thought occurred to her: What would Logan Swan's children look like?

Later, with Swan's gentle snoring punctuating the night, Shenda stared blindly into the night. Sleep wouldn't come. She was on an alien world surrounded by strange sounds: the sound of the rain dripping through the canopy of branches overhead; the sound of horses snorting and pawing nearby; and the sound of a man sleeping at her side. And as foretold by Swan she had begun to feel a painful tenseness invading her muscles. Every time she moved, she discovered a new pain, a new ache. Dammit! She needed sleep. Forcing her eyes closed, she concentrated on the sound of the rain, willing the monotonous sound to drown out all awareness.

Phillip Nagami had been Darren Marnier's aide for some time. It was a position that, for the most part, he enjoyed. Now, his thin Oriental features twisted with effort as he attempted to obtain something that would help them, an impression, some psychic resonance, from the few personal articles they'd found on the *Raven*. They had been unable to obtain anything from either of the Swan ranches without risking bloodshed with people who, technically speaking, were innocent of crime. A skirmish with the guardians in these politically uncertain times would not have been viewed favorably by the powers of government back on Earth. Were any harm, eventually, to be visited upon a member of the Swan family, it would of course have to appear to be the work of felons. But for now, they operated within the confines of the law. Nagami intensified his concentration on the object in his hand. Fleeting, disconnected pictures flashed in his mind, and were as quickly gone. Finally, frustrated, he broke off. "Nothing, sir. I'm sorry."

Marnier's lips twisted with annoyance, but he kept any derogatory words he might have uttered to himself. Nagami was one of the few people in the universe whom Darren Marnier treated with respect. Phillip had a gift that Darren himself craved. Psychic ability. Uncertain though it was, at times it proved very useful. Rising, Darren rose to pace the small suite he had taken in Santon's

149

only respectable hotel. A moment later, he stopped in front of a window and looked down into the street.

His ever-rigid posture gave nothing away, but Phillip knew what he saw. He had studied it himself just a short time ago. Santon was a filthy little frontier city. The roads were barren of any pavement that might have diminished the dust that floated constantly in the air like a haze. The reddish powder seeped through minuscule cracks and holes to settle in a thick layer on every available surface. Small buildings, apparently constructed without prior thought to any uniformity, crowded along the wide, dirty streets. Some edifices boasted a coat of paint, but it appeared that many had never seen a protective coating and their wood had weathered to a homogeneous muddy-gray. Most disgusting of all, animal droppings, teeming with buzzing insects, littered the packed surface of the roads. To give the city planners a small amount of credit, they did apparently have people employed to pick up the droppings and dispose of them, but in a city swarming with almost as many horses as people, they could not possibly keep up.

And the people . . . the people were almost as offensive as the city itself. They wore rugged serviceable clothing, almost completely devoid of style, and enormous hats which served rather effectively to shadow their expressions. For someone adept at and reliant on interpreting facial nuances, the hats were an annoyance. Even more disconcerting, Fortunan men and women alike tended to sport primitive projectile handguns in holsters on their hips. According to what he'd been able to learn about them, these guns were never turned on a fellow Fortunan, and in fact were rarely used on humans—with the exception of the odd pirate or privateer who overstepped the boundaries of acceptable behavior when visiting the world. Rather the weapons provided protection from Fortuna's vast assortment of carnivorous wildlife. Walking the streets of Santon was like being thrust back in time—to humankind's primitive origins. Phillip couldn't wait to leave.

Abruptly, Marnier pivoted to face him. "I cannot afford to stay here any longer. Not only are there too many other things requiring my attention, but by giving this prison escape my personal attention, I may have made an error in judgment. Already there have been questions in the media concerning my possible motive for attempting to apprehend Swan myself. I arranged to have it suggested to the media that Shenda's safe recovery is my motivation. Most seem to accept that. However, two political correspondents who remember Shenda's long-term coolness toward me have questioned that insinuation due to the fact that Shenda has not officially acknowledged our engagement. They are making other suppositions. Thus far, the conjecture has only gone so far as to suggest that my motivation is to preserve the reputation of the Sentran prison. But they are questioning why I didn't pursue the other ship, which contained more than one escaping inmate. All of them have since been apprehended, of course, so the point is moot. However, it mustn't appear that I have a personal vendetta against Swan."

Phillip nodded. "I agree."

"Good." Marnier smiled. "Then you won't mind staying here, incognito as they say, to continue what we have begun. I'm leaving a squad of Legionnaires here under the command of Sergeant

Boltin, but I'm not convinced that their search will prove fruitful. I need an ace up the sleeve, as the saying goes. I'd like *you* to be that ace."

Although the order, couched as a suggestion, caught him off guard, Phillip's characteristically immobile features betrayed not a flicker of the emotion he felt. The idea of staying here in this hellhole of a city was bad enough. But to be asked to do so incognito was distressing. None of the privileges of being a political aide would be his. Still, Marnier usually paid well for assignments beyond the call of duty, and Phillip could always use more credits. He met Marnier's gaze unblinkingly. "The usual bonuses will apply, sir?"

Marnier nodded. He understood greed. "Of course, Phillip."

"Then I will be happy to stay, sir."

As he walked back across the room to resume his seat, Marnier said, "I want you to grease palms and do whatever is necessary to make contact with Andrew and get a lead to Swan before he finds a means of getting off the planet."

Phillip frowned. "Where exactly do you think he means to go, sir?"

"Think about it a moment, Phillip. If you were a fugitive, where would you go?"

"To Earth, I suppose," Phillip returned thoughtfully after a moment. "I'd try to lose myself in the crowds. Join the fringers."

"I've thought of that. But forget Earth for a moment. There's another option that would allow you more freedom. One where you can be paid for work without valid identification."

Phillip suddenly perceived Marnier's concern. It had escaped him because for him personally it would not be an option. "A mining colony," he said, and almost shuddered. He'd rather be dead than live for months in unbreathable atmosphere, forced to constantly wear a bulky, oxygenated suit.

"Exactly," Marnier said.

There was another option: one that hadn't been considered by Darren. Swan could hire himself on as a worker at one of the scientific facilities that peppered the galaxy on moons and asteroids and planets. But Phillip decided he'd keep that possibility to himself. The future was seldom clear, and one never knew when one might be a fugitive.

Nagami nodded. "All will be done as you say, sir."

Logan opened his eyes. It was cold. Dawn had arrived. He didn't quite know how he knew that, for it was still dark in the small tent. Perhaps it was a slight increase in the number of rustling sounds that reached his ears from the undergrowth. Perhaps his internal clock, accustomed to early risings and the lifestyle of a rancher, would have awakened him even if all external stimuli had been removed. Or, perhaps there was a slight lightening of the darkness, an almost insignificant graying around the edges. Whatever it was, even though he couldn't yet see, Logan knew that a new day was breaking. He listened as a spate of water droplets struck the tent surface in an irregular rhythm no doubt provoked by an errant breeze or the movement of small animals in the branches overhead. It appeared to have stopped raining. He closed his eyes and dozed, content to wait a few more minutes for the arrival of the new day. Then he tried to shift position. That was when he noticed Shenda.

In her sleep, she had apparently chosen to forgo her own strict rule concerning physical contact.

In the gray light of the early dawn, he studied her. She lay with her head on Logan's bare chest and her left arm draped across his rib cage. Her left leg, knee bent in a relaxed position, lay across his right thigh. In fact, her entire position could only be described as . . . familiar. If she had not slept fully clothed, the position might have been termed *intimate*.

Possibilities rose in his mind to taunt him, and he felt his body respond. She felt . . . soft, and incredibly provocative, pressed up against him. He could feel the small globe of her right breast compressed against his side. In the pale predawn light that was just now seeping into the tent, he studied her features. Her pale complexion looked as smooth and clear as alabaster. Her delicate raven-dark brows winged upward at the temples, mimicking the upward slant of her eyes. Her lashes, unadorned by cosmetics, did not appear as thick as some he'd seen, yet her beautiful emerald eyes hadn't needed a thick frame of lashes to show them to advantage.

Shenda stirred. Her nose was cold. She turned her head slightly to bury it in the warm fuzziness beneath her cheek. A faint, vaguely familiar musky scent invaded her nostrils. Sleepily, she tried to identify it. It smelled like . . . like deodorant soap. A man's deodorant soap! Suddenly, her eyes opened to encounter a broad expanse of hairy chest. An instant later, a pair of gleaming whiskey-potent eyes fastened on hers. For a frozen instant in time, they stared at each other.

"Good morning, sweetheart." His husky voice rolled over her with the seductive pull of tidewater.

Great stars! She was lying virtually on top of Swan. And after *she* had told *him* to keep his hands to himself. Embarrassment burned her face and flooded it with color. She could only hope that the pale pre-dawn light would prevent him from seeing it. "Morning," she murmured as she hastily tried to roll to the side. His arm was there to prevent it. Shenda's eyes flew to his face. A mistake, for once again she found her gaze trapped by the hypnotic potency of his.

A peculiar tension invaded the tent, thickening the air, making it difficult to breathe. His eyes never leaving her face, he gripped her arms in a firm but gentle grip and slowly pulled her up the length of his body, over the magnificent chest, until she looked down into his face. Whiskers shadowed his jaw with a new day's growth. His full-lipped mouth, free of tension, curved into a slow, devastating smile. His tawny eyes gleamed at her from beneath thick black brows. Slowly, never releasing her from the spellbinding grip of his gaze, he bent his head forward.

Shenda's breath froze in her chest. She could not have moved had her life depended on it. His lips closed over hers, soft and demanding. His tongue touched her lips and, helplessly, she opened to him. Rational thought fled. His kiss was more overwhelming, more thoroughly devastating to the senses than she'd remembered. Her nipples tingled and hardened. Her pulse raced. Her lungs constricted, drawing air in panting little gasps as they sought desperately to keep pace with her pounding heart. She felt lightheaded, breathless and . . . thoroughly, gloriously woman.

He found the fastening on the front of her jumpsuit and tugged it down, baring her breasts. He cupped one of them in the palm of his hand, raking the sensitive nipple with the pad of his thumb. Shenda gasped. In the next instant, he freed her lips and then, with a sudden movement, turned, reversing their positions. Shenda stared up at him. His molten gold gaze roamed slowly from her face, down her throat, to her exposed breasts, searing her with its heat.

"Saints, you're beautiful." The low murmur of his voice drifted over her like a tactile caress. His large, warm hand moved to encompass one small breast. And then his lips closed over the hard little nipple of the other. Sensation lanced through Shenda clear to her toes. A moan clawed its way up her throat, forcing its way between kiss-swollen lips. Her breasts swelled. Her body arched beneath him. And her hands clutched mindlessly at the satin over steel flesh of his biceps.

She was vaguely aware that, even as he lavished attention on her sensitive breasts, he was easing her jumpsuit off her shoulders and sliding it down her body. But, she was too lost in sensation, in unrivaled sexual excitement, to care. His hands and lips roamed slowly over her entire body, stroking, caressing, exploring. Then, the encumbering fabric of the jumpsuit disposed of, he worked his way back up her body until he looked down into her face with glittering, hungry eyes.

She stared at him, mesmerized by the scorching desire reflected in his eyes. Tantalized by the promise of rapture transmitted through his touch. Seduced by the sheer power of his compelling masculinity. When his lips closed over hers again, Shenda clung to him, kissing him as devouringly as he kissed her. Her hands splayed over his splendid chest and she admired the flexing muscles beneath her hands even as she gloried in the soft abrasion of his chest hair against her palms.

He shifted slightly to one side, one of his hands gliding tantalizingly over her breasts before sliding down to her stomach. A finger delved playfully into her navel before moving lower. Instinctively, Shenda raised her hips in invitation. But he ignored it. His fingers caressed the small thatch of crisp midnight curls at the junction of her thighs. Moved lower to draw playful, torturous circles on the tender flesh of her inner thighs. Pressed unsatisfyingly against the sensitive bud of her femininity before moving back to begin the torture all over again. She couldn't stand it. She was on fire for him, aching for him to touch her.

"Swan, please . . ." she gasped finally, desperately, against the warm column of his neck. Her voice was so thick she hardly recognized it. His head moved lower, lavishing attention once more on her already swollen and aching breasts, but he continued to ignore the burning need that centered between her thighs. Shenda was vaguely aware that the panting little cries she heard were coming from her own mouth, but she was powerless to control them. Stars, she felt like she was going to explode. "Logan—" she cried again, urgently.

And then finally that coveted hand began to move in a more satisfying manner. His fingers deftly stroked the tiny bud that pulsed for his touch, and then moved lower. Lingeringly, tantalizingly, he slid a finger inside her body. The sensation was exquisite. And as he slowly withdrew that pleasure giving finger, her body instinctively arched in renewed invitation.

"Saints, you're hot," he murmured. "How long has it been for you?"

Shenda was beyond comprehension. Forcing her eyes open, she looked at him. "What?"

"How long has it been since you made love?"

His finger pressed its way back into her body.

"Nine years," she half moaned, half whispered, responding to the question without forethought.

She realized the magnitude of her confession in the next instant when his fingers froze in mid-maneuver and he stared at her in astonishment. "Nine *years*?" he echoed.

It was too late now to retract the statement. Slowly, Shenda nodded. "Yes."

"Why?"

Why the hell did he want to carry on a conversation now? Her senses were in chaos; she couldn't think. "I . . . I don't like men." She instinctively used the same explanation she'd used over the years to explain her solitary existence. Somehow, under the circumstances, it rang a little false.

He withdrew his finger from her body, and once again her hips arched in involuntary enticement. "I see." A tender smile hovered on his lips. "And you never availed yourself of an erotica booth?"

"No!" Her brows shot almost into her hairline. She was scandalized by the suggestion that she might have frequented such a device. Erotica booths were for . . . the unrefined.

And then, as his finger plunged slowly back into her body and Shenda was unable to stifle a soft sigh, mercifully he stopped talking. A moment later, he rose above her and began to unfasten his trousers. As the cold morning air moved greedily into the confines of the slumber bag to caress her body, a brief moment of lucidity stabbed Shenda. What was she doing? But as the soft morning light eased its way into the tent and her eyes caressed the magnificent male body before her, the moment passed. Feeling bereft, Shenda allowed her gaze to roam over him hungrily.

Then Swan was moving over her, kneeling between her legs as he leaned forward to lavish attention on her supine body once again, fanning the flames of passion into a raging inferno that all but consumed Shenda with its scorching intensity. She cried out. And then, he was entering her. Huge and hot and hard, he filled her. Thrusting, caressing, stoking the inferno of desire into an all-consuming firestorm that fused their flesh and touched their souls. Shenda cried out. Her muscles clenched, gripping him. And release came. A volcanic explosion of heat that radiated outward from the center of her being in pulsing waves to every atom of every extremity in her body. A fraction of a second later, Swan's hoarse shout melded with hers and they lay exhausted in each other's arms.

A short time later, he rolled to one side, holding her close to him. "Saints alive, sweetheart," he murmured as his breathing slowly returned to normal. "You are one hell of a woman. I think I could get used to this."

Shenda opened her eyes and, in the next instant, bolted upright. Scooting back onto her own side of the tent, she sat staring at him. "This is not going to happen again, Swan. Ever. Do you understand?"

He stared at her, pinning her with those amber-hard eyes. "I was under the impression that you enjoyed it as much as I did."

Heat flooded her face. "That's beside the point. I have no particular use for men, and I refuse to begin a relationship with one. Especially a fugitive."

"Maybe you'd do well to remind yourself of that before you snuggle up next to one again."

Eight

She stared at him for a moment longer and then, without a word, she retrieved her jumpsuit and scrambled into it as efficiently as possible. Grabbing her boots from the corner, she jerked them on and wiggled her way out of the tent, giving Logan a tantalizing view of a shapely derriere.

As he continued to watch the tent flap through which she had disappeared, his ego swelled slightly. She might hate men in general, but if she had hated *him* quite as much as she tried to let on, there was no way she would have had any contact with him, even in her sleep. And she certainly wouldn't have responded to his lovemaking as enthusiastically as she had. So as much as she might deny it, Shenda Ridell was as attracted to him as he was to her.

Shenda, after braiding her unruly hair into a semblance of neatness, had secured the braid with a piece of the twine from her pack. Now she stood in the small forest glade, eating another Vegetable Medley ration bar without tasting it and staring at the glowing flame coil. It was throwing off enough heat to cause steam to rise from the damp ground of the clearing. With nothing left to do, she watched the steam and found her thoughts returning to Swan.

How could she have been so stupid, even in her sleep? It was as though, since meeting Logan Swan, she had become a different person. Someone she didn't recognize, and certainly didn't like. Soft, she thought scornfully. She was becoming soft. She shifted position and muscles in her thighs and posterior screamed in protest. In more ways than one, she reflected, determined to bear her pain stoically.

The horses snorted and stomped. Shenda eyed them with distaste. The thought of climbing back onto the equine instrument of persecution, intensifying the distress she already felt, was torture unto itself. How people could actually ride the creatures for enjoyment was totally beyond the limits of her understanding. A rustling behind her signaled that Swan was leaving the tent. Dread flooded her. How could she face him now?

Dammit! Why did she have any feelings at all for him? Why did she care what he thought of her? The man was nothing more than a convicted felon, a fugitive, and a colonial fugitive at that. He was . . . beneath her. She winced inwardly, immediately shamed by the prejudicial thought, an echo of her father's philosophy. The snobbery with which she had been raised was showing through, and Shenda had vowed never to subscribe to such bigotry. Still, in a matter of a single day, Swan had managed to achieve much too prominent a position within the scheme of her life. She wanted nothing more than to terminate any and all association with him. But fate had conspired against her. In order to safeguard her own future, she had to accept Swan in her present. A trade-off that she could have endured without qualm if only . . . she had never begun to see the convict as a man. Her face flamed with the heat of a blush. And she was as much to blame as he was for what had happened between them. Stars! How was she going to endure the next few days?

"I'll just grab a bit of jerky to eat and then we'd best be on our way." Swan's bass voice rumbled across the clearing. "We have a long ride ahead of us to get to the *Eagle*."

She nodded without comment. He looked at her appraisingly. "I hope you're up to the ride. Not too sore, are you?"

He certainly hadn't worried about that earlier. Renewed heat flooded her face at a question that she suddenly perceived as too personal after what they'd shared, and she turned away. "I'm fine." Her tone was cool and cultured, revealing not a hint of the turmoil she felt.

He grunted—that generic, noncommittal sound that men sometimes make.

The new day that emerged was cool and dismal. Although the rain had ended, clouds continued to rumble threateningly overhead. Fingers of thick mist wound their way through the ancient giants of the forest like enormous phantom serpents. The luminous undergrowth seemed somehow pathetic in the dense gloom, adding to the eeriness of the day. Shenda was wet. She was cold. She ached in muscles she didn't even know she had. And she hated rain forests. Directing a hard, cold glare at the back of the man responsible for her predicament, she found a measure of comfort.

How could he seem so nonchalant? Didn't he feel the chill dampness?

As the day wore on and the sky overhead began to clear, it did warm up somewhat. And slowly, as she felt less chilled, Shenda's spirits lifted enough to allow her to take more notice of the world around her. A ray of sunlight somehow managed to sneak past the thick canopy of branches overhead. Like a spotlight, it captured and displayed all of the small pieces of nature in its path. The prismatic glitter of a raindrop trembling on the edge of a leaf. The shimmering, gossamer strands of a spider's web stretched between two branches. The brilliant color of a flower peeking defiantly from beneath the bulbous root system of one of the forest's oldest inhabitants.

Before long, Shenda noticed that the trees began to grow less densely. Shortly after midday, Swan drew up. They had reached the edge of a steep grassy slope littered with gigantic boulders. Only the occasional tall tree continued to maintain a foothold on the embankment. And beyond the plateau lay an enormous body of water. Shenda eyed it suspiciously. "I thought the ocean was behind us."

"It is," Swan answered. "But it's in front of us, too. The land we've been traveling is a large peninsula. Down there"—he pointed to a particularly rocky section of the slope—"is where the *Eagle* is."

Shenda studied the area carefully. "I don't see anything."

Swan just looked at her. "That's the idea. It's a perfect natural hangar. Come on." He spurred Dancer forward, tugging on Star's reins as he went. He never had bothered to show her how to guide the horse herself, Shenda realized, as she grabbed the pommel and canted back in the saddle to balance as the horse began down the slope. Oh, well, she hoped never to have to ride one of the creatures again anyway.

A few minutes later, Swan secured the horses to a small bush and, moving to Star's side, looked up at Shenda. "Let me help you down," he said, reaching toward her.

Shenda took inventory of the various aches and pains which plagued her muscles, and wasn't certain she had the fortitude to force them to move. But she couldn't, and wouldn't, stay on a horse for the rest of her life, so there was really little to do but grit her teeth, accept Swan's aid and dismount.

With her left foot still in the stirrup, she managed to rest her weight on her left leg while she swung her right leg over the beast's hind end. But when it came time to extend that right leg toward the ground . . . something went wrong. The muscles in her left thigh screamed so loudly and so painfully at her attempt to bend the leg that she froze, unable to move. In the next instant she felt Swan's hands at her waist, lifting her free and setting her firmly on her own two feet.

Pain. It burst through the shell of her facade for an instant, fracturing her composure. And she gasped.

"Are you going to be all right?" he asked.

Gritting her teeth, she willed the pain under control and, cursing her moment of weakness, met his gaze. He looked honestly concerned. "I'll be fine," she responded, although her normally cool cultured tone almost deserted her. The knowledge that she would not have been able to dismount without Swan's aid was . . . humbling.

She watched as Swan removed all the gear, including the bridles, from the horses and stowed it, with the exception of the two helmets, in a small cave-like depression to their left. "Are you just going to leave them here?" she asked, nodding in the direction of the horses. "Will they be safe? Won't they run away?"

"There's nowhere for them to run but home," he said. "And they'll be safe enough. Most of the carnivores range further inland. The horses will graze around here for a couple of days and then, if no one shows up to ride them home, they'll make their own way back to the comfort of their stable." He looked at Shenda. "Come on. The *Eagle*'s over here." He gestured with a hand containing one of the helmets and moved off to the right.

Shenda looked ahead of him, but saw nothing other than an almost vertical cliff face. Unwilling to try moving just yet, she stared after Swan incredulously. If he thought she was going to climb that, feeling the way she felt, she would cheerfully split his skull with one of the numerous boulders littering the ground and take her chances with Marnier.

Suddenly Swan dropped from sight. Shenda frowned. Had he faded again? An instant later his head reappeared. "Are you coming?" he called. He sounded impatient.

Not bothering to reply, Shenda shot him a poisonous look and took a cautious step forward. It was as she'd suspected. Every muscle in her body screamed out in protest. But since she couldn't stay standing in the middle of nowhere until her body healed itself, she forced herself to keep moving. Every step became an effort of willpower. Finally she reached the spot where Swan's head had again disappeared, and she discovered why she'd been unable to see the *natural hangar* of which he'd spoken.

The cave entrance, perhaps 25 feet wide and 17 or 18 feet high, sat in a depression hidden by the ridge of earth in front of it. The basin in front of the cave's mouth was flat and about 20 feet in diameter. Shenda studied it critically. If Swan viewed the cave as a *perfect* natural hangar, then he was a much better pilot than she. Which, she conceded, wouldn't be difficult.

A tachyon scout's external dimensions measured approximately ten feet in height and 20 feet in length. That meant that when Swan landed the *Eagle*, which would need at least two feet beneath it for its thrusters to work, he had roughly five or six feet to spare above the craft when he eased it into its hangar. A tight fit. Very tight. Not many pilots would have attempted it.

Slowly, cautiously Shenda stepped down into the depression and made her way into the cave. Just within the mouth of the cave and to the right, partially concealed by the shadows, she could make out the outline of the tachyon vessel that Swan had christened the *Eagle*. She paused to allow her eyes to adjust to the dimness, and then stared in wonder. The ceiling of the cavern soared overhead to a height of at least 30 feet, probably closer to 40. Glittering stalactites speared downward toward their counterpart stalagmites. In a couple of places the two had met, forming natural pillars of luminescent stone. The cavern was enormous, capable of holding at least two, possibly three ships the size of the *Eagle*. It *was* a natural hangar.

As she continued to attempt to convince her muscles that movement really was the best course of action for them, a sudden action caught her eye and she saw Swan poke his head from the open hatch of the ship. He watched her move toward him. "Would you like some help?" he asked with exaggerated solicitude. In truth, he looked thoroughly exasperated.

Shenda gritted her teeth, this time in annoyance. "I told you I'm fine."

"So you did," he said. Just as he pulled his head back inside, Shenda heard him mutter something about *stubborn females*. She received the distinct impression that he didn't believe her.

A moment later, she finally managed to make her way into the ship. The *Eagle* appeared to closely emulate other tachyon-style vessels, despite having never seen a factory. Looking aft along the corridor, Shenda saw three narrow doors. The two on the left would lead to the tiny cubicle-like staterooms. The third, straight ahead, would lead to the small, functional galley and a lavatory scarcely large enough to turn around in without inflicting grievous injury on some part of one's anatomy. Looking forward along the corridor, she could see Swan standing before the pilot's console frowning furiously. She stepped into the ship and moved toward him. "What's the matter?" she asked, not certain if she really wanted to know.

"The damn tracker's gone," he muttered. "Saints above! What else can go wrong?"

Saints? Shenda wondered. A fragment of the Kanisi belief system in Swan's background, no doubt. She'd heard him use the expression a couple of times now. Aloud, she asked, "Who else knows about this place?"

"Just about everybody from the dig site, but they'd have no reason to take the tracker. No further shipments have been arranged since my arrest."

"You're certain of that?"

He shrugged. "Well, there's one way to find out. Computer on!" he barked. A series of lights flashed on the console. Sitting down in the pilot's seat, Swan placed the palm of his hand on the identification pad. Within seconds, the word AUTHORIZED came up on the monitor. Using the key pad, Swan punched in a series of numbers. "Site two, come in," he said. "This is Eagle one."

There was no response. Frowning, Swan tried again without results. Leaning back in his chair, he glanced at Shenda. "That's strange. There's almost always *someone* manning the communications, unless . . ." He broke off.

"Unless what?" Shenda prompted.

"Unless they've made an important discovery, or something is wrong."

Moving slowly forward, Shenda concentrated on lowering herself gingerly into the copilot's seat. She looked up to find Swan's unreadable eyes on her.

"You're fine. Right?"

She nodded. "Right."

Shifting his gaze, he stared thoughtfully through the steelglass viewscreen at the mouth of the cave. "I sure wish we knew more about what we were up against." He muttered the comment so quietly that Shenda almost didn't hear him. She wondered if he knew he'd spoken aloud. Abruptly he turned to her. "It looks like we're going to have to take a run out to the site." Quickly donning one of the helmets, he lowered the visor and made a few remarks, too muffled for Shenda to hear. Then he removed the helmet once more and looked at Shenda. "I've transferred Lais to the on-board system. On the way to the site, I'd like you to use the computer to find out more about that Obsidian Order." He manipulated a series of controls, and the ship began to vibrate slightly as the engines warmed.

Shenda bristled a little at the peremptoriness of his tone. She might be accustomed to taking orders, but she wasn't accustomed to taking them from a convict. However, since fate had chosen to make them allies, she forced herself to overlook his brusqueness. "I only have access to the database on Apollo and the computer at home." She looked at Swan. "My father's home, on Earth," she clarified. "I'd need to access at least three jump satellites to connect with Apollo and . . ." She paused thoughtfully. "Probably four or five to connect with Earth. Can your computer handle that?"

"As long as you know which satellites you want, she can calculate their exact coordinates and contact them."

Shenda shook her head. "That could be difficult unless you happen to have the most current map. I'll need orbit and trajectory information and . . . frequency variables."

Swan nodded. "We do a lot of business with Earth, so we have to keep on top of that." He depressed a series of buttons on the console, and a holo map shimmered into existence in front of them. "You choose which satellites you need to use, and using the date of this map along with orbit information, the computer can calculate their present positions."

As Swan fired the thrusters and began to maneuver the small ship through the cave mouth, Shenda studied the map with its dozens of scattered jump satellites. Next to each satellite a range of numbers shone. She had to find three satellites, using the same frequency as the database she'd been authorized to use on Apollo, each successively nearer to Apollo than the last. It took a minute. "All right," she said. "I think I've got it." She looked at Swan. "Can you put the computer on verbal response mode? I'll need voice access when I get through."

Swan nodded. "Computer, activate voice mode and create a voice-print file on Shenda Ridell complete with voice authorization." Shenda noted that Swan appeared to be heading the *Eagle* out to sea, but she didn't have time to ask about it.

"Acknowledged," the computer said.

Swan indicated with a gesture of his hand that she should begin. She looked at the computer. "Corporal Shenda Ridell."

"Age?" queried the computer. The age query aided the computer in classifying the voice. As people aged, subtle changes occurred in the voice. By storing an age, the computer could predict and make allowances for slight modifications that might occur over time.

"Twenty-five Earth years."

"Voice-print created. Authorized."

A few minutes passed before Shenda, with the aid of the *Eagle*'s computer, was able to make contact. In the next instant, the space station identification came up on the computer screen and the words *INPUT ACCESS CODE*. "Access delta-theta-three-zero-two-nine-omega," she said.

There was a wait. Much longer than usual. Probably because of the distance, Shenda mused. Finally the computer said, "Corporal Shenda Ridell. Security level four. Access granted." The words *Space Station Apollo* adopted a horseshoe shape around the reproduction of a naked statue representative of a Greek god who looked disconcertingly like Swan had looked in the prison loin-cloth. "Request?"

Shenda wasted no time. "Library archives. Search for any reference to an Obsidian Order."

"Searching." The silence in the small space craft stretched.

Shenda looked out the viewscreen and saw nothing but miles and miles of ocean. White-capped waves swelled and rolled. "Swan, where exactly *is* site two?"

"It's on an island in the middle of the Messenian Ocean. The nearest land is five hundred miles away."

The sight of the swelling, surging water made her nauseous. "Why didn't you choose to excavate some ruins a little closer to home?"

"There are no ruins closer to home. Apparently, the only continent on this world that was ever in-habited by intelligent life prior to our arrival was the island of Sendiri. Both of the intact cities and all of the ruins we've excavated are there."

The computer beeped, signaling it now had the information Shenda had requested, and then be-gan speaking. "The Obsidian Order was the name adopted by a group of black youths in the early twenty-first century to promote the education of Third World children."

Shenda frowned. That didn't sound like what they were looking for. "Computer, are there any other references?"

"One. It refers to a discovery made by geneticist Dr. Nathanial Tredway during recent anthropo-logical DNA research. The obsidian order refers to a distinctive string sequence in the DNA of certain individuals. The sequence is consistently black and follows the same pattern, hence the term *ob-sidian order*."

Curious. Shenda looked at Swan.

"Ask if there's any indication of what this string is supposed to indicate." he said. Since he'd never been granted access to the Apollan computer, he could not ask himself. It would be deaf to his voice. Shenda complied.

"That information is classified: security level one."

"In other words, there is, but we can't access it," Shenda elaborated for Swan. Shenda stared thoughtfully through the viewscreen, but her gaze was turned inward. Finally she asked, "Computer, what is the doctor working on now?"

"Dr. Nathanial Tredway is currently involved in performing DNA comparison tests relating to the primitive species of Earth and their possible connection to the species of other worlds."

"And where is the doctor conducting his research?"

"He is currently based on the Duana Moon research station orbiting Dendron II."

Shenda raised a brow at Swan. "Anything else you want to know?"

"Everything," he scowled. "But there's nothing I can think of that the dammed computer will tell us."

Shenda nodded. "Computer, access news releases over the past"—Shenda paused, calculating how long it had been since she had seen Marnier—"two months. Search for any reference to the name Shenda Ridell."

"Searching."

Although she was reasonably certain that Swan had told her the truth concerning the news release announcing her engagement, Shenda needed to confirm that such a thing existed. Its existence would prove that she wasn't being manipulated, at least not by Swan.

An instant later, the article flashed up on the screen complete with a picture of Shenda and Marnier together at some society function. Shenda stared at it. She remembered the instant that Marnier had put his arm around her. Remembered the smell of liquor on his breath when he'd couched his ridiculous proposal in an undertone at the charity ball. And she remembered how quickly she'd escaped his embrace. The bastard had had it all planned, even back then. He had gone so far as to hire a photographer to catch that one quick moment in time. Why? Why did he suddenly want her so badly? And why the covert manipulation? Had he decided not to use the coercion tactics she'd seen him use on others, or was he just biding his time? He didn't know she feared him. After all, he had never known about the scene she'd witnessed.

She'd been 16 at the time, immature and unsure of herself. Mere hours after he had left her, closing the door in her face and shattering her heart, Shenda had decided that she had to talk to him once more, to attempt to convince him that her love for him was something he should not cast aside.

She'd dressed in her most fashionable outfit. The mirror had told her she looked beautiful. But did she look mature? Did she have that indefinable something it took to become a political asset rather than an encumbrance? Without knowing the answer, she had gone to Darren's office and, finding it empty, she'd hidden in the inner office to await his arrival. She hadn't had long to wait.

Within moments, she heard him arrive. But he was speaking to someone. In all the fantasizing she'd done of what she would say and how she would say it, they had been alone. She decided to stay hidden in the hope that whoever was with him would leave. And that was when she began to listen to what they were saying.

"That black bitch knows too much about my extracurricular activities. She's determined to ruin me." It was Darren's voice, but his tone held a quality that she had never heard before. Cold brutality.

"I assume you're speaking of Minister Valencia," a woman said. Her voice was absolutely emotionless.

"Who else?" Darren snapped. "I want her stopped. Permanently. Do you hear me?"

"Loud and clear," said the woman. "I'll arrange something as soon as possible." Although Shenda didn't understand the nature of the conversation completely at that point, its vicious undertone had frightened her. Staying hidden, she had sidled forward to peer around the corner of the inner office and view Darren and the woman. She saw a beautiful blonde in possession of all the traits that 16-year-old Shenda lacked. Poise. Maturity. Style. And cool hauteur. A moment later, she saw them kiss.

It was at that moment that she finally accepted the fact that Darren Marnier did not love her and probably never had. It was then that she began to hate him. Secreting herself in the inner office, she waited until all sounds in the outer office had ceased and she knew they had left. Then she returned home. Within three days, she saw a story on the news-vid speaking of Minister Valencia's untimely death at the hands of burglars. The crime had never been solved. But Shenda knew who was responsible. The knowledge that Marnier could reach out and have the lives of powerful and influential people snuffed out so easily had terrified her.

Suddenly Logan spoke, his voice pulling her from her thoughts. Shenda looked at him with distant and uncomprehending eyes. "What did you say?" she asked.

"Check for any references to me in the last couple of days," Swan prompted again.

She nodded. "Computer," she said. "Scan news releases and Legion Bulletins for any reference to Logan Swan of the planet Fortuna."

"There are seven news articles concerning Logan Swan's escape from the Sentran prison. Did you wish to see them in sequence?"

"Yes."

The articles flashed up on the screen. The press had made much of the fact that Marnier had involved himself personally in the pursuit of a criminal. Some journalists had attributed his uncharacteristic action to the fact that his purported fiancée had been taken hostage. Shenda, knowing Marnier as she did, knew that he would not have crossed a hall to rescue her. He'd have sent a squad of Legionnaires while playing the concerned fiancé for any nearby camera. The remaining stories drew suppositions that perhaps it was a personal vendetta directed against the first man who had successfully escaped a prison of which Marnier was the director. Whatever his motivation, the journalists were right. Marnier's actions were completely out of character. Marnier was a controller. He liked to stay nice and safe in his office and control people's lives from a distance. Shenda's eyes narrowed. She had been so concerned with her own situation that she hadn't seen that immediately. And again she had to ask: why?

The last of the articles appeared on the screen, a model of its predecessors. "Computer, display any Legion Bulletins."

A single Bulletin flashed on screen. "Hell's universe!" Shenda exploded. "They've ordered you shot on sight."

Nine

Logan shrugged, although the thought filled him with dread. "It's what I expected."

"Well, it's not what I expected. How are we supposed to search for . . ." She almost said *proof against Marnier,* and caught herself. "For your figurine if we run the risk of being shot at every turn? There are Legionnaires everywhere, you know. If you go into a bar or restaurant, you can be shot. If they see you in a corridor, you can be shot. They haven't been ordered to arrest you, Swan. They've been ordered to kill you—*on sight.* Your likeness is probably being passed around like cheap wine. There won't be a Legionnaire in the galaxy who doesn't know what you look like. The whole thing is impossible."

"Nothing's impossible," he argued. "It *can't* be impossible."

Shenda stared at him without seeing him. They had to think of a way to make the Legion adjust or revoke the Bulletin. Something. But what? "We have to think of some way around this death order," she said. "Or we're going to be in trouble."

"Well, we don't have any time to worry about that right now," Swan said. "We're almost at the site. Can you access the other computer?"

Shenda nodded. She could feel Swan's eyes on her as she terminated communication with Apollo and initiated contact with the jump satellites again. "Got it," she said a moment later. "Computer access personal memos and appointment calendar for myself and my father. Search for the term Obsidian Order."

"That term is not in my data bank. Would you like to alter or expand search perimeters?"

Shenda frowned. "Yes. Search for the word *order* or the word *obsidian* separately."

"I have three references using the word *order*."

"Let's see them."

"Anything?" Swan asked a moment later as Shenda continued to stare at the screen silently.

She shook her head. "I'm not sure. Two of the references are just notes to order items. The third is confusing. It's the word *order* followed by a set of numbers." She frowned. "They look like they could be coordinates."

"I think they are."

"Computer," Shenda said. "What is located at these coordinates?" She repeated the series of numbers on the screen.

"Searching." There was a pause during which the only sound was the soft drone of the *Eagle*. "The planet Dendron II is located at the given coordinates."

Logan frowned. "Wasn't there a reference to Dendron II when you contacted the Apollan computer?"

"Yes. The genetic scientist who discovered the DNA strand that he called the Obsidian Order is stationed on the Duana moon orbiting Dendron II."

"Almost too much of a coincidence. Wouldn't you say?"

Shenda nodded. "You think we should pay a visit to Dr. Nathanial Tredway?"

"I think that should be our first port of call. But I can't leave without knowing why the site is not answering communications." He frowned thoughtfully. "I sure hope Zach took the tracker. I'd hate to think that someone else got his hands on it." He shrugged. "We can go on without it, I suppose. But I'm still hoping that the tracker will lead us to the artifacts."

Shenda watched Swan's sure hands fly over the console. "Who's Zach and why would he take the tracker?"

"Zach is my grandfather. And I have no idea why he might have taken the tracker, but he's done things I haven't understood before, so I'm not ruling it out." Abruptly he pointed through the viewscreen. "There's Sendiri Island."

At first Shenda saw nothing more than a bluish outline in the distance, but within seconds the outline manifested itself as two snowcapped peaks.

"The mountains you're seeing are actually near the center of the island," Swan elucidated. "But, because they are so massive, we see them first. Sendiri actually has a fairly unique terrain. If you were to approach by water, it would be extremely difficult to land on the island. Except for a few exceptions, the coastline consists of thousands of miles of sheer-faced cliffs."

As they neared the island, Shenda saw a strange

black formation consisting of needle-like black spires and tumbled stone. It appeared to rise from another small island just off the coast. "What is that?"

"We call this area the Devil's Backbone. See how the small islands curve like a backbone?" Shenda nodded. Now that they were almost on top of the area, she could see that a number of islands formed a half circle that almost touched the coast of Sendiri. "At one time, those islands and the shoals around them were part of Sendiri. The black spires you see are all that remains of another alien city. It's extremely difficult to do any extensive excavating there, but from what we've seen we don't think that the beings who created this city were of the same race as those who created the other two cities we've found."

"Why not?"

Logan shrugged. "The construction is different. Black instead of white. Haphazard and disjointed rather than uniform and symmetric. It just *feels* different. But since ninety percent of it or more is underwater, we haven't really concentrated on this site much, so we could be wrong." He frowned as the discussion reminded him of the one item they'd retrieved from the Devil's Backbone site which he now wished he'd retained. It was a large crystal that appeared to contain a recording, partially holographic, of somebody's personal life and work. But they'd been desperately in need of funds at the time in order to continue their work, and they'd known that the linguistic scientists back on Earth would be scrambling for it, so they'd auctioned off the crystal. He didn't even remember the name of the company who'd purchased it. It had been one they hadn't dealt with previously.

But he did know that once again, the crystal had been stolen en route.

Shenda looked back over her shoulder for one last glimpse of the peculiar jet-black spires. As she swung her gaze forward again, she happened to catch a glimpse of a huge shiny object in the water directly beneath them. "Swan?" she said, suddenly afraid to take her eyes off the water.

"Yeah?" He was busily adjusting dials on the console.

"What kinds of creatures live in this bay?" she asked.

Swan looked out the window. "This is called the Sea of Serpents. Probably thirty percent of the entire worldwide sea serpent population comes from this area. Most of them migrate back here to breed."

Shenda wished to hell that he'd stop his educational dissertation and just answer her question. "So what you're saying is that this bay is full of water snakes?"

He nodded.

"And just how big do these snakes get?"

"The biggest we've seen was seventy or eighty feet long and about three feet in diameter. Scientists think that there are larger specimens in the deepest parts of the ocean."

Shenda swallowed. "Just what I wanted to hear," she muttered.

"Pardon me?"

"Nothing. I was talking to myself."

"Oh." He looked at her quizzically. "We're coming up on the coastline of Sendiri now."

Shenda looked eagerly ahead, suddenly anxious to be over land rather than water. She saw a wall of towering white and mauve cliffs. Beyond them, the snowcapped peaks of the twin mountains shone in the brilliant light of Fortuna's two suns like goddesses overseeing their domain. Within seconds, they were beyond the cliffs and Shenda looked down at the most amazing sight she'd ever seen. Her mouth dropped. It was beautiful. Absolutely extraordinary.

"Fire Falls," Swan said. She glanced at him long enough to see that he, too, stared at the sight with appreciative eyes. *Fire falls*. And, that was exactly what it was. A fall of molten lava that flowed endlessly into a lake of fire at its base. "There's a rift in the planet's crust here that's centuries old, according to the scientists. At the rate that it's healing itself and cooling, it will take another hundred and fifty years before the falls stop flowing."

Shenda looked at the terrain bordering the huge bowl-like depression into which the lava flowed. The vegetation looked almost tropical. Enormous trees, bountiful brilliant flowers, verdant plateaus and masses of clinging vines. "The lava seems to have affected the climate," she remarked.

Swan nodded. "The Sea of Serpents has an average temperature of twenty-seven degrees centigrade."

"How far are the excavation sites from here?"

"Site One is on the opposite side of the island. It's subtropical there, too. But naturally so. Site Two is just a couple of hundred miles from the base of the Gemini Mountains."

Shenda stared at him. "Exactly how big *is* this island?"

"Roughly five hundred and fifty thousand square miles." A short time later, Logan nodded toward the viewscreen. "You can just make out some of the towers of Site Two now."

The towers Logan spoke of were needle-like spires much the same as those she'd seen as they approached the island. Only these, rather than black, appeared to be constructed of some almost crystalline substance. "You can't actually go inside them, can you?" she asked.

He shook his head. "No, they're pretty much solid."

"So what are they?"

"To tell you the truth, we're not absolutely certain. They appear to be part of a solar lighting and heating system incorporated into the buildings. But we think there's more to them than that." He banked the *Eagle* and keyed in a complicated series of numbers.

"What are you doing?" Shenda asked, staring at the gibberish on the screen.

"Deactivating the security system. Just a few of the artifacts from the sites on this island are worth enough for a few disreputable types to retire for life. It's not something you can leave unguarded if you expect to be able to have the chance to appreciate its scientific impact."

"No, I suppose not." Shenda eyed the alien city with new appreciation. "So what would happen if you didn't shut it off?"

"We have a radar system that works in conjunction with a number of automated blasters."

"What you're saying is that we would have been shot down."

He nodded and they began approaching a large, flat depression within the city confines. "This appears to have been some type of stadium. But thus far, we can only guess at what type of entertainment they enjoyed. Despite the well-preserved quality of the city itself, its inhabitants left very little behind. We know virtually nothing about them. Not even what they looked like."

"You haven't found any drawings or physical remains?" Shenda asked incredulously.

Swan shook his head. "Nothing. It's as though they just packed up and left." There was a very slight jolt as he landed the *Eagle*. He immediately keyed in the code that would reactivate the security system.

As they left the craft a moment later, Shenda stared around in awe. The stands surrounding the field on which they stood would have held thousands of people. Knee-high grasses rustled as they moved through them. The sky overhead looked somehow larger, like a huge inverted blue bowl. Fortuna's suns blazed unrelentingly down upon them. It was hot here. Very hot. She could see how Swan had obtained his tan.

"Come on," he said, grasping her arm. "We need to find Zach."

They moved through a door in the stadium stands into the streets of the city itself. The deserted thoroughfares were paved with a yellow-gold stone.

"What kind of stone is this?" she asked, poking at it curiously with her toe.

"We call it diamond stone because of its incredible durability. It's endemic to the Sendiri continent. So far, we haven't found it anywhere else on Fortuna."

Shenda nodded and continued to look around them with wide eyes. The city felt alien, and yet it didn't. It had a very *human* feel to it. Large white buildings with arched entries rose on either side of the wide avenues. Time had weathered them somewhat, but not nearly as much as one might expect in five hundred years.

"This way," Logan said. "We'll check communications first. Make sure the problem isn't something technical." He led her across the street and down a slightly narrower avenue. Gray powdery dust rose to hover around their ankles at each step. Heat shimmered in mirage-like waves ahead of them. Unidentifiable creaks and groans broke the ghostly silence of the ancient city. But there were no voices, human or alien.

The buildings on either side of the narrow street lay derelict. Yet were it not for the years of accumulated filth—in some areas the dirt and dust had collected to a depth of two feet or more—Shenda could almost have believed that the owners intended to return. Through one window opening she saw what appeared to be the remains of flowers. Desiccated into petrification, their skeletal stalks rose from a bowl-like vase on a table laden with years of soil deposits. Through a doorway, a child's toy lay discarded on a stool in the center of the room next to a circular device that, to Shenda's uneducated eye, appeared as though it might be some kind of cooking appliance. She could almost see the ghostly presence of the beings who'd lived here. Almost hear the laughter of the children. A chill raced up her spine. "Do you think they intended to come back?" she asked.

Swan looked down at her with his enigmatic whiskey gaze. "Who?" he asked, the sound of his soft bass voice mere vibration in the intense silence.

"The people who lived here?"

"Who knows?" He shrugged. "The city was obviously constructed to stand the test of time, so it's possible, I suppose."

Shenda continued to study the architecture on either side of them. "How much of this did you actually have to excavate?"

"*Excavate* is a bit of a misnomer when it comes to the two main cities on this island. Basically we've only had to do some extensive and gentle cleaning. What you're seeing now, we've barely touched. From the size of the city, we think it had a population somewhere in the range of three hundred thousand people. We started with the larger buildings, the public places that could tell us something about the culture. My grandfather has spent a lifetime studying both major cities on this island. He's explored them in a general way so many times that he could probably draw you a map with his eyes closed. But when it comes to detailed analyses, we're still working primarily in the heart of the cities."

They approached an intersection and he grasped her elbow, prompting her to turn. "We erected a pre-fab shelter"—he pointed at a nondescript gray rectangular structure a couple of hundred feet ahead—"to serve as head of operations and communications. There's almost always someone in the area."

Brushing at a trickle of perspiration worming its way down her forehead, Shenda searched the area. "I don't see anyone." She did, however, see a large number of smaller pre-fab structures that mimicked the communications center in uniformity if not size. It appeared that the archeological team had erected their own small village within the ancient city.

He frowned. "Neither do I." He scanned the area. "Anybody home?" he called loudly. Startled, Shenda flinched at the invasive sound of his voice in the intensely silent city of ghosts.

They approached the communications building, and Swan cautiously opened the door. Slowly, they stepped into the room. A long narrow table laden with computers and other electronic equipment stretched from one wall to the other.

Enough space had been left at each end to allow someone to circumnavigate the table, but that was all. It didn't appear as though anything had been sabotaged. In fact, one of the computers appeared to be in the process of running some type of analytical program.

Strolling slowly forward, Swan studied the place thoroughly. He stopped abruptly in the center of the room and stood scowling down at the table. "Now I know what happened to the tracker," he muttered.

"What?" Shenda asked, looking at him.

He held up a couple of electronic parts sporting dangling wires. "Somebody took it apart."

"Oh." Shenda took one more look around. "So now what?" She was beginning to get impatient. Marnier seldom worked slowly. The longer they took to get proof against him, the more nervous she would get.

"Well, we can't just leave without knowing where everyone is. And I need the damn tracker if we can reassemble it." He sighed. "So I guess we search. Eight weeks ago, they were working in the castle. We'll start there."

"Castle?" said Shenda.

"Yeah. At least that's what we call it. When you're working here, you find you have to identify the buildings in some way to serve as a reference in conversation. The building with the ten crystal towers near the center of the city is the one we call the castle."

Shenda nodded, and followed him from the communication center. She followed his gaze, easily locating the enormous crystal spires spearing into the sky above the city. "How far is it?"

Swan's mouth twisted in an expression that Shenda couldn't categorize. "A long way if you're walking." He looked at her. "Which we're not. We'll take the skimmer most of the way." He gestured to the craft. "If the *Eagle* was a little smaller, we could have used her. But she kicks up a pretty good wind, and I didn't want to risk damaging anything."

A couple of minutes later, humming along in the skimmer at little more than three feet above the ground, Shenda watched Logan's deft manipulation of the controls almost jealously. He seemed to handle every mode of transport he touched with expertise. Although Shenda could pilot a skimmer proficiently, she had never attained a level of comfort that would enable her to be quite so . . . confident.

Ten minutes later, they approached an unusual sight distracting Shenda from her unconscious observation of the play of the muscle in Swan's forearm. It was a white brick wall stretching off endlessly in either direction. "What is this?" Shenda asked curiously as they neared the arched gateway.

"We're not sure," Logan replied. "The city is divided into three distinct circular areas. A large outer ring—the stadium is part of that—then a slightly smaller ring inside that, and finally, the circular center of the city. Each area is separated from the others by one of these walls. There are only four arched gates in each wall, one in each direction. We've just entered the inner ring. The castle is in the center, so we'll see another wall in a few minutes."

"Strange." Shenda studied the arched gate as they moved through the wall. There was a thin line of some crystalline substance implanted into a depression in the arch. "Is that quartz embedded in the stone?" she asked.

Swan nodded. "The molecular structure of the crystals is a bit off, but quartz is the closest identifiable material."

"So what you're saying is that it's a quartz derivative? Do you think these people knew how to manipulate matter at the molecular level?" she asked incredulously.

Swan looked at her, his eyes unreadable. "Scientists on Earth have been experimenting in that direction for years. They've had moderate success with crystalline substances. And if you believe that the beam affecting me is a transfer beam working at a molecular level, it doesn't take much more of a leap to imagine them working with matter at the molecular level in other ways."

Shenda frowned. "No, I suppose it doesn't." But for some reason the thought frightened her. If someone had the ability to control and exploit the properties of matter to the point that they were able to *create* alternate resources, what was to stop them from going beyond the precepts of morality and playing god? Early in the 21st century, the governments of Earth had found themselves in the position of legislating morality to the scientists of the time experimenting with DNA programming. What if the alien race had possessed the technology to go beyond even that capability? The idea terrified her. Yet she was at a loss to explain why, even to herself, so she didn't voice her thoughts.

Immersed in her somber reverie, Shenda only took cursory notice of the second gate—it was identical to the first—as they passed through into the inner circle of the deserted alien city. Parking the skimmer, they disembarked and Swan led her toward the *castle*. As they drew nearer, she couldn't help but stare in awe. A flight of stone steps, perhaps 30 feet wide at the base and easily as high, rose to meet a set of four arched doors placed side by side at the top of the stairs. The edifice was large, and beautiful. The architecture, impossible to classify, consisted of fluid lines. Gentle curves rather than corners. Subtle grandeur rather than bold affluence.

Swan began ascending the stairs. "The last time I spoke with him, Zach was still working in here."

At the top of the flight of steps, Shenda turned to look back. Her mouth dropped in awe. Although the steps themselves weren't that high, the building must have been constructed on a high point within the city, for the entire metropolis lay before her. She imagined what it must have looked like peopled and prosperous. It would have been one of the most beautiful places she'd ever seen.

Logan, about to enter the building, turned around to say something to Shenda, and found her observing the city with shining appreciative eyes. Despite his desire for haste, he let her have a moment. He was used to the sight, but for a newcomer it could be quite awe-inspiring. "It's beautiful, isn't it?" he said a moment later.

Shenda turned to him, her gaze focusing gradually as though emerging from a trance. "Yes," she said simply. "It is." Words simply could not describe the simple grandeur of a city built to withstand the ravages of time. From this vantage point, it was obvious that its architects had not merely dealt with immediate needs of its people. Rather they had sought versatility and quality, constructing to serve the needs of generations.

"Ready?" Logan asked.

She blinked. "Yes. Yes, of course." Turning, she followed him toward the doors of the castle, but she couldn't resist casting one more glance over her shoulder at the gleaming white city bathed in the light of Fortuna's suns.

They approached the white arched doors of the building, and Shenda wondered just how they would gain admittance. There were no pressure plates in evidence, no knobs or levers. In fact, the doors looked as solid as the walls. Only the four arched recesses that held them betrayed their obvious location. She looked questioningly at Swan, and observed as he extended a hand toward a design, merely a subtle shading of gray-white, etched into the upper third of the door. As he touched one portion of the design, a note sounded. Musical. Mystical. Completely alien. He touched another part of the motif. Another note. Deeper. Peaceful. Then his fingers traced a gentle curve in the pattern. A short sweeping series of notes drifted along Shenda's nerve endings. And then the door disappeared.

She stared in astonishment. She looked at Logan. "A holographic door?"

"More like a holograph combined with a force field. You can't walk through one until you know the combination that opens it. We've tried." He met her gaze. "And even then there sometimes seems to be a type of residual energy that some people find uncomfortable. We don't know what it is."

"What happens?" Shenda asked, nervously eyeing the innocuous-looking doorway.

Swan stepped through the doorway and looked back at Shenda. "The worst that's happened is that one of my people became quite disoriented. He almost lost consciousness."

"Nice," said Shenda, giving the archway overhead a distinctly wary look. Then, taking a deep breath, she stepped through to join Swan. Nothing happened. She looked around.

They stood in an enormous corridor, easily 20 feet wide. It seemed to go on forever. Overhead, the ceiling rose fully three stories in the air. On each side, occasional balconies from the upper two levels overlooked the central corridor. Gold-veined marble flooring peeked through the dust and grime of disuse in patches cleared by the passage of archeological feet.

"Zach!" Swan's shout in the preternatural silence of the ancient alien edifice shot Shenda's blood pressure off the scale. The single word echoed and re-echoed endlessly.

"Stars! You could give a person a little warning," she gasped, clutching her throat in an attempt to persuade her heart to slide back down to its normal station.

"Sorry," Swan said, but he didn't sound very repentant. "This place is so large we could search for a very long time without finding them. It's easier to call, and let Zach come to us." He paused, and added, "If he's here."

They strolled slowly forward along the main corridor. Shenda studied the nature of the embellishments added to the walls. "It's strange," she murmured to herself.

"What is?" Logan's voice made her jump.

"That none of the artwork appears to reflect the likeness of the beings who lived here."

Swan shrugged. "We find it odd by *our* standards. Most of Earth's societies, no matter how disparate, have made representations of themselves in their art. Who is to say what standards these beings set for themselves?" Walking at her side, Logan joined her in her examination of the wall. Virtually no color, with the exception of a few subtle shades of gray, had been used in the design. It was a nature scene; trees, flowers, sky and clouds, all created with a white plasterlike substance on a white background.

"Logan!" a deep voice bellowed, reverberating back and forth within the building.

A tall barrel-chested man approached them from the opposite end of the corridor. Swan quickened his step, and Shenda hurried to keep pace.

"Hello, Zach," Logan said affectionately, walking into the older man's embrace. Zach's thick white hair stood out from his scalp in multidirectional tufts. Although roughly the same height as Logan, he was more burly. His eyes left no doubt in Shenda's mind concerning their blood tie. Logan had inherited his liquid, whiskey-colored eyes from his grandfather.

Zach thumped Logan on the back enthusiastically enough to cause bruising. "Ah, son, it's good to see you. The damn government saw the error of their ways then and let you go, did they?"

"Not exactly, Grandfather. I take it you haven't spoken with Father recently?"

A frown furrowing his brow, Zach leaned back to look into his grandson's face. "No. We've made an important find, and nobody wanted to be stuck monitoring communications. Most of the group are off checking for similar finds in other buildings. Henry, Liselle, Gordon and Sarah stayed with me here. But before I tell you about that, I want to know *exactly* what you would be meaning by *not exactly*."

Logan cleared his throat. "I escaped. Or rather, Brie's Legionnaires rescued me. Now, I have to find that damn figurine. Then, I have to prove my innocence before I catch a Legionnaire laser between the eyes."

A sad and worried expression in his liquid eyes, Zach shook his head. "So they ordered you killed then?"

Swan nodded. "There are Legionnaire search parties looking for me, so you'll have to be careful. I've no doubt that they'll decide to check here for me before long."

"We'll be careful." Zach looked at Shenda. "This pretty little thing escape with you, son? I don't recall seeing her before." It was Zach's way of reminding Logan that he had yet to perform introductions.

"Grandfather, this is Corporal Shenda Ridell. Shenda, my grandfather, Zachariah Swan."

"Mr. Swan," Shenda murmured with a smile. She found the older Swan's personality a bit gruff but endearing.

Zach Swan extended his hand. "A pleasure, miss. And please call me Zach. I've always disliked being called anything else, although I've learned to tolerate *Father* and *Grandfather* when I have to." Abruptly he grasped both Shenda and Logan by the elbow and began to lead them forward. "Now, I know you're in a hurry . . ." He broke off with a frown. "That being the case, what the devil are you doing wasting time coming to visit me?"

"I need the tracker, Zach," Swan explained.

"Oh, that." To Shenda's surprise, Zach actually looked slightly discomfited. He cleared his throat. "Well, it might take a few minutes to arrange that."

"Why's that?" Logan asked, pretending ignorance.

"Well, um, we have another shipment going out soon, and we wanted to be able to track it, too.

Only we wanted to use a different frequency so we could differentiate between the shipments, you know? We couldn't get another tracker like the one Barrington got from Earth, so I had young Henry take apart the one we had to try to make a duplicate of it. He hasn't been completely successful yet."

"I see." Logan shot Shenda a speaking glance. It signaled both his impatience and the respect for his grandfather that restrained that impatience. "We need that tracker before we go on, if at all possible, Zach. How long do you think it will take Henry to reassemble it?"

"He might be able to have it ready this evening. Definitely by tomorrow morning. Can you spare that long?"

Shenda wanted to shake her head vehemently when Swan once again swung his gaze in her direction. She was beginning to feel a distinct sense of urgency. But she'd definitely have trouble explaining that feeling, so she merely met Logan's gaze and left the decision up to him. It was his life at stake, not hers. Well, hers was too—she qualified the thought—but in a different way.

"How important is the tracker to what you have to do?" his grandfather asked, sensing his hesitation. "Perhaps you should go on without it."

"I won't know until I start the search," Logan explained. "That's the problem. If he has all the artifacts stored in the same place . . . then it could be very important. But if they're spread out, then it could be virtually useless. It's the wings I need. Without them, I might not be around to prove anything anyway. Unfortunately, the tracker was keyed to one of the other artifacts in the shipment: a vase." He shrugged. "Finding that could prove Marnier's guilt, though, provided we can link it to him. So I guess the tracker is pretty important either way."

"All right." Zach nodded decisively. "I'll send young Henry back to get to work on it immediately. He won't like it—that young fellow always likes to be in the thick of things—but it can't be helped."

"What exactly are you in the thick of?" Logan asked.

Zach Swan's eyes began to gleam with excitement. "Oh, yes. I haven't told you yet, have I? It's our most exciting and mystifying find yet."

"What?"

"A . . ." Abruptly he shook his head. "No, I'm not going to tell you. It will spoil the impact. I'll show you."

They followed Zachariah Swan through a maze of wide, brightly lit corridors. The light appeared to emanate from recessed ledges in the walls above their heads. Shenda eyed them quizzically. "Did you install the lighting?" she asked Logan.

He shook his head. "No. In fact, we're still studying how it works. They apparently found a means of using crystals to generate light that exactly recreates sunlight. We know from our studies that they also had found a means to control the type of light the crystals emanate. Here." He gestured to the lights above their heads. "We're receiving full-spectrum lighting, just as we might receive it from the sun."

"But," he went on, "there are some rooms in the building across the way where particular colors of light are dominant. One room will have green light, another blue. We think it was a hospital of some type. If so, they used light in their healing just as some of Earth's physicians have started doing."

"Interesting." Shenda looked once more at the lighting overhead.

"Everything about these people is interesting," Zach concurred. "Technologically speaking, you know. I don't know that they were all that much more advanced than we are now, but they certainly moved in different directions. Earth's scientists will be busy for a hundred years just trying to decipher what they've done with crystals." He stopped before a pair of double doors. After he touched one of them in a manner similar to that used by Logan on the main door, they swung open. Shenda frowned, eyeing the portals. Were they holographic images designed to look and act like real doors? Or were these *real* doors simply endowed with the same type of locking mechanism as the main doors?

Logan must have divined her question. "They're the real thing," he said as he followed his grandfather into the room.

The room before them was large, its floor tiled in a mosaic fashion unlike the other floors they'd seen. A number of skylights overhead endowed the images created by the tiles with a unique shimmering effect, subtly changing them. It was a beautiful room, a peaceful room. The atmosphere was something intrinsic to the chamber. But this room did not appear to be Zachariah Swan's destination.

He led them across the floor to a wall. A solid wall? Shenda looked at Logan. He appeared as puzzled as she. "What . . . ?" But he got no further.

Zach held up a hand to forestall him. "Watch," he said.

They watched. Zach extended a hand to touch the wall. As soon as he touched it, the outline of a door became visible. He looked back at Logan, his eyes gleaming. "A secret door," he said with barely suppressed excitement. Then, turning back to the door, he began moving his hands over its surface. "As with all the other doors we've found, this door has four sensitive points generating individual notes, and two curling lines that generate a series of notes. Since they're not visible, the trick with this one was to locate them. Once we'd done that, it didn't take long to decipher the combination. The computer supplied us with the variables and we simply tried them until we found the one that worked." A second later, the door shimmered and disappeared.

"How did you find it?" Logan asked.

Zach snorted. "I bumped into it. Literally. And as you saw, as soon as you touch this section of the wall, a faint outline appears to show you the door. Liselle noticed it, and we experimented from there." Liselle was his grandfather's assistant. She'd been with him almost 30 years now. Logan sometimes wondered if their relationship hadn't developed into something more after his grandmother's death. But if it had, his grandfather had kept the alliance clandestine.

Shenda stepped forward. The room beyond the secret door was something she had never seen, and yet, inexplicably, it felt familiar. It was much smaller than the outer room and circular. Its domed ceiling consisted of one gigantic skylight. But, the most unusual thing about the room was what stood in its center: a colossal crystal as clear as a diamond. It was oblong-shaped and easily the size of a man.

Slowly, Shenda stepped into the room and circled the crystal. Around it almost insignificant depressions, perhaps an inch deep and six feet long, radiated outward from the huge stone. At the apex, nearest the crystal, the depression was perhaps a foot wide. However, it quickly widened to almost three feet. Shenda frowned. It was familiar. So familiar. What was it? The answer came from nowhere: *A communion chamber*. How had she known that?"

"What did you say?" Logan asked.

Had she spoken aloud? "Nothing. I was talking to myself."

He looked at her quizzically, but let it pass and turned to his grandfather. "Well, this is quite a discovery." He moved forward to examine the stone.

"Oh, this isn't *the* discovery." He grinned. "Come on. The others are in here." Once again, he led them toward a door. This one opened at a touch. Beyond was a small closetlike room already crowded with the four people it contained. In its center was a small casket covered with a clear glass-like lid. "Look." Zach led them forward.

Shenda didn't know what she expected to see, but it certainly wasn't what she saw. "A sword?" she asked incredulously. The small sword just didn't seem to suit the advanced society she'd thus far envisioned.

Zach looked at her. "Not just any sword. A *cursed* short-sword. The Sword of Ish'kara."

Logan suddenly pinned him with his gaze. "How would you know that?"

"Because it comes with a warning, delivered in *English*."

"That's impossible!"

"Read it yourself." Zach indicated the top of the casket.

Logan moved forward and looked down. A copper plate had been affixed to the upper edge of the casket. A band of alternating vertical streaks of color stretched across the top. Beneath it was what appeared to be an inscription. Bending forward he read the words that had been inscribed . . . in English. *This sword imprisons the soul of Ish'Kara. It is evil. Touch it and you imperil your race, for Ish'Kara will be freed. Be warned. Defeating her is not easy. Only when this specially constructed blade once again tastes her blood and contacts her soul may you be saved. And even that is not certain for she gains strength with each incarnation.* The warning was signed *C. Barrington.*

Ten

"What the hell is this?" Logan demanded, straightening up and staring at his grandfather. "Somebody's idea of a joke?"

"No joke." Zach shook his head. "I almost wish it were. Nobody quite wants to take the risk of touching the blasted thing. And any ideas about what to do with it are about as scarce as hair on a toad."

"But Chance was never in this room," Logan protested. "He couldn't even have known about the existence of this sword, let alone have engraved a warning about it on this casket."

"It says *C. Barrington*," Zach pointed out. "Not *Chance*. The message could have been made by one of Chance Barrington's ancestors."

Logan stared at his grandfather. "How would someone from Earth have reached Fortuna five hundred years ago? Five hundred years ago, they hadn't even reached their own moon."

Zach Swan scowled at his grandson. "True. But it's the only explanation we've come up with so far. You got a better one?"

Logan, echoing his grandfather's scowl, stared down at the small casket, trying to penetrate the secret of its existence with the power of his gaze. "No," he responded finally. He glanced at Shenda where she stood between gray-haired, steel-eyed Liselle and Henry, the young electronics whiz his grandfather had taken on as an assistant this year. "Do you have a thought on this?"

She swallowed. "I do actually, but given your own situation you might not want to hear it."

Logan continued to stare at her for a moment. Finally he said, "Let's have it."

"Well," Shenda said, "it is possible that the energy field that made your friend, Chance, disappear was not simply a matter-transference system. Perhaps it's also capable of time displacement. Just because *we* haven't figured out how to go back in time yet doesn't mean that they didn't know." She gestured to the room in which they stood as though the *they* to whom she referred might be hovering invisibly nearby.

The room was suddenly so quiet one could have heard the passage of a ghost. Finally Zach cleared his throat. "She may have something there."

Logan looked at him. "Yes. Which means that if I don't find that figurine and find a way to reverse the effect, I could end up more than five hundred years in the past with . . . obliteration"—he made a sweeping movement intended to encompass the entire empty city—"as my future."

Zach cleared his throat. "Well, then, I guess we'd better get that tracker reassembled so you can find the figurine. Hadn't we?" He waved a hand dismissingly at the casket. "This sword was safe here for centuries. It'll be fine for a few more hours or days until we figure out what to do with it."

In was late evening as they stood in the communications center sipping hot cocoa and watching Henry. He'd been working nonstop for hours in his attempt to reassemble the tracker. Initially, he'd promised to have it ready by late afternoon, but he'd apparently discovered something more wrong with it, and the timetable had been moved to the morning. Now he made an effort to satisfy Logan's impatience with a satisfactory explanation.

"See here," Henry said. "This is what's bothering me. This chip shouldn't be here. It's a transmitter. What's a transmitter doing in a receiving device?"

"A transmitter," Logan repeated, astounded. Abruptly he frowned. "Can you tell how long it's been there? Has it been in the tracker from the start?"

"I can't tell for certain, but I'd say *no*. It just seems a little crowded, a bit out of place. That's partially what made me notice it in the first place. That and the fact that I've never seen one quite like it. It must be a new design."

"You *can* make the tracker work without it, though?"

Henry nodded. "Yes. But like I said, it's going to take some time. Whoever added this thing knew what they were doing. They made enough alterations to guarantee that almost any attempt to remove the transmitter would mean extensive reconditioning."

"Is it transmitting now?" Shenda asked.

Henry shook his head. "No. I disabled it when I

dismantled it. But it was transmitting up until then."

"Interesting. I wonder who wanted the tracker tracked," she mused.

Logan looked at her. "I think we know the answer to that. The question is, how was he able to get hold of the tracker to have a transmitter installed. Only my people and Zach knew that the tracker was on the *Eagle*, and where the *Eagle* was. And only Tucker knew for certain where on the ship the tracker was concealed. Zach said it took him over an hour to find it. So somebody must have told Marnier where it could be found. Which would mean that I have one of Marnier's people working for me." He didn't like the thought that occurred to him. If Marnier knew about the tracker, it would be virtually useless. Marnier would have disabled the transmitter at the other end.

"You think it was Tucker?" Shenda asked quietly.

Logan refocused his thoughts. "I don't want to think so, but I can't afford to overlook the possibility. And he was an electronics engineer when he was with the Legion, so he could have installed the transmitter himself." He then voiced his concern about the usefulness of the tracker.

Shenda frowned thoughtfully. "You're right in that Darren would have found the transmitter at the other end. But I doubt if he'd destroy it. He'd find a way to disable it until he needed it."

Logan stared at her. "You mean he could use it to set a trap for me?"

Shenda nodded. "Exactly."

His gaze turned inward, Logan stared at the wall across the room. If what Shenda surmised was true, the tracker still could prove useful in avoiding recapture. It would warn him of entrapment.

Phillip Nagami sat in the dingy frontier-city bar known as *The Barbarian's Lair*—of all the stupid names. He'd asked the bartender, Roscoe Taggart, how the place had come by such a distinctive label. Apparently Taggart—who chanced to also be the owner—had been called a barbarian by some *high and mighty Earther* on one of his business trips. Rather than regarding it as the insult it was meant to be, Taggart had rather liked the brawn implied by the appellation, and had adopted it as his own. Nagami tended to think it was a blatant misnomer. Taggart was a lean sinewy fellow, no more than five feet eight in height.

Suddenly the door opened and a splash of sunlight cut through the gloom of the establishment, spotlighting dancing dust motes. Nagami narrowed his eyes against the brilliance, the better to study the silhouette of the person that entered. So he'd come after all. That was good. Nagami raised a hand slightly to attract the man's attention.

Nodding, he moved toward Nagami. Sliding into the booth across from him, he sat with his hands folded on the table in front of him.

"I had begun to think you might disappoint me by not coming," Nagami remarked quietly.

"I had trouble getting away."

Nagami nodded sagaciously, and wiped the sweat from his glass of Fortunan ale with his fingertips. He watched the man closely as the waiter came to inquire as to his preference. That was the one thing Nagami actually liked about the colonial settlements: Service once again had become personal. No servo droids or androids here. They were too expensive to build and maintain without a ready supply of parts. No matter how many advances were made, scientists had yet to equal the human being for versatility, adaptability and inexpensive maintenance. No, the best tools were human. On that Marnier and he agreed.

Nagami smiled inwardly as he noted the sweat on the brow of the man across from him. It was quite cool in here. Yet the man's perspiration, his demeanor, broadcasted fear. The question was: fear of what was to come, or fear of reprisal? It was difficult to monitor the activities of one's *tools* in such a distant locale.

The waiter moved off. "So," said Phillip. "What can you tell me about the probable whereabouts of Logan Swan?"

The man shook his head. "Nothing. I'm finished with this, Nagami."

Phillip frowned inwardly. So things weren't going as well as he had supposed. "Have you forgotten about the Cobalt Moon, Andrew?" Nagami asked.

"I haven't forgotten anything," he snarled. "I live with it every hour of every day. Because of me five good men—men I called friends—are dead. I was so spaced out on *Paradise* that I couldn't even feel my body, let alone operate a ship. And because of my weakness, they're gone forever. I wish every day that I'd died in that crash too. That's not the kind of thing you forget, Nagami."

Nagami scowled inwardly at the lack of respect accorded him—he was used to hearing the title *Mr.* before his name—but as usual, no emotion showed on his face. "No, Andrew, I don't suppose it is. However, a certain gentleman we both know went to considerable expense so that you might avoid execution. He concealed the evidence against you. He arranged to have your unit shipped here and abandoned so that you could reasonably seek employment in the services of the Swans. And he generously saw to the education of your motherless son. Such . . . altruism does not come cheaply. Have you heard from Taran recently? Perhaps I should have someone look into his welfare?" Nagami allowed a small insincere smile to touch his lips.

The silence stretched as he watched the man opposite him struggle to control his temper. As Nagami had expected, he failed. The Legion trained its people in so many fighting techniques, yet it completely ignored one of the most basic tenets of the warrior: *Never allow emotion to rule.*

"You bastard!" Andrew growled under his breath. "He's just a kid. He had nothing to do with any of this."

"Agreed, Andrew. But you must understand; we will require your continued cooperation." He paused to level an intense stare into Andrew's eyes. "Where is Logan Swan?" he asked quietly.

Silence.

Phillip waited.

Finally Andrew sighed, and Phillip knew the contest of wills was over. "I don't know where he is," Andrew said. "But I know where he's heading."

"And where is that?" Nagami asked.

"To find the golden-winged statue."

Nagami almost frowned. The response made no sense. Swan was a fugitive from the death penalty and, rather than going into seclusion, he intended to follow the trail of an unexceptional artifact into the lion's den, so to speak. "Why?"

Andrew shrugged. "I'm not certain. He doesn't talk about it openly. At least not with me. But . . . something happened to him and Chance Barrington when they found it. Chance died. Swan believes he will too if he doesn't recover it."

Nagami stared at Andrew in surprise. "You're trying to tell me that once again an archeological site has been visited by a curse? Isn't Swan a bit too educated to believe in such things?"

Andrew met his stare. "His friend died. You tell me."

Nagami waved a hand negating the importance of such trivia. "How does he intend to leave the planet? His ship was all but destroyed."

"He has a scout. He'll use that."

"You did not inform us that he had more than one ship." Phillip had almost barked the statement, but managed just in time to maintain the carefully modulated tone of voice he employed at all times.

Andrew smiled. "You didn't ask?"

Nagami's eyes chilled. "In the future, it would be in your best interests—and those of your son— if you remembered to pass on all pertinent information. Whether we ask or not. Do I make myself understood, Andrew?"

The man across from him nodded sharply. "Yeah."

"Good." He paused to paste on another condescending smile. "Now then, is this a tachyon-style scout? Or the old shark model?"

"Tachyon."

"And its name?"

"The *Eagle*." He said each word as though it was being torn from him.

"Now we're getting somewhere. Do you know where this ship is located?"

"On the other side of the peninsula. He'll have gotten to it by now."

"So you're telling me that he's probably off-world already?" Nagami asked.

Andrew nodded and took a large swallow of his ale, finishing what remained in the mug. "Yes."

"I've been informed that his grandfather, Zachariah Swan, resides at the archeological site rather than on the ranch. Is this true?"

Andrew hesitated. "Yes," he said finally, although his jaw was clenched in a manner that suggested he would have liked to imprison the word behind his teeth.

Phillip pondered the ramifications of the piece of intelligence concerning the elder Swan's whereabouts. It might prove . . . useful. Neither he nor Marnier had initially included the archeological site in any of their planning because it had always been well guarded in the extreme with an elaborate security system and human security. Now, however, it was the Swan ranch that was swarming with defenders. Had those guards been pulled from the site? If so, that left the site much more open, and someone for whom Logan Swan carried more than a passing affection would be within their grasp. It was something to consider should Logan Swan continue to be elusive.

"Are we finished?" Andrew abruptly asked in a tone bordering on belligerence.

"I don't know, Andrew. Are we?" Nagami looked deep into the man's eyes, seeking the things that lay beneath the surface. "I take it that, if Swan is once again searching for his artifacts, he'll be using the tracker?"

"Yes."

"And did you perform the alterations on the device that you were requested to?" The reprogramming of the tracker had been implemented contingent upon the eventuality that it might be needed in the future. Darren Marnier believed in being totally prepared. And once again, despite Nagami's personal doubts about the practicality of the gesture, Marnier had been right.

"Yes." The man fairly barked the word. Nagami could see the instant regret on his face, the thoughts for his son. "Yes," he repeated more quietly.

"Then, I believe we are through, Andrew. For now." Rising, he extended his hand as though to conclude a business arrangement. He noted Andrew's hesitation, but knew that the man would not risk insulting him by refusing the gesture. The instant his hand came into contact with Andrew Tucker's larger one, he began receiving a series of disjointed images. Andrew's son Taran as he had been when he'd last seen him. The tracking device, open, being worked on. Logan Swan lifting Shenda Ridell—another unknown quantity—onto a horse's back. He didn't believe that Andrew had held anything back. Satisfied, he released his hand.

Logan sat on a stool in the pre-fab building that served as his on-site quarters, trying to still the shudders that racked his body. It had happened again. Worse than ever before. Longer. He thought he had actually begun to see things. Faint shadows of things he didn't recognize. Moving forms in a thick mist. Sinister shapes. Was it his imagination? Was the stress of continued dematerialization beginning to affect his mind? Or had he almost reached the preprogrammed destination? The thought terrified him more than he wanted to admit, even to himself.

There were so many things he hadn't done yet. So many things he'd never known. His eyes fell on a family photograph he kept on his desk. It had never meant a whole lot to him other than as a nice ornament. After all, he'd always had the real thing any time he wanted it. But now, suddenly, he stared at it with new eyes, memorizing each line and curve in each beloved face.

His father, David Swan, stern and rigid in appearance, his features weathered by hard work and the intense Fortunan sun. Yet you could not find a gentler man in the universe. His mother, Callista, tall and slender, her pale blond hair giving her an almost ethereal appearance. Yet when necessary, she had more intestinal fortitude and strength than any person Logan knew. His sister, Larissa. She, like himself, had inherited their father's dark hair, but she had their mother's brilliant blue eyes. She was married now and very involved in her career as a geographer and cartographer, spending much of her time mapping the world they now called home. Logan hadn't made the effort to see her nearly as often as he should have. His eyes skimmed over his own face to that of his grandfather. It was one of the few pictures for which they'd been able to get the imperious old man to sit still. Logan's eyes roamed the craggy face lovingly.

Dammit! He wanted his own family. He wanted a chance to pose for a picture like that. To hold his son or his daughter near. To love them and feel their love for him. To experience the wonder of seeing the universe through the unjaundiced eyes of his children. What greater blessing could there be? Was he to be denied it all?

In the picture, his father's arm rested lovingly around his mother's waist. Love. The kind of love his parents shared had eluded him. He realized suddenly how much he wanted the *love* of a woman. Not just caring, not the temporary gratification of sexual pleasure. But real love, that rarest of jewels. Clenching his fists in an effort to control another violent tremor, he wondered if he would find love in his lifetime.

Lifetime? Who did he think he was kidding? He didn't have a lifetime. He'd seen the way Zach had looked at him. Discerned the compassion and the fear in the depths of his eyes. Stars, he'd seen the same look in Shenda's eyes. And she didn't even like him. If the damn energy field that had its grip on him didn't succeed in taking him, he had a galaxy full of Legionnaires on the lookout for him. Hell's universe, if he'd been playing a game of Galactic Exchange, *he* would have bet against him.

No. He refused to consider it. Somehow, in some way, he would think of a way to beat the odds. Looking skyward, he sent a fervent silent prayer to all the Saints that he be allowed to fall in love, to marry and to father a child or two before he died or . . . disappeared.

Lying on the portable hammock-cot they'd erected for her in Liselle's quarters, Shenda found sleep impossible. She could almost *feel* Darren Marnier breathing down her neck. She couldn't afford to lose Swan. Not yet. Not until she knew what Marnier had on her. Yet with the death order out for Swan, it was only a matter of time until he was captured or killed by a vigilant, glory-seeking Legionnaire unit. Although she belonged to a fighting unit for only a few months every two years, she knew the high that a Legionnaire experienced when apprehending a criminal. She knew how hard it was to see a situation objectively when the only information you received was that fed to you by your superiors, the news networks— which seldom seemed to know more than the troops—or the occasional underground news release. And the rewards for doing your job unquestioningly were high. Popularity and adulation from the public—until the next hero or group of heroes came along, commendations from your superiors on your record and pay bonuses complete with a leave-of-absence to enjoy them. There was no incentive for a Legion unit to ask questions. They were sworn to *uphold the law in the pursuit of peace and justice for all humankind,* but they were seldom given enough information to make those judgments themselves. It was a facet of the Legion with which Shenda had always disagreed.

Yet she was certainly no angel. She, too, had almost succumbed to that seductive elixir of fame and fortune. Thank the stars, she'd awakened in time. A few others she knew had as well. Brie Tanner for one. But it was a rare occurrence, and she certainly couldn't count on the selflessness of her fellow Legionnaires. They would do their duty as they saw it—just as they must all do, herself included. What else could they do? The way things stood now, Swan would be either captured or killed.

The *capture* of a fugitive offered more prestige, of course. The Legionnaires could march the dangerous felon through the corridors of Space Station Olympus or Apollo to the Hall of Justice and hear the murmurs of admiration along the way. They could achieve their own brief moment in the chronicles of the galactic press association. But executing Swan would also garner a certain amount of distinction, and with the death order out few would hesitate to shoot if they suspected the felon might escape.

And that Shenda could not accept. If Swan was

killed before they found the proof she needed to guarantee a life free of Marnier, she could very easily find herself spending the rest of her days trapped in the prison of a loveless marriage. She knew she couldn't survive that. Just as her own mother had taken her life, so would she. Or . . . she narrowed her eyes. She'd end up taking Marnier's life. Could she live with that? she wondered. Despite her Legion training, killing was something Shenda could not do easily. Oh, she'd killed before . . . once . . . and might do so again. But it had been in the line of duty, impersonally and in self-defense; and even then she had suffered nightmares for weeks. She was not so certain she could kill someone for personal reasons.

So . . . She raked a hand through her wild, unbound hair. As things stood now, she'd arrived at three options. One, she and Swan found the artifact he required and the proof she needed against Marnier. Not very likely. Two, she found herself married to Marnier and ended up killing herself. Unacceptable. Or three, she married Marnier and ended up killing *him*. Again unacceptable. She pounded the cot with her fist. She needed to make herself less desirable as a marriage partner while at the same time making it less likely that they would shoot Logan on sight. An impossible feat!

Damn! She wished she'd married some innocuous young man before Marnier had inexplicably begun to consider her acceptable spousal material.

Marriage? She frowned, grasping the half-formed thought and pulling it into focus. Marriage!

Although he hid his feelings well in the interest of accumulating votes, Marnier hated colonials. His lofty opinions were mirrored by many more in the political arena, her father included. If she married a colonial, it would certainly make her less desirable as a marriage partner. And even if she ended up a widow, she would still carry the stigma of having been a colonial's wife.

Her conscience gave her a painful nip. All right, for some odd reason that she refused to examine, she didn't want to contemplate Logan's death. If they orchestrated everything properly, perhaps marriage to her could also prompt authorities to revoke the death order. She frowned, trying to consider all the angles.

Much as she sometimes liked to forget the fact, she was the daughter of a powerful and influential man—which gave her a certain amount of power in her own right. People were interested in her; they kept themselves informed about her life. The minute she did anything a little strange, or something happened to her that was attention getting, the press milked the story for every last bit of sensationalism they could. Look at the furor that had arisen when she'd joined the Legion. It had taken three months for the story to fade out of the news.

If Logan married her, he would be the husband of a woman whom the public and the press loved to criticize, adore, or sympathize with, depending on the nature of the story. He would also be the son-in-law of the Commissioner of Intergalactic Affairs. And her father always did what was best for himself politically, even if it stuck in his craw personally. So . . .

What she and Logan would have to do was make certain that news of the wedding—and her own *willingness* to wed—was broadcast to Earth. Turn it into a story of star-crossed love or some such nonsense. The Earth woman and the colonial felon. She frowned. She would also have to make it known that she believed, unequivocally, that Swan was innocent. That went against the grain of her Legion training. Although she had certainly begun to lean in that direction, she wasn't one hundred percent certain that he *was* completely innocent. Since she had never been involved in the original trial, she still only had Swan's side of the story. However, for the plan to work, she would have to sacrifice her sense of duty.

All right. She proceeded to the next phase of the idea, working it through in her mind. Assuming that they married and broadcast the story to Earth, and the press picked up the account and ran with it, the public would once again be watching every move that Shenda made. With millions of people observing her and her fugitive husband—people who loved nothing more than a tale of true love—Marnier would have to revoke the death order or risk considerable political repercussion. The people would demand that Swan be retried. Shenda pursed her lips and raked her fingers through her hair. Had she considered everything?

The order for Swan's arrest would not be rescinded, but an arrest order gave them considerably more leeway than a death order. And, hopefully, time. Of course, assuming that everything Swan said was true, there was the consideration that Marnier might, anonymously, hire an assassin. But that would still be only one or, possibly, two people—depending on how badly Marnier wanted Swan dead. It certainly gave them better odds than having the entire Legion looking for him with intent to kill.

She ran the whole thing through her mind

again. Excitement began to build in her, until she wanted to laugh in triumph. She settled for a smile. It could work! It really could. Now there was only one thing left to do. Convince Swan to marry her. The smile faded and some of the excitement began to diminish. How was she going to convince him to marry her without giving away her own position? Could she trust him with the knowledge that, in actuality, she hated Marnier? She hadn't been exactly successful in concealing her dislike for Marnier, but her alleged motivation for agreeing to marry him—social status—rather negated the importance of her feelings for him in any case. She was pretty certain that Logan believed her. Which, in itself, probably contributed considerably to his distrust of her. Could she now trust him with the whole truth?

She shook her head. She wasn't ready to do that. Not yet. Not unless she absolutely had to. Despite his pretense otherwise, she sensed that he didn't totally trust her. If he felt that she was using subterfuge to maneuver him, he might go ahead with his original plan to ransom her to Marnier for the figurine. He was desperate, and she couldn't trust a desperate man to consider her interests.

Rising, she began to pace Liselle's small quarters. Quarks! She refused to abandon such a workable plan because she couldn't arrive at an explanation that Swan would accept. There had to be something. She raked her hands back through her hair, shoving the unruly mass away from her face. The glimmer of an idea began to form in her mind. That was it. Before she could change her mind, Shenda headed for Swan's quarters.

*   *   *

"Come," Logan responded to the knock on his door. Surprised to see Shenda enter, he rose to face her. "Is something wrong?" he asked, hoping against hope that there wasn't. He just wasn't in the mood to deal with anything else right now.

"No, nothing." She stopped a couple of feet inside the door and stood squarely on two feet, legs slightly apart, as though bracing herself against a storm. Then, meeting his gaze, she said, "Swan, I think we should get married."

He couldn't have heard correctly. "Pardon me?"

"I said, I think we should get married." Her jaw had a decidedly stubborn set.

He stared at her, unable to come up with an intelligent response . . . a response of any kind for that matter. If this was the Saints' idea of answering a prayer, then he was going to have to begin wording his prayers more carefully.

"I'm serious, Swan," Shenda said at his continued silence.

He'd made love to the woman once and been informed in no uncertain terms that he was not to repeat the action. Although he was definitely attracted to her, he wasn't certain he liked her, and from the signals he'd been getting, the feeling was reciprocated. So what the hell was going on here? He cleared his throat and found his voice. "Are you sure you're feeling all right?"

"Of course," she snapped. "I'm fine. Just a little stiff. I don't want to ride horses again for quite some time. Now, can we talk about getting married?"

He blinked. Saints! They couldn't even carry on a conversation, and she wanted to get married. As if he didn't have enough on his mind. "Look, Shenda, I don't know about where you come from, but on Fortuna one bout of lovemaking is not considered a courtship. If you've reconsidered your edict, I would be willing to make love to you again." He paused, studying her and trying to determine where her incredible proposal had come from. "But the idea that we have to get married to do so is a bit antiquated."

"Reconsidered . . ." She halted as outrage silenced her, and stared at him open-mouthed. She'd forgotten about the sexual aspects of marriage. But of course, since he was a man, it was the first thing that had popped into Logan's head. "You egotistical idiot!" she snapped when she finally found her voice. "I haven't reconsidered anything." She would have to make it perfectly clear that she expected the marriage to be annulled when it had served its purpose.

"Then, what the hell are we talking about?"

Shenda sighed. "A marriage of convenience. Marriage to me, if we orchestrate things properly, could help you considerably."

How, by all the Saints, could marriage to Shenda Ridell help him find the figurine? "And did this *marriage* idea just come to you in a flash of inspiration?" he asked.

Shenda frowned. "Stop being sarcastic and listen. Marriage to me should prompt them to revoke the death order. That will buy us time to find your figurine." *And the proof I need,* she added silently.

He stared at her, running her little speech through his mind a couple of times. For the life of him, he couldn't see how it could possibly work, but the idea that it might was certainly something he couldn't overlook. "I can see this is going to take a moment. Have a seat." He gestured at a stool near the cot on which he'd been sitting. "Would you like some tea?"

Seating herself, Shenda looked up at him. "Yes. Thank you."

After pouring the tea from a thermal container on the small bedside table, he handed her a cup and said, "All right. Now explain."

And she did. Caught up in enthusiasm for her idea, she began pacing Swan's quarters as she spoke. Less than 15 minutes later she pinned him with her zealous gaze and said, "It *will* work, Swan. I'm certain of it." She drank the dregs of the cooled tea and set the cup on the stand.

He studied her. He couldn't argue. She knew more about the world she had come from than he. And it sounded like it actually *might* work. But there was still something exceedingly strange about her offer. "I think you may have forgotten something."

"What's that?"

"You, Ms. Ridell, are already engaged."

Shenda shrugged as though the matter was of little consequence. "Darren will be upset for a while," she said. "But he'll get over it after I explain it to him."

If she really believed that, then she was crazier than a Morar-stung horse. "He'll get over your marrying another man?" Logan asked incredulously.

"Well, it's not like it will be forever. We'll have the marriage annulled as soon as it's served its purpose."

"Oh, I see." Logan stood, stuck his hands in his pockets and nodded knowledgeably. She obviously knew absolutely nothing about the Fortunan marriage ceremony. But he wasn't about to enlighten her. Not yet. Because this marriage thing might actually work to save his life. "And just why are you willing to do such a thing for me?"

It was the question Shenda had been expecting. "Because I believe you're innocent. I think you deserve the opportunity to sue for a re-trial based on whatever evidence we uncover." Had he accepted her explanation? His features were inscrutable.

"I see. And you're willing to make this sacrifice—marriage to me—for the sake of duty? For an ideal?"

Shenda frowned. Was there a trace of sarcasm in his tone? "Well, I wouldn't exactly call it a sacrifice. Like I said, we can have the marriage annulled. It's more of a strategic maneuver."

"A strategic maneuver," he repeated with a smile. Saints! How gullible did she think he was? There was more at work here than Ms. Ridell wanted to let on. And he intended to find out what it was. Just as you couldn't play Galactic Exchange on a single level, you couldn't make an informed decision based on partial information. Turning, he studied Shenda. And, as always, her unconscious elegance assaulted his senses. Her thick, wavy midnight hair billowed around her face and shoulders like a cloud. Her brilliant green eyes met his gaze and held it, holding him with their seductive appeal. Her generous coral-tinted lips glistened provocatively in the light of the lamp. Damn, she was beautiful. But he had to get past that. He had to know what was in her deceitful little mind.

"I don't believe you, Shenda." He stalked slowly toward her, his golden eyed gaze never leaving her face.

"W-why?" Despite herself, Shenda found herself unnerved. Physically, she was much smaller than Logan Swan, and in the light of the lamp he suddenly appeared . . . dangerous.

He stopped not more than two feet from her. Looking down into her upturned face, he said, "Because I think you have an ulterior motive. Did you really think I'd fall for that noble, self-sacrificing attitude?" He shook his head, answering his own question as he held her gaze with his. "I know you're a Legionnaire, Shenda. And, I know you have a strong sense of duty. But this . . . well, this goes far beyond the requirements of duty. So what's your real motivation? What does marriage to me gain for you?" He stretched his lips into the semblance of a smile.

The predatory display of teeth increased Shenda's nervousness. "I don't know what you're talking about."

"Oh, I think you do." How was he going to get her to tell the truth? He couldn't intimidate her, not with her training. Or could he? There was one thing that Ms. Ridell seemed to fear. He stepped closer. A scant 12 inches separated them. "Are you after my body, Shenda?" he asked in a low, suggestive voice.

"D-don't be ridiculous!" she snapped, but her tone was slightly more breathless than it should have been. He was certain he'd guessed correctly: She feared intimacy. And he would use that knowledge to his advantage.

Shenda saw the gleam in his eyes and, recognizing it, took a hasty step backward. Stars! What had she been thinking of coming to his quarters unarmed? He stepped forward. She retreated. "Tell me, Shenda," he prompted in an intimate tone as he stepped forward again. "What is it you're after?"

Oh, Stars, he didn't believe her and she didn't know what to tell him. Her mind went blank, absorbing stupid details that she'd not noticed earlier. The clean male smell of him faintly tinged with the odor of a man's deodorant soap. The way his overlong chestnut hair brushed the collar of his shirt. The way his facial whiskers had grown during the day to stubble his cheeks and chin with a dark, sexy shadow. Sexy? What was she thinking? His whiskey gold eyes locked onto hers and he matched her step for step, advancing as she retreated.

"Answer me, Shenda."

Her breath caught in her throat. She didn't know what to say. And then, he swooped. Too stunned to react, she stood paralyzed for a fraction of a second too long. And then, it was too late to act. This kiss wasn't anything like the other. It was hard and punishing, pressing her lips back against her teeth as he pulled her into his arms, crushing her against the unyielding solidness of his chest. Yet its result was just as devastating. Instinctively, Shenda opened her mouth to relieve the pressure. His tongue invaded. A multitude of half-remembered sensations besieged her: Her breasts swelled and tingled almost painfully; her blood roared through her veins and pounded in her ears as her pulse raced out of control; molten heat coiled in her abdomen robbing her limbs of strength. She was imprisoned in a spinning vortex with nothing solid to hold on to. Nothing but Logan Swan. Of their own accord, her arms pushed their way up between their bodies to wrap around the thick column of his neck.

She was being devoured by the flames of desire. His? Hers? She was beyond knowing. His hand came up to cup her breast, hot, erotic, a gentle counterpoint to the savage need in his kiss. She felt herself swell into his hand, felt her nipple tighten even more, aching.

The force of his desire caught Logan off guard. Shenda was not supposed to have reacted to his advance quite so enthusiastically. He'd miscalculated. With an almost superhuman effort, he banked the flames. Reluctantly lifting his head, he looked into her passion-dazed eyes and focused on what he needed to know. Cupping her softly rounded bottom in his hands, he pressed her against the hard, heated length of him. "Is this why you want to marry me, Shenda?"

He saw the instant that awareness struck. The passion in her eyes was replaced by blazing anger and she began to struggle in his grasp. Regret and purpose warred within him. But he would not be deterred. Not now. His future was at stake and he had no room for compassion. He countered her struggles with ease, refusing to release her. "No?" He arched a brow in feigned surprise. "I'm devastated."

She stopped struggling and stood immobile and furious within his embrace. "Let me go, Swan. Now!"

"Not yet, my sweet. Not until you tell me the truth."

"There's nothing to tell."

"Really," he murmured, his low voice caressing her nerve endings. His gaze fastened on her lips and, once again, he began to lower his head. He threaded the fingers of one hand into her hair to hold her.

"No! Stop!" She couldn't bear the thought of more of his brand of torture. Because she knew that soon she wouldn't want it to stop. And it would. *He* would stop, leaving her unfulfilled and full of rage at her own vulnerability. He stopped with his lips so close to hers, she could feel the heat of them. "I'll tell you," she said, hoping that she was doing the right thing.

"The truth, Shenda," he murmured against her lips. "I'll know if you're lying."

She closed her eyes and swallowed, defeated. "The truth," she whispered, looking into his hot whiskey-dark eyes.

Eleven

He released her and moved back to lean against the wall, crossing his arms over his chest. His observant eyes never left her. Once again Shenda began to pace his quarters, more slowly this time. Was there any way to tell Swan about Marnier that would still guarantee her own value to him? She nipped at the inner flesh of her bottom lip. If there was, she couldn't think of it. She would simply have to tell him and hope for the best.

Halting in the center of the room, she braced herself, met his gaze and plunged. "I don't want to marry Marnier. I never have. And I am *not* engaged to him."

Whatever Logan had expected her to say, it was not that. Clearing his throat, he eyed her narrowly, suspecting a lie, but uncertain. "Explain," he demanded.

Shenda sighed. "Darren proposed to me the last time I was home, a few weeks before I was assigned to Sentra. The idea was so ludicrous that I didn't take him seriously. I laughed and walked away. It was a mistake." She looked at Logan, knowing it would take a miracle to make him understand. Stars, she didn't even understand it all herself.

"Why don't you want to marry him? I'd think that from your point of view he'd be quite a catch. He's rich, powerful and reasonably young and attractive."

Shenda stared at him incredulously. "How can you ask that? You know what kind of person he is."

Logan nodded sharply. "I do, yes. But how do you know?"

Shenda considered him. "There are only two classes of people who are acquainted with Marnier. Those who know nothing about the kind of person he is and take him at face value, and those who know a lot about the kind of person he is but have neither the power nor the courage to try to do anything about it. Unfortunately, the majority fit into the first category. Only a few unfortunate people ever come to suspect what he is capable of. And only a few know him as well as I know him."

"You still haven't told me *how* you know what kind of person he is," Logan pointed out.

Shenda studied Logan, and knew that only the whole truth had any chance of making him understand. "I'll tell you," she said. "But if you ever tell anyone else, I'll deny it. There is no proof."

"Agreed."

Shenda paced more quickly. "Marnier seduced me when I was sixteen. He was twenty-six at the time. After three months, he ended our affair. I was devastated; I believed I was in love with him. So I plotted to get him back. For some reason, I thought that I might change his mind if I showed him how poised and sophisticated I could be." A wry, self-deprecating smile twisted her lips as she told Logan how she had sneaked into Marnier's office and what had transpired there.

"The idea that Marnier could, without compunction, snuff out the life of another human being horrified me. That he had enough power to get away with killing a very influential person, terrified me.

"I've tried to avoid having any contact with Marnier ever since. It's sometimes difficult because he and my father are colleagues, possibly even friends, if people in that arena can be considered to have friends. I can remember my father telling me when I was just a little girl that I must always keep my mouth shut and my ears open. The adage has served me well. I've learned a lot. I know Marnier is one of the most ruthless men in the galaxy. I . . ." She paused and swallowed. "There aren't many people I fear, Swan," she said, meeting Logan's gaze candidly. "But I'm afraid of him."

"So why did Marnier issue the press release? It doesn't make sense."

Shenda shrugged. "He must have discovered some means of coercing me into marrying him. And until I discover what it is and how to circumvent it, I don't dare face Marnier publicly." She looked at Swan. There was no way she would reveal the real threat Marnier represented to her. It was a secret too long held. "If I'd realized he was serious when he proposed, I might have expected such a move. But I wasn't aware—until you told me about the entertainment news vid—that he had simply gone ahead and announced our engagement as though I'd said yes."

Logan watched her. "Why does he want you so badly?"

Shenda frowned. "That's the one question I can't answer," she said. "I don't know."

"All right," Swan allowed. "So tell me what marrying *me* gets *you*."

"Reprieve, I hope," Shenda responded frankly. "You're a colonial. Marnier hates colonials, and so do many others in the political circle. I'm hoping that marriage to you—even after it's annulled—will carry a stigma that will mark me as an unsuitable marriage partner."

"Well that's flattering," Logan remarked sarcastically.

"You asked for the truth."

"And why aren't you as afraid of Marnier's vengeance for marrying me as you are afraid of his retaliation for simply defying him?"

"Because provided you live long enough for us to find it, I plan to collect the evidence to prove that he is involved in illegal activities, and hold it as security."

"You're going to blackmail him?" Logan asked in amazement.

Shenda nodded. "It's the one language Marnier understands."

"And what if I need to expose that evidence to prove my innocence?"

"Provided it's enough to keep Marnier away from me for the rest of my life, you'll have no arguments." She sat on the edge of the stool she'd vacated earlier and watched him expectantly.

Swan nodded, stuck his hands in his pockets and stared thoughtfully at the floor. He believed her. Amazingly, that put them on the same side. And her plan could well work. There was just one little hitch: the Fortunan marriage ceremony.

Once done, it could not be undone. And no Fortunan priest would perform a fallacious ceremony. Saints! Shenda Ridell was not exactly what he had in mind when he thought of the woman with whom he wanted to spend the rest of his life. He tried to bring that fantasy woman into focus. All he received for his trouble was a vision of a cloud of midnight hair surrounding a piquant face and brilliant emerald eyes. An image of creamy white skin half hidden behind the fabric of a blue jumpsuit. An illusory recollection of elegance and grace. All of which he could enjoy without marriage. *But you may not have your life*—the coldly logical words echoed and reechoed in his mind. What good was his sense of honor, and waiting for the right woman and all that other philosophical pretension going to do him if he was dead? Logan searched for a way to solve the dilemma and found none.

Neither could he tell Shenda the nature of the Fortunan ceremony. She would withdraw her offer and his life would once again be forfeit. He looked at her and tried to see her as his wife, the woman with whom he would spend the rest of his life—however long that might be. The woman who—Saints willing—would bear their children. Surprisingly, it wasn't as difficult as he'd thought it might be. She was not nearly as much like Lilah as he had initially supposed. He could envision her in the role of his wife quite easily. Provided, of course, that she didn't kill him herself when she discovered she was stuck with him forever. He almost grinned. She was going to be positively livid. And when one considered the fact that he would be taking something that Darren Marnier wanted very badly, Logan realized that Shenda's proposal made him a winner all the way around.

And in that instant he realized he'd made his decision. To gain a chance of saving his life, he would marry society's rebel, Shenda Ridell. He could have done worse. Much worse, he conceded, letting his eyes roam her exotic brows, high cheekbones and lush lips with possessive yearning. He wondered how long it would take, after their marriage, for him to seduce her again. Once they were married, there was no way in hell that he was going to continue holding her at arm's length when he wanted her more than . . . well, more than he'd wanted a woman in a very long time. He was a patient man—his occupation had taught him that—but even his patience had limits.

"All right, Shenda," he said, keeping his tone carefully neutral. "I accept your proposal. You will have a husband. But we have very little time, so we had best begin working out the details."

"And you'll take me with you to find the evidence?" She needed to ascertain that her position hadn't changed.

"Of course."

"Good." She smiled slightly and allowed her shoulders to sag a bit with relief. "How difficult is it to arrange a wedding on Fortuna? We won't have to wait for all kinds of clearances, will we?"

Logan shook his head. "The marriage ceremony here is relatively easy and free of bureaucratic involvement."

Shenda sighed. "That's a relief. Do you want to tell your grandfather what we have planned?"

Logan shook his head. "I don't think so. I think it's best if everybody believes this marriage is the real thing. That way, no one can inadvertently divulge information they shouldn't."

"You're right." Shenda nodded. "So what are you going to tell him?"

231

Logan rubbed his brow. He hadn't thought of that. Zach was a dinosaur; his value system belonged in the same age as the ruins he studied. Quaint, honorable, but not always practical. "We'll tell him the same story that we're going to transmit. We fell in love while I was in prison and, despite all the odds against us, we knew we had to be together."

"Will he buy it? It's going to seem awfully sudden."

He would also tell Zach that with things going the way they were, he wanted the opportunity to marry . . . in case that chance never came again. It was the truth. "Yes," he said, looking at Shenda. "I think he'll believe it."

An hour later, Zachariah Swan climbed into a skimmer. He looked through the open hatch at his grandson. "I'll be back before dawn with a priest and your parents," he promised.

"Bring Larissa and Raf, too, if you can find them."

"No promises there." Zach shook his head. "But I'll do what I can."

"Thanks, Grandfather." Logan grasped the gruff old man by the shoulder. "I appreciate it."

"I know," the old man growled. He looked over Logan's shoulder at Shenda and smiled. "I'm gaining another granddaughter. Always did like girls better than boys." With a wink, he closed the hatch on the skimmer. A minute later, he was out of sight. Logan stared after him, and wondered where fate would lead him next. Just six months ago, he would never have believed the turn his life was about to take.

It was still dark when the sound of a skimmer arriving woke Shenda. She looked over at Liselle asleep on her cot, and envied her the ability to sleep soundly. Shenda never had. She had no idea what time it was, but knew that it must be near dawn. And since she would never be able to go back to sleep in any case, she decided she might as well get up. Throwing back the blankets, she hastily slid into the blue jumpsuit she'd worn since leaving the *Raven*. The first thing she was going to do when she and Swan reached a space station was buy a change of clothes, she promised herself.

Slipping out the door of Liselle's quarters, Shenda paused a moment in the dark to get her bearings. There were lights and voices coming from the building Logan had called the mess hall, so she moved in that direction. A moment later, she pulled open the door and entered to find the small building crowded with people. Henry was there, taking a break from his work on the tracker. Zach was talking earnestly into his ear. Callista and David Swan were there, both talking almost simultaneously to their son. A man wearing flowing white robes stood off to one side, watching the gathering with a rather bemused smile on his face. He would be the Kanisian priest, Shenda supposed. And beside him stood a beautiful young woman, with chestnut brown hair and brilliant blue eyes. Her skin was tanned to a deep, dark golden brown. At her side stood one of the most ruggedly handsome men Shenda had ever seen, aside from Logan Swan. He was tall and broad-shouldered, about the same size as Swan, but there the similarity ended. This man had a thick mane of golden-blond hair and deep blue eyes.

As the door closed audibly behind Shenda, all conversation in the room ceased and every pair of eyes in the place turned to her. Logan broke the silence first. "Shenda, come in." He moved forward to grasp her arm and smile down at her. "I thought you were still asleep or I would have come for you." Tucking her hand in the crook of his arm, he led her toward his parents. "You've met my mother, Callista Swan."

"Yes," Shenda murmured with a smile for the attractive older woman. Callista Swan looked much as Shenda imagined her own mother might have looked if she'd been a stronger, braver person. She was tall for a woman, with an innate slender grace that would guarantee that others viewed her as *attractive*, no matter what her age. Shenda extended her hand. "I'm pleased to meet you again, Ms. Swan."

Callista smiled gently. "Please, Shenda, call me Callista. After all, shortly you will be my daughter." She took Shenda's hand and enfolded it in both of hers. "I wish we'd had the opportunity to get to know each other better before you married my son." She looked at Logan, encompassing him in her gentle smile. "But if my son has chosen you, then I know that I will grow to love you as much as he."

Guilt for the deceit they were practicing gnawed at Shenda, and she squirmed inwardly. "Thank you," she managed to murmur.

She was infinitely glad when Logan grasped her arm to move her on. "And my father, David," Logan said by way of renewing her introduction to his father.

Again Shenda nodded and extended her hand. "Mr. Swan."

He studied her with a deep penetrating gaze, nodded and said, "Shenda," in a voice almost as deep as Logan's.

"This is Sire Vashti," Logan said, presenting her

to the white-robed gentleman.

"Sire." Shenda dipped her head in acknowledgment and presented her hand. "I'm pleased to meet you."

"Likewise, my child," he said. "I look forward to discussing the principles of our Kanisian beliefs with you."

Shenda hesitated. She'd forgotten that all Fortunans became Kanisian. "I . . . um, yes. I'll look forward to it."

"Excuse us, Sire," Logan said.

"Of course, son."

As they moved off, Logan looked down into Shenda's face and winked. "And this is my sister, Larissa," Logan said, stopping in front of the attractive chestnut-haired woman. "And her husband"—he indicated the blond man at his sister's side—"Raf Colter, a Guardian. These two spend all their time exploring Fortuna." He glanced at Shenda. "They're geographers," he explained.

"I'm pleased to meet you." Shenda smiled, extending her hand to each in turn. "I thought most geographical work was done by scanners and computers."

"Much of it is," Larissa responded. "But I am also a cartographer, and there are many things that electronic eyes simply cannot perceive, let alone map. Until they improve on them, the human cartographer will still be a necessary component of the mapping process on every new world."

"Thank the Saints!" murmured Raf, drawing Shenda's attention.

Larissa smiled. "We're very passionate about the need for human productivity," she explained. "And our work gives us the opportunity to constantly travel and see new things while at the same time earning enough credits to live on."

"It sounds wonderful," Shenda said.

"Oh, yes. Aside from the aching muscles, biting insects, slithering reptiles, dangerous carnivores and the dearth of bathing facilities, it's heaven."

"On second thought, you can keep it," Shenda said to her.

"I thought you might say that." Larissa smiled. "It only *sounds* romantic. The reality is quite something else."

"And you love every minute of it," Logan said.

"True," she answered. "But it's not for everybody. Most people like to stay around home a little more. If Raf and I hadn't stopped in to visit Mother and Father for an update on your situation, we would have missed your wedding."

At that moment, Callista appeared at their elbow. "If you want to be away shortly after dawn, Logan, it's time we got organized." She looked at Shenda. "I brought you a wedding dress, dear. I'm afraid it's just something out of my own closet. On such short notice I was unable to manage more. But I think it should fit reasonably well."

"I appreciate your thoughtfulness." Shenda smiled. "It will be more suitable than this jumpsuit."

"Come then, dear. Let's get you ready."

The dress was a beautiful emerald satin that brought out the creaminess of Shenda's complexion and the color of her eyes. Its heart-shaped neckline and off-the-shoulder cut revealed slightly more of Shenda than she was used to exposing, but she couldn't deny that the effect was stunning. The hem of the gown reached almost to her ankles—she was a good three inches shorter than Callista Swan. Matching emerald satin slippers completed the ensemble. After only a slight hesitation, Shenda was even able to ignore the luminous embroidery that encircled the waist. Lunar Moss it might be, but it obviously was quite harmless in this state. And it *was* beautiful.

"You look absolutely stunning, Shenda," Callista said as she came into the room that Liselle had graciously agreed to vacate for Shenda's temporary use. "I can certainly see how you were able to turn my son's head so quickly."

Once again guilt nipped at Shenda. "Yes . . . well, thank you. Logan is a very handsome man himself."

Callista smiled. "I know," she said. "And that is not just a mother's pride talking. Are you ready?"

"Yes."

They returned to the mess hall, which seemed to serve as a type of community center for those who lived on-site. "I think if you use the holo-camera from this angle," Logan was saying to his father as they entered, "then Shenda and I can sit behind that table to make our statement." He looked exceedingly handsome in a black suit and white shirt.

"All right." David Swan nodded his agreement.

Shenda frowned. Surely there was a more suitable place available from which they could make the holo? It needed to look affluent, a setting suitable for the fairy-tale romance they were attempting to portray. "Excuse me," she said absently to Callista. Moving up to Logan, she tugged unobtrusively on his sleeve to get his attention. "May I speak with you a moment?" she asked when he looked down at her.

He stared at her for a moment, stunned by the radiant beauty of the woman he was marrying. "Yes, of course. What is it?"

"Privately," she said quietly, and turned to lead

the way to an unoccupied corner. When he joined her, she told him of her concerns. "I think we should be married in the alien temple," she said. "We should make the holo record from there."

"Temple?" Logan echoed, frowning.

"Did I say temple? I meant the building you call the castle. We should use the room with the mosaic tiling and the skylit ceiling. What do you think?"

Logan didn't think that the setting was all that important, but he was willing to humor her—provided it didn't take too long. He shrugged. "It's all right with me."

Three quarters of an hour later, the small group reached the magnificent mosaic room of the alien edifice. "We'll make the holo recording of our statements first," Logan remarked to Shenda as they entered.

"Why?" She had assumed they would be married before making their statements for transmission to Earth.

Logan hesitated. "The ceremony can be rather taxing. I think it's wise to leave it for last."

Shenda heard his hesitation, and assumed that he didn't trust her to make the statement *after* they were married. She would have what she wanted, but nothing that he needed from the association would yet have been taken care of. She could understand his lack of trust, yet it bothered her. Not willing to delve deeper into that emotion, she nodded. "All right."

A moment later, Shenda and Logan stood in front of a mosaic-patterned wall and faced David Swan, who directed the holo-camera toward them. "Ready?" David asked.

Shenda cleared her throat. "Ready," she affirmed with a nod. Logan merely nodded.

"You're on," David said, with a slight flourish that hinted at the sense of humor he would have in other circumstances.

Shenda curled her lips into a soft and gentle smile. "Hello. I'm Corporal Shenda Ridell of the Stellar Legion. Most of you know me as the daughter of Harris Ridell, the Commissioner of Interstellar Affairs. I am making this recording so that you, the people, will know the story behind the circumstance in which I now find myself.

"My last assignment was as a prison guard on the planet Sentra. While I was stationed there, I fell in love with a prisoner. A prisoner whom I *know* has been falsely accused of murder and sentenced to death. His name is Logan Swan; he is a colonial archeologist from the planet Fortuna. When Logan managed to arrange an escape, he took me hostage. But he did so that we might be together while he fought to initiate a retrial.

"Logan Swan is now my husband." She threaded her hand through Logan's arm in a calculatedly possessive gesture. "I love him. Yet our time together may be ruthlessly cut short by the newest Legion bulletin. This bulletin orders all Stellar Legionnaires to shoot my husband *on sight*. It is important that you, the people, know the extent to which your government . . . our government . . . will go to prevent a single man from appealing for his life, for justice. Know, and pray that it does not happen to you, or your son or daughter or grandchild. Know and exercise the power you have to change those who govern us.

"That's all I have to say. Thank you for listening." She turned slightly to face Logan, and observed as David zoomed in on his son's face.

"Hello," Logan said. "I am Logan Swan. I am an archeologist on Fortuna, where my family has lived for three generations. Sometime ago, many of the artifacts my family shipped to Earth began to be stolen. Investigations into what was happening led nowhere. Finally, I took matters into my own hands and began to delve more deeply. Someone took exception to that and framed me for the murder of two museum guards killed when the last shipment was stolen. I've been accused of stealing the shipment myself so that I might resell it. I am innocent.

"I do not expect you to believe that outright. Nor do I expect you to exonerate me. All I ask is the opportunity for a re-trial. The opportunity to present the new evidence my wife and I have uncovered. If I should be . . . if I should die before that end is achieved, I ask that someone out there take it upon themselves to aid my wife in presenting the proof she has. Help her to restore honor to the Swan name. Thank you for listening."

David Swan lowered the camera. His eyes were suspiciously shiny, and he blinked rapidly. "Well, son," he said. "If that doesn't pull some strings and ruffle some bureaucratic feathers, nothing will. You were both terrific."

"Yes," Logan agreed. He looked down at Shenda with a strange light in his eye.

"Is something wrong?" she asked.

He shook his head. Nothing that he could do anything about. But the fact that the lies had rolled so easily and so passionately off of Shenda's tongue bothered him somewhat. He'd suddenly realized that they were seeking to manipulate the people of the galaxy to their own ends much as the politicians they so loved to despise had been doing for centuries. Considering Shenda's background, her facility for manipulation shouldn't have surprised him, he supposed; but despite the inherent truth in it, their little holo message had left him feeling slightly unclean. Still, they'd had no option, so there was nothing to be gained by brooding about it. Shrugging off the unpleasantness, he smiled. "Time to get married."

Shenda and Logan stood before Sire Vashti. The priest still wore his flowing white robe, but he'd added a deep blue stole that reached from his shoulders to the hem of his robe. He looked at each of them with kindly brown eyes and began his address. "We have gathered here on this day to witness the alliance of this man and this woman in marriage. Blessed be our God on High for bringing them together. May the Saints watch over them." His voice droned on, reminding them of their duty to each other; warning them of the small trials they would encounter in life that would test the strength of their love; imparting his prayers that their union would be blessed with children.

Shenda allowed her attention to wander. She saw Raf smile tenderly down at Larissa. She saw David Swan place his arm around his wife's waist and hug her close while still managing to maintain a sure grip on the holo-camera that recorded their marriage. She saw Zach meet Liselle's gaze with a smile and a wink. And she realized that this vast room was filled with love. The perception surprised her. Genuine affection was something she'd rarely witnessed. Such gestures were usually reserved for privacy. And in her case, her father had not been a demonstrative man. She could recall being cradled by her mother, the warmth and security she'd felt. And the scent. She would never forget her mother's perfume. But she could not recall her mother's face from memory.

Suddenly Shenda was filled with a longing so intense that tears stung her eyes, a longing to experience the kind of love that surrounded her. And just as abruptly she ruthlessly shoved the yearning aside. Such love was not for her. She had faced that knowledge long ago.

"Shenda, are you aware of the blood-sharing portion of the Kanisian wedding ceremony?" the priest asked, drawing her out of her reverie.

Shenda looked at Logan. He met her eyes and quickly allowed his gaze to slide away. "No, I'm not," Shenda murmured, confused.

The priest gave Logan a disapproving look. "I apologize, Sire," Logan murmured. "We decided on marriage rather suddenly and..." He shrugged. "It slipped my mind."

Sire Vashti met Shenda's inquiring gaze. "It is nothing to concern yourself about, child." He extricated a small blue crystalline globe from the folds of his robe. "In fact, it is rather like the compatibility blood tests sometimes done on Earth. I am going to ask both you and Logan to place your hand on the sphere at the same time. A needle will extract a small amount of blood from each of you, combine it with the serum in the globe and then re-inject a fraction of the compound into your palm. It is a standard part of the ceremony and quite harmless. If you're incompatible or either of you carry a disease which could harm the other or your offspring, the globe will change color. All right?"

Once again Shenda glanced at Logan, but he was observing the priest. She didn't like the sound of the procedure, but what could she do? She needed this marriage. And the priest said it was harmless. She nodded. "All right."

The priest smiled encouragingly. "Please extend

your right hand, Shenda." He looked at Swan. "Logan, your left." They complied, and the priest placed the sphere in Logan's outstretched palm. Then, taking Shenda's hand, he placed her palm over the globe where it lay in Swan's hand. After curling their fingers securely around the crystalline sphere, he pressed a small lever that remained exposed between their hands. Instantly, Shenda felt a small puncture in her palm—painful enough to cause her to instinctively jerk her arm, but Vashti's hands were there to control the movement.

As he continued to hold their hands in position on the sphere, he began to speak. "As this serum combines thy blood so will thy minds be joined. And for all time two souls will become one." Between their fingers, Shenda noted that the blue color of the globe remained unaltered. The priest depressed another button on the sphere, and Shenda felt the small needle withdraw from her palm. "In the Light of our God and in the presence of the Saints I pronounce thee man and wife." He withdrew the sphere and returned it to the folds of his robes. Then, joining their hands together without the globe between them, he blessed their union and announced it to the assembled witnesses, introducing them as Logan and Shenda Swan.

As they turned to accept the congratulations of Logan's family, Shenda noticed that her palm and forearm tingled strangely. But Shenda found herself enveloped in the perfumed embrace of Callista Swan and there was no time to examine them. "Welcome, my daughter," Callista said. Tears shimmered in her eyes.

Before Shenda could do more than smile tremulously, she was swept into David Swan's arms.

"Welcome to the family, my child," he murmured huskily in her ear.

"Thank you," Shenda managed to murmur. There was a pause in the congratulations as Logan spoke with his father, and Shenda surreptitiously glanced at her stinging palm. Only a small red dot remained as testimony to the blood-letting portion of the Kanisi ceremony. A practice that she personally considered a bit primitive. But she had been left little choice in the matter.

"How do you feel?" Logan asked.

Shenda looked up at him. "Fine. Why?"

"The serum can make you feel a little lightheaded and nauseous. If you begin to feel ill, let me know."

She nodded. "What exactly *is* the serum?"

"Congratulations, brother." Larissa's voice interrupted them. She pressed a glass containing a bronze-colored liquid into their hands.

"I'll tell you later," Logan murmured to Shenda as he turned to accept his sister's felicitations.

Shenda eyed the slightly syrupy liquid in her glass warily.

Noting the expression on Shenda's face, Larissa smiled. "It's Fortunan brandy," she said. "Trust me, it's delicious. One of the few Fortunan brewed spirits worthy of a marriage celebration." As Larissa turned back to Logan, Shenda took a cautious sip. It *was* delicious. Feeling as though she could use the bolstering influence of the liquor, Shenda tilted the glass back. Larissa caught her hand. "Slow down, Shenda. Our brandy is very potent."

As Shenda complied, Larissa switched her gaze to her brother. "Father and Sire Vashti are making the transmission to Earth now," she informed him.

A sudden buzzing in Shenda's ears prevented

her from hearing Logan's response. Their voices merged into an unintelligible murmur. Shenda began to feel strange. The conversations in the room seemed to get louder, yet the tones became jumbled, difficult to understand, as though they were coming to her ears through a lake of water. Shenda shook her head slightly, trying to clear the heavy, cottony sensation from her ears. It didn't work. Either the brandy was *very* potent, or this was the sensation that Logan had warned her about.

"Shenda." Larissa's voice came to her from a great distance. "It's wonderful to finally have a sister. I hope we'll have the opportunity to get to know each other soon."

Shenda forced a smile to her lips; it felt wooden. "Thank you," she said. And the room began to spin. "Logan, I think I'd like to sit down now." Her voice was a faint murmur in her own ears. Blackness hovered on the edges of her consciousness.

"Shenda?" She felt Logan's arm around her waist. Felt him swing her up into his arms. Felt his solid chest beneath her ear. "Shenda?" His tone sounded anxious. She tried to respond, but the words remained locked in her throat. And then, the curtain of blackness fell.

Twelve

Darren Marnier reclined in his chair, a data-log
on his lap. He was so absorbed in the information
revealed there that he was barely aware of his
step-sister, Delilah, lounging on the sofa watching
a vid transmission. His linguistics people had informed him that they'd made a breakthrough in
interpreting the information recorded within the
crystal, but what he had received had exceeded all
expectations. They'd translated and interpreted
close to three quarters of the material. And it was
some of the most fascinating reading Darren had
ever encountered.

The crystal was, in effect, the personal log of a
woman calling herself Ish'Kara. Ish'Kara had
been a scientist of sorts, but she had also ex-
panded her knowledge into the realm of the arcane to an extent which far surpassed attempts
made by her colleagues. In her time, this woman
had held within her grasp the key to ruling forever.

According to Ish'Kara, the Tesuvian race—presumably her species—had been obsessed for generations with finding the secret of eternal life. Their scientists had, in fact, achieved greatly extended life-spans, but their constant bickering and warring with each other over minor issues had prevented them from progressing further. Having been fortunate enough to be born on one of their colony worlds, a place where Tesuvians numbered in the mere thousands rather than the billions, Ish'Kara thought she would be able to complete her work without clashing with her colleagues. But it was not to be. Another woman, a high priestess known as Aliya, had sought to steal her work. Nevertheless Ish'Kara had forged ahead in secrecy. Having formed an alliance with other-dimensional beings who *did* enjoy eternal life, she eventually solved the enigma. Immortality was within her grasp. But too soon, her secret was discovered.

Once again, jealousy reared its head, and her rival's faction sought to destroy her and her findings before the process could be tested. They succeeded. But not without annihilating themselves in the process, for the resulting cataclysm destroyed their island home and ruptured the planet's crust, causing a chain of massive volcanic eruptions. Deadly toxins and millions of tons of ash were released into the atmosphere, ravaging vast numbers of life-forms and plunging the world into a millennia of darkness. This planet was the third from a yellow sun; its coordinates proclaimed it to be Earth.

Ish'Kara's story of the destruction of Atlantis coincided with the other accounts he'd read, with one small but very major difference. It eliminated any mention of the survivors. Survivors from

Christine Michels

whom he himself was descended. Perhaps Ish'Kara had not known of the hundreds of small boats which had escaped the doomed island continent—boats which had carried many of the children of Atlantis across the ocean with little but hope to sustain them. For some reason that Darren had never understood, apparently very few adults had attempted to save themselves. Perhaps, like the captain of a ship, their duty demanded that they stay with the world they'd created.

Although the catastrophic devastation had been the end of most Atlanteans, according to the crystal it was not the end of either Ish'Kara or her rival, for although their bodies perished, their spirits did not. They were destined to meet again and again over the millennia that followed, each time in a new incarnation. *And now, it is the eve of a new battle,* Darren read. *The final battle? This conflict must end so that I can resume my work. However,* Ish'Kara concluded, *if you are reading this, then I did not win and I have not had an incarnation wherein I could retrieve the data held in this crystal. I can only conclude that my rival found a means to kill or entrap me spiritually as well as physically. Find me in whatever hell I am in, I beseech you. Release me and I will be eternally grateful.*

The word *eternally* caught Darren's eye. The idea of having a woman who was on the verge of plumbing the secret of immortality eternally grateful to him was intoxicating. He scrolled through some more information on the data-log: unintelligible gibberish that his people had marked as *possibly scientific formula,* ritual proceedings which he would go over and, if possible, incorporate into the rituals they had already initiated based on past writings, a blank spot where

248

his people had input the words *holo message here*.

Would the holo be another map? he wondered. Or might he be lucky enough to have a video record left by the incredible woman calling herself Ish'Kara? He would have to view it. He refused to take the chance of missing anything she might have recorded. She fascinated him as had no other woman.

"Darren." Delilah's petulant voice intruded on his ruminations. "Are you going to work all evening?"

He glanced over at her, but for the first time that he could remember he was not aroused by her. Of course, half of the allure in making love with Delilah had always been the element of the forbidden. She was his half-sister. Off limits. Untouchable. They had sought solace and the exotic elixir of the forbidden in each other since they'd been little more than children. And in answer to a promise he had made her, Darren kept her with him always. It had been an easy promise to keep. Physically, she knew him better than any other woman could hope to. They served each other's needs.

For years, he had called her his stepsister in concession to the ethically bound voters whose endorsement he had always had to seek. That way, should he and Delilah inadvertently touch in public in a manner that might be considered unseemly for brother and sister, the gesture would at least draw less censure. But the idea that he had been forced to do even that much for his political career angered him. He was so much better than all of them, above them and their inconsequential moralistic perceptions. But soon, he would do what he wanted, when he wanted, with no one to stop him. The information he had gleaned from

Ish'Kara's crystal and other artifacts, along with the data he continued to accumulate, would see to that.

"Darren."

His gaze focused briefly on Delilah's face. Beautiful. Blond. Slender and leggy. Completely uninhibited sexually. Possessing a remorseless ambition exceeded only by his own. She would have made the perfect mate . . . if only she had possessed the distinctive gene that would have marked her as a true descendent of the superior race—the *Tesuvians* that had settled the continent of Atlantis. But it was his mother who had carried that gene, not hers, and unfortunately, not their father.

Tesuvian. The word echoed in his mind. He marveled that he now possessed a name for himself and those like him. Not Earthling or Earther. But Tesuvian. Even the name sounded superior.

"Darren." Delilah drawled his name loudly. Pouting, she lifted her bountiful breasts in the palms of her hands so that the erect nipples pressed against the diaphanous black fabric of her lounging gown.

He frowned slightly at the interruption. "Start without me, Dee," he said. "I'm not in the mood. Perhaps I'll join you later." He barely heard Delilah's angry sigh as his attention shifted back to the data-log on his lap. What had Ish'Kara looked like? he wondered. Of course, she would have looked different in each incarnation, wouldn't she? Such thinking was new to him. It would require adjustment.

"Darren!" He failed to notice the slightly different tone of Delilah's voice.

"What is it, Dee?" he demanded, not bothering to keep a slight edge from his tone.

"I think you'd better see this."

He looked at her. She was sitting up, elbows on knees, leaning toward the vid-screen as though engrossed in a fascinating item. He glanced at the vid, expecting to see nothing of significance, and . . . froze.

Shenda was on the screen. At first he stared at the transmission uncomprehendingly, and then the message behind Shenda's words penetrated. The bitch had married! Not just anybody. She'd gone and married the colonial felon.

Marnier felt the blood begin to pound in his temples as Logan Swan appeared on the screen. Fury pulsated through his veins until he literally saw red. And then he took his emotions in hand and began to listen to Swan's statement. The colonial talked of new evidence. What evidence? What had they found? Marnier racked his brain. Nothing. That's what they'd found. Absolutely nothing. It was a ploy. A ruse to force his hand, but it wouldn't work.

Was the marriage genuine? he wondered. Or, was that too an element of the subterfuge they practiced? He pinned his gaze on the screen. He hadn't long to wait. Footage of the actual wedding ceremony replaced Logan Swan's face; an officious-looking Kanisian priest presided. And the formal Fortunan seal appeared in the bottom right-hand corner of the transmission. Marnier noted the number for reference, but he had little doubt that it was genuine. He would find that Shenda's marriage was indeed recorded in the Fortunan registry. His hands clenched on the arms of his chair, but that was the only outward sign of the intense rage he felt.

He studied Shenda in the green wedding dress, and pondered his next course of action. The bitch

251

was bright. Not brilliant, but definitely bright. He would have to have the Legion death order revoked or risk looking like a hard-liner, a man without compassion. And hard-line politicians hadn't done well in recent years. Still, there was more than one way to kill a convict. There was simply no way that he would allow Swan to sue for a re-trial. Swan would be captured and . . . executed.

Marnier briefly contemplated hiring an assassin to deal with Shenda—he couldn't believe the little bitch had had the nerve to embarrass him publicly, throwing his engagement announcement back in his face. But he reluctantly concluded that he could not afford to have her killed. Not only might it look suspicious, but she was the only unattached female he had found who had the three elements he required in a wife: style, elegance and, most importantly, lineage. He needed her to provide him with offspring. To help him in purifying the blood of the Tesuvian heirs. To be his queen.

He studied her with a possessive longing that had nothing to do with love, or desire, or even lust, but everything to do with ambition. She was the means to an end, and he *would* have her, colonial husband or no. It would merely take further planning. If only his people would get back to him about the missing period in Shenda's life. There must be something there he could use to curtail her independent streak.

The news release faded from the screen and Delilah's entertainment broadcast resumed without Darren taking any notice of the fact. As his fury began to ebb, his mind turned to dealing with this new circumstance. He still hadn't arrived at any definite solutions when a melodious bell chimed three times, signaling an incoming communication.

"Who is it?" he demanded of the computer.

"The communication code belongs to Phillip Nagami," the precise female voice responded.

Marnier sighed. "Very well. Viewer on. Scramble communication." He swiveled his chair to face the screen just as Nagami's thin, imposing countenance appeared. "Have you seen the transmission?" he demanded.

Phillip nodded.

"I hope you have some *good* news."

"Unfortunately not, sir," Nagami responded. "Swan had another ship, a Tachyon scout called the *Eagle*. He has escaped the planet."

"I see." Marnier slowly leaned forward in his chair. "Do you have any idea where he is headed?"

"He is apparently desperate to retrieve a certain statuette, a pair of golden wings. He believes that if he does not retrieve the figurine, he will die. Evidently a colleague of his has already perished, and the death was linked to the wings. I haven't been able to learn the exact nature of this professed curse; our contact did not know."

"Really." Marnier's lips quirked slightly at the corners. "Now that does put an interesting twist on matters." Logan Swan was coming to him. He would have to arrange a suitable welcoming party. Still, Swan had a disturbing tendency to elude the traps set for him. It would take some thought. He didn't want Swan bolting again; this time, he must not escape his execution. Picking up the small transmitter that had been removed from a vase found in one of the appropriated archeological shipments, he considered the possibilities. Nagami cleared his throat, drawing Darren's attention. "Anything else?" he asked.

Nagami lowered his head slightly in a gesture that was, for him, a nod. "Most of the military personnel normally kept at the archeological sites have been reassigned, temporarily, to the Swan ranch. This makes the task of reaching either of the parents extremely difficult; as is reaching Swan's sister, Larissa. She is married to a Guardian and has guardianship protection. Since Swan is, in all likelihood, heading toward you regardless, you may no longer be desirous of a means of persuasion. However, if you are, it seems that the elder Swan, Zachariah, does reside on-site. Currently, they are working at Site Two. At present, the site *is* protected only by a laser-grid alarm. I believe it can be disabled sonically."

Darren stared at Nagami although his vision was turned inward, weighing possibilities. In all likelihood Swan had been trying to retrieve the winged figurine when he'd been caught on Nigeur. An innocuous-looking object whose purpose Darren had still not divined, the figurine had been pictured a number of times in records from both the Atlantean archives and the ruins on Fortuna. Hmmm. He looked at Nagami. "Phillip, I believe we will allow Logan Swan to find his golden wings before springing the trap on him." Marnier pursed his lips thoughtfully and fingered the transmitter. Perhaps Swan would reveal the purpose of the wings before he died. "It is unlikely that he will bother with Nigeur. He knows the artifacts will have been moved by now. So we must assume that he knows or suspects that I am in possession of his artifact." No doubt it was this which had prompted Swan's claim of new evidence, but it was a claim that the colonial would never be allowed to substantiate. "In which case, he will search for it at my residences."

Abruptly Darren met Phillip's gaze. "However, with Swan, nothing is certain. I do believe we should take out a little extra insurance in the event that he eludes us again. Have Zachariah Swan put up in the guest quarters at our facility on Dendron II. I will join you there as soon as I am able."

Nagami nodded. "It will be done."

"And Phillip . . ."

Nagami halted in mid-motion as he reached to disconnect the transmission. "Yes."

"Do remember to mask your features. We want to be able to let the old man resume his archeological duties when this is over if at all possible. His efforts have helped us tremendously over the years."

Phillip nodded. "Of course. Is that all?"

Marnier nodded. "I believe so. Yes."

"I'll be in touch." Nagami reached to flick a switch and the transmission ended.

Shenda opened her eyes to stare at an unfamiliar bulkhead. Her head throbbed painfully. Her mouth felt as though it had been stuffed with cotton. And an annoying buzzing in her ears pulsated in time to the pain in her head. Where was she? Slowly, cautiously, she turned on her side until she faced the room. The chamber was exceptionally small—the opposite bulkhead barely two arm's lengths away—and completely barren.

She tried to remember the events leading up to the present, and found her mind frighteningly blank. The act of trying to remember seemed only to intensify the pain in her head. Giving up for the moment, she closed her eyes and willed the agony away. It didn't work.

She heard the door to the stateroom swish open. "Shenda, are you awake?" a man's voice asked gently, solicitously. She knew that voice. Logan. That's who it was, Logan Swan.

Slowly, she opened her eyes to stare almost directly into his as he knelt at the side of her berth. Golden amber eyes. Potent whiskey eyes. The eyes of the Sentran fugitive. Her husband. As the events of the last few days stormed back into her memory with the force of an assault team, setting little electrical charges off inside her brain, she clutched her head and moaned in misery. She swore that, if she survived, she would never again take so much as a sip of Fortunan brandy.

"I have something that will help," he said softly as he smoothed a strand of hair back from her forehead. He held a small capsule before her. "Can you sit up?" She felt his arm encircle her shoulders to aid her. Clutching the sheet to her with one hand, she dutifully struggled to rise to a seated position, even though she felt as though a two-ton weight lay on her forehead. "Good girl," he murmured. Shenda tried to frown at the phrase which, to her, sounded condescending and sexist, but found she didn't have the energy to do anything but endure. "Here," he said, extending his hand to show her the small pill in his palm. "I even have some hot lemon tea for you to wash it down with."

Shenda popped the small pill in her mouth and took a sip of the steaming liquid Logan held to her mouth. The tea tasted surprisingly good. "Thanks," she murmured, and closed her eyes because the pain seemed to diminish when her brain didn't have to deal with processing her visual perceptions. Then slowly, carefully, she lowered herself to a reclining position again.

"You'll feel better within a few minutes," Logan promised, seating himself on the edge of the bunk.

Not wanting to speak for fear of exacerbating her affliction, Shenda nodded slightly and pulled the sheet up to cover her bare shoulders. Bare? Bare! Her eyes shot open, finding and pinning Swan almost instantly. She winced as the light lanced laser-like through her eyeballs and into her brain. But after only a slight hesitation, she persevered. "Where are my clothes?" she demanded.

"Larissa supplied you with a pair of trousers and a shirt before we left. They're right here." He gestured to the folded clothing on a small chair near the foot of the bunk that Shenda had missed seeing earlier.

"No, I mean where are *my* clothes?"

He appeared confused. "You don't have any," he explained. "You left your uniform on board the *Raven*. Remember?"

"Of course I remember," Shenda snapped with as much force as she could muster under the circumstances. The effort of trying to make herself understood was wreaking havoc on her disposition. "Where . . ." A particularly vicious pain stabbed through her temples and she paused, lowering her voice. "Where are the clothes I was wearing?"

"You mean the wedding dress?" he asked.

Was that what she'd been wearing? Yes, she supposed it must have been. The last thing she remembered was getting married. She nodded.

"I hung it in the reconditioner," he replied.

As her headache began to slowly fade, allowing her to think with a little more clarity, Shenda's concern and chagrin began to escalate. "Who undressed me?" she demanded.

There was a long pause. "Oh," Logan finally said, avoiding her gaze to stare with sudden fascination at the door. She could have sworn she saw his lips twitch slightly with the beginnings of humor, but in the next instant she wasn't certain. "I did," he admitted solemnly. "There wasn't anyone else around to do it. We're on the *Eagle* en route to the Duana Moon, and since you were obviously uncomfortable I thought you'd be more relaxed. . . . " He shrugged and opened his mouth to continue, but never got the chance.

"Shut up, Swan." Shenda tried to gauge, without being obvious, exactly how much clothing she still wore. Except for her panties, she was virtually naked.

"Yes, ma'am."

Shenda shot him a suspicious glance. There was definitely a smile hovering on his lips. Damn him! He was enjoying this. "Well, I hope you looked your fill," she said caustically, "because it's the last look you'll be getting. Now get out of here so I can get dressed."

He grinned openly as he stood and paused to look down at her. "Yes, ma'am."

She rose to a sitting position, carefully maintaining her grip on the sheet. "Stop calling me 'ma'am' in that condescending manner." Her temper was switching into high gear.

He nodded his head in acquiescence. "As you wish . . . my dear," he said with a slight smile and a devilish gleam in his eye. Before Shenda could think of a retort, the stateroom door swished closed behind him.

"Ass!" Shenda directed the derogatory appellation to the closed door. Although she knew he couldn't hear her, it made her feel better. She examined the clothing donated to her by Larissa, and eyed with distaste the bulky gravity boots she would once again be wise to don.

* * *

Logan's smile faded as he walked down the narrow corridor toward the modest-size bridge of his small Tachyon vessel. Resuming his captain's chair, he stared through the viewscreen at the pastel aurora peculiar to hyperspace and once again contemplated how he might tell Shenda Ridell—correction: Shenda Swan—that she was firmly and irrevocably linked to her husband. No particular insights came to mind.

A few minutes later, he was distracted from his reverie as Shenda moved into the seat next to his. "How long until we reach the Duana Moon?" she asked.

"Lais, did you hear that?" he asked.

"Yes," the computer responded. "Unless a more direct network of stable lanes presents itself, we will require a minimum of four days to reach the Hagen Star system."

Swan leaned back in his chair and studied Shenda. She was still a little pale. "Are you hungry?"

She shook her head. "The mere thought of food makes me feel nauseous." Nauseous. The word echoed in her brain. Swan had told her that the serum they used in the ceremony could make her nauseous. Had she been wrong to think that she'd had an adverse reaction to an unfamiliar alcoholic beverage? She frowned thoughtfully. "Swan . . ."

"Yes?"

"What exactly was in that serum they injected us with?"

He hedged. "I'm afraid I don't know its entire composition. Its development is a relatively secret process used by the priests who create it."

She refused to let him off. "So tell me what you do know about it."

"Well, I believe one of the major ingredients is a glucose solution . . ."

"And?" she prompted.

"And"—he met her gaze—"Morar venom."

She stared at him in disbelief. "Morar venom?" she echoed incredulously. "But you told me the venom is poison."

"It is, in large doses. The amount the priests use in the serum is almost negligible."

She continued to pin him with her probing, watchful gaze. "And what purpose does this venom have in a marriage ceremony?"

"In compatible couples, it initiates telepathic communication—rather like when a Morar stings a human and they form a nexus. In fact, the discovery was made when we were researching the effect of the poison on Morar victims. We think that the venom somehow uses the DNA structure of the blood to bind the two minds, but we're not absolutely certain. We do know that the venom acts very quickly on the brain. That's what causes the blinding headaches."

Her mouth opened as if to say something, but she remained silent, searching his face with her intense green gaze as though suspecting him of playing a prank on her. "Pardon me?" she asked finally in a hoarse croak.

"I said that if the couple being married is physically and psychically compatible, the Morar venom initiates telepathic communication between them. It's a process that starts almost at once, but is refined as years pass and they come to know each other well. Initially, the connection is simply a sharing of emotions, feelings, but eventually most couples develop a limited ability to actually communicate."

"I see." Shenda nodded and looked toward the

narrow corridor as though contemplating escape. "And do we know yet if you and I are . . . physically and psychically compatible?"

"Yes."

Once again her gaze pinned him as she sat ramrod straight in her chair, her fingers digging into the armrest. "And . . . ?"

"We are compatible, or the priest would not have concluded the ceremony."

"I was afraid of that," she murmured. "All right. So how long is this effect going to persist after we go our separate directions?"

Swan looked through the viewscreen at the pastel mists that swirled around them. "Forever," he murmured.

"Excuse me?" Shenda demanded stridently. "Did I hear you say *forever*?"

He looked at her. Studied her pale face with its upswept midnight brows and coral lips. She looked so fragile, almost ethereal. An illusion, he knew, but a very attractive illusion. "That's right."

Her mouth opened slightly, revealing a glimpse of pearly white teeth. She shook her head. "Wait a minute! I thought we agreed that this would be a marriage of convenience. We're getting an annulment when this is all over. Remember?"

"A Kanisian marriage cannot be annulled."

"Fine, then we'll get divorced."

"A Kanisian marriage cannot be undone."

Panic lanced through her, catapulting Shenda to her feet as though her chair was on fire. Standing over Logan, she looked down at him, shooting daggers with her eyes. "You double-crossing colonial bastard!" she said through clenched teeth. "If you think I'm going to stay married to *you* for the rest of my life, you've got another think coming. I despise you." She looked at him as though he was nothing more than a particularly loathsome insect.

Logan's eyes chilled as he discerned the bigotry in her tone. "Oh, you may despise me, but that didn't prevent you from planning to use me as a tool against Marnier, did it? So what does that make you?" He raised a scornful brow as he rose to his feet to look down into her angry face. "A colonial I am, but at least I was reared with ethics. I haven't become so used to manipulating the masses that I thoughtlessly tread on the emotions of others to achieve my own ends."

Tossing her head, Shenda turned her back on him as though to walk away.

Fueled by anger, he grabbed her arm and whipped her back around to face him. "Ms. Shenda Ridell." He mimicked the tone of an entertainment news broadcast. "Society's daring rebel." He narrowed his eyes at her. "But when the facade is peeled away, you aren't so very different from the rest of them, are you, Shenda?"

"You don't know what you're talking about."

"Don't I?" His golden amber eyes bored into her soul. "Do you like what you are, Shenda?"

She smirked at him. "And what exactly do you think I am?"

"I think you're a manipulative, egotistical, bigoted little baggage who thinks the universe is her playground."

"I learned from the masters," she said, not bothering to refute his defamatory statement. "You'd be wise to remember that."

"Let me tell you something, sweetheart: This time, you've been out-manipulated. So get used to it. If I'd told you the nature of the Kanisian wedding ceremony, there's no way you would have gone through with it. And as you so generously pointed out, marrying you could provide me with the time I need to save my life. I thought being connected with you was a fair trade-off for my life."

She jerked her arm from his grasp. "Well, you won't think so for long, I promise you. When I'm through with you you're going to wish you *were* dead." She met his implacable gaze. "In fact, there's a phrase that is an integral part of many traditional *Earth* wedding ceremonies that you might be wise to consider. It's part of the promise the bride and groom make to each other." She paused dramatically and bared her teeth at him in a cold mocking smile. "The words are: *until death do us part*." Tossing her head, she walked toward the corridor exit.

"Shenda . . ." She paused and looked over her shoulder. "You're a first-class bitch. You know that?"

She laughed, the sound remote and hard. "*First class* all the way," she said. "That's me. And honey, I hate to break the news to you, but . . ." She paused dramatically and looked him over insultingly from head to toe. "You're definitely economy."

Swan tensed. "Really?" he murmured. His icy, sardonic smile mimicked hers.

Shenda swallowed. Had she gone too far? She'd wanted to anger him, to force him to admit to some way of undoing the Kanisian wedding ceremony. Now Swan's gaze held her immobile as he stalked slowly, purposefully toward her. His muscular body transmitted a message of power and brawn and latent violence that suddenly, forcefully reminded Shenda of the first time she'd seen him in his cell on Sentra . . . a lifetime ago. "Swan . . ."

263

she said quietly, warningly.

There was no response. He was almost upon her. "Swan, don't. . . ." In that instant, he sprang.

Thirteen

His hands closed over her upper arms and he jerked her hard against him, forcing her to tilt her head back to maintain eye contact. Shenda felt the rock-solid expanse of his chest crushing her breasts. Felt the tree-trunk-hard expanse of his muscled thighs bracketing hers. Felt the leashed power in the fingers that held her paralyzed in his grasp . . . and *knew* she had gone too far. He stood staring down into her face with hooded eyes, his gaze roaming her features at a leisurely pace, brushing her brows, cheeks and lips with tactile facility.

"Swan . . ." The word, meant to sound a warning, emerged in a husky, breathy tone.

His eyes returned to hers. She met his potent gaze and read the purpose there. "Shut up, Shenda." The seductive murmur of his voice sent her senses reeling.

"I . . ." But she got no further. With the rapidity

of a predator, he trapped her mouth with his. Ground her lips against her teeth until she had no recourse but to ease the pressure by opening to him. Instantly, his tongue invaded. His hands left her arms and he threaded his fingers into the thick mass of her ebony hair, the better to position her head at just the right angle for his carnal assault.

Shenda's breathing quickened. Her heart hammered. Her legs weakened. Instinctively, she grasped his biceps to steady herself, and immediately wished she hadn't. The sensation of the granite-hard muscle against her palms was somehow dangerously erotic, serving only to accentuate her femininity.

His mouth left hers to trail hot seductive kisses over her cheeks and brows. His hands moved from her head to her back, kneading and exploring until they reached her small, rounded bottom. And then, suddenly, without warning, he lifted her slightly in his hands and pressed her feminine mound firmly against the hard length of his swollen sex. Shenda gasped, sagging in his arms, as every vestige of strength she possessed deserted her.

A floodgate opened; molten heat washed through her. Even as he continued to hold her against him with one hand, the other insinuated itself between their upper bodies. His hand closed over her breast, cupping it, squeezing it gently, sending barbs of pure pleasure darting along Shenda's nerve-endings. His fingertips found the small, erect crest beneath the thin fabric of her shirt and delicately squeezed it. Need, hot and relentless, surged through her. Shenda could no longer contain the pressure that had been building in her throat; half moan, half whimper, the sound escaped her.

"Shenda . . . open your eyes." His voice was a hoarse whisper, coaxing, urgent. Lost in sensation, she didn't comply. And then suddenly, he no longer pressed her body to his. His hands no longer roamed her body. His lips no longer caressed her face. Involuntarily, she cried out at the loss and . . . her eyes opened. She had difficulty focusing on his features. Only the bolstering strength of his hands on her upper arms kept her from sagging bonelessly to the deck. "Good girl," he murmured, moving his hands up to cradle her face between his palms. He planted a gentle kiss on her forehead. Abandoned by intellect, guided solely by instinct and need, Shenda wanted only to burrow herself into his arms. Her eyes began to drift closed. "No! Look at me," he murmured sharply. Her eyes snapped open. "Who am I, Shenda?"

Her brow furrowed in confusion, the blood singing through her veins making her thought processes sluggish. She wasn't certain she could find her voice. "Logan Swan," she murmured finally as he continued to hold her away from him, waiting for her response.

He nodded, but appeared only partially satisfied. "And who am I to you?"

Shenda's mind remained frighteningly blank. She saw the sensuous fullness of his lips, and knew she wanted him to kiss her again. She saw the potent magnetism in his whiskey-colored eyes, and knew that they would be part of her for the rest of her days. She saw the blue-gray tinge of the whiskers beneath the skin of his cheeks, and realized how incredibly erotic his rugged masculinity was.

"Answer me, Shenda," he prompted as the coarse pads of his thumbs roamed the sensitive spot beneath her ears. "Who am I to you?"

Suddenly a deluge of appellations came to mind. Convict. Fugitive. Felon. Husband. Colonial. Collaborator. But she knew what he wanted to hear . . . and somehow it was the only designation that seemed suitable at the moment. "My husband," she murmured.

A smile flashed across the taut planes of his features and was gone. He nodded, holding her gaze captive. "Now . . . tell me what you want, Shenda." He must have read the flash of confusion in her eyes. "Tell me what you want me to do."

Pride woke and reared its head, stiffening her spine and raising her chin. No! She couldn't . . . wouldn't . . . But in the next instant he'd pulled her into his arms again. His lips closed gently over hers, coaxing. His hands roamed her body, caressing her as he rained tempting kisses across her face. His fingers found the turgid peak of her left breast and tugged gently on the eager crest. Sensation, like a bolt of lightning, shot through her, searing her nerve-endings, striking pride a numbing blow. A moan escaped her throat and her eyelids threatened to close.

"Look at me, Shenda," he demanded. As her eyes once again made contact with his, he shook her slightly. "Tell me."

And Shenda conceded to herself that this was one battle she had already lost. "I want. . . . " The sound of her voice startled her. He waited, hard and uncompromising. "I want you to make love to me."

She saw a spark flare deep in his eyes, as though her words in some way freed something within him. Hunger blazed in the fiery golden depths, scorching her, igniting an answering heat. Pulling her close, he devoured her with his lips and tongue and hands. The banked flames of passion she sensed within him fanned the coals of her own long-denied need into an inferno. And as he swung her up into his arms and turned sideways to carry her down the narrow hall toward the small cabins, Shenda could do nothing more than close her eyes and cling to him. Regret might come later, she realized in a brief flash of lucidity, but she had never felt more alive than she did at this moment. It was time to live.

As Swan lowered her to the narrow bunk and stood looking down at her with those incomparably magnetic eyes, Shenda felt a momentary rush of shyness.

A curious half smile hovering on his lips, Logan knelt at the side of the bunk and rested his head on one of his hands. The other he began to trail lazily down the front of Shenda's shirt, leaving a row of gaping buttons in its wake. His gentle fingers brushed the slopes of her breasts, and lingered teasingly before moving on. Why was he moving so slowly when he'd all but ravished her a few moments ago? Gritting her teeth, Shenda controlled her impatience.

When the shirt was completely unfastened, he opened it wide, first one side and then the other, baring her to his gaze as though unwrapping a gift. Still smiling, never taking his eyes from her face, he leaned forward to tease the erect tip of the breast nearest him with his tongue. Shenda struggled to be as composed as he, but as his actions reignited the flames within her, her breathing quickened and her eyes drifted closed. Then, unexpectedly, his hand slid between her legs, firmly cupping her feminine mound through her trousers. A torrent of sensation so powerful that she heard the rush of blood in her ears tore through her. Her fingers clenched on the blanket beneath her, fisting around the fabric as she struggled for control. Of its own accord, her body arched reflexively against his hand.

"Swan . . ." she cried desperately, pleadingly.

"Saints, you're hot," he murmured, and began working her trousers and panties down her legs, trailing hot, erotic kisses in the wake of his hands in a manner that erased all conscious thought from Shenda's mind. Reaching her feet, he divested her of her gravity boots before deftly sliding her trousers the remainder of the way off of her slim legs and kissing each of her slender pink toes. Then, standing, he looked down at her. "Do you know how beautiful you are?" His deep bass voice washed over her with a tactile caress.

Assuming he didn't expect an answer to such a question, and not knowing how to respond in any case, Shenda remained silent. She watched as he unfastened his own shirt, with much more efficiency and economy of motion than he had used on hers, and shrugged it off. Her eyes swept over the bronzed muscles of his biceps to his strong shoulders; clung to the broad expanse of his tanned chest; roamed the soft matting of dark hair that formed gentle swirls across his clearly defined pectoral muscles. He was beautiful. Perhaps not the epitome of male beauty dictated by current standards, but Shenda could no longer deny that, in her opinion, he possessed the most gorgeous male body she had ever seen.

Logan had never had a woman look at him quite so hungrily before. The expressions that flitted across her face as she studied him were enough to swell his ego, and his libido, to the point of bursting. He continued to watch her as he released the fastening on his trousers and skimmed them off of his hips. Her eyes widened as his turgid sex sprang free of the cloth confinement. She hadn't actually seen him before, he realized. The first time they had made love, the dim light of an early dawn had veiled their vision. The admiration and desire reflected in the depths of her beautiful eyes sparked a sudden urgency within him. Quickly he toed off his boots, leaving his clothing in a heap on the deck, and joined her on the narrow bunk.

Gently but firmly, he drew her into his arms. She was his wife for all time—however long that might be—and he was about to make love to her for the first time as her husband. There was something humbling in that realization. Her lips parted eagerly beneath his as he kissed her, plunging his tongue into the warm, moist recesses of her mouth. And then, as she clung to him, he lowered his head to the impudent coral peaks of her small, perfect breasts. He grazed the tip of one passion-flushed breast with his teeth and Shenda arched toward him, her hands clutching at him.

"Logan . . ." His name on her lips was a supplication.

Glorying in her desire, but ignoring her demanding plea, he trailed his hand over the soft skin of her gently rounded stomach to the crisp dark curls at the apex of her thighs. She opened to him eagerly, parting her white thighs to grant him access. He plunged one finger into the tight, hot crevice of her body, and marveled at the slippery succulence of her readiness. As he withdrew the finger to fondle the swollen, sensitive hood of her sex with her own slick juices, she arched her body completely off the bunk. Small, frustrated sounds of lust escaped her lips, and she clutched desperately at his shoulders. This time, he heeded her wordless appeal.

Supporting his weight on his arms, he moved over her, kneeling between her soft thighs. He rained gentle kisses over her flushed face and rosy bosom. The stiff peaks of her swollen breasts enticed him, and he lowered his head to tug the crests, each in turn, gently into his mouth. Shenda's body arched beneath him in invitation, and a groan escaped him as her soft feminine mound brushed the exquisitely tender flesh of his distended shaft.

Raising his head, he looked down at her. She met his gaze with dazed, passion-dark, emerald eyes. Carefully positioning himself at the entrance to her body, he pressed slowly forward. She was as tight as a silken fist. With a tenderness that was exquisite agony, he worked his way deeper and deeper into her hot, moist sheath.

He filled her to overflowing and . . . stopped. The pressure within her was more than she could stand, and she moved against him. Groaning, he heeded her solicitation and withdrew to thrust slowly, deeply into her body again. In that instant, she began to feel it. The joining. The fusing of minds. She sensed his caring, his desire to give her pleasure. She perceived his delight in her, felt the exquisite bliss he experienced in that moment. She knew him, touched him, in a way she had touched no other. The sensation coalesced with her own feelings and emotions until she had difficulty separating them. Startled, she opened her eyes and looked into his intense, amber-gold gaze with a sense of both wonder and fear.

"It's beginning, Shenda," he whispered. "Don't be afraid." She not only heard his reassurance, she *felt* it. She felt the intense pleasure of his next slow, deep thrust from both standpoints. She felt the tension, the building pressure from each viewpoint as the rhythm of their lovemaking increased. The dual perspective was . . . electrifying.

The tempo increased, grew frantic as they strove to reach the summit of shared sensation. Then abruptly, sensing its nearness, Logan slowed. Thrusting himself lingeringly, completely into her body until the walls of her sheath contracted around him and . . . she climaxed. The sensation, unlike anything she had ever felt before, rocked her to the core of her being. In that instant their souls touched. The incredible transcendent feeling of the joining they experienced could be described in no other way. As she rode crest after crest of surging pleasure, she felt the hot rush of his climax filling her as he joined her in bliss.

It was a long time before either of them moved. And when they did, it was simply to curl up together, spoon fashion, and allow exhaustion to claim them.

Phillip Nagami, with the entire squad of Legionnaires that Marnier had left behind to search for Swan, hovered over the ancient alien city in a quantum-style vessel he had managed to purchase. It was old, but functional. The fee he had paid would have purchased a *new* ship had he been anywhere other than on Fortuna. Oh, well, Marnier had assured him that he would be reimbursed for his expenses. The ship was a necessary expense.

"Have you pinpointed the security system targets yet?" he asked a young Legionnaire named Warner.

"Yes, sir. There are five: one central and four in each directional sector."

"And will a sonic explosion take them out?"

"Wingate says *yes*, sir. But with this equipment, it will take a few moments to isolate the effective frequency."

Nagami nodded. "Very well. Proceed." He turned to a console operated by a woman called Kennedy. "Have you found the greatest concentration of life within the city?"

She nodded without taking her eyes from her scanner. "Readings are coming predominately from the heart of the ruins. However, there is also a fairly large concentration in this sector." She pointed to a location on the computer-generated map.

Nagami followed her finger and silently considered their options. Word was that half of Swan's guards were being reassigned to the island today. It appeared that the fight they had expected to unfold at the Swan ranch had never materialized— with the exception of a small personally motivated skirmish between the searching Legionnaires and Swan's ex-Legion employees. What time today they were being reassigned, Nagami didn't know.

The first of Fortuna's two suns was already more than an hour into its daily voyage across the sky, and the second had just pulled itself completely over the horizon. Swan's guards could be arriving at any time. Nagami had little doubt that his Legionnaires could eventually triumph over whatever ex-Legion people or guardians the Swans employed, but battle was not their purpose. Phillip decided that he would proceed on the assumption that Zachariah Swan was within the largest contingent of people and hope for the best.

Even the most carefully laid plans contained an element of chance.

"Sir, we have the frequency." Nagami turned to see Wingate standing behind him.

"Very good," Nagami said. "Fire simultaneously at all five targets until the grid is disabled."

"Yes, sir." Turning, Wingate directed a nod at a man who'd been introduced to Phillip as Corporal Collins. Collins depressed a button, and Nagami felt a slight vibration work its way through the fabric of the ship, gradually increasing in intensity. Then, Collins pulled a lever, and the sonic beams were released. Phillip turned to the screen to monitor the effect of the sonic weapon on the laser-grid security system.

For a moment, it seemed that there was no effect at all. Nagami almost frowned. Was there some aspect to the grid of which he was unaware? And then one of the targets failed and a few of the grid lines disappeared from the screen. The tension within him faded. A moment later, the remainder of the grid collapsed.

He turned to Collins. "Set your course for the largest concentration of life. Kennedy . . ." He glanced at the woman. "Give him the coordinates."

"Yes, sir," Collins and Kennedy said simultaneously.

Satisfied that his will was being carried out, Phillip turned to stare out the viewscreen at the alien city beneath them. He could see why Marnier was so fascinated with it. It had a unique exotic ambiance that was at once strange and yet, indefinably, familiar. His eyes fastened on the crystalline spires that rose from the center of the city-like sentinels. The morning suns bathed them in fire. Beautiful.

The craft banked. "There doesn't seem to be anywhere to put down at the coordinates I have, sir," Collins remarked.

Nagami moved to his side to study the readings. That was the problem with utilizing a craft large enough to carry a squad: To gain size, you sacrificed handling. "Very well, Collins," he said, having confirmed for himself the accuracy of the statement. "Find the nearest available clear space and bring us down."

"Sir." Collins nodded.

A moment later, the craft landed in a small square flanked on four sides by single-story buildings. They had to wait a full five minutes for the dust generated by their landing to settle before they could see the narrow paved roads leading away from the square. Phillip turned to Kennedy. "Hoods will be donned by everyone prior to any contact. Inform the crew that they must carry them."

Her surprise was evident in her fractional hesitation, but her response satisfied him. "Yes, sir." He listened as she broadcast the message to crew members not present on the bridge. Phillip patted his pocket, assuring himself that the hood he had brought along for himself was still there. The hoods were simple, but effective. Uniformly black, they completely covered the wearer's head. Not even the eyes were visible. Yet the fabric was so porous that it in no way hindered breathing or vision. A remarkable achievement that had initially been designed by Earth's Global Intelligence Network.

Nagami left the bridge and headed for the hatch, the crew of Legionnaires on his heels. Leaving the ship, they moved silently through the preternatural stillness, crossing the square and heading down the only road that went in the direction they wanted to go. Nagami noticed that the movements of his escorts seemed unnaturally hushed. Whether it was from respect or fear he didn't know, and couldn't care less, since their silence was desirable in any case.

He looked at Kennedy. "I want to know immediately if anything moves, other than ourselves, within a forty-meter area."

"Yes, sir," she murmured in a near-whisper as she withdrew a motion tracker from her belt and switched it on.

For the next 15 minutes, the only sound was the slight plodding sound of their feet on a cushion of dust that had been centuries in the making. Then they reached a stone wall that seemed to stretch endlessly in either direction. From where they stood, they could see no gate. Neither could the enclosure be easily scaled: Absolutely vertical, it was at least 20 feet high. Nagami paused, studying the barrier with annoyance. Finally he said, "We'll walk along it until we find a gate."

Suiting action to words, he turned right and proceeded to walk along the stone wall. He heard the Legionnaires fall into step behind him. Within five minutes, they came to an entrance recessed within the wall in a manner that made it nearly invisible until you were upon it. Eager to complete his business and be on his way, Phillip stepped through the opening without hesitation. But he would never again in his life step through a door or gate without remembering the agony he experienced in that fleeting moment.

Flaming coals sizzled along his nerve-endings, sending one all-consuming message to every receptor in his brain: pain. Pain, spreading, creeping through his body like molten lava. Pain, burning, reducing his flesh to quivering supersensitivity. Pain, filling the center of his being, becoming his universe. He cried out, or at least he thought he did. And then, he was through and the pain was gone. But the aftermath lingered. Numb, barely conscious, Phillip turned back to look at the gate. He could see nothing to account for the intense misery he'd suffered, but if it was an alien version of an electric fence, it was very effective.

He noticed then that only one of the Legionnaires had been close enough on his heels to follow him through: Kennedy. The others stood beyond the invisible barrier. All of them, including Kennedy, eyed him a little doubtfully. In fact, Kennedy appeared completely unaffected by whatever barrier existed within the alien gate. "Are you all right, sir?" she asked.

Gathering the shreds of his dignity around him, Nagami nodded. "I will be fine." He studied Kennedy. "You didn't feel anything . . . strange when you stepped through the gate?"

She shook her head. "No, sir. Like what, sir?"

"Never mind." He looked at the others. "Well, come on, people, we haven't got an eternity."

Backing up a couple of paces, Nagami waited . . . and watched. He wanted to closely observe the effect of the gate on others as they stepped through. Collins and Warner made it through with as little effect as Kennedy. As did most of the twelve unit members, with the exception of two. Smart, an engineer, leapt and yelped, saying he'd experienced an electrical shock, and Dubrovsky, a tactical expert, complained of his hair standing on end. No one experienced a reaction on par with Nagami's. That bothered him, and he pondered the possible significance as he resumed walking, once again heading in the direction of the crystalline spires that Kennedy had indicated as the area having the greatest concentration of activity.

A few moments later, they emerged into a small square flanked on all sides by large buildings. As Phillip scanned the area, he saw no one. "Where are they, Corporal Kennedy?"

"According to the tracker, sir, they're in there." She gestured to the building with the ten crystal towers.

Nagami studied the steps—there had to have been at least 30 of them—that led to the wide, pillared portico above them. He could barely discern the arched doorways. "All right," he said. "We go in."

He had barely taken one step forward when Kennedy's voice halted him. "Sir," she called. "They're coming this way, sir."

"Quickly," Phillip said. "Put on your hoods. I want six of you at the top, aligned on either side of the door as they come out. Use the pillars as cover. You will use your weapons to prevent their escape back into the building, if necessary."

"Yes, sir," Collins, Warner, Dubrovsky, and three other Legionnaires whose names Phillip had not bothered to learn raced up the stairs, pulling the hoods over their faces as they ran. Since the flat of each step was perhaps two to three paces wide, it was not an exercise that could be accomplished by leaping the stairs two at a time. Each of the Legionnaires stood panting slightly in the marginally heavier Fortunan gravity when they finally reached their goal.

Phillip looked at the Legionnaires flanking him. They too had donned their hoods. Satisfied that all was well, Nagami removed his own hood from his pocket and pulled it down over his distinctive Oriental features. Suitably disguised, he began mounting stairs to meet—he hoped—his quarry. "How far away are they, Corporal?" he asked Kennedy.

"Nineteen meters, sir. They are moving slowly."

Phillip gauged the horizontal distance from Kennedy's position to the anterior of the building. "They are almost to the door then." Having ascended half the distance to the portico, Phillip halted to wait. Characteristically, he carried no weapon. He never had. In addition to his marginal clairvoyant abilities, Phillip had discovered at a young age that he possessed the capacity to kill by manipulating the life force of his opponents. In fact, he was one of the few people in the galaxy who'd mastered that rare power he called the *Death Touch*. But then, for him, the facility had always been there, buried in the depths of inherited memory.

A moment later, the arched doors above him shimmered and faded into nothingness. Interesting, Phillip thought in that fleeting second before his attention centered on the people emerging from the alien edifice. There appeared to be a large number of them attempting to crowd through the doorway at once. In their midst, a long narrow box rested on a stretcherlike device.

"Be careful now," Nagami heard a gruff voice bellow. "The damn casket might be metal, but we don't know what the lid is made of. It could break if you drop it. Then, who the hell's going to pick it up?"

If there was a response to the crusty inquiry, Nagami didn't hear it. A group of 11 people had emerged from the building, and the doors had shimmered back into place, before the old woman noticed him. When she did, she started and reached out to grip the arm of the burly older man at her side. He shook off her hand and continued to mumble dire warnings to those carrying the strange case. Grasping his arm again, she tugged on it rather forcefully.

"What is it, Liselle?" he barked in ill-natured inquiry.

"Be quiet for two seconds and look," Liselle retorted, pointing at Phillip.

The man, a large, brawny individual of advanced years, raised his gaze from the box. Having studied a number of holographic representations prior to the mission, Phillip recognized him as Zachariah Swan. Swan, momentarily taken aback to discover a stranger in his domain, recovered quickly. "Who the hell are you?" he bellowed in a tone that Nagami was beginning to suspect was generated more by character than by temperament.

Phillip, who disliked raising his voice, mounted a few more steps, never taking his eyes from Swan. When he was within conversation distance, he responded. "I am merely an emissary, Mr. Swan. My employer requests the honor of your company, as his guest."

Swan's eyes narrowed. "Why would an emissary arrive masked?" he demanded. "And who is your employer?"

"The mask is merely a component of my instructions, Mr. Swan."

Swan snorted. "And I'm supposed to just take your word for this and calmly walk off with you?"

"No, Mr. Swan," Nagami responded. "We anticipated that you would not. However, unless you want innocent people hurt, it is the most expedient course of action for you." Nagami raised a hand and armed Legionnaires stepped from behind the pillars, ranging themselves threateningly on either side of the archeological group. Phillip knew without looking that the Legionnaires flanking him had brought their weapons to bear as well. "We came prepared to persuade you." Nagami stepped slightly to the side and, with a friendly beckoning gesture, said, "Please join me, all of you." His eyes ranged over the small group, and fastened with curiosity on the casket they carried.

Swan's people looked to him for guidance. Ignoring them, Zach stood silently considering his options for endless seconds, studying his adversary with wary eyes. Had he had only himself to consider, he might have challenged the man before him. He'd lived a long, happy and fulfilling life; death was no longer something he feared. And his instincts told him that this enforced visitation had something to do with Logan. He didn't want to be placed in a hostage situation where he could be used against his grandson.

However, his assistants, with the exception of Liselle, were young. They had their lives ahead of them, and he had no right to ask them to follow a course of action which could deprive them of that life. With a sense of fatalism, Zach decided that he had no choice but to surrender. He could only hope that Logan was smart enough not to fall into whatever trap these people were creating for him.

What worried Zach now was the sword. He'd been in the process of having it sent for study by scientists and theologists together at the Kanisian archives, a place where it could have been examined in controlled conditions. The thought that it might end up in the hands of this man's employer struck dread into him. Even if the curse was mere fancy—which no one had been willing to presume—the sword itself was an exquisitely valuable artifact forged from an unknown metal alloy. But Zach had no means of concealing it.

If only he'd waited for the arrival of the guards who were to escort the sword to the mainland before removing it. If only this hooded man and his companions had arrived a couple of hours later. But *if only*'s had never amounted to a hill of beans, and they still didn't. The fleeting hope that this man might not have an interest in the artifact was quickly negated by the acknowledgment that all of Logan's problems seemed to be connected to their archeological finds. He could not allow the sword to fall into the wrong hands. His only hope lay in the fact that his host was not interested in it. With an abrupt gesture, Zach directed his assistants to set down their burden and come forward in response to the man's demand.

"No! Bring the case," Phillip directed, instantly countermanding Swan's instruction. He looked at Zachariah. "What is in it?"

Zach shrugged. "A simple sword."

"A ceremonial device?" Nagami asked, knowing Marnier's fascination with such things.

Swan shook his head. "No. No gold or jewels. As I said, it is a simple sword."

"Let me see it."

Zach glanced at his assistants and nodded his permission for them to acquiesce to the man's demands. Slowly, with Zach in the lead, they began moving down the stairs toward the hooded figure dressed in black. The hooded Legionnaires fell into step behind them. The man they approached was lean and tall but, other than that, Zach was able to discern little about him. Damnation! He wished he knew more about what they were dealing with here.

As they drew abreast of him, Phillip halted them

with a gesture, and stepped forward to view the ancient weapon through the transparent lid of the metal casket. At first glance, he saw only an unremarkable weapon, as Swan had indicated. He was about to tell them to leave it when he thought to wonder why they were carrying an unexceptional sword in such a guarded manner. He leaned forward to study the case rather than the weapon, and that was when he saw it. Briefly, as he read the curse inscribed in English, his lips curved in an uncharacteristic smile. Marnier would reward him handsomely for such a find. Handsomely indeed.

He looked up and met Zachariah Swan's forthright gaze. Despite his hood, he had the impression that the older man could see right through him. It was a disconcerting sensation. Without so much as turning his head, he directed his next comment to the Legionnaires. "Do any of you have an anti-grav lift in your packs?"

A second of hesitation. "I do, sir." The speaker was one of the Legionnaires whose name Nagami did not know.

Phillip looked briefly in his direction. "Use it to aid you in carrying the case. I doubt that it's particularly heavy, but I don't want to risk it's being dropped." Then, turning his gaze back to Zachariah Swan, he said, "We will take the casket." Lowering his voice to a bare murmur, he spoke solely to Swan. "And the evil spirit within it, if it exists." Then more loudly: "Come, Mr. Swan. We have a long journey ahead of us. Say farewell to your colleagues."

Fourteen

Logan awoke, and automatically sent his hands exploring the curvaceous form snuggled next to him. Shenda's alabaster-fair skin was as soft as velvet, as smooth as satin. He trailed his fingers over her small breasts and ribs to her navel, exploring, learning. It was just below her navel that his sensitive fingertips encountered some slight striations that he'd not noticed during the height of passion. They were familiar in nature but completely unexpected. He paused, wanting to examine the faint marks visually, but knowing that he couldn't move without waking Shenda; her head rested on his left arm. And so he continued his gentle unobtrusive exploration of her beautiful body, memorizing each delectable detail with his hand.

Moments later she stirred, and he settled back to await her return to wakefulness. With a sigh, she turned to face him. As wakefulness restored awareness, her cheeks flushed a becoming shade of pink. He reached to brush a strand of midnight hair from her delicate features. "Welcome back," he murmured with a tender smile.

She smiled a little uncertainly and said, "We should get up."

"There's no hurry. We're still days away from Dendron II." Now that she was facing him, he swept her body with his gaze and saw the faint striations that he'd only sensed with his fingertips. A million half-formed questions milled around his brain, but only one formed on his tongue. He hoped it was the right one. "Shenda, where is your child?" he asked gently.

She avoided his gaze, but he sensed her sudden tautness in every fiber of his being. She licked her lips. She brushed at an itch on her collarbone. She cleared her throat. Finally she met his gaze, and he was startled to see tears in her eyes. Shenda crying? She was so fierce, so independent. Her tears stirred a protective instinct within him that he'd never before experienced.

"Since you're obviously an observant man, I won't attempt to lie to you and tell you I've never had a child," she murmured as she hastily blinked the tears away. "But I haven't seen my son, except in pictures, since I gave him up at birth, and I prefer not to talk about it."

"You gave him up?" Swan echoed, genuinely confused. "Why?" There were so many reproduction controls in place that unwanted pregnancies were virtually non-existent. And in those rare cases where a pregnancy wasn't planned, few people would give the child up due to the constraint concerning the number of children a woman was authorized to bear: two on Earth; four on Fortuna, because of its less-populated status.

Shenda searched his eyes as though debating whether or not to answer his question. "Because I couldn't allow anyone to know that I had a child," she said softly. "You are the only living person who knows."

Logan reared back, staring at her incredulously. Pushing himself to a sitting position, he considered her. "How is that possible?" he asked doubtfully.

Sliding past him, Shenda retrieved her clothing and began to dress. "You're not going to let it go, are you?"

Logan tried, he really did, but there were just too many unanswered questions hovering on his tongue. "I'm sorry, I can't," he said. "I will promise you that if you explain it to me, I'll never speak of it again . . . if that is what you wish."

Fastening her shirt, Shenda turned to him, searching his face for an endless moment. Finally she nodded. "Very well. You already know too much, so I suppose telling you the entire story will make little difference. I have your word that you will never speak of it to anyone?"

Logan nodded, and rose to pull on his trousers. "My word," he promised in a murmur as he fastened the waistband and resumed his position on the bed.

"Were I not so certain that you and Marnier are on opposite sides, I would kill you rather than reveal any of this to you. I want you to be aware of that."

Logan nodded. "Point taken." It was in that instant that he began to piece together some of Shenda's story. She'd been seduced by Marnier when she was 16, little more than a child herself. Three months later he'd abandoned her. And she'd said she hadn't made love in nine years. Mathematics took Logan back to Darren Marnier; he was the father of the child she'd given up.

"All right. You asked *why* I gave my son up," Shenda said, drawing him from his illuminating ruminations. "It's a long story; there were so many things in my life that affected the decision I made." Shenda began pacing the small cabin, her eyes glued to the floor as though searching for something. "I'll have to start at the beginning, with my mother's story."

Finally she began. "I hardly remember her. She died when I was very young. I remember her gentleness, her flowery scent and the coolness of her hands when she brushed the hair off my face, but that's about all. At the time that she died, I remember a lot of commotion: raised voices, whispering voices, people rushing all over the place, rooms and rooms of flowers, and a sense of isolation, of standing back watching it all from a distance without understanding."

Shenda frowned thoughtfully, her staring gaze turned inward to a time that only she could see. "It was shortly after that that my father sent me off to boarding school. I would come home each holiday season, dutifully kiss him on the cheek, and be hustled off by a new nanny or housekeeper to be entertained for the duration of my visit home. My father was a stranger to me." She looked at Logan. "He still is in many ways. But I think I know him better than anybody."

She returned to pondering the floor with an intense sightless gaze. "Then, the holiday season after I had turned fourteen, my father suddenly seemed to notice my existence. He told me that I was a beautiful young lady with tremendous potential." Shenda snorted indelicately. "I was foolish enough to take the compliment at face value.

"Shortly after that, he had me brought home from school and informed me that I would complete my education at home under his direction and that of the tutors he would hire." Shenda glanced at Logan. "I wasn't happy. I had never been an outgoing child, and the few friends I had were at school. I balked, but I was forbidden contact with my friends until I completed my studies to my father's satisfaction. And since my father is never satisfied, I lost contact with all the young girls my age."

"Did you ever try to contact them?" Logan asked.

Shenda nodded. "Of course I did. But it was almost a year before I was able to so, and when you're young that amount of time is an eternity.

"I had been immersed in politics, quite literally. I ate, drank and slept the workings of the political machine. I had begun to view the universe with a jaundiced eye. And I matured. I no longer made impulsive decisions. I learned to choose my clothing, my makeup, my hairstyles with an eye to the statement I'd be making."

She looked at Logan and shrugged. "My friends were still consumed by inconsequential things. In molding me, my father isolated me from others my age, be they boys or girls. Before long, I soon acquired a reputation as an aloof, mysterious young woman. I didn't understand why at the time, but my father was as elated by that as I had ever seen him."

Shenda swallowed and looked at Logan. "Would you mind if we moved to the galley?" she asked. "I'm very thirsty."

"Not at all." Rising, Logan pulled on his shirt and boots and led the way from the small cabin.

Scant minutes later, they sat across a table from

each other sipping cool, soothing Fortunan iced green tea. "Where was I?" Shenda asked.

Logan considered. "Your father had molded you into an aloof young woman, I believe." He had assimilated more about Shenda's life in the past few minutes than he had ever expected to learn, and knowing her fierce independence, he had carefully concealed the pity he felt for the lonely young woman revealed, layer by layer, in the narrative.

Shenda nodded and stared silently into her glass of tea. Finally she sighed. "I was about a month short of my sixteenth birthday when a package arrived for me. To this day, I don't know how it got past all of my father's staff to reach me without being confiscated. But it did, and it changed my life." She fell silent, staring at the table surface, her gaze turned inwards.

Finally Logan could stand the suspense no more. "What was in it?" he asked quietly.

Shenda started, as though she'd forgotten his presence, and looked at him. "A holodisk made by my mother," she murmured. "A message she'd made specifically for me before she'd committed suicide."

"Ah, Saints!" Logan murmured under his breath. "It must have been tough learning that."

"Yes, it was," Shenda agreed with a brittle smile that betrayed just how close the pain was to the surface. "But not as tough as learning to accept the message she'd left for me."

Logan waited, knowing that Shenda had to deal with the painful memory in her own way. She stared at the iced tea, running her fingers through the beaded moisture collecting on the exterior of the chilled glass. Then she began. "I look a lot like my mother. I didn't realize that until I received the holo; my father had had all traces of her wiped from our lives. But there are differences, too. My mother's appearance was warmer, more gentle. There is an expression, a hardness, in my face that my mother's lacked." Shenda glanced at Logan, and her lips twisted briefly in self-derision. "No matter how hard I try to deny it, I can see my father in me as well. The hardness comes from him." She shrugged and looked back at her glass. "Perhaps that's the way it was meant to be."

Rising, iced tea in hand, she began to pace the small galley. "The story my mother told me on that holodisk horrified me—still, to this day, disgusts me—but it was one I had to hear.

"I always knew that my father was a cold, unfeeling man. Listening to the other children in boarding school talk about the relationships they had with their parents had taught me that." A small, self-deprecating smile curved Shenda's lips. "I used to make up stories about the things my father and I did together so that no one would know that he was a stranger to me. But it was the holodisk that revealed exactly how cold he was."

Shenda's mind replayed the disk. A disk that she'd watched so often that she'd memorized every line of her mother's face, every nuance of her voice and every word she'd uttered.

Shenda, my darling child, I love you more than life itself. You must always remember that. And know that you are not to blame in any way for the things that have happened. It is an evil world and . . . No, I won't tell you how to feel about your father. You alone must learn to judge the people around you. Never adopt another's feelings as your own.

To know that these are the last words you will ever hear from me is a difficult thing. But I felt I had to explain my decision to you, to warn you, and this is the only way I can think of to accomplish that. I hope it will be enough. I hope you will grow up stronger than I, my darling child. And I hope you will forgive me for my cowardice.

Her mother had bowed her head then, to brush at the sparkling tears that tracked down her fair cheeks. When she'd looked back at the camera, she'd squared her shoulders as though summoning some hidden well of strength, and continued. *I didn't begin to really know your father until after we'd married. And then, little by little, he began to reveal his true character. He is an ambitious and dictatorial man, Shenda, and you will have to be very strong to become your own person. He likes to control everything around him, including people, and he usually finds a means to do so.*

Kalenta Ridell paused and closed her eyes, swallowing. *This is so very difficult. I don't want you to hate your father, Shenda. He is, after all, your father. But, I want you to know him, to understand him as no one else does so that he doesn't turn you into a . . . a shadow or, like me, an automaton. And escaping that fate will be extremely difficult because it means you cannot allow yourself to care about anyone or anything. As soon as he knows you care, he has a means to threaten you, to control you, and you will be lost.*

He used you, Shenda, to control me. He threatened to have you removed from my care, to have you raised far away where I would never see you if I did not comply with his demands. The thought of losing you terrified me. He is a rich and powerful man, Shenda; he can do almost anything. So I did what he asked of me for as long as I could. But I can't do it anymore.

Her voice broke and she squeezed her eyes shut, taking a deep breath before continuing. *Unfortu-*

nately, for me there is only one escape. I will take my own life. Forgive me, Shenda, for leaving you alone. But you will be safe for some years yet. I have timed the delivery of this disk to coincide with your sixteenth birthday; I hope it will be soon enough.

I know you're wondering what he had me do that drove me to such lengths, and were it not necessary for me to tell you in order for you to fully understand, I would never speak of it. She paused, looking directly into the camera. It had always seemed to Shenda that, in that instant, the holographic image of her mother had looked straight into her eyes. *He turned me into a thief, Shenda. A thief and a political whore. I don't know if you know what that word means. It's when you sell your body or your principles in return for something, usually wealth. In my case, I sold myself in return for contact with you.*

When we were invited to political or society functions, I was directed to excuse myself as though going to the washroom, and find the offices belonging to Harris's opponents. Once inside, I would access their computers, placing a small transmission device in place as I'd been taught. These devices enabled Harris to know everything his opponents were doing. But as the years progressed, some of his colleagues, aware of the problems others had had with computer integrity, installed virtually foolproof security systems. That was when he came up with the idea of . . . of placing me in their beds, of insinuating me into their confidence.

He would stage an argument with me in a place which seemed relatively secluded but which had been carefully chosen to be within view of his opponent. Then Harris would stalk off, leaving the party and . . . me. In most cases, he judged his opponent's character accurately. They comforted me, whisked me off into seclusion, and seduced me. Many had Harris's idea in reverse. They thought that by seducing me they would have an inside track into Harris's activities. And for the most part, I managed to get enough information to keep Harris happy while feeding his opponents inconsequential details.

Kalenta bowed her head, clasped her hands demurely before her and licked her lips before looking again at the camera. *I don't like who I am, Shenda. And I can't do this anymore. Forgive me. Remember I love you. And please, guard yourself well. Become your own person. Don't let anybody force you to do anything you know is wrong.*

At that point, the image had faded, and Shenda was left staring at empty space. Now she looked at Logan. "Love and hate warred within me for a long time. I couldn't decide how I felt about either of my parents."

Logan knew how *he* felt. He disliked the woman who had sentenced her daughter to a lifetime of self-imposed loneliness because of her own weakness. He despised the man who had made such a sacrifice necessary. And he marveled at the inner strength of the young woman who was their offspring. But he knew he would never voice those feelings.

Shenda drained the last droplet of tea from her glass and cleared her throat. "It was at that time in my life, when I was so uncertain about everything, that Darren Marnier entered my world." Shenda looked at Logan. "You already know that story except for the fact that when Darren left me, I was pregnant. It was my mother's experience that prompted me to keep that information secret . . . from everyone. I refused to take the chance that someone would try to control me through the love I had for my child. So I used the extensive education my father had given me to hide my pregnancy."

Logan frowned. "Surely the medical archives recorded your pregnancy. Somebody had to deliver the baby."

Shenda shook her head and resumed her seat, setting her empty glass on the table. "No. I knew that if my child was born in a licensed facility, there would be an account of his birth. So I accessed the SubNet and found a list of doctors operating outside the law." SubNet was the name given to an extensive underground computer network that somehow always managed to stay one step ahead of those who tried to shut it down. "When I checked their backgrounds, I found one doctor whose sole reason for operating outside the law was a strong sense of morality. She was instrumental in championing the morality legislation as it now exists, but she claimed it hadn't gone far enough. She continued to argue against involuntary organ harvesting from condemned criminals. She argued against the genetic labs getting aborted fetuses, even consensually. And she argued against the practice of genetic programming—which as you know is becoming rather commonplace. It was that last which lost her public support—people consider it their right to be able to have a child with blue eyes and blond hair if they so desire. The *take what you get* mentality frightened some of them. So, due to pressure from influential quarters, her license was revoked and she moved underground. For my purposes, she was the perfect doctor.

"I was only three months pregnant when she took me in without even knowing my identity. Since everything within me recoiled at the idea of aborting my child, I lived with her until Gavin was born. Then, just three days prior to his birth, another woman birthed a child who died within hours of being born . . . her second such loss. She was entitled to no more children. But since she was wealthy, she could afford to have records altered. She paid to have the records show that her child had not died, and she adopted my son. I have no idea who she is. That was part of the agreement. But I do receive progress reports, via the SubNet to a numbered address, each year on his birthday. He is healthy, intelligent and handsome. That's all I need to know."

"And the doctor?" Logan prompted. "She must know who you are now; your face is widely recognized."

Shenda shook her head. "The doctor died in a shuttle accident about a year later. It looked like sabotage, but it was never proven. If she suspected who I was, she never told anyone."

She frowned abruptly. "My greatest concern now is that Marnier has somehow learned of my son's existence.

"Logan?"

He met her anxious gaze. "Yes?"

"Do you think Marnier has found out about Gavin?"

Logan recognized the question as the plea for reassurance that it was. Only he wasn't so certain he had any to give her without lying to her, and he knew she wouldn't appreciate that. He hesitated, forming his words carefully in his mind before speaking. "I think there are two possibilities for Marnier's actions. One, as you suspect, he may have learned that you have a child. Or two, he may—for some reason that we do not yet know— be so desperate to wed you that he simply took a chance that there would be something in your past that you did not want known and you'd assume that he'd already found it."

"You think he's bluffing?" Shenda asked incredulously.

Logan shrugged. "It is a possibility."

Shenda's eyes narrowed thoughtfully. "Yes, it is."

"Shenda, can I ask you something?"

She looked at him and nodded once, sharply. "Last question," she said. "I'm tired of talking."

"If you think Marnier knows about your son, why did you come up with the plan to marry me? Aren't you afraid he may retaliate by using the child?"

Shenda nipped the inner flesh of her lip thoughtfully. "It was a chance I felt I had to take. If Darren has learned about Gavin, then I also have to assume that he will come to the conclusion that Gavin is his. My solitary nature is common knowledge in many quarters." She shrugged. "I have to believe that he won't harm his own son. And aside from physically hurting him, about the only thing he can do to hurt me through Gavin is to cut off all connection I have to my son. The thought of that bothers me, but since I have always been distanced from him, it holds less power over me than it might for a mother who'd actually raised her child. Do you understand?"

Logan nodded. "Yes."

Shenda took a deep breath. "Then you also understand why I cannot possibly stay married to you. I cannot be linked to anyone."

A peculiar stillness settled over Logan as he studied her. Had the telling of her tale of woe merely been a ploy, a device to seek a means of undoing the marriage? He suspected that, had he not married Shenda, he would never have heard the story of her life . . . or her mother's. The telling of it had not been a gesture of trust, but of manipulation. Damn her! Damn him for a fool, for believing even for an instant that she might allow herself to begin a relationship with him. He returned her gaze now with a cold and uncompromising look.

"The marriage cannot be undone, Shenda. *Until death do us part*. Isn't that what you said?" He raised a sardonic brow and smiled mirthlessly. He leaned back, lacing his fingers behind his head as he considered her. "But then, with your education, I'm certain you'll be able to arrange a very effective and melodramatic introduction to widowhood."

"Damn you, Swan, that's not what I—"

Logan interrupted her protestations. "But until that happens . . ." He rose and stood staring down at her. "I intend to enjoy the circumstance of being married to an attractive woman."

Shenda rose to face him, and held up a hand as though to ward him off. "Swan . . ."

"And, whether you want to admit it or not," Logan continued undaunted, "you'll enjoy it, too. I sensed your feelings, remember. And if I concentrate, I can detect your feelings now."

Shenda's eyes widened in alarm and, much as she hated the necessity, she retreated a step. "Swan, we can't keep doing this." She tried for a reasonable tone. "It will only intensify the bond between us. Please understand. We have to find a way to undo the marriage as soon as we find your figurine."

"You want this as much as I do, Shenda. You're afraid, but you want me."

Shenda shook her head and retreated another

step. "No. You're wrong, Logan."

He didn't bother to respond to her desperate lie. As her back came into contact with the bulkhead, he reached for her and pulled her into his arms. Looking down at her, he let his eyes roam her beautiful, exotic features. "Until death do us part, Shenda," he murmured in his seductive bass voice. "However long that might be . . . that's how long I want you."

Shenda closed her eyes and swallowed, trying to block out the newly developing sense that allowed her to feel the extent of his desire for her. Trying to shut down the powerful response within her that insistently broadcast her own yearning. But it was useless. He was right. Whether she understood it or not, she wanted him. Wanted him as she had never wanted another man. And reawakened passions would not be denied. "Logan—" she murmured. But she couldn't remember the words of the desperate argument she'd been about to make.

"What?"

Shenda opened her eyes and allowed herself to drown in his potent whiskey gaze. "Kiss me." As his lips came down on hers, Shenda allowed herself to drift, a willing hostage in fugitive arms, on a sea of sensation.

The Duana Moon hung in the sky, dark and cold like indigo ice, barely visible as its inky surface absorbed more light than it reflected. Beyond it, the luminous surface of Dendron II glowed in the light of a warm, yellow sun, its single pencil-thin ring of dust as radiant as a halo. Dendron II was very like Earth had been in its infancy, or so scientists theorized. However, there was one major exception: The planet's atmosphere contained a toxic gas that made it impossible for humans to breathe without special filters.

Since they were not concerned with Dendron II at the moment, but rather its single satellite, Duana, Logan began to study the moon. Unfortunately, since virtually all of its facilities had been constructed underground, there was little to be gleaned from an examination of its surface. He glanced over at Shenda. "Have you any idea what kind of security system they have in a place like this?" he asked.

She shook her head. "I've never been to a non-Legion scientific facility."

Logan spied the docking bay doors and compressed his lips on a sigh. "All right, here goes," he murmured. "Lais, see if you can contact their computer. Transmit ship classification and identity, and request permission to dock."

"Acknowledged."

Two minutes later a distinctly mechanized, sexless voice responded. "*Eagle*, you are clear to dock in bay four. Please use forward thrusters to slow to one-quarter propulsion speed prior to entering the docking bay area."

"Acknowledged," Lais replied, and Logan realized that he still hadn't transferred to manual control. Since he much preferred being in control of his landings, he made the switch and began to guide the ship toward the open docking bay door. Firing thrusters at regular intervals, he carefully monitored their speed and adjusted trajectory. Cold, luminous, green lights lit up the docking lane within the bay, looking like nothing so much as inverted lime icicles.

Moments later, they settled to the thruster pad with a gentle thump and Shenda took the opportunity to study the area. With the exception of the docking lane lights, the entire bay consisted of unrelieved, unadorned blue-gray metal. The massive metal doors closed behind them like the jaws of a giant maw. She looked ahead. Three doors, all currently closed, provided exit from the bay: one on each side, which probably provided access to neighboring docking bays, and one a substantial distance in front of them, which would undoubtedly prove to be the access to the station.

"Lais," Logan said, startling Shenda from her perusal, "check exterior pressure and atmospheric conditions."

"Checking . . . Exterior pressure is at standard. Oxygenated atmosphere has been re-established and gravity is at forty-five percent of Earth normal."

Logan studied the door ahead of them. "It doesn't look like anyone is sending a welcoming committee, so I guess we go in."

"I guess," Shenda echoed doubtfully. "This seems awfully easy. What's to keep these science centers from being raided if this is the extent of civilian security?"

Logan looked at her and shrugged. "Maybe they don't believe they have anything to steal. Their computer is programmed to authorize landing without human intervention."

She met his gaze incredulously. "There's always something to steal. Even *ideas* are marketable, and a place like this must be full of revolutionary concepts."

Logan nodded. "We're probably going to need human authorization to get past whatever security system they *do* have in place." He looked at the monitor. "Lais, access the station's computer again, and send a message to Dr. Nathanial Tredway. Tell him that he has two visitors waiting in

301

docking bay four who would very much like to see him."

"Sending."

A moment later a woman's face appeared on the screen. "I am Fawna Bolten, Dr. Tredway's assistant. May I help you?"

"Ms. Bolten." Logan nodded, imitating her tone and formality. "I am Dr. Logan Swan, an archeologist from Fortuna. It is imperative that I speak with Dr. Tredway as soon as possible on a matter of some urgency."

"I'm sorry, Dr. Swan. Dr. Tredway is in the middle of some very sensitive work and cannot be disturbed. If you care to tell me the nature of your visit, perhaps I can help you?"

"No, I don't think that is possible," Logan answered smoothly, noticing as he did so that the assistant's attitude cooled even more at his words.

"Very well, Dr. Swan. If you care to wait, I can give you access to the public lounge, but it may be some time before he can get to you."

"You will tell him that it is urgent?" Logan pressed.

"Of course, Doctor," Ms. Bolten assured him coolly.

"Then we will accept your invitation to wait in the lounge."

"Fine. Please progress through the door ahead of you and follow the servo-droid to the designated area. It will direct you to any refreshments you might require."

"Thank you, Ms. Bolten."

The screen went blank as Dr. Tredway's assistant cut the communication link. Shenda looked at Logan. "Dr. Swan?" she asked.

A smile tugged at the corners of Logan's lips. "I

do have a doctorate, Shenda, so I am qualified to use the title."

Shenda stared at him. There were more facets to this man than a Martian Euro-crystal. "I suppose next you're going to tell me that you know six languages and govern your own small country?"

Logan grinned. "Not at all." He retrieved his small arsenal of weapons and strapped them around his waist beneath his jacket. Just as Shenda was about to attempt to satisfy her curiosity about an unfamiliar Fortunan weapon, he knelt and removed another item, depositing it hastily into her hands. Shenda looked down to see her own laser and stunner. Swan looked searchingly into her eyes. "Put them on quickly," he said. "Before I have second thoughts."

Shenda nodded, and clipped the stunner to the waistband of her trousers. Since she had no holster for the laser, she slid it into a pocket.

When she'd finished, Logan extended his hand and said, "Shall we go?" Without forethought, she grasped his strong, warm hand. They had grown comfortable together in the preceding days. Shenda flushed as memory reminded her just *how* comfortable. Somehow, being at his side, taking his hand, seemed right and natural. That it would all change in the near future Shenda acknowledged, although she knew that Logan didn't. In the days past they had reached a tacit agreement to disagree and left it at that. But whether Logan acknowledged it or not, there was no future for Shenda with a man . . . any man—though had she the choice to make, she now felt that she *might* choose a man like Logan Swan.

"Four, actually," Logan said as they ducked through the hatch.

"Pardon me?"

"Four," he repeated, looking at her. When her expression remained blank, he elaborated. "Languages," he said. "I don't know six, I know four."

"Oh." Shenda's face cleared as understanding dawned. She skipped a step to keep up with Logan as they crossed the enormous bay. "Which ones?"

"New-Modern English, Mid-Modern English, Kanisi, and Japanese. And of course, I've also studied hieroglyphics, pictographs and cryptographs."

"Of course." Shenda nodded, although her attention had focused on his previous sentence. "Kanisiism has its own language?"

Logan nodded. "The linguists say it's an amalgamation of many languages, but . . . yes, it's now a language unto itself."

"Say something in Kanisi," Shenda said as they neared the door that would take them from the docking bay.

"I already have."

"When?"

He gave her a speaking glance, and she vaguely recalled his saying something to her at the height of passion that she had not understood. At the time, it had not seemed important. Now it did. "Say it again, please."

"Now?" he asked incredulously. She nodded, and he looked over his shoulder as though to make certain there was no one around to hear him. *"Ci tha'lassa hava,"* he murmured quickly.

She frowned. "What does it mean?"

Logan shook his head. "That you will have to discover at another time." The door opened before them, and they stepped into a corridor. The contrast between the dull blue-gray of the docking bay and the brilliant shade of orange that currently assaulted their eyes from all sides caused them to blink reflexively.

The servo-droid, a barrel-shaped creation that was perhaps the most versatile of the robotic inventions to date, awaited them. "Come this way, please," it said in its synthesized male voice, and immediately took off down the corridor without waiting to see if they followed.

Within minutes, they were ushered into a large, comfortable lounge. An exterior viewscreen showing a portion of Dendron II occupied the whole of one wall, and Shenda wondered how they'd managed to get so close to the surface when she'd not sensed them ascending. A glance at Logan's countenance as he stared at it told her he noticed the same thing. "They must have constructed the facility into the side of a mountain," he commented.

Before Shenda could respond, the servo-droid spoke. "You will find a food and beverage dispenser on the wall," it informed them. "Is there anything else you require?"

"No," both Shenda and Logan said simultaneously, and the droid left on whisper-quiet wheels.

"Now what?" Shenda asked, turning to look up at Logan.

"Now we wait . . . for a while. Let's see if we can determine the layout of this place." He walked to a recessed monitor set into the wall near the door. There didn't appear to be any kind of a switch in evidence with which to activate it. "Computer," he said. The monitor flickered on, revealing the logo belonging to the scientific station, and Logan smiled. "Display a map of the facility, please."

"Please state clearance code."

Logan frowned. "On second thought, I don't need to see the whole facility; just show me my current location in relation to docking bay four."

A map flashed onto the screen. The lounge and the docking bay both were highlighted with a red star. Many chamber identities were conspicuously absent. "Good," he said. "Now can you expand this to show Dr. Nathanial Tredway's position in relation to my present location?"

There was a split second of hesitation, and then the map redrew itself, highlighting three locations. Shenda moved nearer to peer at the display. "He's just around the corner!"

"And down a level," Logan added. "See how the computer has drawn these areas in a different color." He indicated a number of areas. "This appears to be a stairwell."

Shenda nodded. "Still, it's not far."

"No, it's not. If we're left to wait too long, I think it might be worth a little foray into the unknown. What do you say?"

"He's moving."

Logan followed her gaze back to the monitor. The doctor had moved into the next chamber. He paused a few moments there and then moved back to his original position. "Computer off," Logan said.

"I wonder what's going on," Shenda murmured.

They didn't have long to wait to find out. Within two minutes, Fawna Bolten appeared in the doorway. She was a tall, slender woman with light brown hair secured in an untidy chignon and intense blue eyes. "Dr. Swan," she said as she moved into the room and extended her hand in introduction. "I'm Fawna Bolten," she said with a cool, formal smile.

"Pleased to meet you," Logan murmured. He nodded to Shenda. "My assistant, Shenda."

A little slowly, perhaps reluctantly, Ms. Bolten extended her hand to Shenda. "Shenda," she said.

Shenda had never heard her name spoken with such condescension. She mimicked Ms. Bolten's smile, added a measure of ice and said, "Fawna," tone for tone. She was rewarded by a slight widening of the other's eyes.

Then, dismissing her, Fawna Bolten turned back to Logan. The appreciative glint in her eye as she quickly looked him over could not be mistaken. Shenda felt a sudden, inexplicable urge to drop-kick the other woman. While she was examining the unfamiliar impulse, she almost missed Fawna's next words. "I'm afraid I have some bad news for you, Dr. Swan. I've informed Dr. Tredway of your presence, but he insists that he will not be able to see you today."

"You informed him that it was a matter of some urgency?"

She nodded. "I did, Dr. Swan. If you care to stay at the station as our guest, we can arrange accommodations. That way, as soon as the doctor is free, he can see you."

Logan shook his head. "No, that won't be possible. I'm afraid we have pressing matters to attend to elsewhere." He frowned, and draped an arm over Fawna Bolten's shoulder as he headed for the door. "Very well, Ms. Bolten, we appreciate your time on our behalf. Please don't allow us to keep you from your duties any longer. We can find our own exit."

Ms. Bolten hesitated uncertainly in the doorway. "Well, if you're certain?"

"Quite certain. Thank you." Logan smiled disarmingly. Under Fawna Bolten's watchful gaze, Logan and Shenda headed down the corridor, back the way they had come. As soon as they rounded the first corner, Logan pressed himself to the wall and hauled Shenda up beside him.

"What are you doing?" she demanded in a whisper.

"Waiting for Ms. Bolten to return to work."

Shenda snorted quietly. "Now who's manipulating?" she demanded.

"I had to do something," Logan whispered in return. He took a hasty glance around the corner. "She's gone," he whispered. "Let's go." Grabbing Shenda's hand, he slipped back around the corner and began heading in the direction of the stairwell.

"What about security?" Shenda demanded.

Fifteen

"We'll deal with that when we come to it," Logan answered.

"Wonderful," Shenda murmured with a wry twist of her lips.

"I don't think we have much to worry about. I received the impression from the map that most of the security is set up on the periphery of the complex."

They reached the stairwell door. After hastily depressing the sensor which prompted the door to slide aside, Logan plastered himself against the wall and peered around the corner. "It's clear. Let's find Dr. Tredway," he said as he stepped into the stairwell.

"Then what?" asked Shenda. "He said he wouldn't see us. Remember?"

Logan shrugged as though the fact was of little consequence. "We'll insist."

Not knowing what to say, Shenda eyed the laser

on Logan's belt and wondered if that was what he meant. She hadn't seen him draw a weapon since the prison break, but anybody who carried one was usually prepared to use it.

Although the stairs dropped for several more levels, they halted at the first landing. Logan peered through the small window in the door, looking as far as he could in both directions, before depressing the sensor. As the door slid aside, he once again grasped Shenda's hand and they slid around the corner to the right. The corridor was empty. They could hear the rhythmic thump of machinery from somewhere down the hall. A faint whir from the overhead camera drew Shenda's attention.

Camera! "Logan," she whispered fiercely.

"What?"

She gestured with her chin to the camera that now hung silently overhead, its single lens focused unerringly on them. It had to have triggered a silent alarm somewhere.

He cursed beneath his breath, and immediately moved off in the direction of the room that the computer had previously revealed as Tredway's location. "Come on," he urged. "Before security arrives."

Trotting along behind him, Shenda couldn't resist a glance over her shoulder at the roving camera. As she'd suspected, it was following them. Logan opened a door to their left, and they ducked inside. Shenda last viewed the camera as it halted outside the door, silently staring at them. When the door closed, blocking it from sight, she couldn't help but sigh with relief. The damn thing was unnerving.

"There he is," Logan said.

"Who?" Shenda asked even as she followed his

pointing finger. Across the room from them was an enormous window constructed of glass thick enough to be steelglass. Beyond the glass, a man worked industriously at a counter laden with a half-dozen computer monitors, computer print-outs, beakers and gadgets of all kinds and what appeared to be skeletal remains. He was lean; a fringe of dark blond hair heavily laced with grey encircled a shiny bald pate, yet his unlined face gave the impression that the untreated baldness was premature. Shenda would have guessed his age at no more than 38 or 39. It was the name on the white lab coat that broadcast his identity. "Dr. Nathanial Tredway," she murmured in answer to her own question.

Logan nodded. "None other."

At that moment the man beyond the glass looked in their direction. For a frozen instant in time, he simply stared at them, surprise etched on his expressive features. And then, with a frown, he strode toward the door. A second later, it swished open and he stalked into the room.

"Who are you?" he demanded in a voice that seemed a trifle high-pitched for a man. "What are you doing here?"

"Dr. Tredway." Logan stepped forward with a smile, extending his hand in greeting. Surprisingly, Tredway automatically grasped it. "I'm Dr. Swan. I believe your assistant mentioned me to you earlier?"

Still frowning, Tredway nodded. "Yes, but I told her I could not be disturbed today. I'm in the middle of some very sensitive work."

"We won't take much of your time, Doctor. Please." Logan brushed aside his jacket and placed his hand on his hip very near the laser he wore. Tredway followed the gesture and his eyes

311

widened as he saw the weapon. "As I informed your Ms. Bolten, we have pressing business elsewhere," Logan continued, as though unaware of the other man's sudden reticence. "We really don't have the time to wait."

"Dr. Swan," Tredway said in an insistent tone, "no one is permitted to wear weapons in a scientific facility. I would think, being a doctor yourself, you would be aware of that stricture."

Logan shook his head. "My work has been done almost exclusively at archeological sites, so I have yet to work on a science station. I am sorry for my unwitting breach of conduct."

"Very well," Tredway murmured grudgingly. "And who is this?" he asked, looking at Shenda with a distinctly interested gleam in his eye. What was with these people? she wondered.

"My wife and assistant, Shenda Swan," said Logan.

"Charmed, Shenda," Tredway murmured. Apparently unfazed by Logan's introduction of her as his wife, Tredway held her hand just a minute longer than necessary. Then he turned back to Logan. "Very well. Since you are here, what is it you wish to speak to me about?"

"The Obsidian Order."

Tredway's brows shot up just as the outer door opened. Logan palmed the laser, directing it unerringly at Dr. Tredway even as he kept it concealed, and spun a half turn that allowed him to keep both Tredway and the door in view. Three security officers in navy uniforms trimmed with orange lightning bolts leveled lasers and stunners in their direction. "Are you all right, Doctor?" the center guard, a robust, almost masculine woman, asked.

"I'm fine. Everything is fine," Tredway hastened

to assure her. "When I've finished speaking to our guests, you may escort them to their ship. In the meantime, please wait outside."

The woman hesitated, obviously undecided. "If you're certain, sir."

"Very certain," Tredway replied with a smile that seemed to reassure her.

She nodded. "Very good, Doctor." With a military style about-face, she and her companions reentered the corridor, and the door closed.

Tredway looked at Logan. "There now. Since you insist on interrupting my work, please come into the other room where I can at least keep an eye on my tests while we speak." Turning, he led the way from the room, and Logan unobtrusively returned his laser to his belt. "Have a seat," the doctor directed as he bent forward to scan the data scrolling by on the monitors.

The seats of which he spoke were four very tall stools. A bit nervously, Shenda perched herself atop one. After a single skeptical glance at the remaining stools, Logan remained standing.

"So then, Dr. Swan," Tredway said, as he turned to face them, "what have you discovered in the ruins on Fortuna that led you to my Obsidian Order theory? Have you finally uncovered some physical remains?"

"Unfortunately not." Logan shook his head. "You're familiar with our work there?"

Tredway smiled. "I keep myself informed. Especially when I suspect a possible link to my own research."

"A link?" Logan repeated, struggling to keep the surprise from his voice.

"Of course. Surely you're aware of the similarity between the sites you've found on Fortuna and the ruins of Atlantis?" The Atlantean ruins had been

313

discovered by seismologists while mapping the faults in the ocean floor during the mid-twenty-first century."

"Yes, of course. But what does that have to do with the Obsidian Order?"

"My theory concerning the Obsidian Order was derived after my work with the skeletal remains found in Atlantis."

Logan hesitated. Tredway obviously expected them to know the details behind his Obsidian Order theory. Would acknowledging their ignorance jeopardize their chances of learning more?

In the next instant, the decision was taken out of his hands. "I found the material available on your theory fascinating," Shenda interrupted. "However, much of the data seems to be suppressed. Would you be kind enough to explain it to me?" She flashed an ego-building smile and looked at Tredway with wide, admiring eyes.

"Well . . ." Tredway cast an anxious glance at his computer monitors and then back at Shenda. "I guess I could summarize a bit." He smiled, unable to resist the opportunity to vaunt his accomplishments before an attractive female. Logan adopted the mildly interested expression of one prepared to listen to a colleague expand on a topic which was quite well known to him.

"My passion began as a student. We were discussing the properties of DNA in class one day when another student introduced the Adam and Eve scenario. She felt that DNA testing should be able to prove or disprove the theory by revealing an underlying genetic fingerprint in the DNA substructure which would prove we all originated from a collective gene pool. I pointed out that early humanoids were not plentiful and would therefore have emerged from the same genetic pool. So, even if we did find a common denominator, it might not necessarily provide proof for the Adam and Eve theory. At that point, we were challenged by our professor to conduct tests to find the common denominator in the gene structure of humankind . . . if it existed."

Tredway frowned. "We almost did, but not quite. In fact, the results were quite confusing."

"What did you find?" Shenda asked, no longer feigning her intense interest.

"I found *two* underlying gene strains in substructural DNA. And due to interbreeding, they are often both found in a single subject. However, one is always dominant, suppressing the traits of the other. The first, which I christened the Lapis Sequence, I now believe to be the primordial strain, inherent to Earth. The second"—he looked intently into Shenda's eyes—"was the Obsidian Order." There was a short, intense pause.

Tredway cleared his throat. "For years I was unable to explain its existence, but despite the scientific community's lack of interest in my work, I persevered with my testing.

"When I compared the traits of people exhibiting the Obsidian Order with those of people exhibiting the Lapis Sequence, I discovered some very marked differences—from a scientific viewpoint, at any rate." The doctor paused to scan the results on his monitor screens.

"Like . . . ?" Logan prompted, before remembering that he was expected to have more than a passing familiarity with Dr. Tredway's work. The breach, if it was one, luckily went unnoticed.

Tredway turned back and replied with an intensity that revealed just how passionate he was about his research. "Those who possess a dominant Obsidian Order genetic sequence exhibit a much higher percentage of extrasensory talents and have a pronounced tendency to display signs of racial memory. They are also taller—statistically speaking—and predisposed to longer life. Of course, at the time I discovered this, I had no acceptable explanation for my findings, and my work was not taken as seriously as I would have liked."

Shenda stared at him, her mind spinning as she tried to interpret the implications. "And you now have a theory?"

He frowned. "Of course. When I discovered the distinctive dark pattern in the DNA substructure of each and every skeleton in the Atlantean archives, it all came together."

"What did?" she prompted. He seemed surprised by her incomprehension. "Please, I find this very interesting, and I have been able to find little material available on the subject."

Tredway looked distinctly unhappy. "I see that I am going to have to speak with the university again." He grimaced. "Very well, I'll spell it out. First"—he held up a finger—"we know that the ruins on Fortuna are alien ruins because, as a species, we didn't even discover the place until a few decades ago. Second, the ruins of Atlantis were found to be so similar in nature that it is now conceded in most quarters that Atlantis was an alien settlement on Earth. Third, the distinctive Obsidian Order sequence was found in the DNA substructure of the skeletal remains found in Atlantis. So . . . the conclusion is . . ." He raised a brow at Shenda expecting her to finish the dissertation.

"The conclusion is that the people exhibiting the Obsidian Order in their genes are descendants of an alien race which settled on Earth . . . and Fortuna."

"Exactly!"

Logan looked thoughtful. "Doctor, if a group of people with this Obsidian Order wanted to, say, intensify their tendency toward extrasensory abilities, could they do so by reproducing only within their own . . ." He paused, seeking the term he wanted. "Genetic pool?" he finally concluded.

Tredway hesitated. "It is possible, certainly. But I would think that the gene pool itself would be so weakened after millennia of dilution by the Lapis Sequence gene pool that any attempt at purifying it would take many generations."

"Have you by any chance heard of a cult calling itself the Obsidian Order?" Logan asked.

Dr. Tredway considered the question thoughtfully. "I believe I did hear about a small group of my test subjects forming an elite little club which they called the Obsidian Order. I did not pay much attention to it at the time, but I vaguely recall that their stated purpose was to continue to seek their origins."

"Would you know, Doctor, if Darren Marnier was ever one of your test subjects?" Shenda asked.

Nathanial Tredway's eyes chilled significantly. "I'm sorry, I will not reveal a test subject's identity." He looked at Logan. "You have still to state your purpose in seeing me, Doctor. Since my time is precious, I suggest you do so now."

"Our primary purpose in coming here was to have Shenda and myself tested for the Obsidian Order. Would that be possible, Dr. Tredway?"

Tredway frowned. "Well, it will take only a matter of minutes, but I fail to see why you could not have had the test conducted at a medical facility."

"We were not certain that they would know

what they were looking for. After all, it is difficult to find information on the Obsidian Order, and we want no diagnostic errors."

"Very well," Tredway conceded with ill grace. "Follow me, please." He moved over to the other side of the lab, clicked on a machine and handed them each a small scalpel. "Since my lab is not equipped for patients, I'm afraid I do not have a blood letter," he offered by way of explanation for the primitive tool. "I will require a small sample of blood from each of you. Although we can do the test with skin or even hair samples, blood has always proven to be the most expedient and reliable. One drop from each of you will suffice." He handed each of them a glass slide and stood waiting.

Giving Logan a speaking glance, Shenda pressed the small, sharp blade to the sensitive tip of her finger and squeezed a drop of blood onto the slide. Logan had apparently mirrored her actions, for when she handed Tredway her slide, Logan was also ready with his.

"Very good," Dr. Tredway said. "Now, while the samples are being analyzed"—he placed them both into the unit which looked much like a small oven—"you may wait here or in the outer room. Please do not disturb me." With that, he closed the door on the analysis machine, depressed a series of keys and stalked back across the room to his ongoing tests.

Shenda and Logan, by tacit agreement, waited right where they were. They watched the digital readouts flash across the screen attached to the unit without understanding the significance. Finally, almost five minutes later, the computer emitted a high-pitched beep and the readout stopped. A second later, Nathanial Tredway made his way back across the room.

Without comment, he opened the door on the unit, removed the samples and examined the display on the monitor. Then, depressing a series of keys, he called up another presentation. "This is you, Dr. Swan," he said after a moment. "You have the Lapis Sequence, the primordial strain. And it is pure. There is no indication that there has ever been a carrier of the Obsidian Order in your ancestry. Unusual really. See here." He pointed to a distinctive blue pattern.

Logan nodded. "And Shenda . . ."

Dr. Tredway keyed in another series of commands and the display shifted. "Shenda has the Obsidian Order," he said a moment later. "There . . ." Once again he indicated the representative strand, obsidian black. "She is descended from the Atlantean strain and it is dominant, although there is considerable evidence of Lapis Sequence ancestry."

Shenda frowned. "But I don't understand. I've never had any extrasensory powers or unusual memories."

Tredway shrugged, obviously at the limit of his patience. "Perhaps you just never bothered to develop them. Or perhaps the Lapis Sequence, although dormant in your genes, exerts some type of suppressing influence. Although I would love to explore the possibilities with you, I'm afraid I simply don't have the time." He turned to face them. "Now, if that is everything?"

"Of course, Doctor. Thank you very much for your time." At Logan's affirmative response, the first positive indication that they were actually going to leave, Dr. Tredway relaxed a bit.

"You're quite welcome, Dr. Swan. Although the

next time, I really would prefer it if you could make an appointment."

A moment later, when they exited the doctor's laboratory, Logan and Shenda were quietly but firmly escorted to docking bay four and their waiting ship.

Shenda resumed her seat on the bridge of the *Eagle* and stared silently, thoughtfully, at the security trio as they made their way back across the bay. "Logan . . ." She looked at him and waited until he met her gaze before continuing. "How did you know?"

He didn't have to ask what she was talking about. "It was the only thing that made any sense. I could tell by the doctor's reaction that Darren Marnier was one of his test subjects. That being the case, if you also carried the Obsidian Order, then Marnier's sudden determination to marry you could be understood."

Shenda nodded. "But that theory only works if you assume that he is out to . . . purify the line. Why would he think that way? How would it benefit him? And what would make him believe that such a thing is even possible?"

"I don't know, Shenda. Maybe something he uncovered among the artifacts. At least we know now why he's stealing them: He's looking for a link to his past, to a lost race of people."

"But why?" Shenda insisted. "You don't know Darren like I do, Logan. He doesn't do things for sentimental reasons. He couldn't care less about his tie to an ancient extinct race unless that tie was, in some way, of value to him. Every move he makes must ultimately profit Darren Marnier."

Logan grimaced. "I'm afraid I don't have any answers, Shenda. Just questions." The docking bay doors opened behind them, and he began powering the ship up. "Let's hope we find the answers on Space Station Olympus." With a burst of thrusters the *Eagle* left the surface of the Duana Moon. While Logan plotted coordinates and returned control to Lais, an unmarked ship flashed by them, heading for Dendron II. "Strange," he murmured aloud to himself.

"What's strange?"

"Hmm? Oh, nothing much," he responded, still distracted. "It's just that I thought Dendron II was pretty much the exclusive province of a few brave scientific individuals. But that ship didn't have any scientific designation."

"Oh."

"Scan for any other ships in the vicinity, will you? I don't want any surprises. Speaking of surprises, you might as well check the tracker too. If it's working, we'll know that Marnier's expecting us."

While Shenda monitored the area, Logan instructed Lais to provide options for the leap into hyperspace and the trip to Olympus. "Nothing on the tracker," Shenda informed him a moment later. "And the only signal I'm picking up is a weak broadcast from a Terminal in the neighboring sector."

"Good." He didn't take his eyes from the console. "Lais, time to the nearest leap point?"

"Five point eight minutes. However, the lane has an instability factor of thirty-six-point-two percent, which may necessitate a premature return to normal space."

Logan hesitated. Instable lanes could prove dangerous, even when the instability factor was as low as six percent. "Is there a more secure lane available?"

"Yes. We are twelve minutes from access. However, use of that lane increases the time to Olympus by six point four hours."

So they either took an unstable lane, or took a stable lane and wasted precious time, or took the stable lane and risked the hazards of time compression for the second time within a matter of days. Logan didn't like any of the choices. He looked at Shenda. "What do you think?"

"You're the one who's going to fade out of existence if we don't find that figurine in time," she responded. "Can we afford another six hours?"

"I don't know. All I do know is that each time I fade, it gets worse."

Shenda looked at the computer. "Lais, can you predict when the next occurrence of Logan fading may occur?"

"According to my calculations, the next incident should occur in approximately thirty-six hours."

Shenda looked at him. "The decision has to be up to you. As long as you have a good supply of tranquilizers on board, I don't mind if you want to opt for time compression. Personally, since we're in no immediate danger, I would rather avoid the unstable lane. I've seen Legion ships disappear forever when a lane collapses without warning."

Logan nodded. "Lais, set course for the stable lane."

"Acknowledged."

Minutes later, cocooned in the timeless silence of hyperspace, Logan noticed Shenda's pensive expression. "What is it?"

Wrenched from her thoughts by his voice, she started. "I'm still trying to figure out what's behind Marnier's sudden interest in archeology. Do you have any idea at all concerning what type of information was stored on the stolen crystal?"

Logan shook his head. "It was pretty much incomprehensible. The only things that looked like they might be readily interpretable were a few maps. There were some recordings that looked mathematical, a bit like scientific formula. But the language used by the person who recorded the data was completely unintelligible, very . . . chant-like." He checked some readings on the console. "At least, if Tredway is to be believed, we now know what the ancient Fortunans looked like."

Shenda glanced at him. "Like us," she concluded for him.

He nodded. "I wish that damn crystal had made it to the linguists like it was supposed to," Swan muttered. "We'd probably know what was on it by now."

"Perhaps it did," mused Shenda. "Just not the linguists for whom it was intended."

Logan looked at her sharply. "You think Marnier has interpreted the data?"

She shrugged and met his gaze. "Something has to have given him the incentive to pursue an ancient past so diligently."

Swan stared thoughtfully through the viewscreen. Finally he shook his head. "No, that theory doesn't work. The crystal wasn't the first item stolen. In fact, it was one of the last. If he's interpreted some ancient store of information, he got it from somewhere else."

Shenda considered. "Still, if we come across the crystal, I think we might be wise to take it, too. Whatever is on it could be very important."

"I agree."

Shenda's eyes widened in sudden inspiration. "Atlantis!" she murmured on a sigh.

"What do you mean?"

"Suppose for a moment you're Darren Marnier.

323

You're an exceptionally ambitious person who has developed and honed your charisma to the point of becoming a cult leader. You thrive on power. Now, you've participated in an experiment which hints strongly at the possibility that you are descended from a race of . . . of super-beings: long-lived people possessing extra-sensory powers—which could include telepathy—and the ability to draw upon an extensive well of inherited memory." Shenda spoke rapidly now, certain of her theory. "Remember, you love power, the ability to outmaneuver and control your opponents. What could be more seductive to you than the idea of increasing your personal power base? Delving into the thoughts of others with your mind? Knowing all that your ancestors knew?"

Logan nodded. "Very good. So, you think it was that lure which prompted him to start digging into the past."

Shenda nodded. "I'm certain of it. When did you start experiencing thefts of artifacts?"

He shrugged. "About three years ago."

"Were there any thefts from the Atlantean exhibits on Earth prior to that?"

"I don't know. I didn't hear of any, but that doesn't mean much. We seem to miss a lot of the news on Fortuna."

Shenda looked at the computer console. "Lais, have you access to the news archives from Earth?"

"Checking jump satellite accessibility." There was a pause. "I have access to the News-Net archives. Other libraries are inaccessible at this time."

"Check the News-Net for any reference to an Atlantean exhibit theft between three and five years ago."

"Acknowledged."

"There are some Atlantean artifacts in private collections, you know," Logan said into the anticipatory silence. "The Cup of Cronus, for example. So the theft would not necessarily have to have been from an exhibit."

"Or," Shenda added, "if he followed a pattern similar to that he used with you, the artifacts may have been stolen during a transition in ownership."

"I find no reference to a theft from an Atlantean exhibit during the stated time parameters," Lais said. "Would you like to alter the search instructions?"

"Yes," Logan responded. "Search for *any* reference to the theft of an Atlantean artifact. Use the same time parameters."

"Searching . . ."

The silence on the small bridge stretched. Without knowing why or what caused it, Shenda suddenly felt an increase in the tension in the air. Logan was looking at her with that hot, hungry look in his eyes, she *knew* it. She *felt* it. But she refused to meet his gaze. To continue this . . . this sexual relationship with a man with whom she had no hope of sharing a future was purest folly, and she was determined to resist.

"There were two thefts involving Atlantean artifacts during the stated time period," Lais suddenly said into the silence.

Swallowing, Shenda welcomed the computer's intrusion and, with a sense of desperation she did her best to deny, focused her attention on it. "What were they?" she asked.

"The first theft involved a number of items sold by private collector, Gilbert St. Jean, to the International Museum. They were stolen while en route to the purchasing museum. The second theft involved a break-in at the residence of Lord and Lady Rutledge, where a single item was stolen."

"Is there any mention of what the item was?" she asked.

"It is referred to as *an ancient tome encased in a solid, glass-like cube.*"

"A book?" Shenda asked incredulously.

"That would be my interpretation, yes," Lais concluded.

"What kind of book?"

"The reference does not elaborate."

"Is there any reference to what kinds of items were missing in the other theft?"

"The article mentions the most valuable object as being a decorative dagger shaped like a lightning bolt. The dagger was created from a rare metal alloy. Descriptions of other pieces are not given."

Shenda frowned and leaned back in her chair. She had hoped for more. "Thank you, Lais. Please store the articles in their entirety for later reference."

"Acknowledged."

"Well, I guess that's about all we can do for now," she said with a sigh.

"Oh, I believe there's something we can do," Logan said.

She looked at him. It was a mistake. Molten gold eyes locked on shimmering emerald, trapping her.

"Come here," he said, rising and extending a hand to her.

Her heart started to hammer. Her breathing accelerated. And her body quickened. All the result of a single potent scrutiny. Like an asteroid drawn inexorably into the sun which would mean its end, Shenda rose to take his hand.

Sixteen

The *Eagle* emerged from hyperspace and Logan fixed his gaze on the light-studded structure known as Olympus with hope glowing in his eyes. "It's here," he murmured. "It has to be."

Space Station Olympus was an imposing structure. Five hundred million tons of revolving metal, it was the size of a small moon; but there the similarity to any natural formation ended. Two large central cylinders formed an X, and each arm of the X was capped by an enormous globular-shaped section. The spherical ends of the station's four limbs sported a total of a thousand spiky columns, each of which represented an adjustable docking bay door for a large space vessel. Unlike the docking bay on the Duana moon for utilization only by smaller ships, these bays were airlocked shafts which attached to a ship's outer hatch anchoring it and providing direct access from the ship to the station.

The docking facilities for smaller craft, like the *Eagle*, consisted of smaller enclosures very similar to that used on the Duana moon. These bays, located on the surface of the spherical ends of the station, occupied every square inch of space available between the bases of the air-lock shafts that sprouted up like tentacles. Despite the abundance of bays, however, with the escalation in the number of small ships traveling the galaxy in recent years, the station was hard-pressed to keep up with the demand for facilities.

Shenda could see a number of large ships in space dock: freighters, passenger cruisers, commercial ore transports and three gigantic Legion star-cruisers. Still, that wasn't an unusual number to be docked at any one time, so the observation didn't particularly concern her. What did worry her was how she and Logan were going to manage to dock the *Eagle*. The second they transmitted the ship's identity, the Station's computer system would tag them as *fugitives*. Luckily, as a small ship, they didn't require direct human intervention from a controller in order to obtain authorization to dock. That at least was in their favor. So many small ships came and went at a station this size that it was impossible for the traffic controllers to monitor them all. And being a small ship, they avoided customs officials. The stations had long since given up on processing smaller ships— which came and went at incredibly short intervals—through customs. Rather, they used sniffers in the corridors. The hallway sniffers were very thorough and usually managed to locate and confiscate any contraband substances. So when the *Eagle* was tagged as a ship belonging to an owner with legality problems of some type, the notification would be added to a hundred others awaiting investigation by overworked station security. Shenda hoped the station Legionnaires were more overworked than usual.

She wanted to be able to land, complete their business, and be away again before an investigation was carried out.

She was probably hoping for too much.

"Are you ready?" Logan asked.

Shenda drew a deep breath and nodded. "Yes," she said, but she felt the tension in every muscle in her body. If they were caught here, escape would be. . . . She caught the word *impossible* and discarded it, refusing to think in such pessimistic terms. Not impossible, *extremely difficult*.

"Lais, transmit identity code and request docking information," Logan said.

"Acknowledged." The silence on the small bridge stretched, increasing the strain. Finally Lais spoke again. "We have authorization to dock on level D, section three. We have been assigned to docking bay three-five-seven."

Logan and Shenda sighed collectively. "Let's go, Lais," Logan said. He looked at Shenda. "I'm going to let Lais handle the entire docking procedure. That way she can respond to any computerized questions and directions."

Shenda nodded without comment; it was a good idea.

The *Eagle* suddenly spiraled toward the space station at an incredible speed. A pair of orange doors opened up before them, and then they were inside. Within two minutes, Lais set the ship down gently on the assigned thruster pad. Impatiently, Logan and Shenda watched the bay doors close and the exterior atmospheric readings slowly return to the constitution necessary to sustain human life.

"All right," Logan said, "Let's go." He picked up the tracker from where it rested on the console and passed it to Shenda. Intercepting her quizzical expression, he shrugged. "If it picks up a signal in Marnier's quarters, we won't go in. At least not until we figure out how to circumvent whatever Marnier has planned."

As she attached the tracker to her waistband, Logan reached to aid her and the weapons he carried beneath his jacket became briefly visible. Once again, the strange weapon that Shenda had labeled *Fortunan* caught her eye. "What exactly *is* that thing?" she asked.

"What?" Confusion written on his features, Logan frowned at her, his mind obviously on other things.

"That?" She indicated the weapon, recognizable as such only because it was shaped similarly to a laser gun.

"Oh." Logan's brow cleared. "It's an antique Earth-style projectile weapon. In many cases we find them more effective for dealing with wild animals on Fortuna than lasers or stunners. They're very loud, and often the noise alone is enough to deter an animal." As he'd made the explanation he'd knelt to open a small compartment to the left of his seat. Now he straightened with a small black rectangular device in hand.

"What's that?" Shenda frowned curiously at it.

He sighed. "A security de-scrambler. Just how did you think we were going to get into Marnier's apartment?" He carefully stowed the item in an oversize inside pocket of his jacket.

"But . . ." Shenda halted as she realized the foolishness of the admonishment that had hovered on her tongue. She'd been about to point out that the de-scrambler was illegal. "Never mind," she said.

He nodded and grasped her arm. "Come on."

Shenda would have liked to learn more about the curious antique weapon he carried, but recognized that now was not the time. "You'd better make certain that your jacket conceals the weapons, or we could end up being detained by an overly zealous corridor security officer." Although the carrying of weapons was commonplace on the stations, authorities did attempt to discourage the practice—especially among civilians. Swatting the sensor panel to close the hatch, Shenda followed Logan from the ship.

Logan nodded without comment, and proceeded to fasten the button on his jacket as they crossed the docking bay. The door to the station opened as the floor sensors registered their approach and ... they entered another world. A world of noise and confusion where arriving captains and crews jostled for space with departing ship personnel weighted down with purchases made while on leave. A world where swaggering, staggering personnel in possession of illegally retained liquor argued belligerently with the overworked Legionnaires currently serving as station security. A world of chaos.

"We need to find a computer terminal that can give us a map of the station," Shenda shouted above the din. "Follow me."

Logan nodded and studied everything around him with observant, wary eyes. It was a full ten minutes before Shenda drew to a halt in front of an establishment calling itself the *Oasis*. Logan stared at her in surprise. "A bar?" he asked incredulously.

She smiled. "You'd be surprised at how much

business is conducted in a place like this. More importantly for our purposes, every table in here is equipped with a terminal." She pushed open the door and they entered a dimly lit, rather gloomy establishment that, despite its obvious popularity, was a few decibels quieter than the corridor.

They paused for an instant in the entry, and Logan used the time to catalog the place and its occupants as he sought a vacant table. The recycled air smelled cool and fresh after the myriad of scents that permeated the corridor outside. A number of servo-droids were in the process of delivering orders to tables, and Logan scanned the faces of the occupants. He saw no one he recognized. "There," he said, gesturing with his chin to a table near the back of the room which would allow them an unobstructed view of the door.

Once seated, Shenda pressed a sensor panel on the edge of the table prompting a touch-sensitive, backlit computer screen to appear within the glossy black surface of the table. "There's a minimum mandatory order in here," she murmured. "But I'm ravenous anyway. How about you?"

Logan nodded, looking warily around. "I could use a meal, as long as it's a quick one."

Shenda nodded. "We'll make it quick." After studying the menu briefly, she ordered a Martian Sunset and a plate of green vegetables with dip. Logan chose a cup of coffee—actually a synthesized blend since the rarity of coffee plants made the real thing more precious than diamonds—and a turkey steak with salad.

While they waited for their order, Shenda used the touch-sensitive display to call up a directory of permanent residents and a map of the station.

A second later, Logan pointed. "Darren Marnier," he said in an undertone. "He's listed on level six, corridor three-A, suite forty-one fifty-seven."

Shenda searched the map. "That's here," she said, indicating a particular section. "We should be able to get there easily enough if we follow Market Alley to this elevator, access level six, and then take this horizontal lift. It's probably the safest course, too. We won't be noticeable in the crowd of shoppers."

"How do we find out if he's there or not?" Logan asked. "The last thing we need is to run into him."

Shenda frowned slightly. "The direct way, I guess. I'll call him." She touched a series of lighted keys on the table surface. "I'll use my father's I.D. code. If Darren answers I'll disconnect. With any luck, he'll think it's just an equipment malfunction."

They waited as the computer placed the call. After a few seconds a brief message flashed up: *Not in residence*. Shenda sighed. "He's not home."

Logan nodded and sat back just as the servo-droid arrived to deliver their orders. "I'll use my debit card," Shenda offered. Removing it from where it hung with her dogtags around her neck, she extended it to the robot. Logan's card would have been confiscated at the time of his arrest, she knew. Her card disappeared into a slot, triggered a brief flash of lights as the appropriate funds were transferred and then reappeared. Regaining it, Shenda slipped it into her pocket and watched the droid until it moved out of earshot. Nothing of vital importance was ever said in the presence of a servo-droid because they made excellent listening devices and could be programmed to record conversations.

A few minutes later, stomachs satisfied even if their palates had not had sufficient time to enjoy the meal, Shenda and Logan left the *Oasis* and headed for Market Alley. Shops of every size and description lined the wide central corridor known as Market Alley for a distance that had to equal almost a mile. Merchants who had been unable to afford shop space had erected licensed kiosks. These stands crowded every available corner as credit-hungry merchants vied with each other for customer attention. Food inherent to every ethnic and religious group imaginable was offered in a variety of formats: on disposable plates, in edible bowls, on sticks, in bags. The scents blended into one unappetizing olfactory assault. There were shops boasting the latest in electronic gadgetry and crystalline technology. Kiosks advertising psychic forecasting. Erotica booths. The variety was mind-boggling. Clothing, as varied and original as its creators could make it, hung from stands or lay folded on tables in colorful displays designed to draw attention and lure the potential customer within range of a rapacious shop-keeper's persuasive tongue. Shenda longingly eyed a pair of jumpsuits that looked as though they'd been created with her in mind. Unfortunately, she would just have to wait a little longer to take care of her personal wardrobe problem.

Shenda drew to a sudden halt at an electronics shop as she spied a sign advertising exactly what she needed: a miniature camera within a very fashionable broach. Perfect! She'd been wondering how she was going to gather the proof she needed. She looked at Logan, who had drawn to a halt at her side. "I think that could prove useful. I'll just be a moment." As he nodded, she withdrew her debit card and quickly negotiated a price with the merchant. A mere two minutes later, her purchase complete, Shenda fastened the attractive piece of jewelry to her lapel.

Logan studied it without comment, his expression grave, his thoughts obviously concerned with what they were about to attempt. "Ready?"

She nodded, and they resumed their journey through the human crush of Market Alley.

"Have the body you've always wanted!" called a Body Shop proprietor wearing only an elaborate lacy tattoo and a metallic g-string. She stepped in front of Shenda, barring her way and forcing eye contact. "In a matter of hours we can create the new you!"

Shenda, left with little choice, halted. She looked up at the statuesque blonde, meeting her gaze. "Alexis Calder," she said. "Promising reincarnation-on-demand again, I see. I thought you'd learned your lesson when I shut you down on Apollo. Keep promising more than you can deliver and you'll end up with another battery of complaints filed against you."

The blonde smiled, but her midnight eyes remained as cold as space. "There's always somebody willing to pay for a dream, Corporal Ridell. And always another place to set up shop. In fact," she said, reaching out to run a finger down Shenda's cheek, "you could use a little help yourself. A tuck here, some augmentation there. I could work wonders. I'd even give you a discount."

"Sorry, Alexis. I'm not foolish enough to let you anywhere near me with a laser."

The blonde's smile widened. "Too bad."

Shenda returned the mirthless gesture. "If you want to stay in business, you'd better make sure the complaints you accumulate don't reach my ears." Without waiting for the blonde to comment, she sidestepped and continued on her way.

"What was that about?" Logan asked.

Shenda shrugged. "I don't like the way she does

business: feeding on people's dreams and insecurities, always promising more than she can deliver. So, when I was assigned to Apollo on my last active tour, I shut her down. Unfortunately, she only has to wait a few months or move on to open up shop again."

They'd negotiated more than three-quarters of the length of Market Alley before the bank of elevators that was their destination came into view. Floor sensors announced their approach and one of the doors in the bank of six opened. Shenda and Logan stepped inside.

"State your destination please," the elevator computer prompted.

"Level six," Shenda responded.

A scant ten seconds later, the elevator doors opened to reveal a wide beige corridor. They stepped across the corridor into the horizontal lift.

"Destination please."

"Corridor three-A," Shenda said.

A moment later, the doors opened. Once again they looked at a monochromatic beige corridor. The only break in the prevalent beige was the occasional potted plant. As they stepped from the elevator, arrows on the wall indicated the direction of the apartment numbers: 4150 and up were to their left.

After the tumult of Market Alley, the deserted hallway seemed unnaturally silent. "Where is everybody?" Logan asked in a hushed voice.

Shenda shrugged. "This is a residential area. There wouldn't be much traffic." Still, she found herself looking around apprehensively. Was it abnormally quiet?

The strain of the situation was beginning to wear on Logan. He had no choice but to be here doing exactly what he was doing, yet he fervently wished he could have been anyplace else. Saints above! Where the hell was 4157? He looked around. Still not a soul in sight. Shouldn't there have been somebody returning from a visit or a shopping trip?

"I don't like this," he whispered to Shenda. "Is there anything on the tracker?"

She checked and shook her head, casting a glance over her shoulder. "Nothing." They walked on in tense silence. "There!" she whispered suddenly. "That's it."

Logan followed her pointing finger with his eyes and nodded: 4157, that was it. Again scrutinizing the area, Logan retrieved the tracker from Shenda and carefully approached the door.

The small screen remained blank. Since the tracker was designed to pick up a signal light years away, they should be safe . . . for the time being. Returning the tracker to Shenda, he set to work with the security de-scrambler. Directing the device at the palm-print identifier, behind which lay the security system, Logan depressed a series of buttons—programming into it exactly what type of security he believed they were dealing with. Within seconds, numerical codes began to flash across the tiny display.

"What's it doing?" Shenda asked in a hoarse whisper.

"Security computers store everything in numeric sequences. The de-scrambler is seeking the numerical pattern that matches the record of one of the handprints authorized to open this door. When it finds it, the door will open."

Shenda nodded, and glanced anxiously over her shoulder to ensure that the corridor remained clear. "Will it take long?"

Logan shrugged. "There's no way of knowing."

A moment later Shenda sighed in relief as the door to Marnier's apartment clicked and swished open. Activating the newly purchased camera pinned to her lapel, she cast another hasty look in both directions down the corridor before following Logan into the apartment. The minute they set foot on the sensor panel inside the apartment, the door closed behind them and the lights came on. Surprise immobilized them. The suite that lay before them was magnificent . . . and immaculate.

The entry on which they stood was approximately ten feet wide and just as deep. To one side, against the wall, a small trickling fountain had been installed. Green plants flourished where they'd been planted on the artificial rock face at the edge of the fountain.

Descending three steps, Logan and Shenda entered the living area of the apartment. Already large and opulent, the snow-white carpeting and furniture made it seem even larger. On the wall to their left, a huge holographic wall mural alleviated the colorlessness of the chamber. It depicted a tropical paradise of white sands and a gently rolling ocean in an unusual shade of aquamarine. Other items in the chamber picked up the same blue-green hue of the ocean: cushions, vases, sofatables.

Shenda thought it was beautiful.

"Not exactly the kind of place where you can see yourself throwing a birthday party for your child, is it?" Logan whispered drily.

Shenda drew to a halt, struck by the sudden realization that their thoughts had been so different, and stared at Logan's back for a moment as he moved ahead of her. Then, she viewed the chamber again, seeing it with new eyes. No. No, it wasn't the kind of place where you'd give your child a birthday party. But . . . it was exactly the kind of place in which she'd been raised. She had always had her birthday parties in the kitchen, with the household help. And if she was lucky, her father had stopped by to give her a peck on the cheek and a present. Most times, she'd simply received the present, relayed through her nanny. Looking again at Logan's back, she hastily moved forward to catch up.

Her heels clicked momentarily on the aquamarine tiling of the floor in the dining area, and the noise startled her. She realized that the uneasy feeling that had haunted her in the corridor was still with her. Why? She attempted to alleviate the unproductive worry by once again focusing on her surroundings, studying the dining room. The difference in the flooring of the living area and the dining room was in fact the only separation between the two rooms, for there were no walls. A large white lacquered table and buffet gleamed, perfect and unused from the center of the dining area. As she moved quietly past it, Shenda found herself trailing her fingers admiringly over the surface of the table. She recognized the quality when she saw it. But Swan was right. She eyed the clay bowl with its bouquet of aquamarine roses and white baby's breath. This apartment was not the kind of place ever meant to see a child's sticky fingers. She studied Logan's broad back. What kind of birthday parties had he had? she wondered.

"I think that's the office," Logan whispered over his shoulder, pointing at a door ahead and to the right.

Shenda nodded and frowned thoughtfully. "Why are we whispering?"

Logan shrugged. "Because it's appropriate."

He was right. It was. Despite her attempt to ignore it, her apprehension increased.

They moved past the doorway to the kitchen. A single glance inside told Shenda that it was unoccupied and equally impeccable. The countertops had been constructed of gleaming stainless steel. The walls, floor and cabinets were pristine white. Not a single misplaced item marred the order. Logan disappeared through a doorway, and she hastily moved after him.

What struck a person immediately upon entering the office was the contrasting darkness of its decor. Richly varnished wooden bookshelves occupied three walls, every available shelf filled with rare, antique books. Even Shenda would not have dared to hazard a guess as to the value of the collection. *Inestimable* was the only word that came to mind. The fourth wall consisted of a backlit holographic light panel designed to resemble a large window, camouflaging its true purpose: the provision of full-spectrum lighting. A huge, highly polished teakwood desk occupied the center of the room. As Logan moved toward it, the bookshelves drew Shenda.

Her eyes roamed the ancient titles at random, picking out works with which she was familiar only through a disk-reader: *Uncle Tom's Cabin, Tom Sawyer, Jurassic Park,* classics all. There were history books and science books and books on social issues. More books than Shenda ever before had seen except within the confines of a library vault. Tenderly, almost reverently, she extracted a copy of one of her favorite classics, *Gone with the Wind,* from the shelf and opened it. To her surprise she had difficulty reading some of it. Of course! The books themselves had been written in

Mid-Modern English. The versions she had read had been translated into New-Modern. Logan had said he knew Mid-Modern English; he would be able to read them. Carefully replacing the book, Shenda determined to take a class in Mid-Modern English as soon as it was feasible. Then, she turned to examining the bookcase and its contents for anything pertaining to their search.

Logan, seated at Marnier's desk, searched it for anything useful, either the artifacts themselves or something that would lead to them. So far nothing. He checked the drawer on his right again. Did it seem a little shallower on the inside than its outside dimensions suggested? Removing a stack of files, he placed them on top of the desk and examined the drawer more thoroughly. As his fingers moved along the edges of the drawer, they brushed against something and he heard an almost inaudible click. The front half of the drawer bottom lifted slightly. A false bottom! He'd been right.

Opening the compartment, he peered into it. A single small item occupied the space: a holodisk case. *Dendron II* had been scrawled across the case in a man's bold writing. Lifting it carefully from the drawer, Logan checked it to ensure that it did indeed contain a disk, then gave a hasty glance around the room. Not finding what he sought, he looked at Shenda. "You haven't seen a holo projector, have you?"

Shenda looked over her shoulder at him. "No. Why?"

In answer, he held up the small silver disk.

"I'll check the credenza," she volunteered. A moment later she straightened from her search of the low cabinet, holo player in hand. "Here it is." She set the small electronic device on the desk in front of him.

Logan studied the unfamiliar model briefly before finding the means to activate it. Then, dropping the disk in the slot, he turned it on. Almost immediately a miniature representation of some type of ceremony being enacted shimmered into existence. They studied the depiction carefully. It was impossible to tell the sex of the ceremony participants, each of whom wore a shapeless black robe complete with hood, as they moved in a strange dance-like formation. The sound of their voices chanting alien syllables filled the room, swelling and receding and swelling again in a manner that raised gooseflesh on Shenda's body. This was familiar. Somehow, in some way, she had seen this before. Yet she knew she had never seen it with her own eyes.

Abruptly she was reminded of Dr. Tredway's certitude that she would have inherited fragments of memories from the lives of her Obsidian Order ancestors. Was this such a memory? She observed the scene more closely. The walls of the chamber in which the robed figures danced seemed to be as black as their robes. Near the front of the chamber, a small dais containing three pulpits rose above the participants. Behind each pulpit stood another cloaked figure. Her gaze fixed on the central figure as he raised a dagger which had been twisted and tortured into the shape of a lightning bolt. *Kris*. The identity of the object came to her from an untapped source deep in her mind. Her eyes moved beyond the kris to the figure holding it. He, too, was familiar; this realization did not come from the distant past, but her own instincts.

"That's Darren," she murmured to Logan.

"Who?"

"In the center."

He nodded, and they returned to their observation.

The more Shenda watched of the strange ceremony, the more certain she was that there was something . . . off kilter about it. It wasn't completely wrong, yet it wasn't right either. Frowning, she tried to determine what bothered her about the scene, but it eluded her.

She watched Marnier, wondering what he was up to. What had this strange ceremony to do with his ambitions? What purpose did it serve?

Before she could find answers for any of the questions in her mind, the representation pulled back, revealing the orderly exit of the participants from the cave into a wide cavernous corridor. As each of the cult members exited the cave, they went down on one knee to brush their lips against the hands of three men. Shenda assumed they were the same three men who had occupied the pulpits. And, as she perceived Darren's position of power among these people, she began to understand his purpose in reviving the Tridon. Reviving *the Tridon*! Those words, too, had surfaced unexpectedly. Suddenly, Shenda realized what had been wrong about the ceremony. The robes of the leaders. They should have been gold, the embodiment of all that was bright and good.

The next scene revealed a number of people wearing breathing masks as they exited the cavern and entered a steaming jungle clearing brilliantly illuminated by the rising sun of a new day. A new day on Dendron II.

The holo ended abruptly, winking out of existence, and Shenda turned to Logan. She saw the disappointment in his eyes. They hadn't even seen so much as the shadow of anything that could be likened to one of his artifacts. Shenda rested her hand reassuringly on his shoulder. "If we don't find what we're looking for here, at least we've added another possibility to our list of locations. Of course, Dendron II is not exactly the type of place we want to go wandering around on, which is probably exactly why Marnier chose it."

"Yeah," he said in a low voice, and glanced around the room. "Did you find anything even remotely questionable?"

Shenda shook her head. "Nothing. No hinges on the bookshelves. No safe that I can find . . . unless one of the books themselves is counterfeit, but that would take too long to check. Not even an ornament that could be Fortunan."

Logan sighed. Damn! He'd been positive that if they were going to find anything, it would be in the office. "All right. Then I guess we search the rest of the place." Removing the small holodisk from the projector, he replaced it in its case and returned it to the drawer. "Here," he said, passing the projector to Shenda, "you'd better put this back where you found it."

Leaving the office, they moved, by tacit agreement, into the first of the bedrooms. This room, in stark contrast to the orderliness of the rest of the apartment, looked as though it had been torn apart. Lacy clothing lay discarded in careless heaps on the teal-green carpeting. Jewelry lay strewn over the surface of a dresser tangled in and around expensive perfume bottles and exclusive cosmetics. Shiny candy wrappers littered the surface of a bedside table. Even the bed remained unmade. This chamber was obviously inhabited by a less fastidious person. Quickly, Logan circumnavigated the room, checking behind the two pictures that hung on the whitewashed walls, reaching into the closet to examine the shelves there. Nothing.

Deciding to give the dresser a more thorough examination for some of the jewelry which had been stolen from his shipments, he moved back to it, shoved aside a tangle of gold chains and froze. There, beneath the jumbled mass of jewelry, was a picture of Lilah. What was it doing here? Who was she to Marnier? Carefully extracting the photograph, he lifted it to examine it.

"What's the matter?" Shenda hissed anxiously from across the room as she noticed him standing there.

He looked at her. "Do you know who this is?" he asked, flipping the photograph around for her to see.

She frowned at him. "Sure. It's Delilah Marnier, Darren's step-sister." She eyed him suspiciously. "Why?"

Logan swallowed. Stepsister? Stars above, how deep did this conspiracy of Marnier's go? Thank the Saints he had never allowed himself to consider her as spousal material. He was astute enough to realize that the hurt he had felt at Lilah's leaving stemmed from a sense of betrayal rather than love. He looked at Shenda, who was still waiting for a reply to her question. "It's nothing," he said, shaking his head. "I thought I knew her, but I guess I was mistaken."

"Well, come on," Shenda urged. "Let's hurry. I want to get out of here."

They moved into the other bedchamber, which was quite obviously Marnier's. The walls, carpeting and ceiling were completely white, and the furniture black lacquer. The bed, covered with an aquamarine satin spread, had not a wrinkle. The dresser, devoid of ornamentation with the exception of a man's jewelry case, was spotless. Even the suits hanging in the closet seemed to be hung at precisely spaced intervals.

Once again, Shenda and Logan searched the room swiftly, carefully and thoroughly. There was nothing of use in any of the drawers or closets. Even the locked armoire, once opened, failed to yield anything of interest. A single huge picture hung over the bed. Shenda knelt on the bed to peer behind it. As she lifted the frame away from the wall, two things happened almost simultaneously. They heard a faint click, then a soft whoosh as a concealed door to the left of the bed slid open. And the tracker, which had inadvertently been left on, began to beep insistently. The noise sawed at Shenda's raw nerves, prompting her to grab the device from her waistband and shut it off.

For a fraction of a second, she and Logan stared at each other. Then, concurrently, they arrived at the same conclusion. "It's a trap!"

Aware that Marnier could arrive with a squad of Legionnaires within scant minutes, Shenda felt a stab of panic. She forced it down. Barely aware of her action, she leapt over the bed without care for the expensive spread. Instantly, Logan was at her side. Uncertain just what form Marnier's trap might take, they looked warily into the hidden vault. There, on six sturdy, velvet-sheathed shelves rested a number of the missing archeological items. And directly in front of them rested a figurine of a pair of golden wings. "Is that what you're looking for?" Shenda asked.

Logan nodded, studying the door with anxious eyes, as aware of the need for caution as he was of the need for haste. "I'll stand in the doorway, to prevent the door from closing on us, while you step in and get the figurine."

Shenda nodded, and moved forward without hesitation. As she lifted the gold statuette, a small transmitter fell from its base. Marnier's idea of a joke. Furious, she picked it up, threw it on the floor and ground it beneath the heel of her boot. A quick glance at the rest of the shelves revealed that the crystal was not in plain sight. Damn! She needed something, anything to take with her. She needed proof. The need for speed gnawed at her as her eyes desperately raked the shelves. "Point out something that isn't yours," she demanded. "Anything that could have been stolen from somewhere else."

Logan's eyes skimmed the shelves. "There." He pointed back along the shelves. "That ring." The ring to which he pointed contained a huge ruby and appeared to be made of platinum.

Shenda handed the winged figurine to Logan and raced to grab the indicated ring. Shoving it unceremoniously onto the middle finger of her right hand, backwards to conceal the stone, she exited the vault and ran toward the bedroom door. Instantly, Logan was on her heels, the precious figurine cradled in the crook of one arm. Subliminally, they heard the vault door close behind them as soon as the sensors no longer detected Logan's presence, but their attention was now focused ahead. On escape.

"Is there another way out of one of these apartments?" Logan asked, no longer attempting to lower his voice, as they rushed through the opulent living room.

Shenda shook her head. "Not that I know of. But if we can make it to the elevators, we'll increase the odds. We'll have an entire station to hide in."

She leapt up the three stairs at the entrance and

ran forward. The sensors detected their approach. The door opened. And Darren Marnier, arms folded casually across his chest, stood there to greet them, a dozen Legionnaires at his back.

Seventeen

Her mind racing, Shenda could only stare at him as four Legionnaires moved forward, two to grasp Logan's arms and two to flank her. "Disarm them," Marnier ordered in the same tone one might expect him to order breakfast.

Abruptly remembering the small concealed camera on her lapel, Shenda unobtrusively reached up to shut it off before the Legionnaire body scanners could pick up its faint signal. She couldn't afford to have it detected.

She had just completed the action when Marnier pinned her with his intensely cold blue-eyed gaze. "Abandoning my hospitality so soon?" A small, satisfied smile curved his lips. "Perhaps a prison ambience will be more to your liking? You are, after all, aiding and abetting a convicted criminal."

Shenda knew she must immediately take the upper hand, at least verbally. "Don't be absurd,

Darren." She injected every bit of icy hauteur of which she was capable into those few syllables, although it was difficult with Legionnaire hands roaming her body seeking concealed weapons. Self-preservation was the key here. She could not allow herself to be imprisoned—either in a facility or in a marriage. If she was incarcerated, both she and Logan were as good as dead. There was nothing she could do to help him right now, but if she remained free, she could seek a means to aid him later.

Determined not to appear frightened or cowed in any way, she looked down her aristocratic nose at Marnier—a skill in itself since he was several inches taller than she—and continued in a voice dripping with censure. "We both know that, had your people done their jobs properly, this situation would never have progressed to this point."

Meeting Logan's gaze briefly, she tried to send a message of apology for what she was about to say, a message of reassurance and trust, but she was uncertain if she succeeded. And there was no time to hesitate. She returned her gaze to Marnier. "If I had not used every bit of ingenuity at my command to stay alive, in all likelihood I would not even be standing here before you." Her voice crackled with ice. "I deliver a criminal into your very hands, and you reward me with talk of prison. Thank you so very much for your concern."

She saw Marnier's features tighten slightly at the sarcasm in her voice. Had she gone too far? Would the embarrassment afforded him by allowing the assembled Legionnaires to hear her words jeopardize her position even further? But she'd had no choice.

The seconds that had passed since the door

opened stretched into a minute. Finally, with his eyes fixed unblinkingly on her face, Darren nodded. Without a word to her, he looked at Logan, stepped forward to remove the gold figurine from the grasp of the Legionnaire who'd confiscated it and spoke to the assembled squad. "Take him to the interrogation room. Await me there."

Marnier had just turned back to face her when all hell broke loose. There was a horrible masculine scream of rage, the thud of flesh meeting flesh, and two unconscious Legionnaires on the entry floor. Logan stood tall and poised at the bottom of the steps. In the instant before the remaining Legionnaires blocked him from her view, Shenda's startled gaze met Logan's. Desperation swam in the depths of his eyes, and the beginnings of a hurt that stabbed her with its potency. The sudden cognizance that he believed she had betrayed him lanced through her in the form of an intense emotional pain that constricted her breathing. Yet she could do nothing but watch with an impassive face as the Legionnaires fought to subdue him.

So intensely was she concentrating on the facade of her own dispassion that, for a number of minutes, she had only a vague awareness of the battle taking place in Marnier's once-immaculate living room . . . and the extent of Logan's deadly skill. Shenda realized that she was observing the combat process of a Kanisi guardian. He moved with an economy of motion and a lightning speed not even approximated by any training to be had in the Stellar Legion. It was obvious that his combat proficiency far outweighed hers, and had he ever truly been desirous of it, he could have killed her almost effortlessly.

As it was, he disabled six of the Legionnaires

before he was subdued. Yet even when it was obvious that he could do no more damage, blows continued to rain down on him, delivered by vengeful Legionnaires in response to the affront he had presented to their defeated comrades. Shenda's hands curled into fists as she struggled to control the urge to intervene. Her nails cut crescent moons into her palms. And still the beating went on.

Finally, carefully schooling her expression, she looked at Marnier. He was watching her with the intentness of a predatory cat observing its prey. This was a test, Shenda realized. He was waiting for her to intercede. "I don't know about you, Darren, but witnessing a murder before dinner tends to ruin my appetite." Even as her instincts screamed at her to do something, her tone conveyed only casual disgust. She stepped around Marnier as though to leave.

Catching her arm in an iron grip, he flicked his gaze from her to the debacle taking place in his once-immaculate apartment. "Enough!" His voice, although barely raised, cracked whip-like through the room. Almost instantly, the sound of the blows ceased. "I need him coherent enough to speak. Take him." With a jerk of his chin he indicated the exit.

Slowly, trying to prepare herself for the sight she would see, Shenda turned to watch the Legionnaires drag Logan from the room. The sight was no better and no worse than she had expected after such a battering. Blood ran from his nose and a cut high on his cheekbone. One of his eyes was rapidly swelling shut. His lips were split and bloody. And he moved in a way that told her his ribs had been injured. Her heart ached for him, but she knew he would heal—the prison officials would see to that . . . unless they received specific orders to the contrary. As a condemned prisoner, Logan's organs were too valuable to allow him to die in an uncontrolled situation. And that could undoubtedly work to his advantage. The time it would take him to recuperate, combined with the public awareness of his situation, might grant him the time he needed to successfully sue for a retrial. Provided, of course, that Marnier did not decide to use his influence to hasten the execution. But Shenda was betting that he wouldn't risk that while the case was in the public eye.

Logan gasped in pain as the Legionnaires steered him roughly toward the door. Again, Shenda clenched her hands, driving her nails into her palms to control the urge to go to him. A moment later one of the Legionnaires deliberately jostled his side and he stumbled, clutching his ribs. Shenda gritted her teeth and took note of the man's face, engraving it in her memory should the opportunity to exact retribution ever arise.

Just as Logan was about to be dragged from the room, he seemed to summon strength from some inner well. "Shenda!" he called loudly in a voice hoarse with agony and desperation. Her name became a stabbing weapon aimed straight for her heart. "Shenda!" Fighting off the restraining hands for a fraction of a second, he looked back over his shoulder, meeting her gaze. And with that one tortured glance he communicated a message of hurt and love and hope and despair. It was a plea that tore her soul in two. An entreaty that nearly shattered her control. And then he was gone, hauled unceremoniously from the room.

The sight of him in that moment would be forever engraved upon her memory. She knew that somehow, in some way, she would free him. Not because she believed he was innocent, although she did. Not because it was the right thing to do, although she felt it was. Not even because she had come to care for him as a friend. But because part of her had gone with him out that door . . . because she loved him! That realization, coming as it did in the midst of what was already a traumatic experience, was almost beyond her capacity to endure. Forgetting to school her expression, she stared at the backs of the departing Legionnaires with a stunned expression on her face.

Marnier studied her. "Are you all right?" His cool tone was devoid of any pretense at solicitude.

Shenda jerked her eyes back to his coldly handsome face. "What? Oh . . . yes. Yes, of course." She swallowed, desperately seeking her next move and managed a composed smile. "Well, if we're through here, I think I'd better be going. I haven't been home in some time, and I really would like a change of clothing."

Darren allowed a tight smile to curve his lips as he shook his head and moved into his living room. "Shenda, Shenda. You do amuse me." Righting one of the living room tables, he set the winged figurine upon it and turned to pin her with his gaze. "Did you really think I would allow you to escape the consequences of your actions that easily?"

"What do you mean?"

He shook his head. "You're simply not that obtuse, my dear. However, this once, I will explain. You may bathe and change your clothing *here*. I'm certain Delilah won't mind, and you are of a similar size. Then, Shenda, you will make a statement retracting your earlier transmission. You will state for the populace, as you implied to me, that your marriage was a ruse to facilitate your escape from the colonial." His lips twisted with distaste on the final word. "Do I make myself understood?"

A sense of stillness invaded Shenda, the extraordinary calm of someone in danger. She could not do as Darren demanded. A retraction could well seal Logan's fate. Despite his physical condition, Marnier could have the execution date moved up. Yet she too was in danger, and right now she was Logan's only hope of liberation. She would have to tread boldly, but carefully, to triumph.

Strolling slowly forward, trailing her fingertips over the surface of a white lacquered sofa-table, she held Darren's gaze. "Why should I?" she sneered softly. "I don't like the way you've acted lately. What made you think that by simply announcing our *non-existent* engagement you could force me into marrying you when I had already declined your proposal?"

She gloried in the brief flash of uncertainty in Marnier's eyes. He had not expected her to attack. She could see the impotent anger grow in him. "You will do as you are told or you *yourself* will suffer, Shenda. The colonial is, after all, already dead. His death is a mere formality now."

Once again, Shenda smiled, trailing her fingers over the back of the sofa. "I'm not afraid of you," she said. "What can you possibly do to me?" Her mind supplied pictures in answer to her belligerent question. Pictures of her body thrown casually in a refuse heap—robbed. Pictures of her body floating in space—the victim of an unfortunate accident. Pictures of her body in the jaws of some jungle denizen on Dendron II—an untimely disappearance. But her face remained cold and impassive.

"Don't push me, Shenda. You *will* do as you are told."

"Or, what?" Shenda stilled the tremor within her. She had to push. She had to know the extent of what Marnier knew about her. "You'll spank me? Revoke my generous allowance?"

Darren watched her with narrowed eyes. A pulse leapt in his temple, betraying the depths of the anger he camouflaged beneath his cultured tone. "I've had you investigated, Shenda. Thoroughly." His vigilant gaze catalogued every nuance of her expression. Shenda waited. The silence stretched.

"And . . ." she prompted with a sardonically raised brow. "Let me guess." She tapped her chin thoughtfully with one long elegant finger, never taking her gaze from Darren's face. "Are you blackmailing me with the murder of a frog in biology class?"

Marnier's brow darkened, a definite sign of anger on a face that rarely revealed emotion. It was almost enough to make Shenda retreat a step, but she dared not. "There is a seven-month period in your late teens when you disappeared, Shenda. Need I say more?" His eyes clung to her face with hawklike intentness.

Oh, stars, he knew! Panic almost shattered her equanimity. And then she perceived the peculiar watchfulness of his expression. Or did he only want her to think he knew? "So . . ." she said breathily, nodding as though she finally understood. "You're blackmailing me for taking a holiday."

Marnier struck with almost blinding speed, taking Shenda completely by surprise. Grasping her throat in an iron grip, he simultaneously twisted her right arm painfully behind her back. Agony shot through her shoulder, slammed into the base of her skull, robbing her of strength. His grasp on her throat tightened, choking, constricting her breathing. "Bitch," he hissed, his face a scant inch from hers. "You will curb your viperous tongue and do what you are told. Do you understand me?"

Shenda stared at him, exultant even through her pain. He didn't know! He'd been bluffing, banking on the supposition that he would come up with something to use against her.

Frustrated by her silence, Darren tightened the hold on her throat and wrenched her arm a little higher. Despite herself, a gasp of pain escaped her. "It hurts, doesn't it?" he asked rhetorically, his eyes fixed with gleaming satisfaction on her face. "Now . . . answer me!"

Shenda stared at him, and could not believe she had ever believed herself in love with him. He was ugly, inhuman. A loathsome caricature of a man. She wanted nothing more than to drive her knee into his groin and watch him writhe on the floor at her feet. Unfortunately, she doubted that doing so would aid her situation. Thanks to him, she was unarmed. He had no doubt re-programmed the computer to open the door only in response to his voice, rather than the sensor. And although she had once been trained to kill with a blow to the nose, she had never done so and the details of the instructions escaped her. So even should she successfully disable him, she only invited a more violent and certain retribution for her temerity. No, she would wait . . . endure. He did not want her dead, not yet at any rate. So she would not fight back . . . but neither would she capitulate to his bullying tactics.

Looking him in the eye, steadfastly trying to ignore the agony in her shoulder, Shenda told him to do something particularly vile to himself, and braced herself for an increase in the intensity of the agony he inflicted. It never came. Instead, he studied her with an almost musing expression on his face and loosened the grip on her throat slightly while maintaining the pressure on her arm.

"You know, Shenda, I do not need to keep you alive to get what I need from you. I can get a wife anywhere. All I need from you are a few eggs. Once fertilized, they could be implanted into the womb of any woman I choose." He nodded and smiled slightly as though the idea pleased him. "And you, my dear, depending on how we get along within the next few hours, can either go your own way, or suffer an unfortunate accident on the operating table."

Horror numbed the pain in Shenda's arm. He was mad, she concluded. Absolutely, certifiably insane.

"And now," he said, releasing her and stepping back, "I really must see to your colonial friend. I want to learn more about the curse he believes is attached to the winged figurine. In the meantime, I suggest you use my absence to think about what I have said. You may, of course, avail yourself of the amenities." Nodding to her in the manner of a proper host taking his leave, he began walking toward the door. Shenda followed his progress with a feeling of incredulity. She'd heard of mercurial temperaments, but this . . . And then, as though suddenly struck by a thought, he pivoted to face her. "Do *you* by any chance know the nature of the curse?"

Shenda couldn't believe her ears. Did he really think she would tell him? Grant him access to the power of such a device? Besides, the secret was Logan's to reveal or not as he chose. "No," she said, and was immediately disgusted by the slight tremor in her voice. "I don't," she said more firmly.

"Oh, well, I'm sure the colonial will tell me. Eventually. Computer, open the door." Then, with a cold smile, he left the apartment.

The threat to Logan implicit in Marnier's words almost made Shenda wish she *had* told him, but her instincts insisted she had made the right decision. She waited three minutes, giving Darren enough time to reach the elevators, and then approached the door. "Computer, open the door." The door remained closed, the sensor panel immune to her presence, the computer tuned only to Marnier's voice. It was as she'd suspected: Marnier had imprisoned her in his apartment. Damn!

Pacing the apartment with determined strides, she sought a new course of action. "Computer," she said suddenly into the silence.

A short chime sounded. "What is your request?"

Shenda raised a brow. She still had some computer access then, but how extensive? "Contact the computer on board the *Eagle*, docking bay 357, level D, section 3."

"I'm sorry. All communication with that ship is restricted due to an impound directive."

Frustrated, Shenda struck her thigh with a fisted hand. All right, there was nothing she could do at the moment. She would simply have to stay vigilant and orchestrate her escape as soon as possible. She refused to consider the possibility that she might not escape. While she was here, she might as well take advantage of *the amenities*.

Stalking into Delilah's quarters—where was Delilah anyway?—Shenda hastily rummaged through the few items still remaining in the closet to find something suitable to wear. The task was not easy. Delilah apparently had a predilection for frilly, lacy clothing. Shenda wanted something functional, capable of withstanding the rigors of escape. She finally settled for a pair of opaque black hose with a subtle sheen and a fitted knee-length belted tunic, also black, with its sides slit to the waist. It had a large collar to which she could attach her camera, and a pocket into which she slipped the ring that Marnier's guards had overlooked. Then, aware that the finery would hardly look right with her combat boots, she searched the closet for some slightly dressier but serviceable footwear. Spying a pair of black flats, she thought for an instant she'd found just what she was looking for, until she looked at them more closely. They were huge; her feet would slip right out of them. Combat boots it was then, she decided with a grimace.

Feeling a strong identification with a caged animal, Shenda paced the apartment for almost two hours after completing her ablutions. Torturous questions echoed over and over in her mind. Where the hell was Marnier? What was taking so long? What were they doing to Logan? How soon would they transfer Logan back to Sentra? How was she going to manage to effect Logan's escape, a second time, from the Sentran prison? More importantly, how was she going to escape Marnier's clutches herself before she ended up on an operating table at the mercy of some unscrupulous surgeon?

The door chimed and opened. Shenda swiftly schooled her expression as Darren entered, his step-sister Delilah on his heels. Shenda hoped that Delilah's presence meant that the entire term of his absence had not been spent interrogating Logan.

Darren had barely nodded in her direction

when the computer spoke. "I have a private communication for you, sir."

"Source?"

"The communication code belongs to Phillip Nagami."

"I'll take it in my office," he said. Then, looking at first Shenda and then Delilah, he said, "Lilah, make our guest comfortable, will you?"

The statuesque blonde shrugged, eyeing Shenda with dislike. "Of course." As Darren strolled across the apartment in the direction of his office, she indicated the sofa. "Sit down." The invitation sounded like an order, but Shenda decided to sit. Delilah plucked a remote control from the floor where it had been thrown during the fracas and, pointing it at the tropical wall mural, depressed a button. Immediately, the mural split in two, each half sliding into the wall, to reveal an extensive and well-stocked bar. Delilah looked at her. "What would you like to drink?"

Knowing she could ill afford muddled wits, Shenda decided to forgo anything alcoholic. "Some vegetable juice would be fine, if you have it?"

Delilah shrugged. "Of course."

A moment later, she handed Shenda a glass of juice and then, her own drink in hand, chose a seat directly across from her. She proceeded to sit there, quietly sipping her drink and staring. Shenda stared back.

Delilah's blond hair was of a shade very similar to Darren's pale platinum, perhaps a couple of shades darker. Her blue eyes were definitely darker. She was tall and slender, her shapely form currently displayed most advantageously in a white, figure-hugging backless dress. Her light-golden skin revealed that she spent some time in a sunbed, for she was far too fair to come by the skin tone naturally.

Delilah sighed and placed her glass on the surface of a nearby table. "Logan makes an excellent lover, doesn't he?"

Shenda almost choked on a mouthful of juice. She lowered her glass to stare at Delilah. "Pardon me?" She couldn't have heard correctly!

Delilah's eyes widened innocently. "Oh, didn't he tell you?"

Shenda waited. The silence stretched as Delilah eyed her watchfully. She obviously wanted to provoke some kind of reaction. "Tell me˙ what?" Shenda asked finally.

"Why, that he and I had an affair. It lasted some time actually. Of course, it had to end when he was arrested, but . . ." She shrugged gracefully. "I was quite fond of him."

Suddenly Shenda remembered Logan's interest in Delilah's photograph. "How fascinating."

Delilah smiled. "Hmmm. I thought you might find it so."

But if what Delilah said was true, why hadn't Logan known who she was? "I find it odd, though, that when Logan saw your picture earlier, he didn't know your identity."

The blonde frowned slightly. "Where did he see my picture?"

"On your dresser."

"I see." Her eyes skimmed Shenda's face thoughtfully. "Well, the explanation is quite simple really. When we met, I introduced myself as Lilah, Lilah Myles."

"Why?"

Although she continued to watch Shenda observantly with her cold blue eyes, Delilah shrugged as though the matter was quite inconsequential. "It was Darren's idea."

Shenda set her empty juice glass down. "He wanted to insinuate you into Logan's life anonymously, to keep him informed of any major finds the Swans made. Correct?"

Delilah smiled. "How astute of you!" She sipped her beverage. "Yes, my association with Logan was . . . arranged."

No wonder Logan had assumed so readily that she'd betrayed him. He'd already been betrayed once.

"But I can't say that I didn't enjoy the alliance," Delilah continued, unaware of Shenda's thoughts. She licked her lips and the edge of her glass in a fashion that Shenda could only describe as suggestive. "As I said earlier, he is an excellent lover."

The blond bitch was trying to get a rise out of her. And dammit, it was working. Shenda wanted nothing more than to tear every strand of her lank blond hair out by the roots, but she controlled the impulse. Matching Delilah sophisticated smile for sophisticated smile, she shrugged. "I don't know. Actually, I thought him a bit, shall we say, prosaic."

"Really!" Delilah raised an artfully shaped brow in disbelief. Sipping her drink, she looked Shenda over from her carefully coiffed head to the tip of her combat-booted toes. "Perhaps the poor man simply lacked incentive." She clicked her meticulously manicured nails against the side of her glass.

Bitch! Shenda thought, but she only laughed softly and raised a raven-black brow. Ms. Delilah Marnier was obviously a master of the verbal dual; however, Shenda was no novice herself. "Touché, Delilah. Have you considered, however, that your own tastes—"

"Enough!" Darren's voice cracked whip-like through the room, startling both women. Shenda saw that he stood at the edge of the living room. How long had he been standing there? "I refuse to serve as referee." He looked at his step-sister. "Delilah, your tongue can be very useful, but I suggest that in the future you keep it leashed until I unleash it."

Delilah smiled. "Of course, my dear brother."

Darren's eyes narrowed marginally. "Shenda and I are leaving. If you promise to behave yourself, you may accompany us. Otherwise . . ." He left the alternative hanging in the air.

Delilah's eyes narrowed as she pinned her step-brother with a cold, hard stare. The contest was lost before it was begun. "Oh, all right," she capitulated churlishly a moment later.

Darren smiled. "Fine. Then, you have two minutes to ready yourself." As Delilah stalked from the room, he looked at Shenda. "Bring the figurine." With a gesture of his chin, he indicated the winged figurine that was so important to Logan.

"Why?"

"Because it is supremely important to the colonial and I don't plan to let it out of my sight." Which meant that he'd been unable to get Logan to tell him anything about it, Shenda surmised. "Bring it. And don't get any ideas." He removed his hands from his pockets long enough to show her that he carried both a laser and a stunner.

"Sure." Shenda picked up the statuette and stood waiting with Darren for Delilah. It didn't matter to her if he wanted to keep the winged figurine with him. In fact, it could actually work to her advantage. When she escaped she wouldn't have to come looking for it a second time.

A half hour later, after two elevator rides and a long walk down a virtually deserted corridor, they entered directly into a docking bay, stepping onto a metal-mesh ramp high above the floor. Once again, Darren had thwarted any hope Shenda had of fleeing. She had planned to create a diversion and escape when they traversed the busy docking area corridors. In hindsight, she realized that she should have anticipated that someone of Marnier's stature would have private access. She was going to have to start thinking smarter if she wanted to make a successful escape. Quarks!

From her position high above the docking bay floor, Shenda scrutinized Marnier's ship. It was a quantum-class ship very similar to the *Raven*, with the exception that it had been painted in four shades of blue. On its side was the representation of a black lightning bolt bisecting a huge red rising sun. Symbolism that meant something to Darren, no doubt, but at the moment it escaped her.

"Please." Darren directed her to the metal staircase and indicated that she should precede him.

Wordlessly Shenda did. Five minutes later, they were securely ensconced on Marnier's personal ship, the *Seeker*. Darren had taken the figurine from her and confined Shenda to quarters with orders to stay there until they reached their destination. A destination which, at this point in time, Marnier refused to reveal. With no idea of where they were heading, Shenda could not even plan. She lay on the hard, narrow berth in her assigned quarters and worried.

The more she thought about it, she had to concede that there was no way she was going to be able to get Logan out of Sentra alone. She'd need the help of the Legionnaires—Logan's Legionnaires—and a good-sized ship. The *Raven* was no longer an option. Marnier's ship, the *Seeker*, was the right size, but his computer would not be programmed to respond to her voice. So even if she managed to hijack it, she'd have to fly manually, locate a lane and plot the leap to Fortuna with minimal computer assistance. Flying a quantum-class ship alone, even with full computer functions, was not something she'd be particularly confident doing. Without them, she would need a miracle.

By the time Shenda felt the ship return to normal space, which she hoped indicated arrival at their destination, she had arrived at two possible courses of action—neither of which would be easy. Her first option was to get Marnier to program her voice and handscan into the computer. How she would accomplish that, she hadn't a clue. Her second option was to steal a weapon and kidnap somebody who could either control the computer or fly the ship manually when she escaped. Since she had no idea where they were going, nor who might be available to kidnap, she hadn't a clue as to how to accomplish that either. However, she was certain some course of action would present itself, and she would be ready when it did.

Hours later, Shenda felt the thrusters fire, and knew they had landed. Sitting up on the berth, she waited anxiously for Marnier to come and let her out. He didn't. At least not for quite some time. And by the time he did, Shenda had fallen asleep from sheer nervous exhaustion.

"Shenda, you may join us now." His voice jerked her unwillingly from her slumber. "You'll have to wear this." He handed her a mask.

Shenda studied it. It appeared to contain a number of different layers of filters, two venting areas and a small electronic device. "What is it?"

With a sigh, Darren clarified, identifying one of the vents as an intake vent, the other as output. "The mask filters out the harmful and excess gases. Put it on."

As she slid the mask into place, Shenda deduced exactly where they were: Dendron II, the place where the Obsidian Order met to conduct their rituals. She wondered if her father was here, and what he would say about the situation if he was. She grimaced inwardly. Why did she still harbor that tiny hope that someday he would prove everything she believed about him to be false? No, she couldn't count on any help from that quarter. She was on her own.

Logan winced as he was jerked roughly to his feet. He felt cold, and realized that once again he wore nothing but a prison loincloth. "Move it," a voice barked in his ear. Pain stabbed through his forehead as he tried to open his swollen eyes enough to focus on his tormentor. He could just make out two blurry shapeless forms. They grasped his arms and propelled him from the shipboard cell. It was agony simply to put one foot in front of the other as they escorted him down the corridor. Still, when compared with the Legionnaires that had comprised Marnier's personal guard, these two were models of consideration. As long as he kept moving, they did not force him to move any more quickly than he was able. They even aided him in descending the companionway to the shuttle bay area.

Shuttle. Saints! In a few minutes he'd be back on Sentra. Like a person lost in a forest, he had done nothing more than travel in circles. A sense of fatalism weighed him down. This time, there would be no rescue. Pain stabbed him in the region of his heart, a pain that was more intense, more agonizing than any physical hurt he suffered. Shenda. He had felt so certain of her. How could he have been so wrong?

"Come on, con. Move it!" The growled command made Logan aware that he had halted. He blinked. At least his eyesight was improving. He took a step in the direction of the nearest shuttle. "Not that way," one of his escorts hissed, grasping Swan's arm to pull him to the left.

They walked along the periphery of the shuttle bay. "Hey, Ford, are you being stationed on Fortuna?" one of his guards asked the other.

Fortuna! Although he carefully maintained his bruised and disoriented mien, Logan's ears perked up.

"No, Lovel is, though. And he isn't too happy about it. He's packing his stuff for the rotation now. I told him to quit complaining. He could have been assigned to Sentra."

"Yeah, tell me about it. I just got my orders."

"Not Sentra?" Ford asked incredulously.

"Yeah. Next stop and I'm off."

"Hell, I'm sorry, Coop." There was a pause. "I pulled Apollo this tour. Couldn't believe how lucky I was."

"Don't suppose I could pay you enough to trade?"

"No way, Coop. Why don't you ask Lovel? He might be just stupid enough to take you up on it. He's never pulled Sentra."

"Maybe I will." Logan could here the grin in his voice. "I'd much rather stay here."

Here? Here! Did that mean they were orbiting Fortuna? The way the guards were talking, a Legionnaire squad was being rotated off duty and another assigned.

One of the guards grasped Logan by the arm to pull him to a halt in front of a small round hatch. The words *EMERGENCY ESCAPE POD* were stencilled over the hatch. A stillness invaded Logan. His heart hardly dared to beat. What was going on here? Were they planning to kill him during an attempted escape? He turned to face the guards. Quite deliberately, they turned their backs on him and stood facing a shuttle. Logan looked beyond them, squinting against blurred vision to perceive what they were looking at. The identity of the Legion star-cruiser to which the shuttle belonged was emblazoned on its side: the *Trojan*. Talk about coming full circle.

The guards began to speak again. "Hell's universe, Ford! Captain Carvell told us *not* to turn our backs on the prisoner, and look what we've gone and done."

Ford shook his head. "With our luck, he'll escape in the damned pod before we can stop him."

Coop spoke again, this time over his shoulder. His tone was barely above a whisper. "You won't be able to navigate the pod, Swan. But it's got a programmable-frequency emergency beacon. You'll be able to record a call for rescue."

Swan hesitated. "Why are you doing this?" he asked quietly.

Coop shrugged. "Captain Carvell's orders. I figured you two were old friends or something."

"Go, man!" Ford hissed. "Before somebody comes. We can't stand here forever."

Swan went. If they took him to Sentra, he'd die for certain. If their plan was to shoot him out of the sky during an escape attempt, at least it would be a swift death.

Eighteen

Escorted by a number of armed men, Shenda followed Marnier down a barely discernible path in the jungle. Night had taken a firm grip on this side of the planet, and there was not a single source of natural light visible. As they lumbered slowly along the trail in Dendron II's heavy gravity, only the lightcells carried by the guards kept the darkness at bay. Walking through the jungle at night, on Dendron II, was not an experience Shenda wanted to repeat. It was *alive* with sound. Slithers and scrapes and rustles. Howls and screams and growls. Sharp cracks and loud crashes and soft snorts. For someone totally unused to the wild, the sounds alone were a thoroughly terrifying experience. She longed desperately for the solace of a weapon.

Perspiration trickled down her forehead and into her eyes. She wished she could wipe it from her face, but the mask prevented it. She could hear the soft rasp of her breathing in her ears beneath the constriction of the mask; the sound made her feel isolated. To take her mind off of the imagined horrors that surrounded her, she attempted to concentrate on the conversations taking place around her. Unfortunately, due to the mask's interference, she found herself able to catch only a few phrases. She then took to watching her escorts closely, noting how they moved through the jungle. They didn't even try to move quietly but hacked at the jungle plant-life almost continuously with huge knives as they walked.

So, she concluded, she would need a knife when she escaped. She tried to take note of landmarks, but the darkness made the task virtually impossible. Provided that there was only one path to follow, that wouldn't be a problem. She could only hope.

Abruptly, they emerged from the jungle into a small clearing. Before them was the cave entrance Shenda had seen on the holodisk in Darren's office. Off to their right, a short distance away, she could see a number of lights. As she drew abreast of Marnier, who had halted to allow her to precede him into the cave, she pointed to them. "What are those?"

He glanced at them. "That's one of the research outposts." He shook his head. "Idiots!"

Shenda followed him into the cave mouth. The passage along which they walked was well lit. "Why do you say that?"

He shrugged. "They came here without proper preparation, with absolutely no idea what they would face in an *alien* prehistoric-type jungle. I can't begin to tell you how many scientists died before they decided to clear that small hill you saw and fortify it with electric fence."

"What killed them?"

Marnier looked at her and smiled. It was not a pleasant smile. "This world is full of all kinds of wildlife, ranging from bird to reptile to some we haven't characterized yet. Almost all species are extremely large, and at least half the species appear to be carnivorous. Get the picture?"

Shenda didn't deign to reply. Her vivid imagination furnished her with a surfeit of graphic pictures. It might be wise to carry a blaster before making her way through the jungle alone, she decided. If she could manage to get her hands on one.

They passed through a small entrance and entered another inner cavern. Darren paused to wait for his escort. Once they were all within, the men slid their long knives into a case that sat on the floor and one of them depressed a switch on the wall. Immediately, a clear steelglass barrier dropped into place, sealing the inner cave. A moment later, Shenda heard the hiss of air through concealed venting. Concluding that Darren must have had atmospheric conditioners installed, Shenda merely took note of the switch location and waited. Before long, a tonal ring sounded and the men removed their masks, hanging them on hooks embedded in the stone of the cave wall. Shenda followed suit. Then, once again, she was quickly herded after Darren, who had moved on. Almost immediately they encountered another steelglass barrier, which was opened and then closed again, effectively sealing the second section of the cave, creating, in effect, an airlock area. Ingenious but expensive.

Shenda quickly discovered that, beyond the outer and inner cave entrances, lay a labyrinth of passageways and caverns. She focused her attention almost desperately on finding and memorizing small oddities in each passageway, anything that would help her find her way out . . . alone.

As Darren strode ahead of Shenda his mind reeled with the choices and possibilities confronting him. The sword with which Nagami had returned from Fortuna was the most priceless and promising artifact so far. He weighed the curse in his mind. The Earth-raised, scientific-minded part of him decried it as nonsense, but the open-minded seeker within him wasn't so quick to scoff. After all, under the tutelage of ancient writings, he had already journeyed far along the paths of the arcane in recent years. And in the translation of the crystal, Ish'Kara herself had hinted at a possible trap. *Find me in whatever hell I am in,* she had said. If the soul of Ish'Kara was trapped within that modest sword, then he was in a position to release her. *Release me and I will be eternally grateful.* In the dawn of a new age, who better to stand at his side as his queen than the woman who knew the secret of eternal life? They could rule the universe together . . . forever. Forever—the word itself was an intoxicating elixir.

Now he had only to solve one problem, a small problem in the grand scheme of things. The woman who carried the genes that, together with his, could strengthen the Tesuvian line walked behind him. The woman who possessed the mind and the power that he craved was imprisoned in the sword in a chamber in front of him. In theory, the solution was simple: Use the body of the one as a vessel for the other. The trick would be in having Shenda pick up the sword. She was neither stupid nor credulous. And no one else dared pick it up to pass it to her. No one else could touch it without risking his own life and the success of Darren's plan.

He veered to the right, traversing the cata-combed interior of the cavern instinctively. Sub-liminally, he was aware of Shenda following just a little behind him and to the right. Behind her, only four sets of booted feet continued to follow. The other six men had turned off to go about di-verse duties assigned them. Darren knew this, without checking, because he'd relayed orders to that effect before even returning to the ship to re-trieve Shenda. He never had problems with dis-obedience.

He had arrived at a tentative plan before retriev-ing Shenda from the *Seeker*, and it was still the best he had. Although he despised the element of chance it involved, he would have to go with it and hope that all worked out. Reaching his destina-tion, he halted, opened the door that he'd had fit-ted to the rock surface of the smaller cavern's entrance and turned to Shenda.

With a mocking flourish of his hand, he bade her enter the small chamber. "Make yourself at home, my dear. I regret the necessity of confining you, but I'm certain you can understand my re-luctance to trust you."

Shenda stepped into the small cave, noting at a glance that it contained a small cot, a table with two chairs and a porta-toilet. Shenda's lips curled, parodying a smile. "How exciting! The very latest in cell furnishings."

Marnier's eyes chilled a degree. He grasped the door handle. "I'm glad you like them. Someone will deliver the evening meal to you shortly. Per-haps later, you may join me." With that, the door closed and Shenda heard the sound of a lock click-ing into place. She studied the solid rock walls of her prison. So much for immediate escape. She knelt to study the locking mechanism on the door. It could be opened without a key, provided one had the tools.

Tools. Shenda set about searching her cell thoroughly, even going so far as to examine the mattress and blanket provided as she lifted them from the cot. Nothing. The cot was nothing more than a solid sheet of plastic with legs. The table and chairs, also constructed of molded plastic, had not a single removable piece that could serve as a tool. She turned to the porta-toilet. The only thing even remotely likely was the plastic hinge securing the lid, but further study revealed its diameter to be too large. She would need a knife to whittle it down. A knife she didn't have.

Muttering a particularly vile curse under her breath, Shenda sank back on her heels fingering the broach on her lapel. The broach! Removing it, she studied it. It had a short pin-style fastening with a small clip-on back. Useless for her purposes. Stars, would nothing work out? She had no choice but to wait. Marnier had said that he would have a meal delivered to her. Her stomach growled, reminding her that it had been a long time since it had received sustenance. She ignored it. Perhaps, she could catch whoever arrived by surprise. If she could gain the upper hand long enough to steal his weapon, then she could escape. She knew, though, that the heavy gravity of Dendron II would slow her down and she would have to compensate for that in any scenario. Her one consolation was that it would slow her captors down as well.

Her next course of action firmly in mind, Shenda sat down cross-legged on the cot to calm herself and clear her mind using a simple meditative technique she'd learned as a cadet. It seemed that only five minutes had passed when a knock sounded at the door and a key began to scrape in the lock. Reflexively, she leapt to her feet to take up a position next to the door. A quick glance at her wrist chronometer revealed that, in fact, almost an hour had gone by.

Shenda stood beside the door, expecting it to open slowly. Expecting to see a tray of food balanced precariously on someone's arms as they fumbled with the keys to the door. Expecting to be able to kick that tray up into the person's face, taking that person by surprise long enough to confiscate a weapon and make her escape. Instead, the door opened swiftly and completely, banging back against the opposite wall. No one entered.

"Corporal Ridell, move in front of the door where we can see you." It was a man's voice, hard and uncompromising.

We? There was more than one then. And both armed, no doubt. Another opportunity for escape foiled. Hell's universe! This was really beginning to get aggravating. Temper showing in the stubborn set of her jaw, Shenda moved cautiously into the center of the room until she could see through the open door. There were two men, both large: One carried the meal tray that Marnier had promised; the other carried a laser, fully charged and ready to fire if the malevolent brightness of the red indicator light could be trusted.

As Shenda moved into view, the man carrying the laser aimed it directly at her. "Back up," he directed. "Over there." He gestured to the side of the room farthest from the table. As soon as Shenda had complied, his compatriot cautiously entered the room to place the tray on the table.

He did not appear to be armed. Perhaps her plan was salvageable.

"All this caution for one small woman?" Shenda asked, beginning to stroll slowly forward.

"Halt right there," ordered the man with the laser. As Shenda complied, his partner sidled his way back to the door without taking his eyes off her.

This was ridiculous! They acted as though she was one of the most dangerous criminals around. Obviously Marnier had told them that she was a Legionnaire—probably ex-Legionnaire by now, she supposed—but . . . "What exactly did Marnier tell you about me?"

"He said that you were tricky and extremely dangerous, ma'am." This from the man who'd carried her supper tray.

"And you believed him?" Shenda asked incredulously.

"We're paid to believe whatever he chooses to tell us, Corporal," the man with the laser responded as he and his partner backed out the door. "Enjoy your meal." The door closed, and once again Shenda heard the lock click into place.

For once ignoring the rules of decorum, Shenda allowed a fierce scowl to settle on her features. She was furious; her blood boiled hot enough to exterminate any bio-nanites that might be in her system, that was certain. Stalking toward the table, she noted the glass and pitcher of water before lifting the cover from the tray to examine the contents. Stuffed trout smothered in sauce rested on a bed of asparagus spears. It smelled delicious, and Shenda's stomach growled hungrily. She lifted the fork, about to sample the cuisine, when something made her hesitate. With a slight frown between her brows, she set the fork back down and sat on the cot to think.

Marnier never acted without purpose. So why had he brought her to Dendron II? She'd been so focused on escaping his custody that she'd not stopped to wonder about his motives. She now knew that his sole reason for wanting to marry her was to have children by her. He had threatened her with a surgical means of accomplishing that task. So his reason for bringing her to Dendron II could be: one, that he planned to marry her in a ritual ceremony—in which case he would have to drug her; or two, that he planned to have the surgery performed here by some black-market surgeon—in which case, again, he could want her at least partially drugged to facilitate the administration of anesthetic; or three, something she hadn't thought of yet. Shenda looked at the meal provided for her with longing eyes. Regardless of his motivation for bringing her here, one thing was certain: She couldn't risk eating anything he provided. There was at least a 75-percent chance that it was drugged. That being the case, she would have to dispose of the meal and act sleepy and thoroughly befuddled when Marnier came for her. She would know soon enough if that was the condition in which he expected to find her.

Her decision made, Shenda cut the mouthwatering meal into tiny bits, stirring it and mashing it until it looked like a regurgitated mess, and disposed of it in the porta-toilet. That way, if anyone thought to check to see if she'd consumed the meal or not, they would not know for certain that she hadn't. Then she reclined on the cot, willed her gurgling stomach not to betray her and began practicing a drugged and compliant demeanor. The most telling thing probably would be her pupils. Drugs always showed in a person's eyes, didn't they? She didn't know for certain, but in any case there was nothing she could do about that. She would simply have to hope that Marnier, or whoever he might send, did not check.

Shenda awoke with a start when she heard the faint sound of a key in the lock. Even though she had allowed herself to doze, her plan had stayed at the forefront of her mind. Now, she quickly triggered the button on the small broach-style camera on her lapel, schooled her features into relaxation and pretended sleep. She heard footsteps enter the room, more than one pair, she thought. There was a slight rattling sound at the table as somebody checked her supper tray.

"Shenda." It was Darren's voice. Shenda didn't respond, didn't move a muscle. She sensed him draw near the cot, felt his gaze on her. "Shenda," he said again. She could hear the scowl in his voice. She decided a moan and a slight frown of annoyance were in order. "I told Carl I wanted her dazed and compliant, not comatose." Although his tone was even, displeasure crackled in every syllable. The man or men with him did not respond. Shenda decided it might be wise to wake up a bit. With a groan and a deeper frown she turned her head on the pillow. "Shenda," Darren said again. Shenda thought she detected a hint of anxiety in his voice. So this plan of his, whatever it was, was very important to him.

Shenda opened her eyes slightly, and turned toward him. "Hello, Darren," she said in a low voice, smiling sleepily at him.

"It's time to get up, Shenda."

"Sure," she murmured, nodding her head like a little girl. And then she frowned. "But I am very tired."

"You can sleep later."

"All right." Slowly, she pushed herself into a sitting position and swung her legs over the side of the cot so that her feet rested on the floor. But despite Marnier's expectations, she wanted him to think that she was virtually incapacitated. That way he wouldn't be expecting an escape attempt. So when she stood, she wobbled alarmingly and sank back on the cot with an inebriated little giggle. "Sorry, Darren. But my legs don't work," she murmured in a thick voice. "I think I'll sleep now." Falling sideways on the cot, she curled herself into the fetal position and closed her eyes. There were four men in the room, including Darren. Darren and one other wore the Obsidian Order robes; two were armed guards.

There was a short period of absolute silence during which Shenda could feel the waves of cold fury emanating from Marnier. Then two words. "Bring her."

Almost immediately, two men grabbed her arms and hauled her unceremoniously to her feet. Groaning, she opened her eyes marginally, noting the positioning of the two guards, one on either side of her. Good. A laser rested in its holster not six inches from the fingers of her right hand. The two guards began dragging her toward the door, following in Marnier's wake. But where was the other robed man? Shenda twisted slightly as though resisting the grip on her arms and caught sight of him. He was bringing up the rear, his Oriental features cold, his eyes vigilant. Damn! She wished he'd been in front with Marnier.

She carefully registered every slight change in the passage they followed as they worked their way deeper into the warren of caverns. She would have to make her move soon, before she became hopelessly lost. She was just steeling herself for action when a loud, demanding voice thundered into the corridor from a door on her left. "I hear you sons o' bitches out there. Let me out. You hear me? You can't keep me here."

Zach! Zachariah Swan? What was he doing here? What could Marnier want with him? Shenda's mind raced.

A crash reverberated through the passage as the person on the other side of that door struck it with something solid. And it was that crash that provided the momentary distraction that kept Shenda's temporary lapse into a vigilant and undrugged deportment from being noticed. She slumped in her captor's grasp, struggling to reformulate her plan to include Zach. She couldn't just leave him here.

She'd need the keys to open his door, and a weapon for him. Beyond that, she didn't think there'd be much problem. He was a robust and capable old man who would probably be more of an asset than a hindrance. She wondered if he could fly a quantum-class ship.

And then, her captors abruptly steered her into a large cavern and halted. The chamber reeked of burning incense. "Put her over there," Marnier directed. *There* turned out to be a small dais that reminded Shenda disturbingly of an altar. Her two escorts sat her on it and stood, one on either side of her, waiting for further instructions. Shenda used the short reprieve to open her eyes slightly wider and examine her surroundings. She would have to make her move soon, or it would be too late.

The chamber was lit entirely by candles. Its black stone walls shimmered in the flickering light. A blue haze generated by a combination of the candles and the incense hung in the air. Three pulpits to her right identified the chamber as the same one she had seen on the holo. Now, though, a table sat near the pulpits. On the table rested a number of ceremonial devices; one of these was the winged figurine that Logan needed. Near the rear of the room a small group of people wearing the long black hooded robes waited, apparently involved in idle conversation. Yet they spoke very quietly, for Shenda could not hear so much as a murmur. There appeared to be a second chamber behind them. The two guards who comprised her escort appeared to be the only armed people in the room. Although, due to the voluminous nature of the robes, she couldn't be certain of that.

She switched her gaze back to her guards. Her seated position gave her a clear view of their backs and the equipment secured to their belts for the first time. Her eyes widened as she spied and recognized one of the latest pieces of technology attached to the belt of the guard on her left. So new, in fact, it had not yet become standard issue for the Legionnaires, who invariably received the best equipment. A sonic emitter. The sound discharged by the device traveled out in an ever-widening cone-shape from the source, paralyzing anyone caught within its field. In effect, it was a wide-angle stunner that could also be used as a sonic grenade. When thrown, the impact caused the conal emission field to oscillate in a 360-degree range.

Unfortunately, neither of the guards carried a blaster, and that was something Shenda had really wanted before facing the denizens of Dendron II's jungle. Quarks! All right, she would just have to do without it. But where were the keys? She'd need the keys to free Zach. If it came down to it, she supposed she could try burning a hole through the locking mechanism with a laser, but she'd risk simply melting the thing in a locked position. It was a risk she didn't want to take. The guard on her right shifted slightly, and she heard the slight sound of metal clinking in his pocket. The keys? She'd have to hope so.

Now, to come up with a plan. She'd have to out-maneuver Marnier and his people because she certainly couldn't hope to triumph strictly on physical terms. She contemplated their position-ing. About 15 feet to her right, Marnier and his black-robed Oriental cohort were involved in some type of discussion which appeared to con-cern a case resting on the table near the three pul-pits. Everyone else other than her two guards was at the rear of the room, 30, maybe 35 feet away. She doubted there would be a better time to act than now. She tensed, preparing to grab a laser from one guard and the sonic erupter from the other, roll backwards off of the small dais where it could serve as a shield and . . . fire. Before she could act, Marnier and his companion moved.

Lifting the small case between them, they came toward her. Stars! Already? She thought she'd have some time before the ceremony began. Per-haps she'd be best to wait until they were all in-volved in whatever ceremony or rite they were about to perform. She'd just have to wait to see where the marble stopped, she decided, drawing an analogy to the game of Galactic Exchange. Slumping slightly, she eyed the toes of Darren's shoes as he halted before her.

"Shenda."

Shenda moaned and stared blearily up at him.

"I have a present for you. Stand up, dear." His voice was soft, coaxing, but Shenda detected a nu-ance in it she didn't like. She didn't move. "Help her up," Marnier ordered.

Immediately, Shenda felt her arms grasped and she was pulled to her feet. Darren and his friend held a metal case before her. Within it rested a plain, unadorned sword. A sword? What was the likelihood of her seeing two such weapons within the space of a week? Despite the missing lid and its warning, Shenda knew it had to be the same one. Now she knew why Zachariah Swan was imprisoned here. And Darren, unscrupulous bastard that he was, had decided to test the veracity of the sword's curse on her. Shenda stared down at the weapon, probing the farthest reaches of her mind in search of a way out of this.

"It's for you, Shenda. Take it."

Shenda shook her arms free of the guards' grasp as though she meant to comply, but only continued to stare at the sword. She fancied that she could see a malevolent greenish aura hovering over the blade as though it was aware of the ambience of ambition in the room. Even though she immediately dismissed the observance as a stress-induced delusion, she continued to see it. Nothing on this world or the next could induce her to willingly set a finger on that virulent blade.

"Isn't it beautiful? Don't you even want to touch it, Shenda?"

If she didn't touch it soon, she knew he would have the guards force her hands into contact with it. She had to act now. There was no more time.

"Shenda, look at me." Continuing to hold his end of the metal case with one hand, he reached forward with the other to place a finger beneath her chin. Before her eyes met his, she moved.

Bringing both of her clenched fists up from her thighs, she smashed them into the noses of her two guards with all her might. Before they had done more than gasp and begin to lift their hands toward the source of the pain, her hands were already down again. Grasping the laser from the one guard's holster, she simultaneously kicked the sword case from Marnier's grasp and grabbed the sonic erupter from the other guard's belt.

She vaguely heard Darren bellow, "What the hell?" as she dropped, flipping backward over the dais before the heavily muscled guards could grab her. When she resumed an upright position, she noticed that as Marnier's end of the case dropped, his compatriot hastily released his end and moved aside. Unfortunately, this meant that the sword stayed in its case. Shenda had hoped to provide Darren with an additional problem: how to retrieve the weapon without releasing its spirit. Quickly pointing the sonic emitter at Marnier, who now stood in a direct path in front of the robed figures in the rear of the chamber, she depressed the button. Although she continued to hold the emitter in hand, button depressed, she didn't have time to observe its effect. The two guards and the Oriental were too close to her to be within the range of effect, and they were turning.

Reflexes, honed by her years in the Stellar Legion, reacted without conscious direction. As the Oriental extended his hands toward her in a manner she could only judge as reminiscent of a martial-art maneuver, she leveled the laser and fired. Before she had an opportunity to assess the result of her shot, the guard on her left began to raise his weapon. It took only an instant for her to move the muzzle of her laser the fraction of an inch necessary to ensure that he never fired the shot. He dropped. Dead? She didn't know. But he was at least disabled for the moment. She swung to direct her laser at the other guard just as he pulled his own weapon from its holster.

"Don't try it," she warned, surprising herself with the cold calmness of her voice. She backed up a step, out of reach of his long arms. "Put it down," she ordered, indicating the dais. If looks could kill she would have been dead on her feet, but after only a slight hesitation, he complied. "Now keep your left hand up and slowly put your right hand in your pocket and take the keys out. That's it. Slowly," she barked as he seemed about to jerk them from his pocket. The last thing she needed was to have them flung into her face. "Put them down next to the laser. Slowly, no tricks." Again he complied. "Good, now keep your hands up and back away."

Arms upraised, he looked over his shoulder at the people on the floor. Some writhed in sonically induced agony, while others lay still, stunned into unconsciousness. "Are you crazy?"

"They're alive," Shenda pointed out. "Or would you rather join your friends?" She could see quite clearly now that the men were dead. A small black-edged hole marked the base of the throat of the guard, and the Oriental man had taken her shot in the chest. Refusing to allow herself to acknowledge that yet, she centered her attention on the other guard. "Your choice," she said without a trace of compassion. These men, after all, would have stood by and watched her killed or killed her themselves if they'd been so ordered. "But make it quickly." The man hesitated a fraction of a second too long, obviously stalling for time. Shenda leveled the laser.

"No, wait!" Hastily, he backpedaled a couple of steps, immediately clamping his hands over his ears as he stepped into the emitter's area of effect.

Before he'd even sunk to his knees, Shenda was moving. There was no time to waste. She dared not release the button on the emitter, not yet, and she didn't want to leave it here unless she had to, so she shoved the laser she carried into the belt of the tunic, freeing her hand in order to retrieve the keys and the laser left on the dais by the guard. That done, she raced to the table, picked up the winged figurine, cradling it in the crook of the arm holding the emitter, before turning to race from the chamber. As she leapt over Marnier's prone form, she reflected incongruously that he would never forgive her for placing him in such an ignoble position. At the doorway, she hesitated a fraction of a second. How long would the emitter's effect last? She tried to remember her briefing. She was almost certain that the sergeant had said five minutes. It would have to be enough. She absolutely refused to negotiate the jungle with only a laser as a weapon.

A minute later, her legs already tiring from the stress of being forced to run rather than walk in the heavy gravity of Dendron II, she entered the corridor where Zach Swan was incarcerated. Stars, she was fast growing to hate this planet almost as much as she hated Sentra. Reaching the door to Zach's cell, she kicked it, calling his name, even as she fumbled with the keys.

"Is that you, Shenda?"

"Yes," she responded breathlessly. "Yes, it's me."

"What in blazes are you doing here?"

She didn't bother to answer. She tried a third key in the lock. Where was the damned thing? She began to consider the possibility that perhaps the guard didn't even have a key to this particular door. No, she refused to think that way. It would be here because it had to be. The fifth key fit; it grated slightly in the lock as she turned it, but it worked.

The door swung open immediately, revealing a disgruntled-looking but otherwise unharmed Zachariah Swan. "Here!" She thrust a laser into his hand. At that moment she heard running footsteps echoing through the corridor. Damn! That hadn't been five minutes. "Come on," she urged, grasping the fabric of his shirt to urge him on. "They're coming." "Don't you worry about me." On the final sentence, Zach's words were already beginning to sound a bit breathy, and Shenda made an observation that she'd not heretofore considered: The strong gravity was going to be harder on the burly old man than it was on her. She hoped he was up to it.

They reached a junction in the passageway and Shenda hesitated a fraction of a second, peering in both directions, looking for something familiar. There, on the right. A small red blotch at shoulder height on the wall identified it as a passage she'd seen before. The next turn took her back into the corridor that housed the cell in which she'd been kept. She glanced over her shoulder. The sounds of pursuit were growing closer. Zach's face was red with exertion.

"Are you all right, Zach?"

"Fine. I'm sure glad . . . you . . . know the way out," he panted. "I was blindfolded . . . when they . . . brought me in."

That little piece of news generated almost instant worry in Shenda. So why hadn't Marnier blindfolded her? The answer when it came was one she'd rather not have known: because he never expected her to leave this place *alive*. For the first time, she comprehended fully that Marnier now wanted her dead. She suddenly felt very afraid. One of the greatest ironies of the universe was that he, a man who cared nothing for justice, occupied the position of the Commissioner of Justice. As such, he was a powerful man with enormous resources.

They had almost reached the first steelglass barrier. In fact, if Shenda remembered correctly, it was around the next corner. Zach was falling a little behind and had begun to wheeze. Shenda slowed slightly, allowing him to catch up. It was at that moment that their pursuers rounded the corner behind them and began firing. A laser beam struck the rock wall of the passage just in front of Shenda's face. Another just narrowly missed her right arm. She couldn't risk turning to return fire. Not when they were in the open. Grabbing Zach's arm in her free hand, she did her best to pull him along. Just three more steps and they'd be at the junction. She heard another laser blast. Immediately on its heels she felt Zach jerk. And then they were around the corner. Without a pause, not bothering to check her targets, Shenda fired a couple of wild laser blasts back the way they had come. Then, in the lull that followed, she grabbed the sonic blaster from her belt and directed a blast down the corridor.

She studied Zach, trying to see the extent of his injury even as she continued to focus the emitter blast. "How badly are you hurt?" He was clutching his right shoulder with his left hand; there was blood on his blue shirt.

"Just my shoulder. I'll live."

Shenda nodded, and risked a glance back the way they had come. Only three men lay on the floor in the corridor. The others must have managed to back around the corner out of the path of the blast. Damn! That meant they wouldn't be slowed for long. She looked at Zach. "Ready?"

"Lead on, little lady." His grin was strained but, since they had no choice in any case, Shenda did as he bid.

They made it through the next corridor to the steel-glass barrier without incident. Shenda found the lever to raise the barrier without any problem and pulled it. She stared at the steelglass barrier expectantly. Nothing happened. "No, no, no, no," she murmured litanously, denying the evidence supplied by her eyes. Hastily placing the lever back in a starting position, she pulled it again. "You can't do this to me. Open, damn you. Open."

"It must be locked," Zach supplied helpfully. "What's in that case above the lever?"

He directed Shenda's gaze to a small gray metal box on the wall. Grasping the handle, she opened it. It contained a single keyhole above which were a green light and a red light. Currently, only the red light was illuminated. Muttering a particularly unladylike curse under her breath, Shenda drew the ring of keys she'd confiscated from the small pocket of the tunic.

"Here." She passed the sonic emitter to Zach. "Just point it down the corridor and hold this button down. It'll keep them back while I try these keys."

"Yes, ma'am," Zach responded with a humorous glint in his eye despite the situation and his obvious pain. Shenda didn't have time to puzzle it out as she set the winged figurine down on the floor out of her way and began fitting keys into the lock. She certainly saw nothing humorous in their situation.

This time, it took only three tries to find the right key. The lock turned, the light turned green, and Shenda pulled the lever down. Immediately, the steelglass barrier lifted. "Yes!" Exultant, Shenda retrieved the figurine and looked back the way they had come. She saw that the emitter had indeed incapacitated one man who had walked unwittingly into its path. "Come on, Zach." Relieving him of the emitter so that he could effectively use his blaster, she hastily tucked it into her belt and pulled him into the air-lock cavern. As soon as they were within, she searched for the lever on the other side and found it. When the barrier once again had lowered into place, Shenda felt safer. Laser fire couldn't penetrate steelglass unless it was concentrated.

Moving around the corner into the other section of the cavern with Zach at her heels, she took down two gas-filtration masks and handed one to him. "We're going to need these to get to Marnier's ship. Can you fly a quantum-style ship?"

The old man shrugged. "I'm no master pilot, but I've flown them before. I can again."

Her mask firmly in place, as was Zach's, she pulled the lever to open the exterior steelglass barrier. "Good. We'll only have minimal computer support because I wasn't able to obtain access, so we're pretty much on our own." She pulled two of the long knives from the case in which she'd watched them deposited earlier, and handed one to Zach.

Zach held it up, looking at it admiringly. "Ah, a machete."

Shenda nodded absently, "Yes." Examining the cumbersome figurine, she tried to determine what to do with it. She couldn't risk being impeded by it in the jungle. Lifting the front panel of her tunic, she managed to tie the figurine into it, thereby freeing her left hand. As the air finished hissing out through the vents, the barrier lifted. Now to try to slow down their pursuers just a little.

With that in mind, Shenda aimed the laser at the exterior barrier-control mechanism and fired. There was a satisfying sizzle and then the barrier began to lower into place again.

Stars! Scrambling forward, she grabbed Zach and pulled him beneath the descending steelglass barrier.

"Whew! I haven't had this much excitement in years," Zach muttered as they stepped out of the cavern into the predawn light of the jungle.

"That way," Shenda said, seeing the remnant of the path she had walked just hours earlier.

Zach took the lead and Shenda brought up the rear, keeping a careful watch for any sign of their pursuers. They had gone, in Shenda's estimate, perhaps half the distance to Marnier's ship when she noticed that Zach was showing signs of exhaustion. Sweat streamed from his face and neck, wetting the collar of his shirt. He was breathing extremely heavily, his barrel chest seemingly incapable of supplying him with an adequate supply of oxygen. And the bloodstain on his shirt grew steadily in size. Still, he continued to hack away at the jungle undergrowth, clearing their path and moving as quickly as was possible. Even Shenda's legs had begun to feel like heavy tree trunks. Stars! She could not imagine actually living on a world where the mere task of moving became a chore.

There was still no pursuit behind them. She had just begun to make out the blue color of Marnier's ship at the end of the path when it happened. A huge something leapt into their path, lifting the robust Zachariah Swan in enormous claws as though he were a child's toy.

For an instant, Shenda froze. Her brain grappled for recognition, understanding. The creature was huge, at least five meters tall. Its shape was similar to that of a gorilla as it stood on its powerful hind legs, but it seemed to be covered with greenish scales—which accounted for the fact that they hadn't seen the enormous creature until it pounced—and it had gold reptilian eyes. In the second that it took her brain to absorb this, the creature had begun to turn away, its prey in hand.

Drawing her laser Shenda fired. The creature barely flinched, but it did turn back to find the source of its irritation. "Zach!" Shenda shouted. There was no response. He hung limply in its clawed hands. She hoped he was still alive.

Suddenly spying her, the creature dropped Zach into the undergrowth at its side, discarding him like so much garbage, and fixed its malevolent reptilian gaze on her.

Nineteen

"Oh, stars," Shenda breathed. The creature took a single huge lumbering step toward her. Unable to take her eyes from it, she backed up along the path, fumbling for the sonic emitter at her belt. "Please, please, please," she muttered frantically as she lifted the emitter, directing it at the creature's head—where she hoped its ears would be, if it had any—and depressed the button.

For an instant, nothing happened. The creature took another plodding step forward, watching her, stalking her. And then, it shook its head and lifted its clawed hands to swat at the air. The emitter *was* having some kind of an effect. Shenda dared to hope. The creature backed up a step. Shenda advanced, keeping the emitter trained unerringly at the creature. It continued to swing its head and slap the air around it with increasing rapidity until . . . it seemed to forget all about her. Finally, with a roar of frustration that sent droplets of ice coursing along Shenda's veins, it gave its head one final shake and turned to flee through the jungle.

Shenda lowered a shaking arm and replaced the emitter at her belt. Then, remembering the treatment Zach had received from the creature, she rushed to the spot where he'd been thrown. After shoving aside an abundance of leafy foliage, she found him lying facedown, eyes closed, apparently unconscious. His shirt had been shredded, and his back was covered in blood. Thank the stars, his mask was still in place.

Scrambling forward, Shenda felt for a pulse in his neck and held her breath. Finally she felt it. A little weak maybe, but definitely there. The trouble was, it might not be there for long if he didn't regain consciousness. There was no way that she would be able to get him to the ship alone without an anti-grav stretcher, and the nearest one of those was probably a few light years away.

Keeping one ear trained on the nearby jungle for sounds of pursuit or another reptilian gorilla, Shenda shook his shoulder. "Zach. Zach, it's Shenda." There was no response. She repeated the action a little more forcefully. "Zach. Can you hear me?"

He groaned, attempted to lift himself and fell back.

"Zach, you have to get up. Do you hear me? I can't get you to the ship alone."

"I hear you, little lady. I hear you." Once again he struggled to lift himself. Shenda helped him. After a couple of pauses during which Shenda managed to brace his weight sufficiently for him to remain relatively upright, Zach made it to his feet. "I thought I was a goner."

Shenda grimaced. "Me, too. Are you ready?"

He nodded, and they set out. The clearing containing Marnier's ship was only about 30 feet away; Shenda could see its blue color through the foliage at the end of the path. It felt like a mile. She kept looking back over her shoulder expecting to see their pursuers, but they weren't there. Surely it wouldn't take them this long to raise that barrier unless she'd done more damage to it with that laser strike than she'd imagined. With a mental shrug, she decided to accept providence at face value.

They made it to the ship and onto the bridge before Zach's willpower gave out. Shenda had just managed to get him into the one of the seats when he slumped forward. For the first time, Shenda saw the true extent of his injury. His back had not been hurt in the fall as she had initially assumed; it had been lacerated by the creature's claws. There were four parallel wounds, each almost three inches apart, gouged deep into the flesh of Zach's back. Blood drained from them in a steady trickle. Looking down, Shenda realized that the arm that she had wrapped around Zach's waist as she supported him was soaked with blood. She swallowed. There was so much blood. "Don't die on me, Zach," she murmured under her breath. They had to get off this hellish planet before she could get him any help. She glanced through the steelglass, peering in the direction of the cave. They had to leave quickly. The problem was, she didn't have much chance of succeeding alone. She lifted the remnants of Zach's shirt away from his back to examine the inch-deep gashes.

Quarks! She was no medic. Feeling desperate and frustrated, she rummaged through all the compartments she could find until she unearthed the first-aid container. All she'd ever taken was basic first aid. Her memory told her she had to disinfect the wounds and wrap them tightly to stop the bleeding. Beyond that, she didn't have a clue what to do. Zach needed a doctor, badly.

At that moment he stirred and sat up with a groan.

"Be still. I'm going to bind your wounds."

"You can do that once we're under way." He reached for the controls. "Come on, little lady. It's my turn to give the orders. Take your seat."

It was 15 hours later—and they were some of the most harrowing hours of Shenda's life—when they returned to normal space within sight of Fortuna. Zach was now not only unconscious, but delirious and burning with fever despite her ministrations. Thank the stars he had managed to stay conscious long enough to enter hyperspace. The *Seeker*'s computer had supplied them with lane information, but they had had to accomplish the leap manually. When Zach had lost consciousness, she had placed his seat in a reclining position rather than trying to move him to a berth— which probably would have proven to be impossible in any case—because she wanted to be able to monitor his condition and she couldn't leave the controls.

In the hours of silence just past, Shenda had tried to come to grips with the knowledge that she had killed not one, but two men. They had been somebody's sons, perhaps somebody's fathers, and they had died for no reason other than that they were doing the jobs they had been paid to do. Every time she closed her eyes, she saw them lying on the floor of that cavern. Dead. It didn't matter that, had she not taken their lives, they would have taken hers. It didn't matter that she had reacted purely on instinct, without malice or forethought. Her emotions were in a tangle, and she suffered an agony of guilt.

Finally, knowing she had to think of something else or go mad, she had deliberately filled her mind with thoughts of Logan. Logan as he'd been when she first saw him, an arrogant and intimidating prisoner. Logan speaking with passion and dedication about his archeological finds. Logan making love to her. *Ci tha' lassa hava.* The phrase had echoed in her mind. What did it mean? She'd remembered the expression on his face as he'd been dragged from Marnier's apartment, and tears had filled her eyes. Would he ever say it to her again? she wondered.

Now, with Fortuna looming on the viewscreen, a huge and welcoming sight, Shenda set her mind firmly on the future. Flicking a switch on to activate communications, she turned a dial until the computer display indicated that she had accessed a channel to the surface.

Unaware of the correct access code for the Swan ranch, Shenda merely hailed the planet on the open frequency. Within a minute, a Fortunan customs official shimmered into view on her screen.

At sight of her, he frowned. "Consular Brahn here. How can I help you?"

"Consular, I am Shenda Swan. I need authorization to dock at Santon and an emergency medical team standing by."

"Pardon me, Ms. Swan, but your ship's code translates as the *Seeker*, a ship owned by the Commissioner of Justice. Can you explain this?"

Shenda decided that there was no sense in trying to camouflage the truth; it would only cause a delay that she could ill afford. The unpopularity of Earth's officials with the colonials might actually help her. "Of course, Consular. I borrowed the ship."

"I see." He didn't bat an eyelash. "And who is the injured party?"

"Zachariah Swan, my grandfather-in-law."

He nodded shortly. "You are authorized to land at Santon, Ms. Swan. Docking bay five. A medical team will be standing by. Can you tell me what type of injury the team should be prepared to deal with?"

She couldn't explain that the primary injuries had been caused by some gigantic beast without generating more questions. "Lacerations, Consular. Deep lacerations and a laser wound."

"Understood." He made a move to end communications.

"Consular . . ." He looked back at her. "Before you go, would you be able to supply me with the access code for the Swan ranch?"

He frowned slightly, a busy man inconvenienced. "I'll have to look it up. One moment, please." The screen switched to displaying a representation of the planet. A minute later, Consular Brahn returned, supplied her with the access code and switched off before she could even thank him.

Shenda glanced at Zach. His condition hadn't changed. He was breathing rapidly and shallowly. Thank the stars, medical help was now only minutes away. Already, Fortuna filled the viewscreen.

Punching in the access code Consular Brahn had supplied, Shenda placed a call to the Swan ranch. This was the call she most dreaded, but she refused to allow herself to think about it.

Within a moment, David Swan appeared on the

screen. "Shenda!" He could not have looked more surprised.

She wasted no time on preamble. Within a very short time, she was going to have to land this ship . . . alone. "You heard that Logan had been recaptured, sir?"

"Yes. But . . ."

Shenda interrupted, knowing she had neither the time nor the words to explain. Not yet. "I have Zach with me, sir, but he's injured. I don't know how badly. A medical team will be standing by in Santon to care for him." Her instruments started beeping, signaling atmospheric entry. "I'm going to have to go, sir. Could you please tell Brie Tanner that I would like to speak with her as soon as possible?"

"Of course," David said. "We'll meet you in Santon."

Terminating communications, Shenda focused all her attention on bringing the *Seeker* down in one piece. Stars! She wished she'd paid more attention in flight training.

Logan grimaced as the Morar's mind touched his, rousing him from a cramped sleep in the bobbing pod. The motion had told him immediately that he'd landed on one of Fortuna's vast oceans. He had no recourse but to wait for rescue. After recording a brief message, he'd set the beacon on the same frequency as the Swan ranch and attempted to find a comfortable position in which to sleep while he waited. The task had been a near impossibility. And then, just when he'd almost found recuperative sleep he'd faded again. And this time he knew for certain he had almost not made it back. Computer estimates aside, the next time, or at the outside the time after that, would be his last fading. Then, he would be gone from this life forever. The irony of that was that he couldn't seem to summon enough energy to care. Lethargy gripped him in an iron fist. He frowned against that insistent touch in his mind. *Go away,* he willed.

But, the sensation was unrelenting. *Wake, brother. Wake!*

What is it, Tlic? Let me sleep.

Logan felt a wave of anger wash over him from the Morar. It surprised him. He had never felt emotion from Tlic before; had not known the Morars were capable of it. *Only a *&%$(* surrenders to death before it arrives. Wake. Listen.*

And then Logan heard Brie's voice, slightly altered, but still recognizable. "Swan, we're coming." Almost instantly a vision of her, elongated and angular, appeared in his mind. "We have the beacon on our sensors. We should make visual contact within a few minutes."

They were coming! The next moments seemed to stretch into hours, but finally Logan could make out the sound of a skimmer hovering outside the pod. Slowly, laboriously, he ascended the short rope ladder to the overhead hatch and released the catch. The hatch hissed open and the fresh scent of ocean air struck him full in the face. He took a couple of deep appreciative breaths and immediately felt his head clear.

"Swan!"

He looked up at the sound. The skimmer hovered overhead. A rope ladder dangled from its open hatch, swaying dangerously in the stiff ocean breeze. The pod slid down the other side of a huge ocean swell, and for a moment Logan lost sight of the skimmer. All he could see was a 15-foot wall of water with a small patch of blue sky

overhead. And then, the skimmer reappeared with
Brie and Striker looking anxiously down at him
from the open hatch.

"Hurry, Swan," Striker bellowed, waving his
arm expansively in encouragement.

Logan didn't understand the reason behind
their desire for haste, but accepted the need.
Blocking the sight of the blue-black ocean waves
from his mind, he crawled onto the surface of the
pitching, rolling pod and braced himself against
the open hatch. He was going to have to catch the
violently swaying rope ladder before he could go
anywhere.

He watched it, waiting for it to come within
reach. There. He took a swipe at the vacillating
contrivance. Missed. Saints! He was going to have
to stand up. The only problem was if he missed
from that position, he wasn't likely to get another
chance.

He looked up. Brie and Striker looked distinctly
worried. And then a huge silver-gray body rose out
of the ocean, blocking the sight of . . . everything.
It was at least ten meters across. The sea serpent
seemed to hover over him. Even though he could
perceive no eyes, he had the curious sensation
that it was studying him. And then, it began to
drop. Logan watched in horror as the huge body
came closer . . . closer. He could see the individual
plates of scale on the huge body. Smell the fishy
odor. Hear the scrape of its leathery scales against
the sides of the tiny pod.

Throwing up his arm in a meager attempt at
self-preservation, Logan waited. Within fractions
of a second, the huge snake would fall onto the
small pod, crushing him. But it didn't happen.
Looking up, Logan realized that the serpent had
merely arched its body over the pod as it dove into

the ocean depths. This time . . . He decided he didn't want to hang around to see what would happen the next time it decided to investigate the curious object that had invaded its domain.

Echoing the urgency of his rescuers, Logan crawled up onto the surface of the pod as far as he dared without risking losing the security of his grip on the hatch. The rope ladder swayed closer, but it was too far over his head. Casting an anxious glance at the seething sea, he waved them lower.

It swayed within reach. He grazed it with his fingertips just as the pod pitched the other way. Frustration sawed at him. And he girded himself for the next try, determined to catch it or die in the attempt.

The ladder swayed almost within reach. Forsaking the security of his support against the open hatch, Logan lunged. His fingers closed over a rung. Yes! But before he could pull himself up, the pod rocked out from under his feet and Logan found himself dangling in midair. Injured muscles and cracked ribs screamed in protest. Biting his lip until it bled, Logan contained the agonized cry that pressed against the back of his throat, and stretched his hand up until he could grasp the next rung. He didn't bother looking up to see how far he had to go, instead focusing all his attention on the next rung. And then the next. Rung by torturous rung he crawled up the violently swaying ladder. And then, finally, his muscles gave out. He couldn't seem to summon the strength to move. Just when he thought that, after everything, he would fall from the ladder to his death, he felt hands on his arms. Hands pulling on him, drawing him into the sanctuary of the skimmer. And he realized that Brie and Striker had hauled the heavy and unwieldy rope ladder with him on it into the ship. They had saved his life . . . again.

With a groan of relief, he rolled onto the ship and lay panting on the floor. He heard the hatch close. Felt the ship begin to move. Sensed the concern of his rescuers.

"Logan, can you hear me?" It was Brie's voice.

He forced his eyes open and nodded.

"Can you tell me what happened? Who did this to you?"

Memory flayed Logan with the sharpness of a Morar's talons. He closed his eyes against the pain of another betrayal. "Shenda," he murmured. "She exposed me to Marnier. Marnier's people did this."

Brie's features hardened. "Well, you just stay right here and rest, all right?" She tucked a blanket around his prone form, and another folded one beneath his head. "We're taking you straight to the hospital in Santon. Striker and I can take care of things."

He nodded and, as she was about to turn away, grasped her arm. "Thanks," he murmured.

She smiled. "You're welcome, sir."

He lifted his head slightly, craning his neck to see around her. "Striker?"

"He's up front."

"Tell him. . . . " A renewed onslaught of weakness stole Logan's voice.

Brie gripped his shoulder. "I'll tell him," she promised. "Now rest."

Three hours later, after Logan had been injected with medications and bathed in accelerated healing energy, Doctor Canjhi pulled him from the warmth of a healing tube to face his visitors. Brie and Striker were there along with his mother, father and sister.

"Hello, son." Callista Swan smiled tremulously. She looked as though she'd been crying. "How are you feeling?"

"Almost as good as new." Logan returned her smile a bit sheepishly. He hadn't expected so much attention.

"Good." She placed a small stack of clothing—black slacks and a green shirt—on the foot of his bed, and watched as Canjhi exited the room. Then everyone simply stood there, looking ill at ease.

Logan frowned. "Is something wrong?" His mother avoided his gaze. "Father?"

David Swan cleared his throat. "There's no easy way to say this, son. Your grandfather has been injured. It doesn't look good."

Logan pushed himself up in bed. "What do you mean? What happened?"

"He was attacked by some creature. Apparently its claws were poisonous. The doctors are trying every antidote and variation of antidote that they can think of, but . . ." David Swan broke off, swallowing convulsively against the intense emotion that rose in his throat.

Logan stared at his parents in confusion. "What kind of creature? Where was he?" He'd heard of no such creature on Fortuna, let alone on Sendiri Island.

His mother stifled a sob, and then looked back at him. "We'll tell you all we know, Logan. But right now, we'll leave you to dress. Striker will stay here to show you to Zach's room when you're ready. All right?"

Slowly, Logan nodded. He didn't like the sound of this at all. What the hell had happened while he was away? His parents left the room, and Brie turned to follow them out. "Brie."

She halted.

"Where was Zach when he was hurt?"

Brie shared a glance with Striker. As the chamber door clicked shut behind his parents, she looked back at Logan. "On Dendron II," she said. "Shenda brought him home."

"What?" Logan barked.

Brie didn't flinch. "Striker can fill you in while you dress." With that, she opened the door and left.

Grabbing the trousers that his mother had placed on the foot of his bed, Logan threw aside the blanket and turned to begin pulling them on. "All right, Doug, start talking."

Tears burned in Logan's eyes as he looked down on his grandfather. Even though Zach's eyes were closed, the dark shadows that ringed them made them seem sunken. His flesh was tinged an unhealthy gray. His breathing was rapid and shallow. His strong hands lay limp and lifeless at his side. The figure in the bed was only a pale imitation of the Zachariah Swan that Logan had always known.

That his grandfather suffered thus because of Marnier and his interminable ambition stoked the fires of Logan's hate to the point of conflagration. Marnier *would* pay for this. Marnier and all his followers. Grimly, he leaned forward to kiss his grandfather's cheek. "I'll be back, Zach," he murmured. "You hang on, hear me?"

Then, gesturing to his parents, he stepped away from the bed. "I have something to do," he said quietly. "I'll return as soon as I can."

Outside his grandfather's sickroom, he spoke with Brie and Striker. "Did Shenda say where she was going when she left?"

A quick, meaningful glance passed between Brie and Striker. Brie cleared her throat. "Shenda hasn't left," she said. "Not yet anyway. She said she wanted to speak with you." Brie shrugged. "I told her that you'd have nothing to say to her, but she insisted on waiting."

Logan's eyes hardened. One of Marnier's people was within reach. "Where is she?"

"She said she'd wait aboard her ship. I believe she said it was docked in Section F, Bay 53. Why? You don't really want to see her, do you?"

Logan stretched his lips into a predatory smile that almost made Brie shudder. "Oh, yeah, I want to see her. We have some unfinished business between us."

Twenty

Logan watched Tucker's progress across the docking bay with thoughtful eyes. Unable to live with the guilt of his duplicity any longer, Drew Tucker had decided to tell Logan about his part in the problems Logan now faced. Logan could understand his motivation: A child was precious. But he wasn't certain he could ever forgive Tucker. And he *knew* he'd never be able to trust him again. So he had offered to pay him out and let him go. No legal recourse. That was as magnanimous as he felt he could be just now.

Leaving Brie and Striker with the skimmer—they had insisted on accompanying him—Logan entered the ship emblazoned with the name *Seeker*. "Shenda," he called.

She appeared almost immediately, her sudden presence like a physical blow to Logan's solar-plexus. Her eyes glowed like luminous emerald moonstones. Her complexion, so translucently fair even in the gloom of the ship, seemed to shimmer with an almost ethereal light. "Logan—" Her soft voice knifed through him, taunting him with what he wanted and could no longer have. Unbidden, the image of her that he carried in his heart surfaced to torment him. Shenda naked and surrounded by a gossamer halo of billowing midnight hair. Her full red lips curved into an uncertain smile. "It's good to see you. How are you?"

Logan hardened his heart. "I'm fine, thanks to some caring people. Are you disappointed?"

The smile trembled and faded from her lips. Without comment, she turned and walked away from him.

His anger unappeased, he was left with no choice but to follow her. A moment later, he stepped onto the bridge to find her seated at one of the consoles.

"Marnier's ship!" he barked at her. "Did you think I was so dense as to not know my enemy's ship?" His eyes narrowed, pinning her beneath a wave of suspicion. "What's going on, Shenda? What the hell are you up to now?"

Shenda lifted her head and met his angry gaze. His obstinate mistrust angered her. Jaw set, she rose to face him. "I thought you had been incarcerated on Sentra again," she said. "What is going on," she repeated with an edge of sarcasm, "is that I came here to ask your people to help me rescue you from Sentra. *That's* what I'm up to. Is that satisfactory, sir?" She added the title mockingly.

His face darkened. He moved toward her. "I want to know everything, Shenda. Now! Why did you betray me to Marnier? Why would he allow you to stage a rescue using his ship?"

"Allow?" Shenda stared at Logan incredulously.

"You think this is all some elaborate plan of Darren's?"

"Are you telling me it's not?"

"Of course it's not." Shenda shook her head slowly in disbelief. "You know, for an intelligent man, you certainly can be obtuse."

"Then explain the things you said in Marnier's apartment." He was standing over her now. Shenda had to tilt her head back to maintain eye contact.

Looking into his potent-whiskey eyes, she almost capitulated. But her desire to force him to see her as she truly was, to trust her because of what they meant to each other, strangled any explanation in her throat. "Stop jumping to conclusions and think for a minute, Logan. I'm certain you'll be able to figure it out."

"Dammit, Shenda!" Grasping her by the upper arms, he jerked her against the hard length of his body and looked down into her face. "Don't play games. Talk to me."

But Shenda didn't think she could have spoken if her life depended on it. She was conscious only of Logan's hard thighs pressing against hers; of the rock-solid wall of his chest a scant hand's breadth from her breasts; of the fullness of the mouth that hovered mere inches from hers. Without thought, her left hand rose to caress his stubbornly set whisker-shadowed jaw.

He jerked his head away from her touch as though he'd be burned. "Oh, stars, Logan," she murmured, too conscious of the pain she'd felt when he'd been taken to acknowledge his reaction to her touch. "I almost lost you." Tears rose to shimmer in her eyes, but pride refused to let them fall.

For an instant he stared at her. Shenda met his

gaze, saw the battle being waged in the tawny depths of his eyes. Then, with a groan that was half growl, half moan, he crushed her to him. His thighs bracketed hers as though he would absorb her into himself if he could. His lips closed over hers in a searing kiss. His hands roamed her body as though he sought to memorize the feel and texture of every curve. And his body heat branded her forever with the need to have him near.

"Shenda," he murmured into her ear. "Saints, I need you. Help me to understand."

And then, they cried out in unison as a million tiny needles pierced their skin. Shenda looked around them to see . . . nothing. Absolutely nothing. Logan was the only form in existence. They floated, still locked in each other's embrace, on a sea of grayness as dense as the center of a cloud.

"Logan!" she cried. But the sound never left her lips. There was no sound around them; nothing to see or hear or touch or smell; the only sensation was that of falling through an endless spiraling void. Terrifying.

But with the terror came a strong feeling of déjà vu. And suddenly Shenda knew that she had been in this place before. She remembered the tingling agony of having every cohesive element in her body ripped apart as she was reduced to nothing more than a mass of individual molecules. She remembered how it felt to be in the grip of a portal. She remembered that she had once helped to design such a device, and—she *knew* how it worked.

The portal had been designed by a race of people who hated death and fought its certainty with every available resource. Therefore, its configuration incorporated every possible safe guard against the unanticipated. Anyone dematerialized by a portal was tagged by an isotope peculiar to that particular portal. The isotope was not removed from the molecular pattern of the person until the transfer was complete or until the party being transferred deactivated the program. Invariably, as a key element in their initial calculations for each transfer, the portals maintained enough reserve power to return the party being transferred to the point of origin should anything interfere with the transfer. In order to accomplish this, the point of origin was also tagged with a radical element each time a new transfer was initiated. Should the transfer be completed without problem, then this radical would dissipate within hours. If the transfer had to be terminated before completion, the person was returned to the point of origin for that particular transfer. The portal would then renew its power reserves before attempting another transfer. She suspected there were two reasons for the portal's protracted delay in transferring Logan: One, it had not gotten a proper pattern from his initial transfer because he had jumped into the area of effect after a transfer had already begun. And two, because he'd consistently traveled, unintentionally increasing the transference distance and the power necessary to accomplish it.

Even as Shenda remembered all of this, she knew that the unanticipated addition of her molecular pattern to the beam would deplete the power levels. The portal, having conserved its power to transfer a solitary pattern, would not be capable of completing the transfer of the two of them; it would return them to the ship. However she, like Logan, was now also tagged by the isotope.

Slowly the grayness surrounding them began to thin. As they gained substance, the sensation of falling ended and they felt the deck of the *Seeker* beneath their feet. Collapsing to their knees in each other's arms, they sought to regain the strength of which they had been robbed by their futile and ineffectual battle against the beam. From somewhere deep within Shenda came the knowledge that, had they not feared the portal, not tensed against its invasion with every fiber of their being, they would be scarcely affected now.

She looked up at Logan. "Are you all right?"

Swallowing, he nodded. "Yeah. It wasn't as bad this time."

"It didn't have enough power to hold the two of us for very long."

Logan rose to his feet and held a helping hand out to her. "How do you know that?"

"I'm not certain." With a thoughtful frown, she took his hand and got to her feet. "It must be one of those inherited memories that Doctor Tredway talked about."

Logan looked at her, a peculiarly intense expression in his eyes. "If holding onto you slows it down, I'm not letting you out of my arms again. At least not until I recover that damned figurine."

Giving him a small smile, Shenda walked across the bridge to a cabinet occupying a corner near one of the console stations. On its shelf rested the camera broach, the ring, and the golden-winged figurine. Removing the figurine, she turned and held it out to him. "It's yours," she said.

Taking it from her, a look of incredulity on his face, Logan studied her expression as though needing confirmation of her sincerity. He took a couple of thoughtful paces away from her, and then turned to look over his shoulder. "You said those things in Marnier's apartment because you didn't want him to use me to try to coerce you into something. Didn't you?"

A soft smile curved Shenda's lips. "Like I said, you're an intelligent man," she murmured.

"But how did you get this ship?" His eyes swept the chamber. "How did you escape?"

"Zach and I did it together," she said. And she proceeded to tell him everything, haltingly at first and then, as she perceived that he didn't blame her for his grandfather's injury, more steadily. "I'm sorry, Logan. I know how close you are to Zach. We just have to be positive."

His mouth thinned and he nodded. His eyes searched her face. "I guess I owe you an apology, and my thanks. I'd hate to think of Zach still being in Marnier's hands when he discovers I've escaped again."

Shenda shook her head. "No thanks are necessary. I couldn't have gotten off of Dendron II without Zach. I'm not that capable a pilot."

Nodding wordlessly, he gripped her arm. "I want to call Brie and Striker aboard and go out to the site right now. All right?"

"Of course."

It was 45 minutes later when Brie, Striker, Shenda, and Logan—with Tlic clinging obstinately to his shoulder and the figurine in his hand—disembarked from the skimmer they'd taken from the communications area and stared up at the alien cathedral. They'd left the *Seeker* in the stadium area where they'd set the larger ship down.

After mounting the huge flight of stairs, they paused outside the doors. Rather than performing whatever magic it was that opened the force-field doors, Logan lifted the golden wings and stared at them. "Saints! I keep thinking: After all this, what if it doesn't work? What if it's too late to reverse it?"

Shenda gripped his arm in silent reassurance, knowing exactly how he felt, knowing that nothing she could say would ease that fear. "Let's go," she murmured.

Looking at her, he nodded and opened the doors. As they walked through the cavernous alien edifice, that one question kept rebounding in their minds: What if it doesn't work? The fear, felt by both of them, became inseparable in their minds, as unifying a force as all else they'd shared.

Finally, Logan lead them into a huge chamber, empty save for an elaborately carved pedestal in its center. Winged motifs marked the walls at regular intervals. "This is it," he murmured. Removing the Morar from his shoulder, he passed it to Brie, and motioned for them all to stay back. Brie and Striker obeyed; Shenda did not. As he began walking toward the alien device, she rushed forward a couple of steps to intertwine her hand with his. He glanced down at her, a frown of displeasure on his face, but apparently her expression told him that arguing would be futile. With an exasperated shake of his head, he walked on with her at his side.

A faint circle, only a slight variation in the color of the mosaic flooring, marked an area perhaps six feet in diameter surrounding the carved column. "Wait here," Logan said, firmly positioning her outside the circle. "I want you to stay outside the area of effect while I replace the figurine."

Shenda nodded and studied the carvings on the pedestal. They were both familiar and alien to her. There was something about them she . . . needed to remember, but what was it? Then Logan stepped into the field, and her attention focused wholly on him. "Be careful."

Logan, his concentration centered on the pedestal, gave no indication of hearing her. Slowly, he reached out to place the figurine on top of the column. The second he removed his hand from it, a peculiar sparkling energy charged the air within the circle and . . . Logan disappeared.

"No!" Heedless of Logan's cautionary words, Shenda leapt through the energy; her hands made contact with the pedestal before her feet touched the floor. That was important, she knew. And time was of the essence. Instinct propelled her; without conscious direction, her hands began to probe the carvings there, searching for anything that would reverse the polarity of the beam. And as her hands traveled the carvings, she remembered the sensation of having done this before. Her palm passed over a small stone inset into one of the carvings, and enlightenment flooded into her mind. Hastily, before she had time to question or deny the knowledge granted her, Shenda pressed the stone. Immediately there was an alteration in the air around her: She felt a tingling in her extremities that seemed like thousands of tiny electrical shocks. And then, Logan reappeared.

Shenda closed her eyes for a moment in brief thanks to the powers on high, whoever they might be, and then leapt to her feet to enfold him in her embrace. As his arms closed around her she felt a sense of calm, of finality, seep into her soul. Logan was back for good . . . and so was she. The transfer program had been terminated.

Relaxing his tight embrace, Logan drew back slightly and looked down into her face. "I was almost there, Shenda. I think I saw people, a strange room." He looked around. "Not like this one." His eyes grew distant. "I wonder why they've never come back here?"

"This is a one-way portal."

Instantly, Logan's head bent as he searched her face with quizzical eyes. "How do you know that?"

She shrugged. "The same way I knew how to reverse the polarity on the beam to bring you back before the transfer was complete. If I had been even one second too late, you would never have returned."

"Oh, Saints!" He hugged her close to him, cradling her head beneath his chin. *"Ci tha'lassa hava,"* he whispered.

"Tell me what that means?" she asked as, eyes closed, she basked in the warmth of Logan's embrace.

"The nearest translation would be *soul of my soul*. It means: I am nothing without you."

Shenda lifted her head to look up into his face. *"Ci tha'lassa hava ,"* she murmured.

Suddenly the sound of a throat being cleared . . . loudly, echoed through the chamber. "Are you about finished here, Logan?" They looked quickly in Brie's direction, to see both her and Striker grinning widely. "Or would you like some privacy?"

Logan smiled unself-consciously. "We're coming." As if on cue, Tlic flew to resume his accustomed position on Logan's shoulder. Logan entwined Shenda's fingers with his, and they walked together toward two of the people who had made his continued existence possible. Friends, good friends, were life's greatest treasure.

As they walked back toward the entrance of the building, Logan and Shenda were forced to endure some good-natured ribbing concerning the precipitous nature of their marriage. But since neither wanted to reveal the true reason behind their hasty nuptials—a reason which no longer applied in any case—they submitted to the witticism gracefully. In fact, the atmosphere around them was lighter than it had been in some time. Although the somber spectres of the charges against Logan and his grandfather's health still hovered in the backs of their minds, one fear had been lifted: Logan no longer had to worry about disappearing forever into a strange alien realm.

They had reached the main corridor and were walking toward the doors when, suddenly, something stepped out of an alcove into their path. The smiles froze upon their faces as they stared uncertainly. It was tall, at least as tall as Logan. To Shenda, it looked like nothing so much as a giant, scaly seahorse on two short, fat legs. The creature had two huge wings near its shoulders, and two small arm-like appendages sprouting from beneath the wings. Its iridescent scales seemed to come in almost every color imaginable, but the primary colors were metallic: gold, copper, and silver. Before anybody managed to overcome their paralysis, Tlic made a strange sound and flew from Logan's shoulder to light at the creature's feet.

Shenda looked at Logan. "What is it?" she whispered.

"A Morar queen," he murmured. "As far as I know, the first live queen ever seen." He couldn't seem to take his eyes from the creature, so homely by human standards, and yet so beautiful.

You are Swan. I have seen much through your eyes. The words resounded in his mind, the voice clear and deliberate, the tone solemn. *Tlic is your nexus to the hive. Through him and others like him we come to know humans. Your race differs from*

418

those who passed before you in this place. She made an expansive gesture with her head and two small arms that encompassed the city in which they stood. *Yet your actions may resurrect past mistakes. This must not be allowed to happen. Do you understand?*

Logan shook his head. "I understand your words, Queen, but not the meaning behind them."

Shenda, Brie and Striker, obviously not privy to the queen's side of the conversation, all glanced at him in surprise.

I have seen through your eyes a large crystal. It contains much information. Yet the knowledge the crystal holds is immoral. Those who created it sought to enslave the essence of life itself with no thought for the life forms devastated. The crystal will propagate this evil. It must be destroyed.

"I no longer have the crystal." Almost instantly, Logan felt a touch in his mind that he recognized as different: It wasn't Tlic.

Then, the Morar queen spoke again. *I am aware of that. I see in your mind that the crystal is now in the hands of humans who will use the knowledge it contains. It, and any translations gleaned from it, must be recovered and destroyed.*

"How do you know this, Queen?" Logan asked.

The queen considered him for endless moments with golden eyes that seemed to look right through him. Finally she spoke. *I will tell you if I receive your promise that what I impart will never be passed on to another. If you were to do so, it could mean the end of the Morar species.*

Logan hesitated at the seriousness of her tone. Perhaps he would be better off not knowing such volatile information? But the Morar's golden eyes rested on him unwaveringly, expectantly. "You have my promise, Queen."

She seemed to nod slightly although the movement was so insignificant that he couldn't be certain. *A Morar's vision is not limited by time. In fact, the way humans viewed the world was very difficult for us to understand when we initially came into contact with your kind. Morars need only stand in a location to see all that has gone before in that place, the now, and what is yet to be.*

Logan stared at the Morar incredulously. *So you know the future?* he asked silently.

Yes. Because of this facility, it is forbidden for us to interfere in the lives of other beings, for in doing so we risk our very existence. However, human experimentation has cost us much in the past, and in this instance we have no choice but to intervene. If the current course of events unfolds unaltered, we will perish regardless. We cannot stand by a second time and allow ourselves or the creatures of this world to suffer near extermination for the sake of human greed. She studied him and those with him with a penetrating gaze that made Swan wonder what human arrogance had prompted the Fortunans to think of Morars as something less than themselves.

Her eyes shifted back to him. *Only by the destruction of the crystal and the information it contains can you save this world, Swan.*

"How do we do that?" he asked, more comfortable with vocal communication.

Your mate will help you. Join with her now.

"Pardon me?" Logan choked out incredulously as a vision of himself and Shenda making love beneath the watchful eye of the Morar queen, not to mention Brie and Striker, materialized embarrassingly in his mind.

Within seconds he heard a strange alien squeal in my mind. Observing the queen, he noticed that peculiar tremors racked her body. *I did not mean physically, human.* And then Logan recognized the nature of the sound in his mind: laughter. Morar laughter. *Join your minds so that I may speak with both of you.* Her mirth faded from his thoughts as she once again became serious.

"We do not yet have the ability to join our minds at will."

You do, the queen insisted. *You need only touch and close your eyes. Concentrate on each other; block out all else.*

Logan held out his hand to Shenda and quickly relayed the queen's instructions. Shenda took his hand and closed her eyes, trying to erect a barrier against all external stimuli. Soon, she felt an unusual sensation in her mind: Thoughts, peculiar and alien, began to form in her mind. But they weren't just thoughts because she could *hear* a voice, recognize its tone as belonging to another. It was the most unique sensation she had ever experienced.

You are Swan's mate. The statement, uttered firmly in her mind, needed no confirmation. *I have instructed Swan that the large crystal taken from the ruins on this island must be destroyed. It was created by people who committed great evil, and the knowledge it contains will perpetuate that immorality. You will help Swan destroy it and any copies made of it. Now, so that you may understand why this must be done, I will reveal some things to you.*

First, I will show you what has gone before, the past. Pictures began to form in their minds, like clips of a holographic movie, stark and terrible in their significance. People fought; people ran in fear. Chaos. A giant crystalline stone exploded. Poisons leeched into the atmosphere. Animals died. A cataclysmic eruption tore an enormous hole in the planet's crust. The years of healing as the world and its creatures slowly recovered.

Now, I will show you the near future as it will be if the crystal is not destroyed. A large black shadowy something hovered always at the periphery of their vision. *It is the gate to another plane,* the queen explained, *opened by those who seek to enslave the life force. Watch!* Horrible, ugly insubstantial beings, not even remotely human, poured through the gate and entered the bodies of human beings. The galaxy degenerated into war as the oppressed and enslaved fought against those who had seized power with the creatures as their allies. And Fortuna, too, was swept into the chaos of the war against evil.

And now, I will allow you to see Fortuna as it will be in the more distant future. Into their minds flashed a picture of a cold, barren world devoid of all life save a few clumps of tortured, twisted vegetation and a few insectizoid life forms.

Logan opened his eyes and looked at the Morar. *How distant is this future, Queen?* he asked silently.

A very short time for us. Perhaps five hundred of your years.

And we can stop this by destroying the crystal? Shenda asked the voice in her mind.

Yes. The Morar leader looked at Shenda. *You are of their race.* Suddenly, Shenda saw herself through the eyes of the queen. *See the light that surrounds you.* A strange pulsing aura of rainbow-hued light enveloped her. *This type of cadential aura is unique to those that have gone before. We thought they had all left our world, but you are here. You know how to destroy the crystal.*

Shenda shook her head. "No, I don't," she murmured quietly.

She could almost sense a frown in the queen's next words. *Your race does not forget what has gone before as do Swan's people. You have the knowledge in your mind: you need only release the barrier of time to access it.*

"I don't know how."

You will know when the time comes. She looked back at Logan. *I have planted protective shields in both your minds, for you are now more than human, more than Morar, and important to the survival of both species on this world. I do not know how effective the shields will be, but they will provide some protection should you need it.* She paused, and Logan felt sympathy wash over him. *I will do what I can for your elder father. He is my soulmate as Tlic is yours. He will live.*

"Thank you, Queen."

The Morar lowered her head in what could only be called a regal nod and, turning, left them with surprising speed for so ungainly-looking a creature. Tlic, after a single glance at Logan, followed her.

Shenda stared after the departing Morars, still not entirely certain she hadn't been hallucinating. Abruptly a thought occurred to her, and she looked at Logan. "How did they get in here?"

He shook his head. "I don't know. I do know that there is a lot more to the Morar species than we ever suspected." He looked down at their joined hands, and tightened his grasp slightly. Then he gave her a gentle tug and said, "Come on. I want to get back to Zach." He looked over his shoulder at Brie and Striker. "Coming?"

Brie hesitated. "Are you going to let us in on what just happened here?"

"Sure." And, as they resumed their walk to the main exit, Logan—with a few interjections by

Christine Michels

Shenda—related the gist of the Morar queen's concerns. As he'd promised, he carefully edited the information that Morars were capable of seeing through time at will. Not even Shenda had been told that, although, since the queen had shown her scenes from the future, she would naturally assume they possessed some precognitive abilities.

A moment later, the foursome stepped through the main doors of the alien complex. They sighted a large form flying overhead surrounded by a number of smaller forms: the queen and an escort of Morars.

Crossing the portico, they stepped between two of the ten enormous pillars that marked the front of the cathedral, and had begun to descend the stairs when there was a slight noise behind them. "Hold it right there!" a voice called out. "Turn around slowly."

Darren Marnier, Delilah, another man with whom they were not familiar, and a squad of armed Legionnaires stepped from the seclusion of the pillars to confront them. Two of the Legionnaires held the case containing the sword of Ish'Kara; two others held Billy Stang and Kyle Leverton—taken from their on-site guard duty—as hostages. "Drop your weapons," Marnier yelled. "Now!" Since no immediate alternative presented itself, they were left with no option but to comply. With a gesture, Marnier sent two of the Legionnaires forward to collect the weapons.

Twenty-one

For a single long moment in time, nobody said anything. What could they say? The sight of two of Logan's people in Marnier's clutches communicated the situation clearly: They could expect no rescue. Delilah, her blond hair perfectly coiffed as though for a society function, clothed in a lacy, revealing, black pant-suit, fixed her lustful gaze on Logan and licked her lips. Shenda felt an almost uncontrollable urge to flatten the woman, but a single glance at Logan revealed that he was watching Marnier, not his sister.

Marnier's gaze brushed each of them contemptuously, before centering on Logan. "What were those creatures that just left?"

Logan raised a brow. "Fortunan Morars."

"What were they doing here?"

Logan shrugged. "I have no idea."

Marnier contemplated him for a moment, obviously disbelieving Logan's statement, but he decided to let it pass and fastened his gaze on Shenda instead. He studied her with a penetrating stare that swept from the top of her head to the tips of her toes. And then, incongruously, he smiled. "Perfect!" he said quietly.

With a stoicism she didn't feel, Shenda determinedly met his obsessed gaze and, for the first time, detected a trace of insanity in the depths of his eyes. That observation frightened her more than anything else about him, but she refused to allow him to sense her fear. "What do you want, Darren?" Her voice was as chill and arrogant as she could make it.

He smiled. "You!" Descending a step, he looked into her face. "Or rather, your body." Without taking his eyes from her face, he descended two more steps to stand beside her. Refusing to be intimidated by him, she turned to meet his gaze. Without warning, he reached up and yanked the fastening from the knot of hair atop her head. Shenda sensed rather than saw Logan make an aborted movement in her direction. Darren's eyes flicked toward him briefly, and then back to Shenda. She didn't know whether it had been Brie and Striker who had prevented Logan from committing an act of foolish bravery, or the sudden tensing of hands on weapons only a few feet away, but whatever it was, she was glad for its intervention: She hadn't just found him only to lose him again. And then, Darren reached up to rake his fingers through her thick ebony hair, untwining it and adjusting it so that it floated in a cloud around her torso. Finished, he looked into Shenda's eyes and smiled. "Since you so rudely ran out on my wedding ceremony, killing my aide Phillip in the process, I've brought my bride-to-be with me." He gestured over his shoulder with his chin to the case containing the sword. "I'm certain she'll be pleased with you."

Shenda stared at him, anger and disbelief overcoming her fear. "You really are certifiably insane." Marnier's face chilled. Shenda ignored it. "Even if that ridiculous curse contains a shred of truth, do you honestly believe that you could get away with such a farce?"

"So you know of the curse, do you?"

"Of course."

He nodded thoughtfully, and abruptly looked at Logan. "Where is my figurine?"

Logan didn't even try to feign ignorance. "I replaced it."

"Take us to it." As possibilities and options, and the lack thereof, ran through their minds, no one moved. "Now!" Marnier's voice cracked over them.

A scant second later, with Marnier peering intently over his shoulder, Logan began the series of touches on motifs that would open the alien door. As soon as the doors shimmered and disappeared, the Legionnaires, commandeered by Marnier, surrounded them, ushering them into the building with weapons at the ready. At no point during that impossibly long walk back to the portal chamber did those weapons waver in the slightest. In fact, the only thing that distracted Shenda at all from her terrified contemplation of the upcoming moment when she would be forced into contact with that horrible alien blade were the strange looks leveled at Logan and herself by the only non-uniformed, unarmed man who accompanied Marnier. Who was he? Why did he keep looking at them? But no answers were forthcoming, and Shenda resolved to turn her thoughts to more constructive thinking.

Marnier analyzed everything around them with avid, possessive eyes, as though he, more than anyone else, had the right to be here. He engaged Logan in conversation, questioning and demanding answers which Logan either reluctantly supplied or managed to adroitly avoid. Perhaps Darren's obsession with everything here could work in their favour.

They entered the portal chamber. "What is this place?" Darren slowly turned, observing the winged emblems that had been embedded in the walls at regular intervals.

"We don't know for certain," Logan responded.

Marnier gave no immediate sign that he had heard. "Ah, there it is," he said as he spied the gold-winged figurine on the pedestal. Then he looked at Logan. "Are you ready yet to tell me what curse you believe is attached to the figurine?"

Logan remained silent.

"Haven't you learned that your stubbornness gains you nothing?" Marnier asked rhetorically. Then he switched his gaze briefly to the two men carrying the case containing the sword. "Set it down over there." He gestured to a spot near the center of the room, adjacent to the portal.

As they complied, Darren turned back to Logan. "Now then, let's go over this curse idea again. From what I am given to understand, you believed that if you did not replace the figurine, you would die. Is that correct?"

Logan said nothing.

"Hmmm." Folding his hands behind his back, Marnier circled Logan slowly, thoughtfully. "We'll assume that's correct then." He looked at Shenda. "Since you so obviously lied to me concerning your feelings for this colonial, you must know the story behind his desperate bid to recover the figurine. What is it?"

"Go to hell, Darren." She looked down her nose at him.

He smiled. "Would you be willing to bargain for your lives?"

Shenda met his cold gaze and read the purpose there. "You have no intention of letting any of us leave this room with our lives."

He looked at her as a teacher might look at an outstanding pupil. "You're quite right, of course. How astute of you." Hands behind his back, he walked slowly back and forth in front of them. "Well, then, let's work this out rationally, shall we?" He looked from Logan to Shenda and back again. "Whatever this purported curse is, it allowed you a number of weeks to find the figurine and replace it. Therefore, it must be a delayed-action type of spell."

Darren was so involved in exhibiting the extraordinary capacity of his deductive reasoning that he didn't catch the looks exchanged by a few of the Legionnaires he'd commandeered to serve under him, but Shenda did. And she began to hope that perhaps they wouldn't allow the madman to complete his hideous plans. Almost as soon as the hope blossomed, it died. These men would not believe in the curse attached to the sword—it was precisely Marnier's talk of curses and spells that had them wondering about his sanity—so they would not truly believe that any harm could come to her.

Marnier's next words tore into her thoughts like a laser through flesh. "Retrieve my figurine, Swan, and I will allow you to die first. You don't really want to watch your wife die, do you?"

Horror raced through Shenda. If Darren forced

Logan to retrieve the figurine, the program would be re-activated with Logan at its center. He would disappear forever. Carefully schooling her features into a cool, expressionless mask that concealed her inner turmoil, she looked at Marnier and spoke before Logan could. "Your cowardice is showing, Darren." Her voice held just the right measure of scorn. "Are you actually afraid of this *delayed-action* curse?"

Marnier's head swung toward her, and he looked at her as though he would cheerfully have chopped her into tiny bits. Without taking his eyes from her, he said, "The offer is withdrawn, Swan. It's time this little bitch learned some respect." Grasping Shenda firmly by the arm, he glanced at Logan. "And you will observe."

As Marnier dragged her inexorably toward the metal case in the center of the chamber, Shenda couldn't help casting one desperate glance over her shoulder at the Legionnaires. Not one of them looked concerned. A couple of them seemed curious, others disgusted, some downright bored. But not one of them looked as though he'd like to interfere—except . . . the non-uniformed man. He had a definite frown between his brows, and an expression of compassion on his face. If he was on their side, that made seven unarmed people against 14 armed opponents, 13 if you discounted Delilah, which Shenda wasn't at all certain she could do. Two-to-one odds weren't good, but they were the best she was likely to get; there was no way in hell she was touching that sword. She'd just wait for the right moment: the moment when everybody, skeptical or not, would be waiting to see the result of her touching the sword; then she would attack Marnier.

Darren positioned her in front of the case containing the sword. Then, looking back over his shoulder, he barked in that carrying tone that could not quite be termed a shout, "Delilah, get over here." Shenda glanced back to see what had irked him just in time to see Delilah take her long-fingered hand off Logan's arm. Shenda watched as the sulky blonde sauntered slowly toward the center of the room in response to Darren's order.

"Now, my dear Shenda," Marnier said, drawing her gaze back to him. "Be a good girl, and pick up the sword."

Shenda looked down at the weapon in the case. She could no longer see the malevolent greenish shadow hovering over it that she'd seen on Dendron II, but she was convinced that she *felt* a foulness emanating from the razor-sharp unadorned blade. She looked back at Darren and shook her head, desperately seeking a way out. If she could convince him, personally, to retrieve the figurine *before* he forced her to touch the sword, then he would re-activate the portal and . . . disappear. Hopefully forever. "You first," she said quietly.

"Pardon me?" he asked incredulously.

Shenda met his icy blue gaze. "I said: You first. If you want me to touch this thing"—she gestured to the short-sword—"then you have to pick up the cursed figurine."

He stared at her, suspecting a trick and unable to see it. "I could simply have you subdued and the sword dropped onto your outstretched arms."

Shenda's eyes danced with scorn as she nodded and smiled coldly. "You could." And then she laughed shortly. "You've come a long way to retrieve a figurine that you're afraid to pick up, Darren."

"Hell's universe!" he muttered. "Fine! I don't want to have to injure you if it can be avoided."

Turning, he stalked into the portal's circular field and lifted the small statuette from the pedestal. Turning, he looked at Shenda. "Now . . . ahh!" Even as his scream echoed through the chamber, Marnier disappeared and the figurine crashed to the floor.

Shenda stared in shock at the spot where Darren had stood until a second ago: It had been too easy.

"No!" Delilah's scream tore through the complex, shattering Shenda's paralysis and drawing all eyes. "You bitch!" she said, pinning Shenda with her accusing gaze. "You killed him. You killed him." Then, before anybody could make a move to stop her, she rushed forward, grabbed the hilt of the sword and raised the weapon over her head as though she intended to cleave Shenda in two.

"No!" Distantly, Shenda heard the shout, recognized it as Logan's voice and sensed him racing toward her, but she couldn't take her eyes from Delilah.

For an instant Delilah froze in position, her eyes widening in shock and disbelief at something none of the others could perceive. And then a force, almost electrical in nature, seemed to flash out of the metal hilt of the sword and trail down her arms in a coruscation of energy. It danced over her arms and down toward her head and torso. And then, for so brief a time that Shenda was never certain if she'd imagined it or not, she saw an image of another woman's face superimposed over Delilah's. A face startlingly beautiful, yet so infinitely cold and corrupt that it made Delilah's features look innocent by comparison. Then Delilah screamed in rage and, as though in slow motion, Shenda saw the sword begin to descend toward her.

In the next instant, Logan leapt in between them. Grasping Delilah's forearms, he prevented her from striking at Shenda. For a moment, that was all he seemed capable of doing: Her incredible strength surprised him. She refused even to look at him, to acknowledge him in any way as her manic gaze remained fastened intently on Shenda. Logan's hands found the tendons that controlled Delilah's fingers and began to squeeze, hoping to force her to drop the weapon without hurting her too badly. It was impossible. Her eyes, devoid of recognition, shifted to him and . . . she smiled with venomous intent. There was a brief flash in his mind, a blinding white light, and Logan felt his blood chill as, with a violent motion of her arms, Delilah threw him off balance and wrested free of his hold. At least he had accomplished half of what he had set out to do: He had distracted her from Shenda; now her attention had fastened on him.

With a lightning-like speed that he could barely anticipate, the blade suddenly arced toward him. He dove aside, avoiding it, and then rose up inside Delilah's reach to once again battle her for possession of the weapon. Her sheer power was amazing. He tried to prompt some spark of recognition in those cold blue eyes. "Lilah, it's me, Logan. Remember? I don't want to hurt you. Drop the sword, all right?"

Her only reply was a feral smile as she, astonishingly, began to best him in their contention over the weapon. Damn! He had no choice but to get more violent. Marshaling his strength, he thrust her away, trying to throw her off balance, hoping she would lose her grip on the sword. Unfortunately, he had not been able to gauge direction, and she struck the portal column forcefully, her head cracking audibly against the stone. For a moment, her eyes glistened with hate. She raised the sword in her right hand as though to attack. And then, her eyes glazed and she fell forward . . . onto the razor-sharp blade of the short-sword.

As he saw what was happening, Logan ran forward to prevent it, but he was too late. The blade pierced her chest. Delilah's fingers finally relaxed their grip on the hilt of the sword that impaled her body, and she curled into a fetal position around the portal pedestal. As Logan looked down on the body of the woman he'd once cared for, regret weighed heavily on him. Regret for a young life wasted. Regret for her potential, gone. And regret for the obsession that had tied her to her brother, a man unworthy of such devotion.

Turning, he looked into the Shenda's clear and compassionate gaze. Wordlessly, he stepped away from the portal and walked into her embrace. "Thank you for saving my life," she murmured.

Lifting his head, he looked down into her face and smiled. "I owed you one." The love shining from his eyes negated the flippancy of his simple statement.

She smiled. A movement beyond Logan's right shoulder caught her eye. Her eyes widened in disbelief. Delilah's hands, leaving bloodstains in their wake, were trailing systematically over the motifs and ridges of the portal column. "Oh, no!" Shenda murmured.

Pivoting, Logan followed her gaze in time to see Delilah make one final sweeping move with her fingers. The air inside the portal field shimmered with scintillating energy and Delilah's body, complete with sword, disappeared.

Logan frowned. "I wonder how she knew how to do that." He looked down at Shenda. "Inherited memory?"

"Must have been," Shenda murmured in reply, but privately she didn't think that Delilah had had anything to do with the transfer. Even if her body somehow managed to live, to heal, Delilah was dead.

"Lower your weapons, people." Both Shenda and Logan spun around to seek out the owner of the voice. "Since Commissioner Marnier is gone, I will assume command." The speaker was the un-armed, non-uniformed man who had accompanied Marnier.

A chorus of "Yes, sir" met his statement. And some of the Legionnaires present actually looked relieved. Turning, he approached Logan and Shenda. Halting before Logan, he studied him with solemn eyes. "You don't know me, Swan, but I have known of you for some time now, and I admire your colonial tenacity." He stuck out his hand. "I am Captain James Carvell of the *Trojan I*. And I'm pleased to make your acquaintance."

Slowly, searchingly, Logan studied the captain's face. This was the man who had ordered him set free. Logan grasped Carvell's hand. "And I yours, Captain." He smiled. "And I yours."

Epilogue

Shenda stood at her bedroom window looking down on the lake that formed part of her back-yard. Water fowl, some imported from Earth and some native to Fortuna, swam back and forth on its crystal-clear waters. Water lilies and other brilliant water foliage floated on its surface or grew at its edges. It was beautiful, a sight she would never have seen if she had not moved to Fortuna. She tried to absorb the peace of the scene into her soul. As always, it helped, but this time she couldn't avoid her thoughts.

Tears that she refused to let fall burned the backs of her eyes as she looked down on the small silver disk in her hand. It had arrived by special courier on the last freighter from Earth. As she examined it, she recalled her father as she had last seen him, seven months ago.

She and Logan had returned to Olympus and, as the Morar queen had told them they must, they had destroyed the crystal. It was as they'd been leaving Marnier's apartment that Harris Ridell had confronted them. Armed with a laser, determined to stop Shenda from ruining her life and *his* career by marriage to a colonial, he'd decided to undo her *unconscionable* marriage in any way he could. Defiant, Shenda had told him that he was being ridiculous.

In his rage, he directed the laser at Logan. "I could kill your . . . colonial," he sneered.

Shenda acknowledged the veracity of his threat. "But if you do, I will crucify you for it. You taught me how, remember? You will spend the last days of your life on Sentra."

Her father had stared at her in disbelief. "You would do that to your own father?"

"Loyalty and love mean little in the vast scheme of things, Father. That's what you've always said. Remember? I will do whatever I have to do to live my life the way I choose to live it." Reaching forward, she took the laser from his hands and shoved it into the pocket of his jacket. Then she wrapped her arms around her father and gave him one of the few hugs she'd been permitted to deliver. "If you publicly disown me, Father, you will salvage your career with your bigoted benefactors. By doing that, you may ultimately end up sacrificing the votes of those who see my marriage as something to celebrate, but that is your problem, not mine. You cannot force me to live your life." Releasing him, she stepped back. "Good-bye, Father."

Linking her arm with Logan's, she smiled brightly up at her husband. "Let's go, darling." Only Logan had seen how the smile trembled on her lips.

Harris Ridell had made no comment as he

coldly watched the daughter he had fathered but neither raised nor loved walk away from him and the life he'd envisioned. Still, Shenda wished that it could have been different. Wished that her father had just once said he loved her. Wished . . . that her father had been a different man.

She looked once more at the small disk in her hand before flicking it into the garbage. It contained her father's last will and testament. Even in death, he had left her nothing. Not even a caring word. She supposed she should have expected as much. Still it hurt. Just as her father's coldness had always hurt.

The bedroom door opened. She turned to see her husband, tanned and dirty from working with the horses, enter the room. His golden eyes raked her with glowing appreciation. "Feeling any better?" he asked.

She nodded. "A little. I'll get used to it."

He walked across the room and enfolded her in his strong, warm embrace. "You're a strong woman, Shenda. Stronger than you should be at times." He studied her features. "You didn't cry, did you?"

She shook her head. "It would be a bit hypocritical to cry for a man whom I hardly knew. A man who, in the end, despised me."

"You don't know that he despised you, Shenda. He had to have been proud of you on some level. You're beautiful, intelligent and accomplished."

"You think so?" she asked.

"I know so." His hand slipped down between them to splay across her burgeoning abdomen. "Now tell me, how is my son today?"

Shenda smiled. "Vigorously protesting his confinement."

"I'm glad. I'd hate to think he intended to stay

there." Logan brushed a feather-light kiss across her forehead. "I want you all to myself at least *some* of the time." Grasping her hand, Logan led her across the bedchamber toward the washroom. "Care to wash my back?"

Shenda ran her hand admiringly over the rippling muscles beneath his shirt. "Is that all you want me to wash?" She feigned a pout.

Stopping in mid-stride, Logan stared at her with glowing eyes. "Come here, wife." As his soft bass voice washed over her, Shenda met his potent, whiskey gaze. The heat she saw reflected there sparked an answering inferno in her blood, and she stepped willingly into her husband's arms.

"I love you," he murmured.

"And I love you." She smiled and planted a gentle kiss on his full lower lip.

Futuristic Romance

Love in another time, another place.

Don't miss these tempestuous futuristic romances set on faraway worlds where passion is the lifeblood of every man and woman.

Awakenings by Saranne Dawson. Fearless and bold, Justan rules his domain with an iron hand, but nothing short of magic will bring his warring people peace. He claims he needs Rozlynd for her sorcery alone, yet inside him stirs an unexpected yearning to sample her sweet innocence. And as her silken spell ensnares him, Justan battles to vanquish a power whose like he has never encountered—the power of Rozlynd's love.

__51921-6 $4.99 US/$5.99 CAN

Ascent to the Stars by Christine Michels. For Trace, the assignment is simple. All he has to do is take a helpless female to safety and he'll receive information about his cunning enemies. But no daring mission or reckless rescue has prepared him for the likes of Coventry Pearce. Even as he races across the galaxy to save his doomed world, Trace battles to deny a burning desire that will take him to the heavens and beyond.

__51933-X $4.99 US/$5.99 CAN

Dorchester Publishing Co., Inc.
65 Commerce Road
Stamford, CT 06902

Please add $1.75 for shipping and handling for the first book and $.50 for each book thereafter. NY, NYC, PA and CT residents, please add appropriate sales tax. No cash, stamps, or C.O.D.s. All orders shipped within 6 weeks via postal service book rate. Canadian orders require $2.00 extra postage and must be paid in U.S. dollars through a U.S. banking facility.

Name _____

Address _____

City _____ State _____ Zip _____

I have enclosed $_____ in payment for the checked book(s).

Payment <u>must</u> accompany all orders.☐ Please send a free catalog.

Futuristic Romance

Love in another time, another place.

Don't miss these dazzling futuristic romances, set on faraway worlds where passion is the lifeblood of every man and woman.

Prisoner Of Passion by Trudy Thompson. The last of her line, Thea possesses strange and inexplicable powers, yet she can't resist the charms of one virile captive. But with her frozen land facing annihilation, she has to trick the blond giant into risking a daring ruse that endangers her heart as much as her life.

_52001-X $4.99 US/$5.99 CAN

To Share A Sunset by Sharice Kendyl. Although he is nothing but an outlaw, Tynan is Tallia's only hope of crossing the perilous desert to reach her home. He is arrogant and rough mannered, yet in his piercing eyes the beautiful healer sees past sorrows he refuses to share—and a smoldering desire that steals her heart.

_52003-6 $4.99 US/$5.99 CAN

Futuristic Romance
NANCY CANE

DANCE of the FLAME

ELAINE BARBIERI

Elaine Barbieri's romances are "powerful...fascinating...storytelling at its best!" —*Romantic Times*

Exiled to a barren wasteland, Sera will do anything to regain the kingdom that is her birthright. But the hard-eyed warrior she saves from death is the last companion she wants for the long journey to her homeland.

To the world he is known as Death's Shadow—as much a beast of battle as the mighty warhorse he rides. But to the flame-haired healer, his forceful arms offer a warm haven, and he swears his throbbing strength will bring her nothing but pleasure.

Sera and Tolin hold in their hands the fate of two feuding houses with an ancient history of bloodshed and betrayal. But no matter what the age-old prophecy foretells, the sparks between them will not be denied, even if their fiery union consumes them both.

_3793-9 $5.99 US/$6.99 CAN

An Angel's Touch *Where angels go, love is sure to follow.*

Don't miss these unforgettable romances that combine the magic of angels and the joy of love.

Daemon's Angel by Sherrilyn Kenyon. Cast to the mortal realm by an evil sorceress, Arina has more than her share of problems. She is trapped in a temptress's body and doomed to lose any man she desires. Yet even as Arina yearns for the safety of the pearly gates, she finds paradise in the arms of a Norman mercenary. But to savor the joys of life with Daemon, she will have to battle demons and risk her very soul for love.

_52026-5 $4.99 US/$5.99 CAN

Forever Angels by Trana Mae Simmons. Thoroughly modern Tess Foster has everything, but when her boyfriend demands she sign a prenuptial agreement Tess thinks she's lost her happiness forever. Then her guardian angel sneezes and sends the woman of the nineties back to the 1890s—and into the arms of an unbelievably handsome cowboy. But before she will surrender to a marriage made in heaven, Tess has to make sure that her guardian angel won't sneeze again—and ruin her second chance at love.

_52021-4 $4.99 US/$5.99 CAN

Dorchester Publishing Co., Inc.
65 Commerce Road
Stamford, CT 06902

Please add $1.75 for shipping and handling for the first book and $.50 for each book thereafter. NY, NYC, PA and CT residents, please add appropriate sales tax. No cash, stamps, or C.O.D.s. All orders shipped within 6 weeks via postal service book rate. Canadian orders require $2.00 extra postage and must be paid in U.S. dollars through a U.S. banking facility.

Name_____
Address_____
City _____ State_____Zip_____
I have enclosed $_____in payment for the checked book(s).
Payment <u>must</u> accompany all orders.□ Please send a free catalog.

An Angel's Touch

Time Heals
SUSAN COLLIER

Tired of her nagging relatives, Maeve Fredrickson asks for the impossible: to be a thousand miles and a hundred years away from them. Then a heavenly being grants her wish, and she awakes in frontier Montana.

Saved from the wilderness by a handsome widower, Maeve loses her heart to her rescuer—and her temper over the antics of his three less-than-angelic children. As her angel prods her to fight for Seth, Maeve can only pray for the strength to claim a love made in paradise.

_52030-3 $4.99 US/$5.99 CAN